MYTHICALS

DENNIS MEREDITH

MYTHICALS

DENNIS MEREDITH

Glyphus

For information about this title or to order other books and/or electronic media, contact the publisher:

Glyphus, L.L.C.
2947 Mesa Grove Rd., Fallbrook, CA 92028
www.glyphus.com
editor@glyphus.com

Library of Congress Control Number: 2017954667

ISBNs: 978-1-939118-29-5 (Print)
         978-1-939118-30-1 (Kindle)

Printed in the United States of America

Cover and Interior design: 1106 Design

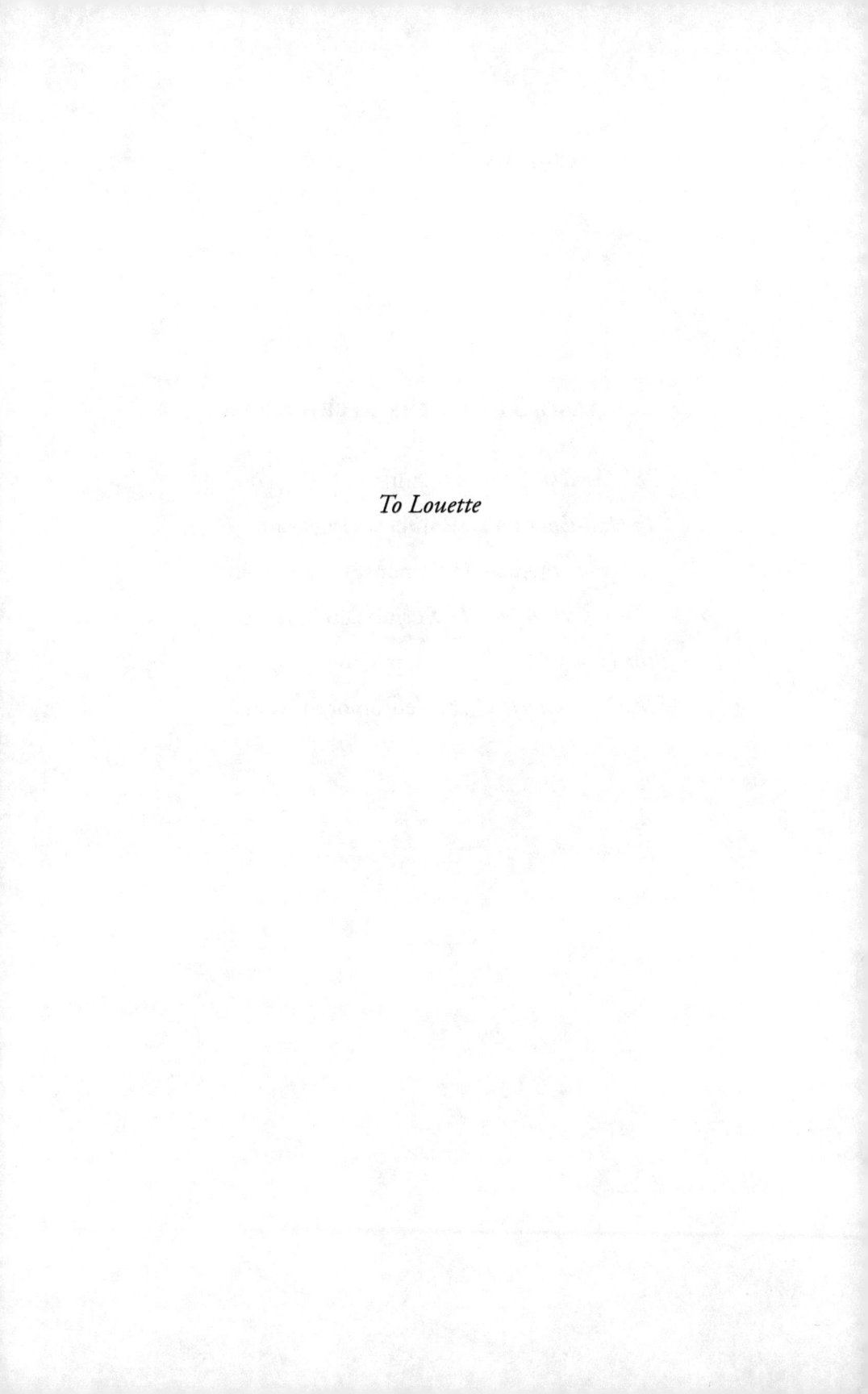

To Louette

ALSO BY DENNIS MEREDITH

The Cerulean's Secret (CeruleansSecret.com)

The Rainbow Virus (RainbowVirus.com)

Solomon's Freedom (SolomonsFreedom.com)

Wormholes: A Novel (WormholesaNovel.com)

The Happy Chip (TheHappyChip.com)

The Neuromorphs (TheNeuromorphs.com)

Chapter 1

"*D*amn! Damn! Damnity-damn! Damnity-damn-damn . . . Shit!*"

Leaning against the bedpost, A'eiio had managed to slide the flesh-suit up over her slim legs and up to her svelte hips. But pulling it over the hips was another matter.

"Nice language," cracked her husband, amused at the sight of her graceful fairy body, with its flawless alabaster skin, gyrating in such a comical way. He sat on the bench of the dressing table in their handsomely furnished bedroom, carefully smoothing the special oil onto his wings. They tended to dry out in the northern winters. The delicate musky aroma of the oil wafted through the room, reminding him of home. It was both a blessing and a curse that the Wardens allowed the exiles to the planet to import small tokens of their life before their sentences. For now, he just enjoyed the sensual oiling process and tried to ignore the pangs of homesickness. They tended to intrude, though, like the memory of his mother smoothing the

1

oil onto his wings as a young one. A'eiio's struggle brought him back from the memory.

"I'm not getting fat! I'm *damned* well not getting fat!" she exclaimed. "The suit shrunk!" She struggled on, wriggling her behind and yanking until the suit slipped over her hips.

"Suits don't—" he started to say, then thought better of it. "Well, maybe the cellular matrix contracts over time. Anyway, a new one's coming through next week."

"Yeah, and it's aged, so I look even *more* like an old lady."

"Well, you are old, for this planet's race." He put down the oil and embraced his half-clad wife, stroking her shimmering silver hair. "But for a fairy, sweetheart, you're young as springtime."

He would have spoken the compliment in the melodic, tone-language of fairies, but they had pledged to only speak the local language, to avoid slip-ups.

She paused in her contortions to briefly hug him back. "You're a good liar. After all, you are a lawyer. Help me get my wings tucked in. I just *hate* having my wings tucked in. They get cramped after a day."

He gently slipped her gossamer, veined wings, which he had lovingly oiled earlier, into the suit. He helped her pull it up to her shoulders, her smooth skin disappearing beneath the flabby, mottled flesh of the living disguise that was a flesh-suit. She slipped her arms into the suit's arms, transforming them from slim, graceful fairy arms into flabbier appendages.

Now all that was left was the head-mask, which hung limply down from her back. She reached behind her, pulled it over her head, and stretched it into place over her face.

The sagging flab of the face mask, like that of the suit, draped loosely over her body. She reached down to her chest and pressed the invisible button that sent the waves of neural signals through the suit, instructing the mesh of living cells to assume their programmed-in shape.

The suit snugged itself obediently to her body and face, becoming indistinguishable from real flesh. She moved to the mirror, but now instead of the feather-light grace of a fairy, she walked ponderously under the burden of the weights built into the suit.

"Now . . . ," she said, peering at herself critically. "The nose is crooked. The damn nose is crooked." She poked a bit and the flesh-suit nose settled into place in the middle of her face over her own nose.

"The worst is when you have to cover those beautiful eyes," said her husband, moving to the closet to pull his own flesh-suit out of its nutrient canister. He hung it over the container to allow it to drain off the syrupy yellowish liquid of the nutrient solution.

"All fairies have these eyes." She pulled back the mask's eyelids and proceeded to pop in the brown contacts over her glistening sapphire-blue eyes. "You *are* being romantic tonight."

"I confess, I am feeling romantic. Let's fly together tonight." He kissed her lightly on the now-fleshy cheek.

"Not quite yet. The moon is still waning. When it's dark. A couple of days, I promise." She kissed him back. She slipped on her matronly party gown and conservative low heels and checked herself in the mirror.

"How's your acceptance speech?" he asked.

She was silent, her expression turning somber.

"What's the matter?"

"This award they're giving me. I really shouldn't accept it. I just don't feel I deserve it."

"You deserve the honor more than anybody. You literally saved thousands of this planet's children . . . *tens* of thousands . . . with the rescue program you created. You traveled the world persuading the leaders to give rescue workers access. Hell, you were almost killed twice by rebels."

"But I can't help feeling like it was just to make the Wardens happy. You know, to fulfill their requirement that part of our sentence is to do good works during exile. I feel like a hypocrite."

He hugged her closely. "I remember when we were home, and you were just as dedicated. Before your sentence. I read about your work with cast-out and orphan fairies before I even knew you. And of course, I read about your crime . . . if you want to call it that. That little one was abused. Taking her, hiding her, was the right thing to do. The magistrate didn't want to sentence you, but he had to follow the law. And when I was convicted for my own crime and met you here, I knew you were genuine. It was easy to fall in love with you."

She shrugged and caressed his cheek, her smile transmitting through the tightened skin of the flesh-suit.

"And it was easy to fall in love with you, my love. Not the least because your 'crime' was to sabotage that horrible mining project that would have devastated vast natural regions." The phone beeped, signaling a call, and she answered it. She uttered a terse "Understood. We're coming," ended the call, and told him, "Get ready, will you? The car will be here soon."

He moved quickly to slip his own flesh-suit over a more muscular male fairy body. He tucked in his now-supple wings and deftly flipped the head-mask over his own full head of silver hair. Snugging the mask into place, he pressed the activation button, transforming himself into a gracefully aging, slightly paunchy, middle-aged male. He donned his elegant bespoke formal suit, tugged the jacket sleeves to smooth them, and took her arm.

"Okay, now we are Senator Deborah Bright and her very handsome husband Marc Bright." He always made that announcement before they left for an evening, as a way to remind them to fully immerse themselves in their assumed identities. One slip would be disastrous. "Shall we see if we can make it through another night with this species without being discovered?"

· · ·

4

Its gleaming black surface reflecting the streetlights, the massive car carrying the Senator and Mr. Bright glided up the circular driveway. It came to a smooth stop under the high, square-columned canopy in front of the official residence of the president of the International Congress of Nations.

The starkly modern mansion sat on an expansive grassy hill on the grounds of the Congress building complex.

The driver quickly swept open the car door, and they both climbed out, to be met by a smiling young assistant in formal dress.

"Ah, Senator Bright, Mr. Bright. So happy to see you," he said. "We are so pleased to be able to honor you tonight."

"See, he knows you deserve it!" whispered Marc to her, grinning triumphantly. *"Dear, you are an extraordinary fairy!"*

"Shush!" she scolded, thankful that the skin of the flesh-suit did not support blushing.

Marc obediently shut up and shook the young man's hand. They walked together into the stark, modernistic reception hall, where other formally attired men and gowned women chatted amiably over before-dinner drinks.

Given that Senator Bright was an honoree, she and Marc were escorted directly to the president of the international body, who greeted them warmly. He was tall and gangly with wispy, thinning blond hair and a magnificent beak of a nose. He gave a courtly bow to the diminutive middle-aged Senator, and he thanked her again for her good works. She responded gratefully, but there was the unspoken shared memory of his somewhat reluctant support of her ambitious and politically risky plan to save children in conflict zones.

Marc had quickly excused himself and wound his way through the elegant throng to the bar. He ordered drinks for the two of them, in particular a strong drink for himself. He didn't have to be sharp tonight. He was merely decorative.

Weaving unsteadily up to the bar next to Marc came a disheveled-looking young man in a rumpled suit, with a tousled mane of blondish hair.

"Gimme a big one, if you please, sir," he declared in slurred speech.

Marc had just taken up his drinks and turned to leave, when the young man's drink arrived. He took a healthy gulp and turned to lean unsteadily against the bar. He grinned drunkenly at Marc.

"Got to take advantage of these parties when you can," he said, grinning. "Free drink, free food, y'know."

"I completely agree," said Marc, starting off. But just as he stepped forward, the young man had raised his glass, and it bumped Marc's arm, spilling the drink all over his sleeve.

"Oh, whoa, I am sorry," said the young man. "I'm really sorry." He grabbed a handful of napkins and proceeded to clumsily rub them on Marc's sleeve.

"No problem, my young friend. I've done the same. Just forget it. And maybe ease up a bit on the drinking."

"Yeah, sorry again," the young man mumbled, ducking his head in apology. "Thank you for understanding. I'm Jack. Jack March. Sorry, not a good day today. Lost my job. Laid off. Budget cuts. Not fair. My first big break outta school. And my girlfriend's kinda mad at me. That's her over there." He pointed to a pretty, blond woman giving instructions to one of the servers. "She works here, and I didn't want to come tonight, but she works here. And it was important to her. Sorry, again." Jack held out his hand, but realized that Marc's hands were full with the drinks. He settled for patting Marc on the shoulder.

Marc nodded his head and smiled. "Got to go, Jack. Again, take it easy."

"Yeah . . . easy . . . right." But Jack drained his glass and turned immediately back to the bar, to order another.

Marc returned to Deborah's side and offered her the drink, apologizing to her for the somewhat alcoholic aroma of his sleeve. By now, she had finished her tête-à-tête with the president and moved on to a group of staff. The talk had just turned to details of her next project to supply food to war-torn areas, when dinner was announced. The guests strolled into the starkly modern dining room, and took their places at the round tables set with glimmering crystal glasses and gold-rimmed plates. The president and his wife sat at a head table on a dais, flanked by Deborah and Marc.

The salad and main courses came and went in a pleasant progression with convivial chatter; as did dessert, a tasty, light cake. Before the award ceremony and speeches began, Deborah excused herself, finding her way to the women's sitting room and the adjoining bathroom. She always worried that eating in public would expose some giveaway wrinkle in the face of the flesh-suit that was their only protection against discovery by the local species. That discovery was considered cause for the Wardens to transform exile into a sentence on a prison planet. A minute examination of her face in the mirror confirmed that all was in order—lips, chin, and the sometimes errant nose.

But she was still distracted as she returned to the dinner, opening the door from the sitting room into the reception hall. She collided with a waiter balancing a square serving pan above his shoulder. The pan lurched forward, and its sharp corner slammed into the side of her head, tearing away the flesh-mask, revealing white skin and shimmering wisps of her silver hair.

The waiter had bent to pick up the pan, perhaps not noticing! Deborah's eyes darted around the room. She couldn't be sure others hadn't seen! She clasped her hand over the torn face and backed away as the waiter came up, uttering effusive apologies.

"Oh, madam, I am so sorry. I hope—"

But Deborah was gone, ducking back into the sitting room. She started to go into the bathroom, to figure out what to do next.

No! She stopped herself. If she returned to the bathroom, she would be trapped! *She needed to have an exit! Not through the front door . . . or any door that would be manned!*

She leaned against the sitting room door so nobody could enter and took out her phone, squinting at the screen. Her brown contacts were purposely nearsighted to remind her to wear her reading glasses at work. She popped them out, and typed a text to Marc, not risking speaking a message. "Torn skin! I'm leaving. Stay. Make an excuse for why I didn't come back."

There was no reply. No doubt the ceremony had begun, and it would be bad etiquette to take out his phone to read the message. She could only hope he would realize she was not returning, check the message, and make a viable excuse why she was not able to make an acceptance speech. Meantime, she had to escape!

•　•　•

Jack was sloppily, unacceptably drunk, so Anna hauled her stumbling soon-to-be-ex-boyfriend up the stairs to the residence floor. She looked desperately up and down the hall to see if they'd been detected. Muttering curses, she shoved him through a guest bedroom door.

"You are not just embarrassing me! You could cost me my job!" She scolded.

"I'm sorry, Anna, I just—"

"Yes, I know you lost *your* job. That is not an excuse! Now you have also lost your girlfriend!"

"Please, please, *please!* I'm sorry. Look, I'll straighten up. I'll take a little time and sober up and come downstairs and be fine." He gestured at the door to the suite's bathroom. "I'll wash up, straighten up. You go on down."

She spat a rude curse and turned and left.

"I deserve that," mumbled Jack to himself. He lumbered into the bathroom and closed the door. He pulled off his tie, jacket, and shirt, ran cold water in the sink and plunged his head into it, submerging his face as long as he could. He raised up to see in the mirror the dripping, bleary-eyed face of a drunken young man, sopping hair in disarray. He plunged his face into the water again, coming up. His head was clearing.

He was drying his face, when he heard a faint thump in the bedroom.

Oh, no! He thought. *Somebody's here! Maybe to go to the bathroom.* He quietly locked the bathroom door and waited. Nobody tried to enter. There were no more noises. He was safe. He put on his shirt and jacket, not attempting to knot his tie. He was still too tipsy. He cautiously unlocked the door and ever-so-quietly opened it.

He peeked out into the room. Nobody there. He eased out of the door, and was turning to leave, when a flash of movement in the corner of his eye caused him to turn back into the room.

He gasped in shock at the sight. Standing by the window was a slim, naked girl, with creamy, smooth skin and lustrous, silver hair. But she had wings!

Wings!

The creature had her back to him, struggling to step out of a rubbery-looking pile of flesh-colored stuff on the floor. Beside the pile lay a dress and shoes.

"Damnity-damn!" exclaimed the creature.

"Jeez!" Jack grunted in surprise at the creature's curse.

The creature spun to look at him with brilliant, piercing blue eyes. She let out her own gasp, freed her delicate feet from the fleshy pile, flung open the large double windows, and gathered everything up, clutching it tightly to her chest.

Her large transparent wings began to beat furiously, filling the room with an intense hum. They became a blur, as they lifted her smoothly off the floor. Hovering, she turned for just an instant to look once more back at him with wide, frightened eyes and sailed out the window into the dark sky.

Jack stood unsteadily for a long moment, mouth agape, stunned into immobility by what he had seen. Then, his reporter's instinct kicked in and he lurched to the window, leaning out into the bracing, crisp night, peering upward.

Nothing. He saw nothing but dark sky lit from below by the glow of the city's lights.

But he had seen *something*. *Really* something!

CHAPTER 2

A'eiio sat slumped on the side of the bed staring into space, her wings drooping, when her husband burst into the bedroom, panic on his face.

"Sweetheart, what happened?" he asked. Still in his flesh-suit and tuxedo, he sat down beside her and enfolded her in his arms. He gently smoothed back her silver hair.

She looked up at him with a stricken expression. "An accident. My face was ripped. I sneaked upstairs to fly out. Somebody saw me. Without the suit."

"Oh, no," he breathed, holding her tighter. "Did they take any pictures?"

"I don't think so. It happened too fast. But he got a good look at me. I don't know who it was."

"Was your flight seen?"

"I stayed over parks and roofs. I had to fly low, but I flew fast. I would have only been a flash in the sky to anybody watching."

"Good . . . good . . . and our neighborhood has a safe approach pattern. That's why we picked it."

"You know what could happen if this gets out? Prison!"

He stood up and took off his clothes, pressing the button that triggered his flesh-suit to relax from his body. He stripped it off and dropped it into the nutrient canister. He saw that her suit still lay crumpled on the floor by the window and immersed it in its own canister. Now, he could comfort her as one fairy to another.

"I'm sure it won't get out. You know these kinds of sightings never do. At most, they end up in the tabloids, and nobody gives them any credence."

"We still have to report it. The Wardens will find out somehow."

"Okay, okay, that's true. But we need to do it the right way. This has happened to other exiles. The Wardens let them stay and relocate, if they identified the witnesses and took steps to discredit the report."

"That would work?"

"Yes, absolutely. What did the witness look like? Was it somebody with the embassy?"

"Young guy, lot of hair, staggering, looked drunk."

He stared up at the ceiling for a moment. "Yes, right! I think I met him. At the bar. He *was* drunk. That's good! Really good!" He knit his brow in concentration. "He said his name, I'm pretty sure. But I couldn't understand him."

"I know what to do," she said, her expression brightening. "I'll have Adele ask for the guest list. Make it a routine request through channels. I'll have her say it's for our files." Then, her expression clouded again. "But my suit. The face is split."

"Not to worry. Remember, it's living cells. It's got repair programming built in. Cuts and abrasions heal. I'll access the repair instructions. We'll just bind the rip, leave it in the nutrient bath, and give it time. At most you'll only have to stay out of sight a couple of days."

Her confidence returning, she rose, wings quivering with renewed energy, taking up her tablet computer and tapping out a message.

"Yeah, and I'll message Adele now," she said. "And I'll set up a news monitor to see if any media reports show up. I'm sure it will be fine." Her husband joined her, and she paused to hug him with one arm. "E'iouy," she said, using his fairy name, "You keep me sane; you keep me so happy. Tomorrow, we fly, sweetheart."

•   •   •

"Please, Anna, *please*," begged Jack, leaning over the restaurant table, trying to look as penitent as he could.

Anna flipped her long blond hair back and glared at him. "You made a fool of yourself!" she exclaimed. "You come running down the stairs in the middle of all the important people. And you rave on and on about this creature you have seen upstairs. This creature with wings that flew out the window. As if being drunk weren't bad enough!"

"I know you're disgusted with me, and you have every right to be. And I know you think I'm delusional. But I am apologizing, and I am saying that it won't ever happen again. The drinking. I was crushed by being laid off. I was stupid. If you do this one thing for me . . . just this one thing . . . I promise to make it all up to you."

He took her hand, and she did not withdraw it. He knew he still had some sympathy from her. He knew she would remember the fun they had together, the way his irrepressible, slightly irresponsible behavior had brought a spice of adventure into her otherwise dead-serious life.

"I don't know if I can get permission to release the guest list."

"You're the assistant social secretary. You don't have to get permission. It's not a state secret. And besides, nobody will ever know it came from you. You're a source. Reporters don't reveal their sources."

"You're not a reporter." Now, she withdrew her hand, but slowly.

He shrugged, his grinning in embarrassment. "Well, I'm a *free-lance* reporter, now. Same thing."

"And you hope this guest list will let you find out more about this flying creature you think you saw."

Jack decided the best course was to lower the craziness level of his claimed sighting. "Well, okay, I was drunk, but I did see somebody go out the upstairs window. And that's suspicious, you have to admit. Wouldn't it be a good thing for you if I helped you identify somebody who did something strange at the dinner? I mean, it could have been a thief . . . or a spy."

Her glare faded to an expression of mild exasperation. "Okay, it could have been some kind of security breach. And it would be helpful to know about that . . . for me to find that out. Look, I'll ask around. I'll ask the staff if anybody left the dinner early."

He smiled amicably, but it was also a calculating smile. He'd successfully used his reporter's wiles to make his request seem beneficial to his source. It was only a slightly underhanded trick to play on his girlfriend—if that's still what she considered herself.

"It sure would help. And I promise I won't tell anybody where I got the list. And when I start making inquiries about what . . . uh . . . *who* it was in that bedroom, I'll report anything I find out right back to you."

• • •

Her body tensed, Senator Bright sat in the cramped office that was of the level assigned to a junior senator and stared intently at the list on the computer screen. *Who* on this list had seen her in that bedroom?

She had already eliminated the servers. They all wore uniforms. She also crossed off the women guests. And the people she had met before and knew by sight. She scanned the result. Ten names left. They were either male staffers or escorts of invited guests.

Now, she could search the online image databases, to see if she recognized any of the faces attached to these ten names as the shocked one that had witnessed her removing her flesh-suit.

She shivered and touched the flesh-suit face that had been ripped. It had healed so nicely over the last few days. No scar at all, thanks to Marc. He'd found in the flesh-suit instructions a section on mending rips. It said to add growth factors to the liquid nutrient medium that bathed the living cells. He'd canvassed other exiles to find another fairy who had a supply of growth factors. He'd meticulously bound up the rip and added the growth factors, and it worked.

She typed the first name into the Image database entry box:

John Duckworth . . . middle-aged guy. No.

Lanny Leslie . . . another middle-aged guy. No.

Paul Stock . . . younger guy, but not the one. No.

Kelley Montoya . . . young guy. Again, no.

Three more names. All no.

Then she came to the name Jack March . . . a common name. She found lots of photos online. She scrolled through them. An old guy . . . no. A baby . . . no. Another old guy . . . no.

Then, *there he was!* Smiling out at her was that young face topped by the blondish hair that she had seen in the bedroom. She went to the online site where that face was featured and read the biographical sketch.

She groaned at the information, taking out her phone and calling Marc, who was at work at his law firm. He answered, and she skipped the usual how-are-you preamble.

"His name is Jack March," she said. "He's the *worst* possible person to have seen me. He's a *reporter!*"

"*Yeah, right!* I'm sure that's the name he said. Send me the picture." She did so, and after a moment, he exclaimed. "Damn! Yeah, that's the guy at the bar. Maybe he won't pursue it."

"Did you look at the most recent entry for his background information? He was with the *Capital Herald*. He was a technology reporter. It says he has an engineering degree, but he decided to become a reporter."

"I see. It says he's a freelance. What does that mean?"

"They just went through a round of layoffs, and he was fired. So, he's an *unemployed* technology reporter. He's hungry. He's got time. He's got connections. He was with Anna Wald at the dinner. She's on the Congress staff."

"So?"

"So, he's going to get as much information out of her as he can. And out of the embassy staff and other guests. He may even figure out I was the guest who disappeared during the dinner."

"He needs to be stopped now," said Marc. "You know how, right?" He answered his own question. "The same way that the Mythicals neutralized that patrolman when he saw Steve out in the desert. It saved him."

"You mean bring in Sam?"

"Yes," said Marc. "Sam will neutralize him. This Jack March won't know what hit him. I'll call Sam."

CHAPTER 3

"Shit," muttered Jack, as he poked the phone screen to end the call. He continued down the narrow, dark street, looking for the address of the server who'd been at the dinner. The call had been to a deputy undersecretary of state, a guest at the dinner, who had uttered only a terse "no comment" to his question about abrupt absences before hanging up on him.

The guests all knew better than to talk to a reporter, much less him, about the event. By the time he'd called a few names on the list, word had almost certainly gotten around the gossip circuit that he was the clown who had been reeling around drunk. And, the one who had dashed down the stairs through the after-dinner crowd hollering about somebody having flown out an upstairs window.

But now, he was pursuing a much better idea for sources: the servers. They were far more likely to sell him information. And the one he was looking for, Geniato Belligrado, seemed quite promising. The catering manager had told him, after having some money slipped into his palm, that one of the servers had some kind of accident with a guest. That guest had then disappeared into the women's bathroom. And the server had taken off after that, said the manager. He had appeared shaken. It was unusual, and a prime rule in the reporters' official rulebook was to go after unusual occurrences. Especially one involving a woman.

For another bribe, the manager had given him Belligrado's name and address. Anticipating more payoffs, Jack had taken more money out of his account, unfortunately drawing it down below his rent payment for the next month.

He reached a set of worn stone steps and looked up to a battered wooden door with peeling green paint. Above it was the number 1719. It was the place.

He paused before walking up the steps, looking uneasily back down the deserted street where he'd come from. He'd had the strange feeling that he was being followed, ever since he'd left his own apartment. He'd glanced back a couple of times, thinking he'd seen movement in the patchwork of shadows cast by the overhanging trees. And once, even movement up in a tree itself, which he persuaded himself must have been some bird settling in for the night. But now, he saw no movement in the shadows, or in the deeper gloom next to the rundown buildings.

He shook off the feeling and entered, finding the name Belligrado handwritten on a smudged card stuck in the name slot on the battered mailboxes. The entry hall was littered with papers and had the musty smell of decades of neglect. He found the apartment up a flight of stairs and knocked.

"Yes?" asked a muffled, accented voice through the door.

"My name is Jack. I was at the dinner at the embassy. Benjamin gave me your name, said you would talk to me. I understand you had an accident."

"Am I fired?"

"No."

"Are you police?"

"No, I was at the dinner, too. Something happened to me there, too. I think the two things might be related."

"Nothing happened to me. Go away."

"Did you see something?"

"Go away . . . please."

"Did you see . . . uh . . . like a mask . . . silver hair?"

After a long pause, there was the metallic clunk sound of multiple locks being unbolted and a cautious opening of the door. The crack in the door revealed a slim, dark-eyed, young man with thick, black hair.

"You saw my accident?" he asked.

"No, but I think I saw the same person afterward. Look, I'll give you money if you'll just tell me your story. I'll record it. But I'll keep your name out of it."

"You saw her?" The young man opened the door wider and backed away, his head bowed. He waved Jack inside. It was a cramped one-room apartment with a kitchen area and a bathroom. The walls were encrusted with layers of old paint, the most recent of which had once been white, but was now a stained brownish. Three mattresses were propped against the wall.

"I saw somebody with wings," said Jack.

"Wings? I didn't see wings." Belligrado retreated deeper into the apartment, standing beside the open window, as if considering bolting out and down the fire escape.

"Then what did you see?" Jack took out his wallet and counted out what would be a generous amount, holding the bills up in front of him.

Belligrado stared at the money for a long moment before licking his lips nervously and answering. "I am carrying tray to kitchen. Lady come out of bathroom. Older lady. My tray hit her bad in the face, and I drop it. I look up, and it was like she had a mask that tore. Like you say . . . *mask!*"

"What was beneath the mask?"

"Very white skin. And like you say, silver hair."

"Would you recognize her if you saw her again?"

"Oh, yes. I can never forget her. Never."

Jack took out his card, a *Capital Herald* card on which he had scratched out the newspaper's name.

"Okay, I'll come back with pictures. Will you look at them and tell me if you recognize anybody?" He handed Belligrado the card.

"You give me more money, and yes I tell you."

"Fine. And call me if you think of anything else. My number's on the card."

Belligrado moved quickly to the door, opening it as he stuffed the money into his pocket, and waving his hand urgently for Jack to leave. In fact, Jack *was* eager to leave. He had work to do. He'd gather as many photos of the older women at the party as he could, and come back. This guy had seen the face of the woman . . . or whatever it was!

He strode away down the street planning his next steps. He would go back to his apartment, search for photos, and upload them to his phone. He had just reached the small store on the corner of the main street, when his phone rang. He stopped in front of the store and answered it.

"Why did you send somebody else?" he heard Belligrado whisper.

"What do you mean?"

"There is somebody . . ." Belligrado paused, and Jack heard a voice in the background, but he couldn't make out the words. Then, Belligrado pleading, *"Please! Angel! Please! Don't take me, angel! My mother needs me!"*

"*What's going on!*" he shouted into the phone. He heard the sounds of the door being unbolted, then a soft female voice in the background. "Geniato, do not leave. Geniato."

But he heard only a faint whooshing sound, and the clunk of the phone being dropped. He stuffed his phone into his pocket and ran as hard as he could back to the apartment, bounding up its stairs to the second floor. The door was open and he rushed into the apartment. It was empty! He ducked into the tiny bathroom, finding it empty, too.

He poked his head out the open window, then climbed out onto the rusty fire escape. Still nothing. Just an empty alley. The window sill showed what looked like fresh scratch marks on it. Something, or somebody, had been taken through it.

He reentered the apartment, shaking his head. What should he do? Call the police? *Yeah, sure,* he thought to himself, *and tell them he was here seeing a guy about some winged creature he'd seen while drunk at a party. And now the guy was gone and said something about an angel.*

The best step right now was just to leave. Leave and think. Go somewhere and think. And get a drink. Several drinks. His hands trembling with increasing paranoia, he wiped the doorknob clean of his fingerprints, and tried to think of anything else he had touched. Finally, his panic trumped his caution, and he sprinted out of the building and down the street, crossing over to avoid a couple walking a dog.

On the way back to his neighborhood—and critically important to his favorite bar—he puzzled over what Belligrado had shouted. Why would he have called the intruder an angel? And why were there no signs of struggle, no chairs upturned, nothing broken? Just a vanished man—a young, strong man at that.

He was *very* thirsty when he made it to the funky-cozy, safe neighborhood bar down the street from his apartment. He settled in on one of his three favorite stools, and prepared to ponder the mysteries that surrounded him with a glass of liquor in his hand.

He would have nobody to talk to really. His work friends had cordially evaporated after he was laid off, as if they might catch some unemployment virus. His parents were at the other end of the continent and had not been happy with his choice of career. Anna certainly didn't want to hear any more about his plight or his activities after his drunken display. And the other denizens of the bar were of the comfortably casual type one talked sports or weather with in boozy chatter.

Phil the bartender had been a good listener, but strangely Phil wasn't there. Jack asked the substitute bartender about the absence. Phil had owned the bar for decades and seldom missed a night. The sub, a round-faced man with a scraggly beard, shrugged noncommittally and mentioned that Phil was sick. Normally, Phil would have automatically poured Jack his favorite brand, but tonight he changed brands, avoiding a minor embarrassment. He would have to drink the cheapest brand. After all, he'd not only lost his job, he was out a considerable sum of money.

He sat for two-drinks'-worth, settling down, letting the warmth of the liquor suffuse his body and soothe his soul. He'd taken out his phone and started searching for pictures of people who'd been at the party, when the bulky guy next to him got up to leave, revealing the presence of a young woman sitting two stools down, sipping a drink and looking at her watch.

He noted that she was model-quality in the looks department. A slim body, but with some shape in the blouse. Silky auburn hair, fine features. She looked up, trying to get the bartender's attention, and he saw the flash of blue eyes. Very blue eyes. Trying to avoid staring, he went back to scrutinizing at his phone.

She took up her phone, and even over the rising chatter of the bar, he could hear her side of the conversation.

"You're not coming? Seriously? That's no excuse! Listen, I know about her. You know who I mean. I don't care! Then don't call me again!" She slapped the phone down on the bar and finished her drink. *"Oh, damn,"* she said to herself, her voice trembling slightly, her head down.

An opening! He thought. He leaned toward her. "Miss, on behalf of asshole men everywhere, I would like to formally apologize," he said.

She looked up at him, slightly startled, then smiled, her eyes still glistening with tears. "Oh, you heard that? I guess I got kind of loud. Sorry."

With a better look, he appreciated even more how truly gorgeous she was, with delicate lips upturned at the ends, a pert nose . . . and those beautiful, wide-set blue eyes. She *was* model material!

"Well, I have to admit, I am a recovering asshole," he said, ducking his head in mock embarrassment. "But I'm two years' reformed. Now a certified nice guy."

"Well, you could relapse," she said smiling again, but still only slightly. "Your sex does."

"Not me. It helps when I meet nice people." He raised his glass to indicate he meant her.

"You're very kind." She had the sweetest, silken voice.

"Look, let me buy you another drink," he said raising his hand to the bartender. "I'll listen, you talk, and I promise I'll apologize as many times as it takes to make you feel better."

After a long moment, she nodded her head agreeably, lifting her glass, turning toward him, and crossing her legs to reveal slim calves and a glimpse of perfect, smooth thigh. She had an undefinable aura about her, an allure, a delicious feminine magnetism.

Jack held out his hand. "I'm Jack." He moved to the stool next to her.

She took his hand in hers, a delicate hand with gold rings on slim, manicured fingers.

"I'm Sam."

. . .

Marc and Deborah—who were now the fairies E'iouy and A'eiio, since they had shed their flesh-suits—lay in an intimate, naked embrace on a blanket in the middle of the utter darkness of the pasture. The huge expanse of land around their country house far outside the capitol gave them perfect isolation for their mating flights.

They had flown wrapped in each other's sylphlike arms and legs, borne on the blur of beating wings, rising slowly up and up, above the trees, into the moonless, velvet-black sky decorated with twinkling stars.

Suspended in the darkness, they had lovingly coupled, their skin becoming luminous as did that of mating fairies, singing the melodious song of love.

Had they been seen, they would have appeared as a softly glowing orb of light, floating in the sky.

Now, a faint glow remained as they separated to lay on their backs playing their guessing game. Which constellation marked the position of their home star? Was their home system even in this universe? Both questions were total speculation, since nobody really knew whether the wormholes used for their interplanetary travel connected regions within a universe, or between universes. In either case, their speculation always made them homesick, although even more thankful that they had each other.

"Twenty-three years, four months, and eight days," she whispered.

"And let's see . . ." He reached over and looked at the time on his phone. ". . . six hours and thirty-five minutes."

"The Wardens won't add to our sentence, will they? For the sighting?" She rubbed the back of her neck, where the Wardens had installed her coma chip. It had been decades since the surgery, but the slight bump of callous reminded her of the chip's presence.

"I'm almost sure they won't," he said reassuringly, turning back to her and stroking her hair. "After all, it wasn't any mistake on your part. And it only involved two creatures. And, I am sure that Sam and the others will neutralize them."

"Thank goodness for Sam."

"And the others, too."

"Remind me, who did she get to help?" she asked.

"Good ones. Very adept at neutralizing. Mike, Steve, Robin, and, of course, Warren."

"Of course, Warren. He loves to neutralize. And he'll hold it over me, I'm sure. At least, we know Sam will handle it as well as it can be handled."

"I feel sorry for the one who saw you."

"Don't," she said emphatically, patting Marc's smooth, bare chest. "He has it coming. He should have just kept his mouth shut."

• • •

His first kiss with the stunning, sexy Sam was beyond wonderful, even magical. Her soft lips against his, her perfect warm body against his, and some indefinable allure—the result infused his soul with an entrancing, erotic warmth. Jack had never actually melted into any woman's arms, but he did in Sam's. They had just left the bar, and she had embraced him, turned up her beautiful face to his, and kissed him deeply. But she was the one who registered the effect.

"Whew!" she sighed, shaking her head apologetically. "I'm *so* sorry if that was too forward of me. I don't do that. Maybe it was because of the state I'm in. Emotional and tipsy."

Trying to recover, he smiled at both her declaration and the effect of the kiss. "Well, I like to think a little bit of it is me," he managed to say puckishly.

They strolled the four blocks to his building, their arms around each other. They reached his apartment and entered. He had just closed the door and turned back to her, when she kissed him again, this time even more passionately. He felt hypnotized once again, but managed to recover enough to remember the proper etiquette for having a prospective bed partner over.

"Uh . . . can I get you a drink? I can make—"

But she interrupted him with yet another warm, deep kiss, and he found himself staring dumbly into those mesmerizing eyes. He remembered them being sky blue. Now they were green. Such a beautiful emerald green. He felt woozy.

Without speaking, she began to gently, deftly remove his clothes, slipping off his tie, his coat, his shirt, his undershirt, his shoes, his socks, his pants, his shorts. He stood there transfixed, watching the disrobing as if he were a bystander.

Then, she stood back, smiling, still mesmerizing him with those luminous, green eyes, and took off her own clothes.

Her undergarments fell to the floor, and he thrilled at the sight of her petite, perfect body, with shapely, perfect breasts and delicate curves. She embraced him, and he relished the warmth and indescribable softness of her skin. She led him into the bedroom, pulling back the covers he'd forgotten to make that morning, and laid him down.

He felt a sharp sting as she embraced him, but she whispered an immediate apology when he winced, declaring it was just "a ring I should have taken off, but I'm so used to it." He forgot the incident immediately, in the warm fog of lust.

Then the room faded.

•   •   •

Sam padded, barefoot and naked, through the living room, rummaging through her purse for her phone.

She dictated and sent the message, "He's out, but he'll be awake soon. You're near?"

As if in answer, a series of loud thumps resounded on the door, and she opened it to reveal a hulking policeman in a dark blue uniform, grinning at her.

"Yeah, I figured you'd take care of him quick," he chuckled in a deep, throaty voice. "You don't waste time."

She smiled. "Neither do you, Mike."

He filled the doorway as he entered the apartment, followed by a hefty young woman in a flowered dress, and a slim, blond woman in hospital scrubs. None reacted visibly to Sam's nakedness.

"He's out?" asked the hefty, young woman in a breathy voice.

"Not for long, Steve," said Sam. "Robin, where's Warren?" she asked the young woman in scrubs.

"He got some kind of call to do with the Senate. He's very *important,* you know," Robin said with a large dollop of sarcasm. "How do you want to do this, Sam?"

Sam wrinkled her brow, as she pondered the strategy. "I think we send in Mike first. Start big. Then Steve—"

"Yeah," said the hefty woman with the incongruous name of Steve. "Ya wanna go from uglier to ugliest," she declared in a breathy, feminine voice.

Sam continued. "Then we go with Robin. By then, Warren should be here, and he can finish him off."

With that, Mike began to shed his uniform, revealing a muscular, hairy body. Steve followed, her short buxom form a sharp contrast to the looming Mike. Then, Robin removed her hospital scrubs, her naked body slim and delicate with pale skin.

The naked Mike tapped his thick chest, and his skin and face sagged away from his body. He carefully slipped his head mask off to reveal a hideous, grinning face with yellow fangs sprouting from a protruding jaw. The effect was like that of a mutant bulldog. His skin fully shed, he stood as a gray-green, hulking monster, scratching his crotch luxuriantly.

By then, the portly young woman, Steve, had shed her skin to become a wrinkled, beady-eyed, squat-bodied male creature with a potato nose and a sparse crop of unkempt white hair. Steve's voice transformed from a softly feminine timbre to a litany of masculine, guttural grunts.

Robin's emergence from her flesh-suit was like that of a butterfly emerging from a chrysalis. She was a slightly more petite version of her dear friend A'eiio. She freed her gossamer fairy wings from the flesh-suit and fluttered them to limber up her flight muscles, shook her matted silver hair to fluff it out, and stretched lithely.

Sam peeked into the bedroom, pausing for a moment before turning back. "He's coming around," she whispered to the group. "You're on."

•　•　•

Jack opened his eyes to behold a bedroom that was moving, shifting, now expanding, now contracting. Was he drunk? No, he'd been drunk. This wasn't like drunk. The room took on vibrant colors that began to slither and undulate across the walls and over the ceiling—orange, blue, green, red, purple.

Panting in shock and fear, Jack peered around the room, looking for the beautiful woman who had just shed her clothes. She had left. Noises in the living room. The colors still swirled madly.

Then, something huge appeared in the doorway made it go dark!

DEAR GOD, A MONSTER!

Looming over him, a hulking gray-green body, a face with depthless onyx eyes. Long yellow fangs jutted from a massive, protruding jaw. He whimpered in fear, his heart pounding. The monster loosed a deep guttural growl.

He cowered against the headboard, whimpering, as the monster backed away into the shadows.

Then a squeal, like a pig's, arose from the foot of his bed. He peered down at the source of the sound. Standing there, a gnarled creature with scraggly white hair, beady eyes, a potato of a nose, and a squat body. It grinned with crooked, stained teeth, and squealed again.

"PLEASE!" He wailed. *"What? . . . who? . . ."* He shut his eyes in hopes that the apparitions would vanish and with it the gut-wrenching fear that he was going insane.

A low, reverberating hum filled the room, and he felt a breeze waft over his naked body. He opened his eyes, gazing upward.

Hovering over him was the winged creature! The same slim, white-winged creature with the sapphire eyes he had seen before. Penetrating eyes! He felt as if her gaze pierced his body.

"You!" he moaned. *"It's you!"*

To preserve some shred of sanity, he shut his eyes again to try to recover himself. He held them tightly closed, trying to block the sound as well, until the bed shook. Something huge had climbed onto it. A bone-rattling, guttural growl rose beside him. He opened his eyes to see a beast from hell. A furred, demonic creature that would haunt his nightmares for the rest of his life. He shrieked in terror, wetness welling between his legs.

The beast thrust its hairy face into his, its eyes gleaming yellow, its bared fangs dripping with spittle. It opened its jaws and howled, it's hot, fetid breath smelling of rotting meat making him choke and gag.

Staring horrified into the face of death, he began to sob piteously, whispering over and over *"Oh no. Oh no. Oh no . . ."*

He felt a pressure on his arm, maybe a jab.

Darkness.

• • •

"I saved you from getting banished, that's for sure." Senator Warren F. Lee chuckled and clasped his hands over his barrel chest, leaning back in the chair and grinning at Senator Deborah Bright. Senator Lee liked all meat, even the red meat of politics. At that moment, he would like some real meat, though, raw. He liked to drag a haunch into the forest surrounding his sprawling ranch and gnaw on it and howl at the full moon. He grinned an appropriately werewolfish grin.

"Well, Warren, the others had a little part . . . Mike the ogre, Steve the troll, Robin the fairy . . . and, of course, Sam the pixie," said Deborah. She sat, across from him in his Senate office. It was larger and more lavishly decorated than hers, given his seniority as a six-term Senator. The walls were plastered with plaques and pictures of him with celebrities—foreign leaders, film action heroes, billionaires, generals.

"Well, I was the climax. He wet himself, y'know. And I had to come in the window. People out front could've recognized me."

Deborah smiled but it was a smile meant to temper her disagreement with this boastful werewolf. "Well, Sam's seduction . . . her pheromones, the hallucinogenic she gave him—"

"Yeah, that little pixie sure knows how to enchant males on this planet, I'll give her that. I hope for your sake that he backs off."

"Well, I hope so. We'll see what the Wardens say. I've reported to them."

"And the other guy? The waiter who collided with you?"

"Wendy took him."

"She'll enlist him. Angels are good at that. But to get back to us. It was dangerous, sneaking over there, takin' off the flesh-suit and all. So you owe me, Debbie."

"Of course." Deborah took a deep breath. Now would come the inevitable cost of any favor given by Warren Lee.

"I want you to support increased funding for my military base. For the new weapons center."

Deborah smiled ruefully and shook her head. "Your military base? Yeah, well—"

"Hey, Debbie, we need those weapons, you know we do. These creatures will be in another war soon, for sure."

"Well, Warren, it means going up against a lot of—"

"Look, Debbie, I know what's coming. I fought in every damn war for the last seventy years, in one identity or another. I have always defended freedom for whoever I fought for."

"True, but eventually, we have to guide the planet toward a lasting, planetary peace."

Lee stood up and leaned his beefy frame over his desk. "I been marooned on this damn planet for almost twice that. Just 'cause I killed a few more of my fellow werewolves than I shoulda. I'm gonna chair the Military Services Committee next term. I like playing with these species' war toys. So, vote for it."

Deborah sat back in her chair, regarding Lee coldly. "And you getting with these 'war toys' means a lot more death and destruction. These creatures are self-destructive enough as it is."

"I do not care! They do it to themselves, and I enjoy the sport. Now, if you don't mind, I got a lunch date with a defense contractor."

She stood and nodded goodbye and, with a grim expression on her face, left.

•   •   •

Jack emerged from the enveloping blackness slowly. Only gradually did he become aware that he was lying on his bed, in his bedroom, and the morning light was coming through the window.

A swirl of horrifying memories rose to claw at his sanity. Terrible, *terrible* memories. Hideous faces, smothering hot breath, flapping wings, piercing eyes.

He experimented with moving his limbs. They were leaden. He tried lifting his head, and the throbbing headache made him give up the idea for now. So, he let himself lie there, trying to piece together his memories.

Finally, he decided to just endure the headache, and hauled himself up to a sitting position, enduring the throbbing. He looked down to find himself fully dressed in pants and shirt. He even had his socks on.

But he thought he remembered being naked, so vulnerable, under the nightmarish onslaught.

He swung his legs over the side of the bed and managed to stand. Holding on to bed, then dresser, then doorway, he staggered into the living room. He scanned the area, seeing his coat and tie neatly draped over the back of a chair at the little kitchen table. He shook his head in confusion. He never did that.

A bottle sat on his sink—the liquor he kept in the cabinet over the sink. It was empty. He thought he remembered buying a new one only a day ago at the liquor store on the next block. Again, confusion.

In the past, he had been known to significantly reduce the level of a full bottle. But not *that* significantly.

The need for coffee rose in his clouded mind. He went into the kitchen and began the ritual of heating water, putting coffee in the coffeemaker . . . an extra scoop today . . . and pouring the water in. As he stood at the counter, waiting for the coffee to steep, he moved his tongue around in his mouth. There was the brown taste of sleep; but besides that, a kind of organic taste. He added that to the other disturbing nuggets of confusion. He took down a cup and filled it, going into the living room to sit on the couch, sip the coffee, and stare dully at the wall for half an hour.

As the memories returned, so did the gut-wrenching fear. He gulped the last of the coffee and refilled the cup. Horrible creatures had either been in his bedroom . . . or in his head . . . including the flying creature he'd seen at the embassy.

Or thought he saw? Had that drunken encounter been merely a first inkling of what would come later? Was he having alcoholic hallucinations? Would he end up like one of those ragged wretches huddled next to the stark government buildings, muttering to themselves?

He needed a shower. Drinking the last of the coffee, he shuffled into the bedroom to take off his clothes. His pants waist was loose, because his belt was buckled on the second hole, not the third. Wrong hole. It nagged at him as he stripped down, turned on the shower, and stepped in. The hot water felt so good, and he let it flow down his head.

Toweling off, he went into the bedroom to get fresh shorts and undershirt. He looked down at the bed. It was made, perfectly. The bedspread was smooth, except for the slight indentation where his body had been. Again, confusion, because he hadn't made a bed that well in his life.

The caffeine was kicking in, a mental fog was clearing, bringing a sharpness. He slipped on his shorts and T-shirt and wrinkled his brow in puzzlement at the anomalies he'd noticed so far. Okay, they were minor, and maybe he was just being obsessive-compulsive, but he decided just to go over his bedroom in minute detail. His bedroom was real, not a dream. If there was some real evidence that something had happened, then his experience was not a dream. He was not crazy. His reporter's juices began to energize his thought process.

The window was unlocked. He never never *never* left the window unlocked, mainly because he had stopped opening it, since he woke up that time to find a bird flapping around in the room, dropping crap all over.

He opened the window and inspected the area, scanning the usual magnificent vista of the dirty alley and garbage cans, and the old brick apartment house across the way.

He was just drawing his head in when he glanced down at the peeling paint of the sill. Caught in a fissure was a dark hair! A long, coarse hair! He took it between thumb and forefinger and held it up to the light from the window. Not his hair; not one of Sam's fine auburn hairs; not one of Anna's long blond hairs. He found an envelope on his desk, took out the overdue bill it held and carefully put the hair into it.

He returned to scrutinize the sill further. Caught in another fissure were dark blue threads from his bedspread!

Why would his bedspread come in contact with the sill?

He was on the fourth floor, with no fire escape. So nobody would use it to pad the sill while crawling in or out of the window. The hair could have been caught on the sill when the bedspread was shaken out the window.

Mysterious hair . . . neatly draped coat and tie . . . empty liquor bottle . . . wrong buckle hole . . . mouth taste . . . *something really, really weird had happened to him in this apartment! And somebody had made it happen!*

CHAPTER 4

"TURN OFF THE LIGHTS, YOU
CURSED ELVES!" roared
Mike the ogre into the radio.
He scratched his bulbous belly and glared up at the gleaming orb
sailing silently across the black night sky against the backdrop of stars.
From his throat rumbled an angry stentorian growl. "Stupid elves," he
muttered. "They mastered wormhole travel, built a technology equal
to any, and they cannot remember to turn off the lights!"

"Other species forget, too, y'know," said Deborah—now A'eiio
because she no longer wore her flesh-suit. She stood expectantly beside
the ogre in the darkness.

"Yes, but the elves are the worst," muttered the ogre. *"One switch!*
All they have to remember is to turn off *one cursed switch* on the other
side of the wormhole to make it dark . . . so it won't look like a light
in the sky. And they cannot remember. Or more likely, they do it on
purpose to frighten this planet's poor creatures."

The light grew larger and larger. In only seconds more it would grow to outshine all the stars, becoming what the planet's indigenous species would call an "unidentified aerial phenomenon."

"The lights! The lights! The lights!" the ogre chanted into the radio, until abruptly, the object blinked out. *"Thank you!"* he grunted sarcastically.

Now the wormhole was a sphere of total light-swallowing blackness that descended smoothly toward them in the wooded valley in the fairies' farm, far beyond any town. The elves, as forgetful as they were about lights, were expert wormhole pilots.

Now the elves switched on the lights, and the wormhole became a luminous sphere casting its light on the desert below. The glow revealed a large cadre of fairies, trolls, werewolves, gnomes, and elves peering upward as the hole grew larger. It halted to hover above them, a subtly hued aurora of red, green, yellow, and blue shimmering about its surface. A faint hiss and crackling enveloped the crowd, telling of air molecules tortured as they impacted with the interdimensional portal. And the sharp tang of ozone told of the cosmic energy being pumped into the atmosphere.

A small knot of vampires lurked well outside the illuminated circle, averse to bright lights. They would wait until the elves obligingly dimmed the lights to conduct their commerce with the various races on the other side of the visiting wormhole.

Mike the ogre continued to manage the process, hitching up the leather loincloth that reached from his belly down to the tree-trunk-thick legs.

"Hold, please," he said, his voice still tinged with sarcastic impatience. He spoke into the radio once more, but this time to the Allies guarding the gates to the sprawling private farm that was their landing port. To any wayfarers, they would appear to be mere farm hands

tending to evening chores at the gates of the farm. "Any interest from the locals?" he asked.

"No traffic," came the answer. "No vehicles. You're all right to proceed."

"Form the aperture," instructed the ogre, and one side of the wormhole flattened, and a ramp extended to the ground from the shimmering globe.

The ogre stalked up the ramp and poked his large head through. "Begin transport," he commanded.

He withdrew, to be followed by three elves, their spindly legs and arms fighting the planet's gravity, which was nearly twice that of their home planet. Their beady eyes also strained to make out the area, given that the light was far lower than what they were used to. Each of them donned light-amplifying goggles that gave their eyes a large bulbous look.

The lead elf emitted a litany of scritchy-squeaks at the ogre—a language that few could understand.

Except pixies. From behind the ogre came the far more pleasant tones of Sam the pixie. "We are terribly sorry," came the translation. "We will take more care with the illumination."

"Let's just begin the unloading," grumped the ogre. "We haven't got all night."

"Well, actually we have," came a lilting voice from inside the hole, and a fairy Warden stepped out, wearing the large, gold chain, with the Control medallion that was the sign of his office. It was covered with glowing colored buttons with which Wardens communicated and managed the exiles who were their responsibility.

The hulking ogre seemed to shrink in size, as he ducked his grotesque head in submission. "Oh . . . sir . . . I didn't . . . I thought . . . Of course, sir. Welcome, sir."

The Warden smiled tolerantly. He was used to such stammering. After all, when he or another Warden wielded the Control medallion, they literally held the fate of all the planet's exiled Mythicals in their hands.

"Please carry on," said the Warden. "I will conduct my business."

The ogre, the elves, and the other Mythicals began to pass the cylindrical cargo containers out of the wormhole, distributing them as required.

For A'eiio, the important containers held new flesh-suits for her and E'iouy, and she hauled them to her waiting SUV. She also pocketed the small test kit, smiling to herself. But the smile faded with the acute awareness that next would come a meeting with the Warden.

She passed by a chilling reminder of what punishment that meeting might bring. As she walked to meet the Warden in a secluded clearing nearby, two barrel-chested werewolves were sliding a coffin-like case through the hole, to be trans-shipped to a penal colony on some barren planet on the other side of the wormhole.

The case held the unconscious body of one of their kind, another exile, who had sought revenge on a citizen of this planet by revealing his horrific snarling face to the victim. The werewolf Warden had triggered the exile's coma chip, rendering him unconscious until he would wake up in a cell, where he would stay for decades to come. The errant werewolf's relatively short exile to this planet for illegal financial dealings had now been extended and made more onerous by his near-violent behavior.

A'eiio approached their meeting spot, her wings twitching nervously. The Warden fairy sat on a rock, a data screen floating before him, no doubt reviewing her records. Unsmiling, the Warden gestured to another rock nearby. But A'eiio indicated she would rather stand. Actually, she would rather rev up her wings and sail away from what would be a very uncomfortable grilling.

The Warden waved the data screen to the side and began to speak in the language of their race—an intricate pattern of chirped tones, modulated in subtle ways to convey meaning.

"You've done well in your sixty-five years here," he sang. "There have been no instances of untoward conduct. You have done good works. Your achievements have helped the other Mythicals here to serve their sentences surreptitiously and productively."

"Yes, I've tried to make exile useful for all of us."

"Well, you did *not* make the best choice in your reaction to the accident."

"I did what I—" Just then a vampire wandered past into the arroyo, seeking darkness and waiting for his turn at the wormhole. They fell silent until he was gone.

The Warden continued his assessment. "Our analysis of your incident report concludes that you should have covered your face in some way, called for your vehicle, and exited as if you had just suffered an injury. That would have increased the likelihood of a successful retreat than your tactic of running upstairs, doffing your suit, and flying away. Your unwise action triggered the need for one witness to be neutralized and another to be dissimulated."

"Both actions seem to have been successful."

"One, anyway. The one who was neutralized . . ." The Warden consulted the screen. ". . . Geniato Belligrado . . . accepted the annuity, has been resettled far away, and has agreed to become an Ally. The other . . . Jack March . . . . It still remains to be seen. He is an aggressive sort. Managing him is now your responsibility. Now, as to the penalty, the Warden Council has decided that you will be placed on probation for five years. Another incident will add thirty years to your sentence."

Before the verdict, she hadn't been able to resist quivering her wings in anxiety. Now, they grew still as she relaxed. *Probation!* Not a sentence to a penal planet. Not even an extension of her sentence. E'iouy would be pleased. She would call him as soon as the hole departed.

She left the clearing and returned to the wormhole landing site, where one last package was being brought through from the other side. It was a large metal cylinder with a folded parabolic reflector on one end and a control panel on the other. After it was hefted through, one of the werewolves managing it, pressed buttons on the panel. Four sturdy metal robotic legs unfurled from the cylinder's body, and with the rising whine of electric motors, the cylinder walked itself to a waiting freight truck and up the extended ramp.

The cargo delivery complete, the lights in the hole dimmed. The vampires were more comfortable in the darkness, and they seemed to glide forward to conduct their business with others of their kind who emerged.

The fairies, trolls, werewolves, gnomes, and elves went to their vehicles, and began to don their flesh-suits, transforming from a menagerie of species into the planet's natives—tall, short, fat, thin, male, female, light-skinned, and dark-skinned.

A'eiio had begun to do the same, but some nagging puzzlement stopped her. That last shipment wasn't the usual cargo container, but some kind of apparatus. She went over to the truck, where a werewolf worked inside the back securing the mysterious metal cylinder.

"That doesn't look familiar," she said to the werewolf. "What's it for?"

The werewolf stood up from its task and glared at her for a long moment, curling his lips to reveal needle-sharp fangs. Then saying nothing, he leaped out and slammed down the truck's overhead door.

• • •

Jack entered the bar with its usual bunch of familiar, woozy local drinkers and sat on the same stool he'd occupied when he first saw

Sam. It might help him sort through the profoundly disturbing previous night. Phil plunked the glass down in front of Jack and stood, eyebrows raised expectantly, waiting for the usual order.

"Yeah, double please, sir," said Jack. He didn't order the cheap stuff. He needed everything to remain as usual as possible, given his traumatic experience. Phil nodded and obliged, then moved off to serve a gaunt middle-aged woman at the end of the bar. Jack motioned him back over. "Say, I was in here last night."

"Wouldn't know. I wasn't. Got sick in the afternoon."

"Yeah, there was another guy here. Not one of your other guys."

"They got sick, too. Roberto was here with me, but we both didn't feel good. Maybe a bad sandwich or something."

"That's weird."

"Yeah, I woulda had to close down and disappoint all my friends . . ." He grinned and gestured at the regulars who were in every night. "But I was draggin' my ass around after Roberto left, and there was a guy here who said he was a bartender who didn't have a shift that night. His name was Anthony. He gave me a reference . . . another bar . . . and I called. They said he was honest and a good worker, so I took a chance and turned over the bar to him and went home. I felt better around midnight, so I did manage to come back and close out the register. The bar had a good night, it turned out. More customers than usual."

"I need to contact the guy. Ask him about a girl I was with."

Phil chortled, his jowly face breaking into a grin. "Jackie-boy, did you forget to get her number? Not like you!"

"Sometimes it happens."

"Well, I paid the guy in cash. He left me a number, in case I needed him again." Phil rummaged around beside the cash register and came up with a slip of paper, handing it to Jack. He went outside where it was quieter and punched the number in on his phone.

"Yeah," a voice answered loudly. The noise of a bar in the background made it hard to hear.

"Anthony, are you the guy who took over for Phil last night?"

"Yeah, can I help you?"

"I wonder if you remember me. I was in . . . with a girl."

"That narrows it down."

"I'm a young guy, blondish hair, wore a coat and tie. She was really good-looking. Cute face. Really blue eyes. Had a red dress on."

"You drank doubles?"

"Yeah, I was here with her for about an hour."

There was a long pause. "Uh . . . friend, you were alone."

"*What?* No, no. She made a phone call. She was really upset, crying because she was stood up. You would have noticed that."

"I did notice you. Okay, pal, I don't want to offend you or anything, but you acted weird. You sat there drinking and talking to yourself. To tell the truth, I was thinking of calling police. But you seemed like a regular, and I was just a temp there. So, I thought maybe you just talked to yourself and that was you being you. And you didn't cause trouble, and you paid, so I thought I'd just leave you alone."

"No, I was with this girl. She—"

"Sorry, bud, you got to deal with your problem. I can't help you." He hung up.

Jack went back into the bar, gulped down his drink and ordered another. He puzzled over the phone call. The guy said he was alone. Was Jack going nuts? Should he go see a doctor? Well, the experience in his apartment *was* hallucinatory. Colors on walls, monsters in his bed. The girl who wasn't there.

But what about the evidence that it was real? Those mesmerizing kisses, her undressing him, her naked. That experience must have been real! But the rest of the evidence was shaky, really shaky. He could have just buckled his pants loosely that day. Funny taste in his mouth?

42

What the hell did that prove? Empty liquor bottle? That argued for a drunken stupor, not hallucinations. Neatly draped coat and tie? That just meant he was a neat drunk. If he were covering a story as a reporter, none of that stuff would make the cut in the first draft.

But there *was* one thing. He took out the envelope, peering into it. The coarse hair was still there. His sanity literally hung by a hair. Fortunately, there was one expert who could help him and who owed him a favor.

. . .

A'eiio rolled over, willed herself to wakefulness, and looked somberly at her husband's peacefully sleeping face. She waited until he stirred, then stroked that face gently, until he opened his sapphire eyes.

"You got in late," he whispered in a voice thick with sleep.

"The unloading took longer. Some kind of accident on the road from the farm. But I got the new suits. And some news that's . . . well . . . not terrible. And some that's great."

Now he was wide awake, wrinkling his brow and rolling to face her, stretching his wings out behind him to unlimber his flight muscles. "Does 'not terrible' news means it's bad? Give me that news first."

"The Warden put me on probation for five years. Another incident adds thirty years to my sentence."

"Oh, no," he groaned, kissing her gently. "Well, we're in this together. I'll go where you go . . . and stay where you stay."

She unlimbered her own wings and began to flutter them faster and faster until they lifted her lithe, naked, white body off the bed and carried her to her feet beside the bed. "Well, if it comes to a longer sentence, you're going home when yours is up. I don't want the guilt of knowing that you remained an exile when you didn't want to."

"Absolutely not, and—"

"And you could take the baby back with you." She smiled. "That's the great news."

He uttered an exultant fairy trill and willed his wings to lift him into the air, hovering and staring at her, wide-eyed.

"Baby?"

"Yes. Well, maybe babies. I sort of felt flutters . . . little baby wings. So, I ordered a test kit. It came in last night, and I tested positive!"

Even in their high-ceilinged bedroom, it was a challenge to execute a loop, but he managed one, returning to an upright position to hug her. "Wow! Well, we'll just have to celebrate!"

"Of course, there are lots of logistics and problems, but—"

"Forget problems! We've got two years to solve problems."

"I'll get fat."

"Yeah, fairy-fat. That's normal compared to these creatures' fat. Nobody will notice. You'll still be gorgeous."

They sat on the bed making plans for a long while, before she roused herself to business. The first task was to find out what was going on with the reporter who'd seen her. After she'd showered, oiled her wings, and donned her new and beautifully fitting flesh-suit, she phoned Anthony the bartender.

He answered sleepily, and she apologized for waking him.

"Don't fairies ever sleep?" he grumped. She ignored the complaint. He'd been a faithful Ally since they'd recruited him. He became an Ally after he had stumbled on a drunken werewolf who had stripped off his flesh-suit and was taking a pee behind his bar.

"Did you hear from the reporter?"

"Yeah, he called last night. I told him what you told me to . . . that there was nobody with him in the bar."

"I really need to know what the reporter said when he heard that."

"Not much. I guess he bought it. But there was one thing that might worry you."

44

She tensed. "What was that?"

"Well, he had a really clear memory of Sam. Described in detail of what she looked like, what she did. I've seen a lot of drunks with memory problems in my time. He didn't strike me as one of them. And Sam . . . She is one memorable pixie!"

• • •

Bernie, a squat, round man with a scraggly goatee, plopped onto the park bench beside Jack. He tapped his battered briefcase significantly.

"So, as of now, I don't owe you *shit*," he declared.

"Well, as of ten minutes from now you don't owe me shit, when you tell me everything that you found," countered Jack.

Bernie leaned toward Jack and pulled his baseball cap down lower, pushing his sunglasses up. "Okay, I was never here. You never saw me."

"Cut the spy shit, Bernie. You're a lab tech. The Bureau doesn't follow its lab geeks."

"Our agreement stands, even though you were fired from the paper?"

"Laid off. And yes, you're still a source. I don't reveal sources. And I obviously won't tell how I saved your ass during the lab scandal. And again, I wasn't fired. I was laid off. Budget reasons."

"Yeah, you saved my ass . . . true. But you screwed my friends."

"They were guilty, Bernie. They're the ones who faked the lab results, which ended up overturning a shitload of convictions. I had to report the truth."

Bernie stared at him for a full minute, then sighed and reached into his briefcase. He pulled out his tablet computer and called up a series of graphs. "Okay, we've got some usual results and some unusual results . . . even abnormal."

"What are the usual results?"

"I ran your urine sample. You were dosed with a hallucinogenic and an anesthetic."

"No shit! I was having hallucinations. I saw . . ." He hesitated to complete the sentence. But he realized that Bernie didn't know enough to realize Jack was on the trail of something really weird. The lab tech would think he was just describing a bad trip. "I saw creatures. A big hairy one. And a flying one."

"Uh . . . well . . . actually, that turns that same result into something unusual."

"How so?"

"It means I may have missed something." He swiped his finger down the screen, scanning through the results. "See, the hallucinogenic you were given doesn't cause the kind of visions where you see things that aren't there. It causes people to hallucinate vivid colors, and see objects, like, melt and distort."

"Yeah, I had those, but I also saw creatures. What would you have missed?"

"I dunno, but there must have been something else in your system besides that drug. Tell me what you saw."

Jack hesitated again, but decided that describing the monsters wouldn't give away the fact that he was coming to believe that they were real. He spent the next ten minutes describing the creatures that had so horrified him, in as much detail as he could remember. Bernie's frown grew more and more pronounced.

"Look, I've got degrees in pharmacology and psychology. I've got to tell you, I don't know of *any* drug that produces these kinds of hallucinations. I'd normally think you were going schizophrenic, but schizophrenics don't have those kinds of hallucinations, either. They hear voices or have delusions, like thinking somebody's after them."

"So, my hallucinations were unusual. You said something else was unusual . . . you said even abnormal."

Bernie took the envelope containing the hair out of the briefcase and handed it to Jack. He then brought up an image on his tablet. "Here's the hair you gave me, under the microscope. It's totally abnormal . . . the ovoid bodies, the cuticle, the cortical fusi—"

"Those are hair parts?"

"Yeah, but . . . well . . . this is shaped like a hair . . . but it's not a known hair."

"What the hell does that mean?"

"It's probably a strand of fur from an animal . . . but not any animal in our database."

"Could it be a werewolf?"

Bernie rolled his eyes in disbelief. "Oh, hell, Jack, are you connecting your hallucinations with this hair? *I am out of here!*" He stuffed his tablet in his briefcase and leaped off the bench as if stung. "You're crazy!" he exclaimed, hurrying away.

Jack cursed himself for blurting out the question. The idea had just popped into his head, and he was stupid enough to express it out loud. If his reporter buddies ever found out that he was trying to prove the existence of werewolves, his career would be ruined. And he might even end up in a psych ward somewhere.

He held up the envelope. This *was* solid evidence, though, that something weird really invaded his bedroom. Now he needed more evidence about the encounter at the embassy. He punched the number for Anna on his cell phone.

Her first words were "You are still an *asshole*." But he could tell it wasn't the emphatic denunciation she'd spat at him before. Her voice was more subdued. "We've been getting calls from the guests saying that you've been trying to talk to them."

"I tried to be as discreet as possible," he said apologetically. "I'm sorry if it caused you trouble."

"Well, something did come up about your . . . person. I talked to one of our assistant protocol attachés. She said that before the toasts one of the guests left the table and didn't return."

"Who?"

"Senator Bright."

CHAPTER 5

D eborah visibly flinched when she found Jack March waiting for her, as she left the committee room. But she quickly recovered her composure, reassuring herself that he couldn't possibly recognize her. The matronly senator was very different from the slender, winged creature that he had witnessed sailing out the embassy window.

"Senator, could I have a minute of your time, please?"

She continued walking down the wide hall, her heels clicking on the marble floor. She tried to calm herself, to not seem too much in a hurry to escape him. "And you are?" she asked.

"Jack March. I'm a reporter."

"With what news organization?" She knew that would slow him down, perhaps fend him off.

"Well, I was with the *Capital Herald*."

"Excuse me. *Was?*" She kept walking, now consulting her schedule on her tablet computer.

"Well, I'm freelance now."

"And who are you freelancing for?"

"Well . . . uh—"

"Mr. March, the usual practice is that when a freelancer has a specific assignment, I'm happy to talk to them. So, when you get an assignment, contact my press secretary to arrange an interview."

Jack kept up with her, weaving his way through the crowd in the hall. "You were at the dinner for the new ambassador."

"Again, when you have an assignment, contact my press secretary."

"And you disappeared before the toasts. You didn't return."

A slight hesitation in the steady click of her heels betrayed the impact of his words. "I didn't feel well."

"I'm sorry to hear that. But you didn't leave . . . at least not by any of the exits. I have it from embassy sources that your car didn't fetch you. And nobody saw you take a cab."

Deborah stared straight ahead, saying nothing, but quickened her pace, making it into an elevator reserved for senators. As the paneled doors closed, Jack noted that her expression was grim, her jaw set.

Jack almost did a dance of delight. It was a bluff! He had no such information! But the bluff worked! *It was her! It was her!*

•   •   •

Jack had just reached a gloomy stretch of the quiet residential street midway between streetlights. His apartment building was two blocks away, so he was on automatic pilot, not paying attention, as he made his way along the familiar sidewalk. His mind was still in turmoil after the events of the day—the encounter with Senator Bright, and what he'd discovered from the hours of research on her in the main reading room of the National Library. To his skeptical reporter's mind, her background was murky, particularly suspicious.

That background became murkier when he'd called the development office at the university she'd graduated from. Using a trick that had worked before, he presented himself as representing an anonymous donor who wanted to endow a professorship at the university in Senator Bright's name. He was immediately transferred to an unctuous fundraiser, who would be delighted to help the donor set up the professorship.

He asked if he could obtain any information on her activities at the university "you know, clubs, organizations, photos, and so forth," he had said. "I'd like to have something to talk about, when we get together to discuss the endowment."

"Of course," said the chipper, young fundraiser. But when she called him back an hour later, she wasn't so much chipper as puzzled. Yes, there was a record of the senator receiving her degree. But the university archives couldn't locate any information on her activities while a student. No membership in a sorority or club, no student government participation, no sports clubs, no articles mentioning her in the student paper.

"Uh . . . well . . . I guess the senator was just a dedicated student," said the fundraiser.

And a ghost, Jack had thought to himself. *Or some weird, winged creature with silver hair and blue eyes.*

Now, he was plodding along the darkened street, head bowed in deep rumination. So he didn't pay attention to the black van stopping past the next intersection to let someone out. And he didn't pay attention to that someone approaching him.

"Hello, Jack," said the lilting feminine voice, jerking him back to attention.

It was Sam! She stood there smiling, her mesmerizing green eyes seeming to glow in the darkness.

It took a moment for Jack to tear his gaze away from her eyes, from her alluring face. "You did something to me . . . that night . . . you brought monsters with you."

She wrinkled her brow and made a puzzled face. "I don't remember that." Still she smiled—the smile of someone confident in their ability to dominate.

"Well, I damned well do. And you're going to tell me what happened." He moved forward and grabbed her arm.

"Sure, of course," she said gently. Her response startled him. He didn't expect such ready compliance. "You can come along with us, and we'll tell you everything."

At first he didn't get what she meant, but the sound of a vehicle zooming up from behind told him something bad was about to happen. It skidded to a halt, and she gently extricated herself from his grip and opened the front passenger door.

"You can sit up here." She gestured an invitation, and he looked in to see a small man . . . a *very* small man . . . driving.

"What if I don't want to?"

She looked cautiously up and down the street. It was deserted. "Well, if you don't want to ride up front, you can ride in back."

The back door slid open. Filling the opening was the same gray-green, hulking monster that had loomed over him that horrifying night in his apartment. It grinned, showing a jaw full of yellow fangs, its face a grotesque horror. It chuckled, making a sound that was a cross between a consumptive hacking and water gurgling down a toilet. A strong animal musk wafted out of the van. He remembered that smell.

"OH, NO!" He backed up against a thick hedge, eyes wide with fright, jaw agape. "HIM!"

"This is Mike," said Sam sunnily. "He's a very nice ogre. He'll be coming along. He'd be glad of the company in back."

Jack stood transfixed, trying to process the stunning sight and sort out the warring emotions that slammed against one another in his mind:

Flee! Get out of here fast and try to forget everything!

Fight! Try to punch, kick, and gouge to escape whatever the hell these things have planned for him.

Stay! Go with them and figure out what is going on.

He realized that the third choice was the only possibility. He almost certainly couldn't escape these creatures. He couldn't fight them. And even amid his panic, his reporter's obsessive curiosity told them this would be the greatest story ever!

If he survived.

The huge ogre just sat there, still grinning, staring at him with black-marble eyes, while Sam held open the passenger door.

Without a word, he stepped over to the passenger door and slid in. He heard Sam step into the back and the door slide shut.

•　•　•

All was darkness for Jack during the long, winding drive out of the capitol. They'd asked him to put on a blindfold, so he could only guess where they were going by the speed of the van and the waning sounds of the city. They had begun on surface streets, then onto a highway, and now on quiet, winding country roads.

The driver said nothing during the trip, but he could hear chattering from the back. Sam had begun talking . . . if that's what it was . . . in a twittering, lilting language that was not only foreign. It was *alien*, like no language he had ever heard. From the pauses in her conversation, he could tell she was talking on a cell phone.

Then, another pause, and she turned to English, still on the phone.

"Yes, he went willingly," she said. "I think he will accept. I don't know. You will have to show him the alternative, I think."

The aroma in the van was decidedly mixed. There was, of course, the musk emanating from the massive Mike. But there was also the delicious scent emanating from Sam, whatever that was.

The van stopped, and he could hear the metallic rattling of a large overhead door. The van rolled forward, and the echo of its engine noise told him they had entered a large building.

The driver slipped off Jack's blindfold, and with urgent gestures and in a squeaky, raspy gibbering—again like no language he had heard before—the driver indicated that he was to get out of the van.

He found himself standing in a cavernous building that had probably once been a factory. There were windows, but they had been blacked out, and the only illumination came from overhead lights.

With grunting and growling, the gray-green Mike hauled himself out of the back, followed by the sprightly Sam. She immediately began to remove her clothes.

"Hello," said a familiar voice, taking his attention away from the naked Sam. And thankfully from the hulking ogre Mike, who was now engaged in thoroughly scratching all parts of his body.

Jack turned to see Senator Deborah Bright, standing beside a table loaded with a buffet and bar service.

Beside her stood a large-chested man in an expensively tailored shirt and a red silk tie. Incongruously, he wore a broad-brimmed hat, the kind hunters wore. "You want a drink?" he asked. "We have some excellent choices." The man took a healthy drink from a glass of amber liquid.

"Uh, I don't think so."

The man chuckled. "Well, you'll sure want a big damn drink in a little while!"

That booming voice triggered Jack's recognition of the man. It was Senator Warren F. Lee, the ultraconservative, whose outsized presence dominated most events he attended. But perhaps not this one.

Senator Bright stepped forward. "We usually introduce prospective Allies to ourselves gradually, so as not to terrify them. But we think you're able to take the . . . well . . . the shock. After all, you've already had one encounter with Mythicals."

"Mythicals?" asked Jack.

"That's what we call ourselves." She motioned for Mike and Sam to come forward. "You've been introduced to Mike . . . an ogre. And you certainly know Sam, but you don't know that she's what your culture calls a pixie."

Then emerging from the shadows came the squat, ugly creature that had crouched at the foot of his bed. He shuddered at the memory.

"This is Steve. He's a troll. And . . ." She waved her hand, and a humming rose from the building rafters. The slender, milky-skinned creature with silver hair that had hovered over him spiraled gracefully down to the concrete floor, her glistening wings fluttering to rest as she landed. ". . . this is Robin. She's a fairy. Like me."

Jack felt a panic overcoming him. He was barely managing to hold it together at the sight of all these creatures surrounding him. This was no experience he could explain away by drugs! There were no swirling colors or melting, undulating objects.

This was mind-melting real!

"Now, we'll show you something that not a lot of your species have seen," said Bright, smiling gently. Both senators began to disrobe, ending up as a pair of naked middle-aged people—one a plump, pale woman, and the other a large, hairy man. Both pressed their fingers to their chests.

Their skin seemed to sag off their bodies!

Jack felt his knees buckling, but as he crumpled, he was caught by Mike's powerful arms and held up. A chair was brought, and he flopped onto it, panting, hyperventilating. He managed to recover himself, remembering the flesh-colored rubbery pile he'd seen in the bedroom. It was some kind of disguise!

Both senators grasped their scalps and pulled upward. Their faces stretched out into distorted caricatures and popped off, dangling down their backs. Now, Senator Bright's face became the delicate-featured visage he had seen in the bedroom. She removed brown contact lenses, to reveal the hypnotic sapphire eyes he had seen flashing with fear.

And Senator Lee, shed of his flesh, became the hairy, fanged beast that had terrified him that night!

Both continued to strip off their fleshy coverings, Bright narrating. "These are flesh-suits. They're actually biologically engineered tissues of living cells tailored to our specifications. They allow us to live normally among your race. It was not always so. Before the suits were developed, we had to live in isolation."

Finally, she was out of the suit, dropping it into a nearby barrel. She was totally, comfortably naked, he noted, with high firm breasts and the other normal female parts—except for the graceful, transparent wings.

Senator Lee, now free of his suit stretched and yawned. He pulled out false teeth, to reveal the fangs that the terror-stricken Jack had feared would rip this throat out that night.

"As you might have surmised, I'm what you call a werewolf." Again, he stretched his thickly-furred, muscular body and growled in animal pleasure.

Jack leaned forward, rubbing his face with both hands, then shook his head in disbelief. "Okay, you call yourselves Mythicals. But what are you? Where are you from? Senator Bright?"

"Call me A'eiio. That's the name I've taken here. In your language, anyway. We're from other planets. Many other planets."

"Why are you here?"

"We're all exiles. We committed some offense on our planets. We were sentenced to yours as punishment."

"Sentenced?"

"Our races use your planet as a prison . . . well, to be kinder, a place where we can atone for our transgressions."

Jack's mind roiled with questions. He had so many, he was nearly catatonic with curiosity.

"I . . . I . . . really have to process all this. Organize my—"

"Now do you want that drink?" interrupted Senator Lee.

"Yes, please," Jack replied, with a faint groan. He accepted a tumbler of liquor from Lee's large, clawed hand and drank it down, thankful for the familiar warm feeling and the comforting buzz. He gratefully took another. He looked up dully at the werewolf. "What are you called? In . . . werewolf."

"Flaktuckmetang," is the closest English pronunciation.

"What do they call you for short?"

"Flaktuckmetang. No nicknames, either. Werewolves consider shortening a name as demeaning. The equivalent of shortening their manhood. Cause for a fight. You'd better learn full pronunciations."

"We know you have a thousand questions," said A'eiio. "And they'll all be answered. We want you to stay here tonight. There's a very comfortable suite here. Steve, Robin, Mike, and Sam will stay with you. They'll help you with questions. Flaktuckmetang and I have to attend to business. Tomorrow, we'll take a trip. And we'll ask you to make a decision."

"What decision?" asked Jack, taking another grateful drink.

"Whether to become an Ally or not."

"What's an Ally? And what's the alternative? And why do I—"

"Tomorrow," she interrupted. "You'll have your questions answered by then."

The whisper of wings from a large open window interrupted them. A snowy white figure sailed into the cavernous building, its feathered wings spread wide. With powerful strokes, the figure lowered itself gently down to the floor. The creature had the luminous face of a beatifically smiling woman with golden ringlets and wearing a billowing, filmy tunic.

"Ah, here she is," said A'eiio. "Jack, this is Wendy. She's an angel."

．　．　．

Jack's hands still trembled slightly, and he had to use both to take a healthy drink of his fourth round. But they were shaking less than before. The alcohol had helped blunt the smothering panic that had shrouded him since his abduction. It didn't help, though, that he was sitting at a large dining table with an ogre, a pixie, a fairy, a troll, an elf, and an angel. The table was in a large apartment built into the factory floor, where he'd been "invited" to stay the night.

He still found himself transfixed by the sight of the angel, her ethereal presence calling to mind the rapturous descriptions of radiant angelic appearances in the world's religious texts. Angels had saved lives, changed lives, brought faith to the faithless. And now, one of the hallowed beings was sitting right there at his table! And now he knew it was an alien from another planet!

He took a deep breath, to help the alcohol further its job of steadying him. All the creatures were eating. Well, Mike the ogre was *devouring*—stuffing handfuls of random foods into his mutant-bulldog face. At least he was making appropriately appreciative grunts. The angel, however, was not eating, but sitting quietly, smiling warmly at the others.

"What's going to happen to me?" he managed to ask. "What are you going to do?"

Sam paused in the graceful act of daintily transferring morsels of a translucent, golden substance to her mouth. "A'eiio will answer that. She'll come back tomorrow. We're just here to answer other questions. We . . ." She paused and wrinkled her nose at him. "You're staring at us."

Jack realized his attention had been riveted on the naked pixie, the naked fairy, and most disconcerting, the naked angel. "Oh . . . sorry . . . I, uh—"

"Are you uncomfortable with seeing our . . . *parts?*"

"Well, we don't usually go around naked."

"You creatures are so odd," said Robin, her wings gently wafting open and closed. "You are ashamed by the natural beauty of your own bodies. You hide them with needless artificial decoration. Very well, we'll cover, so you won't be so disturbed." She left and returned with a towel, which she wrapped around her slim body. Sam put her dress back on, and Wendy the angel wrapped herself in her long, white, feathered wings.

"Better?" asked Robin.

"Thanks."

"Wanna see my balls?" asked Mike in his gurgly, water-flushing-down-the-toilet voice. He'd paused in his gluttony.

"Not one little bit," said Jack emphatically.

"Mike is very proud of his balls," said Robin. "Do you know ogres decorate their balls?

"I do now. Still, I'll pass," said Jack as he finished his drink and felt comfortably drunk enough to begin eating. Mythicals were good cooks. The seafood casserole was delicious. He'd have to ask about their talents. He had so many, many questions.

He asked Robin the fairy, "The name 'A'eiio'. Does it mean anything?"

"It's the closest she can come to her name in our tonal language."

"Werewolves have long names," observed Jack.

"Not compared to elves," said Sam, gesturing at the gray-skinned elf, to whom he'd been introduced as Ryan. "His elf name is Cvjmgrowfjhvvglehjhiiorddvmgtohq. Elves pass down their names and add a letter for each new generation.

Cvjmgrowfjhvvglehjhiiorddvmgtohq paused in his eating long enough to make a scritchy-screeching sound, like an excruciating chorus of a badly tuned violin, fingernails on a chalk board, and a cat with its tail caught in a blender.

"Elves prefer not to speak your language. It hurts their vocal cords."

"Well, the sound he just made would hurt mine," said Jack. Now that he was full of alcohol and food, Jack felt his fear waning and his journalistic impulse taking over. "Okay, I've seen fairies, pixies, angels, trolls, werewolves, ogres, and elves. Are there others?"

"Oh, yes," said Sam. "Just about all the creatures of your mythology."

"Goblins, vampires, witches, warlocks?"

"Yes."

"Leprechauns, mermaids, demons, cyclops?"

"Of course."

Jack plumbed his memory for more. "Gnomes, satyrs, bigfoot, sirens?"

"All of those, at one time or another. Some served their sentences and were allowed back to their home planets. Others periodically arrive to begin their exile."

"Now, you're all kind of shaped like us," said Jack, waving his arms in illustration. "Why aren't there any weird Mythicals, y'know, that look like blobs or octopuses?"

"Yes, there are . . . on other exile planets," said Sam. "Each species chooses an exile planet that that species can more easily blend into." She laughed a melodic laugh. "But, of course, weird is in the eye of the beholder. It takes some of us quite a while to get used to your peculiar shape."

"But there have been *really* different creatures here . . . dragons, sea serpents, and so forth," said Jack.

"*Pets,*" growled Steve, running his fork through his scraggly white hair. "Centuries ago, some exiled Mythicals were allowed to bring pets. Bad, bad idea. They escaped."

"You said you all are exiles. What crimes did you all do?"

There rose a chorus of protestations, each creature declaring its innocence, until Robin raised her hand for quiet. "Of course, none of us deserves to be here. But our justice systems accused us of various violations of our law. Theft, sedition, embezzlement, and so forth."

"But you're not violent, right?"

"Well, some species are naturally . . . aggressive, I guess you'd say. Especially werewolves. But we weren't sent here for violent crimes."

"Do you have jobs?"

"Sure," said Sam. "We blend in. Lots of pixies are ballerinas, actresses, spies, queens."

"Actresses, spies, queens?"

"Yes, for some reason, we enchant your species. It seems to be some chemical attractant. So we tend to be very successful."

"Are there any well-known women today who are pixies?"

"Well, I don't want to name any. But you've seen them in movies, on magazine covers, in commercials. The ones who just rivet your attention."

"Ogres are football players, basketball players, bouncers, wrestlers," interjected Mike.

"Fairies are lawyers, legislators, professors," said Robin.

"Angels do caring jobs . . . social work, nursing, doctoring, and so forth," said Wendy.

A scritchy-screech emanated from Cvjmgrowfjhvvglehjhiiorddvmgtohq.

"He says many elves are jockeys," said Robin. "They also masquerade as kids. They say they're home-schooled, so they don't have to interact too much with you creatures."

The liquor, the food, and the trauma of the day were causing Jack to begin to nod off.

"Let's get you to bed," said Sam gently, helping him up and guiding him, stumbling, toward the bedroom.

"So, it wasn't just the drugs that you gave me that made me so . . . goofy."

"No," she said, smiling tolerantly. "You were what you would call enchanted." She pulled back the covers, sat him onto the bed, and removed his shoes, jacket and shirt.

"You said chemicals?"

She laid him down on the bed, and pulled the covers up. "Something like pheromones. Our race evolved natural substances that just happened to lure your race. You can tell when we're emitting them. Our eyes turn green."

"Um . . . are you wearing one of those suits? Are you going to take it off and be some kind of slimy thing?"

"No, this is me." She took his hand and ran it over the soft skin of her face.

"Yeah, that feels like it's you." His eyes were closing. "I love you," he murmured.

"I know," she said gently.

"You're amazing." His eyes closed. He was asleep.

"You ain't seen nothin' yet," she whispered, kissing his forehead and tucking the covers around him.

CHAPTER 6

J ack peered out the window, as the private jet swept over the tan desert landscape and gently touched down on the isolated runway. He was thankful for that. He didn't need any jostling or bumping. His head had only just cleared of his hangover, after drinking lots of water and eating a good meal on the trip from the capitol to . . . *somewhere* in the desert. His host didn't divulge that information. He was not yet trusted. Not until he made his "decision," whatever that would be.

He allowed himself to daydream about the mesmerizing pixie, Sam, as he watched Senator Deborah Bright sitting across from him, putting away her laptop. And beside her sat her husband, Marc, sliding a sheaf of legal papers into his briefcase.

Jack apologized for his drunken behavior at the embassy reception, and Marc accepted, clapping him jovially on the back.

They exited the plane into the brilliant glare of desert sunlight and the dry heat that sucked the moisture from his nose, mouth, and eyes. He squinted as he scanned the flat, barren landscape stretching into the distance, all around them. The only buildings were a large hangar and a sprawling adobe house. They had explained to him that they were taking him to a central interplanetary transport terminal for the Mythicals. There were locals, for example, on the Brights' property near the capitol. But they wanted him to experience the full extent of the Mythicals activity on the planet.

Senator and Mr. Bright showed him into the cool shade of the house's entry hall, and he was invited to clean up in one of the bedrooms. There, he found a change of clothes, sunglasses, a wide-brimmed hat, and desert boots . . . his size. They had done this exercise before.

He emerged refreshed from the bedroom to find, not the Senator and her husband, but two graceful fairies. They had shed their flesh-suits, and stood fanning their wings, lifting themselves off the floor and settling back down, as if eager to soar. In deference to Jack's discomfort with exposed "fairy parts," A'eiio wore a filmy tunic, and her husband wore a pair of swimming briefs.

Jack stood silent for a long moment, watching them. It was a revelatory moment. These were beautiful creatures, he thought. The world was a richer place because of them, even though his race believed them to be only diverting myths . . . fairy tales.

Marc was now introduced as the fairy E'iouy.

"It's the closest to your name you can come in our language?" he'd asked.

"Yes," he answered. "We feel rather badly for you. Your language is rather . . . shall we say . . . un-melodic."

"We hope you're rested," said A'eiio. "We have a trip to make, and you have things to see, a decision to make."

"Decision? Look, I still don't understand."

"You will. You need to see some things first. Then we'll talk."

A white off-road vehicle waited for them outside the house, and it took them speeding across the desert floor for miles, ending up winding along a dusty road into a steep-sided canyon. They passed several other vehicles on the roadside, beside which stood people scanning the horizon, presumably for intruders. Those were other Allies, A'eiio explained.

As they reached a broad expanse of desert surrounded by steep mountains, he saw perhaps a dozen other off-road freight trucks and other vehicles parked around the periphery. The driver eased their vehicle in among them.

A single ogre stood in the middle of the expanse, peering upward. He held up his meaty gray-green arm in a signal, and a menagerie of creatures emerged from the vehicles.

Jack, still sitting in the back seat, experienced a *really* bad case of the jitters. He *really* didn't want to get out to face that weird throng! A flight of fairies emerged from a limousine, fanning their wings and lifting smoothly off the desert floor, raising small dust clouds, soaring in gentle circles overhead. Trolls, werewolves, and elves crowded around the large circle, all peering upward. An angel alighted from a van, spreading her gloriously white, feathered wings.

Then there were creatures he'd never seen before. Gnarled, ugly beings that might be goblins, or perhaps gnomes. Small, elf-looking creatures that weren't elves. Leprechauns?

A group of perhaps a dozen creatures stood huddled together, in black capes, hoods, and masks, sunglasses covering their eyes.

"Don't be afraid," said A'eiio, interrupting his awestruck reluctance. "They're used to seeing your kind. After all, they live among you. Come on out."

Jack managed to unfreeze himself and climb out to face the throng. "What are those?" he asked, pointing to the hooded group.

"Poor things," she said. "Vampires. They absolutely hate sunlight, but it's a daytime landing, so they have no choice."

"Landing?"

She pointed upward, where the crowd of Mythicals was staring, and far above them was a hole in the sky. A black dot growing larger.

"ON!" Bellowed the ogre into a radio. "NOW TURN THE LIGHTS ON!"

Abruptly, the dot almost disappeared against the sky, showing a faint white spot that could just as easily have been a wisp of cloud.

"*Elves!*" spat the ogre.

"What *is* that?" asked Jack.

E'iouy had come up on the other side of him, and they all watched the white dot become a globe whose image shimmered in the desert heat, an aurora of faint colors swirling around it.

"The technical term for what you're seeing is a spontaneous trans-dimensional aperture," said A'eiio over the hiss and crackle emanating from the globe. "Common name, wormhole. In some galactic regions, the space-time fabric periodically weakens in spots, and allows these holes to just pop open."

"And they're holes to . . . where?"

"We don't really know. Maybe to other regions of this universe; maybe to other connected universes . . . like a froth of soap bubbles. All we know is that more than a thousand years ago, a few races discovered how to use magnetic fields to capture them. Basically, they used gigantic shells to enclose them and the magnetic fields to hold them open. And, they found the same fields could guide them, so they could use them for transport through space. And those races taught those on the other side of the wormholes how to use them, as well. More and more races were connected. Now, there are fifty-three races in the transdimensional network, part of what we call the Alliance. We think there may be more races that we don't know of yet."

"You mean there may be other races you don't know about coming through wormholes to our universe?"

A'eiio didn't answer, but gave E'iouy a worried glance.

Jack realized there would be no answer, so he kept going. "And they can move through our space?"

"Yes, they are basically spaceships that aren't affected by gravity or inertia; *and* they can transport matter, including living creatures, between worlds . . . or perhaps universes. The elves have proved to be the best pilots. They're most adept at using magnetic fields to steer the holes through space on either side."

The shimmering white globe descended close enough that Jack could see the small figures of elves within it. The globe settled to just above the desert floor. From a perfect sphere, one side began to flatten slightly. A ramp emerged from it, its edge settling into the dusty desert floor.

"They use the magnetic field also to temporarily flatten one side to become an entrance or exit," explained A'eiio. "The only way to pass through a wormhole safely is directly perpendicular to the interdimensional plane. Otherwise, the hole would shred whatever it touched, like an infinitesimally sharp blade."

Jack shivered, as an elf stepped carefully out of the hole and down the ramp to the ground. He wore a large medallion, whose surface was studded with colored buttons, and carried himself with authority—if that could be said of such a small, wizened creature.

"That's a Warden," said A'eiio. "They oversee all the Mythicals' sentences, monitoring our conduct . . . and meting out punishment, if necessary."

With the elf Warden watching, the ogre who greeted the wormhole was joined by four more of his hulking kin, and they began to haul large cylinders from the hole, arranging them in a line. The strange collection of Mythicals began to mill around the cylinders, opening them and removing cargo, carrying boxes and packages to the waiting vehicles.

"How ironic," said Jack. "We've dreamed about aliens for decades, listened for signals from space, and they've been coming and going here the whole time. Amazing sight!"

"Well, Jack, you're not just here to watch," said A'eiio.

"What do you mean?"

"There's a decision I'm going to ask you to make. And in order to make it, you'll need to go through this wormhole."

• • •

Jack backed up to steady himself against the vehicle they'd arrived in, staring at the shimmering globe of the wormhole, trying to prevent himself from hyperventilating in anxiety. The ogres had finished unloading cargo, and now there emerged from the globe a line of Mythicals—fairies, ogres, werewolves, gnarled creatures that might be goblins, small, bearded men that were probably gnomes, red-eyed devilish-looking beasts that might be demons.

"New exiles," said A'eiio. "Coming to serve their sentences."

"I can tell," answered Jack.

Even though many were creatures he had never seen before, he could tell they were downcast. They moved ploddingly, heads down, past the elf Warden.

They trudged to waiting vehicles, meeting others of their kind who presented them with the large canisters that must have held their flesh-suit disguises. The mournful procession ended, and the elf Warden standing beside the wormhole gestured impatiently for a happier group to come forward.

"These are free?" asked Jack.

"Yes," said A'eiio. "Some have been here for many decades. Now they're going home."

The freed Mythicals stepped eagerly forward, babbling in their native languages—a cacophony of alien noise to Jack's ears—and stepping lightly up to the wormhole.

One by one, they mounted the ramp into the hole, and the elf Warden reached into a cylindrical trunk and drew out a crystal skull, which shimmered in the light.

"What are those?" asked Jack.

"Long, long ago, the custom became to bestow upon a freed Mythical a symbol of the end of their time on your planet. A crystal skull was decided on. It symbolizes the Mythicals' efforts to adapt to the planet's most advanced species."

"Well, it seems a little weird, but—" Jack started to say, but realized that now the wizened little elf Warden was waving at him!

"You can go through now," said A'eiio softly. "Another Warden will be waiting for you on the other side. You'll go through a series of wormholes in transit to our planet." She said the last words with a subtle catch in her voice.

"You're not coming with me?"

"No." Now her face grew somber. "I'm under sentence," she said, her voice tinged with melancholy longing. "I can't go back."

"Well, I just can't go without you," he said. "And I still don't understand why . . . what this decision is I have to make."

"Just go." A'eiio voice failed her, and tears rolled down her alabaster cheeks. E'iouy saw her grief and stepped forward, putting his arm around her and helping her away from the portal that could take her home.

The ogre tromped forward and grabbed his shoulder, shoving him forward, and growling, "You must go. They cannot stay on the surface."

He allowed himself to be manhandled up the ramp and through the shimmering hole. He found himself in a huge, white chamber, whose smooth interior surface was studded with metal probes. There, a helmeted elf dressed in what he took to be a spacesuit poked unceremoniously at him, shoving him toward an airlock door. He obediently stepped through, and chattering in screechy elvish, the elf swung the door shut behind him and locked it.

He was just beginning to suffer a combined fit of jitters and claustrophobia when the other airlock opened to reveal an elderly fairy waiting for him. The fairy's naked, pale flesh was sagging and wrinkled, his silver hair sparse, his sapphire eyes slightly dimmed with age. A gold chain with a large medallion hung around his neck. His wings—not as crystal clear as the other fairies Jack had encountered, were fluttering open and closed. This fairy, he guessed, was a bit perturbed at the process of traversing wormholes.

"I am . . ." He began to introduce himself, but instead of a spoken name, he sang a brief melodic phrase. "I am a Warden, and I will guide you."

"Thank you, but can you tell me what this is for? Why I'm doing this?"

The Warden sang another melody, presumably a name. "She will discuss everything with you. Come with me."

They had emerged into a chamber that was apparently a control room for the wormhole. An elf stood before a console festooned with a glittering array of colored lights, each emblazoned with other alien symbols. Floating above the console was a large, translucent, three-dimensional map of interconnected colored spheres, with a small whiter sphere at its center.

Jack followed the elderly fairy out of the control room, and to Jack's stunned surprise, into a vast hangar-like building lined with rows of house-sized white spheres like the one from which they had emerged. They were on another planet!

The fairy walked slightly unsteadily ahead of him, Jack guessed because he was not used to walking. Indeed, overhead, fairies flitted past, easily sailing along in the warm, humid air. Jack and the Warden passed a steady stream of various Mythical species wheeling cargo cylinders, and entering and leaving the control rooms of the spheres.

"This terminal houses wormholes that connect to planets with oxygen atmospheres like yours and ours," said the Warden. "There are other such terminals that house wormholes to planets whose atmospheres would be deadly to those of us who breathe oxygen. Here we are."

They reached a sphere with an inscription above its hatch that was an array of graceful symbols, none of which resembled letters. Entering the control room, the Warden consulted with an elf who stood before the wormhole's console. The elf touched several of the control panel lights, and the hatch door unlatched with a metallic clang and swung ponderously open. The elf twittered to them with seeming annoyance.

"Fortunately, we only have two transits to make to reach our system," said the Warden, beckoning him to enter the airlock leading to the wormhole.

"Transits?" asked Jack, but the Warden merely smiled tolerantly.

Jack's anxiety ebbed as the inner airlock door opened, and they made another transit through a wormhole, and through an airlock into another similar terminal, and then through yet another. As he transited, each terminal was clearly on another planet, the suffusing light yellower or bluer; the sounds strange to his ears, the aromas metallic or sweet or pungent.

"This transit takes us to our home," announced the Warden finally, as they made their way across an expanse of black crystalline floor in another terminal to a waiting sphere. His wings grew still, seeming to relax as they entered the final wormhole chamber.

"Do you have to travel much?" Jack regretted the question the instant he asked it. It was stupid small talk, but he couldn't think of anything else to say. Some journalist he was!

But the Warden nodded his head tolerantly. "Too much. The duties are not pleasant. But I have committed myself to them." He moved quickly to the wormhole, from which shone a rich amber light, and stepped through. Jack followed.

They exited the airlock to find themselves in a soaring crystalline dome, bathed in that warm light. Overhead flitted hundreds of fairies—male and female, young and old, large and tiny—their glimmering wings reflecting the light in evanescent flashes. The dome was filled with the harmonious hum of vibrating wings, and with a musical counterpoint of the intricate, intertwining melodious polyphony of singing voices. He felt enveloped in a continual, rich symphony.

The air was warm and moist, and rich with a mélange of fragrant, spicy, and sweet smells that reminded him of a combination bakery and florist shop.

A flight of fairies sailed down, came lightly to rest in front of him, and began to sing to the Warden. He replied with a short melody and turned to Jack.

"We can only stay a brief while, but they want to show you where we live."

Their wings folded, the fairies led Jack and the Warden to the dome entrance and outside it.

There, Jack looked out over a lush green landscape of rolling hills dotted with soaring clear crystal spires. The spires were adorned with translucent decks in colors of ruby, sapphire, emerald, amethyst, and citrine. Swirls of fairies landed and departed from the decks, swarming in a sky that was not the blue of the sky he knew, but an intense turquoise.

A silver airship the size of an ocean liner cruised silently overhead, slung beneath it a gleaming golden cargo carrier. On the ground, sleek translucent vehicles of different vivid hues glided along roads that appeared to be made of glass-smooth obsidian. They had no wheels, but floated just above the surface.

Peering upward at the vista, mouth agape, he had trouble catching his breath. He was feeling faint. He felt a steadying hand on his shoulder. It was the Warden.

"Take your time. Your race often has a moment of panic, or perhaps euphoria, or perhaps both, when they first arrive."

"I . . . uh . . . I think—"

"And don't try to talk. Just relax."

A ground vehicle eased up to them, and the group boarded it and sat in backless chairs that enabled them to stretch out their wings. The driverless vehicle accelerated smoothly along the obsidian road toward the tallest of the crystal buildings.

They passed what appeared to be shopping stalls, made of shimmering glass and alive with fluttering fairy customers. They passed broad lawns, where teams of young fairies competed in aerial versions of the ball games he had played at home. They passed an arena, where perhaps a thousand fairies watched two naked fairies, closely embracing, performing intimate aerobatics. Their movements suggested a sexual tryst, but he couldn't be sure. At one point loud, sing-song cheering rose from the audience.

Jack managed to recover himself from the panorama and revert to his journalist mode, but perhaps too eagerly. *Is this your only planet? Is this the biggest city? How many are you? What are your principal exports? How long do you live? What are—"*

"Just savor the experience," interrupted the Warden, patting his shoulder. "Just look, and listen, and smell, and taste, and feel. Just experience."

The vehicle eased to a stop at the building entrance. Some of the fairies launched themselves aloft, flying upward to a high floor, but the Warden and another fairy shepherded him inside, to a transparent clylindrical elevator, whose doors closed. Jack noted that their fellow passengers were either frail, ancient fairies that had probably lost their ability to fly, or fairy mothers holding tiny infant versions of themselves, who had perhaps not gained the ability to loft to the heights necessary to reach upper floors.

The elevator accelerated skyward, soaring to the top of the dizzyingly tall spire. Slightly acrophobic from the rapid rise, Jack emerged to find the group that had accompanied them, and to his surprise, several men and women.

He was introduced to a trim, young woman named Zorah, a middle-aged man named Porter, and two middle-aged men, Anton and Ben. He found it difficult to concentrate on them, as he marveled at the apartment's panoramic view, which showed miles of rolling forested hills, punctuated by spires. He could see in the distance a shining collection of the spires, of all shapes, like a gallery of crystal sculptures.

He managed to return his attention to the group, as Zorah shared that she and the others had decided not to become "Allies," a designation that Jack immediately queried her about. But she fell mute, shaking her head and glancing at the fairies with a smile.

"We've been asked to answer any questions about our lives here," she said. "But they've asked that they be allowed to explain everything to you later . . . not to prejudice your decision."

He asked "what decision?" but none of them would say more, as they moved out onto the spacious balcony. They sat at tables made of a glimmering green crystal, perhaps emerald, and piled with foods he had never encountered. As they watched the fairies flitting through the turquoise sky, he was invited to eat. He steeled himself for the possibly unpleasant tastes of an alien world. But all the dishes were delicious—the orchid-like flowers tasted like crisp lettuce; the spiral-shaped green vegetable tasted like squash; the delicate meat in the steaming stew tasted like lobster. But these were only approximations. The foods all had an exotic flavor all their own.

The three told him of their lives among the fairies—of their comfort, the many kindnesses shown them, the many entertainments, their fulfilling jobs, and the contentment of their daily lives. They declared that their days were rich and fulfilling among a civilization at peace with itself and with its planet.

Finally, the Warden told Jack it was time for them to leave, as one of their suns was setting, the other to rise after a few hours of night. The sunset revealed three moons, and the spires were illuminated in a rainbow of colors. They made their way back to the vast clear dome, now glowing in the night, that housed the wormhole chambers.

Jack was silent during the trip, but as they were about to enter the first wormhole transit back home, he balked.

"Look, this has been amazing," he told the Warden. "Your planet is stunning, your race extraordinary. But now, will you please tell me what this is all about. Why have you brought me here?"

The Warden bowed his head, considering his question, then turned to regard him with a benign tolerance.

"Because this may become your home."

• • •

"What if I try to escape?" asked Jack, as he sat across from A'eiio and E'iouy on the private jet flying them back to the capitol. Now, however, the two wore their flesh-suits, becoming Senator Deborah Bright and Marc Bright.

"We don't kill people, if that's what you're thinking. What we're offering you will be two perfectly benign choices."

"But what if I don't want either one? What if I try to escape?" he repeated.

"Let's concentrate on your options. Let me explain your options."

Jack leaned forward in the leather seat, his jaw set, impatiently awaiting an explanation. "One thing about our species," he declared. "We can be pains in the ass. We don't like being given options that are more like ultimatums."

"You had a headache when you woke up in your apartment."

"Yes?"

"Warren Lee, as you know him, implanted a coma chip at the base of your skull. It's about the size of a grain of sand. Very benign. But it means you can't escape."

"A werewolf implanting a coma chip? Doesn't sound benign."

"It is. All of us have them. It enables the Wardens to pinpoint our locations. And should any of us . . . exiles or Allies . . . become unruly, they can trigger it to cause us to lapse into unconsciousness. You become very sleepy at first, so you can lie down without being hurt. Then you just go to sleep."

"So, I'm a prisoner, like you."

"Look," said Marc, "In a real sense this is your own fault. After you saw A'eiio you could have just kept your mouth shut. Many witnesses have encountered Mythicals and while they were shocked, they decided nobody would believe them and kept quiet. We watched them for a while, then let them go on with their lives. You, however, came roaring downstairs into a crowd, drunk, hollering about seeing a creature. I happened to be in the entry hall when it happened."

"The waiter, Geniato, didn't say anything, and he disappeared. Is he dead?"

"He did say something. To you. And he's very happy. And you could be, too. Let me tell you about the options."

Jack shook his head in resignation. "Fine, I'm listening."

Deborah began what sounded like a recitation she had done before. "We give those who have discovered us two options. You may choose to live on our home planet, which you have seen. It is a pleasant life, with no worries, no pressure."

"And it means leaving my home, my family, my job."

"That's why you may choose to become an Ally."

"I heard that word on your planet."

"Being an Ally means risk, but it means a rewarding, challenging life on your home planet. It means that you pledge to keep our secret and to help us remain anonymous, in whatever role you find acceptable and gratifying."

"And betraying my race?"

"Not at all. You'll find that Mythicals are contributing to society. You'll help us do that."

"Okay, what do I get out of it, besides the possibility of being labeled a traitor?"

"You tell us what you want out of life. We help you get that."

"You mean make me rich, make me powerful?"

"Maybe. If riches are what you *really* want. Actually, that's where the myth about leprechauns and their pots of gold came from. Centuries ago, somebody caught a Mythical leprechaun, and he gave them riches. But when you think about it, that's probably not what you'll want."

"No, probably not." Jack sat back in his seat, his expression contemplative.

"We're like the genie giving you wishes. As a matter of fact, that's another old tale that involves Mythicals. We simply ask Allies what they hope to achieve in their lives, and we help them achieve it. We don't give it to them; we help them."

"I grew up in a small town in the north. Way back in the woods. Very isolated. But my parents had big ambitions for me. They sacrificed a lot to send me to school to be an engineer like them. They were frankly disappointed when I wanted to be a journalist. I want to prove to them that I'm successful."

"We can do that."

"I want to report on you."

Marc laughed sarcastically. "So you basically want to expose us all to your species? *Impossible!*"

"No, not at all. Here's the deal. You're a clandestine group . . . now. Nobody knows you exist, except for your Allies. But this is a new era of instant, global social media. If just one video of what I saw in that bedroom goes viral, you're revealed. It's going to happen. Until then, I'll protect your secret. Absolutely. But what I'm asking is that you let me cover everything you do. Everything. I'll cover the good things, but I'll also cover the bad. And if you are revealed, I'll put out the whole story. It'll be to your advantage."

"That's unprecedented," said Deborah, shaking her head. "Nobody has ever been given such knowledge. You could put us at grave risk . . . even put your species at grave risk."

* * *

Jack sat on his couch in his apartment, his phone in one hand, a drink in the other. He was trying to drink his way to bravery. Over the last few days, he'd seen things that had shaken him to his soul.

He took a drink, his hand still trembling a bit. He still occasionally got those shivers when he thought about the trip through the wormholes and the "options" he'd been given.

But he'd also summoned the courage—even without alcohol—to assert himself. And now, A'eiio was talking to her Warden about whether to grant his audacious journalistic request. If they let him cover them, he could go down in history.

An abrupt signal from his phone startled him out of his reverie. It was a text from Sam! His day had just gotten much better. Then he read the text, and it got much stranger.

"I'm dancing tonight. The City Ballet. Left you a ticket. Please come! You'll meet some friends."

She was a ballerina! She'd mention that some pixies were ballerinas, but he hadn't realized she meant herself. He was eager to see Sam again. *Very* eager! But meeting her friends? He didn't know whether he could withstand the charms of more than one pixie. Sam was intoxicating enough. And why had she contacted him now?

He decided that, after what he'd been through, sitting quietly in a dark theater watching a pixie dance was a piece of cake. He messaged her back, accepting with pleasure.

Now to make a call he'd dreaded. Anna and he had been dating for about six months, and until his drunken behavior at the reception, had enjoyed each other's company. And the sex was great. But for both their sakes, the relationship had to end.

She answered quickly, and with accusation. "Jack, you didn't call. You didn't return my calls. What's going on with you?"

"I'm sorry. Look, Anna, I'm involved with something that you don't need to know about." He stopped himself. *How stupid of him!* He absolutely regretted telling her that the instant it came out of his mouth. Now she would be suspicious.

"What do you mean? Does it have something to do with that intruder you said had wings? *What the hell, Jack?*"

"I'm sorry, Anna. I like you a lot. You're a great person. And that's why we can't see each other anymore."

"What did you find out, Jack? What's this all about?"

"Anna, you take care of yourself. I've got to go."

"Jack!"

He ended the call, cursing himself. He had left her suspicious. She might tell her boss about her suspicions, who would notify the government's foreign affairs department. Or maybe the intelligence agencies. They would make it their business to investigate an unknown intruder in a friendly embassy. And to investigate a laid-off reporter who knew something he wasn't telling. *Shit!* He'd have to figure what to tell the Mythicals, if anything.

He worried over his stupidity until it was time for him to leave for the ballet. He took care to dress in his best suit. He took a cab to the Capital Performing Arts Center, picked up his ticket and made his way to his seat, fifth row, third seat from the aisle in the soaring, warmly lit theater with its gold curtain. *Nice seat,* he thought absent-mindedly. He was deeply involved in mulling over his foolishness and the decision he had to make.

So he did not pay attention to the tall, somewhat sinister-looking four men who took the seats on either side of him.

The lights went down, the curtain swept open and the ballet began. It was a drama of love and betrayal. On a dimly lit stage, the dancers writhed and gyrated through ominous scenes. Jack scrutinized all of them, looking for Sam. But when she appeared, there was no doubt it was her.

As an alluring temptress—an appropriate role—she was riveting, elegant, sensuous, as she seemed to float across the stage in a tattered, diaphanous dress.

"That is our mutual friend," he heard a rumbling voice in his right ear. He flinched and turned to see looming beside him a large man in a black suit, black shirt, and blood red tie.

"Uh, excuse me?"

"We are friends of Sam," said the man gesturing at the four men flanking Jack, two on either side.

He suddenly felt hemmed in.

From his left came a similarly deep, stentorian voice, muttering "Good ballet. I like the dark themes."

"Uh . . . if you say so." He tried to concentrate on the stage, as the ballet continued through its first act, its foreboding atmosphere adding to his growing discomfort at being boxed in by these men.

Intermission didn't bring any relief.

"Won't you join us for a drink?" asked the man on his left.

He couldn't very well refuse, since they'd advertised themselves as friends of Sam's.

As they made their way out of the theater, he couldn't help noticing that all four were dressed in black, except for a splash of red—a red tie, a red cravat, a red pocket handkerchief, a red scarf. Some kind of signal? And all four were preternaturally tall, towering over the other theater-goers.

They entered the soaring foyer, with its crystal chandeliers and red carpeting, and headed to the bar. The glittering crowd in formal dress was milling tightly around it, seeking an alcoholic libation to add a pleasant glow to the evening. But Jack knew that no amount of alcohol could stem his growing anxiety.

The four towering men seemed to part the crowd. Whether the person in their path was an imperious dowager or a silver-haired mogul, the objects of their attention would take one look at the phalanx approaching them, grow quiet, and back away.

Jack wondered whether they had some pheromonal power like Sam's; only theirs was the power to intimidate, even frighten.

"We'll have something that's blood-red" said the one that had been to his right. Then abruptly he laughed, and the others grinned and chuckled. "Just kidding. We'll have what you drink. We will like it."

"Uh, okay. How did you know what I like?"

"A little bird told us. She dances like a lovely bird in flight, does she not?"

"Yes, she's amazing." He took his drink and tried to avoid slugging it down. "How do you know her?"

"We *all* know each other. I'm terribly sorry, I didn't introduce myself. I'm Vlad . . . short for Vladimir."

Jack shook his hand, finding it cool, even room temperature. The other three introduced themselves as Radomir, Milorad, and Gennady. Jack shook their room-temperature-cool hands.

"You will have dinner with us afterward, won't you?" asked Vlad, grinning toothily. "Sam said you would join us."

Jack was severely conflicted. Dinner with these four could be unsettling. But then, being with Sam would be a great antidote to that. He was noncommittal. He would ask Sam about these guys first.

The intermission ended, and they made their way back into the auditorium, watching the second half of the portentous ballet. Periodically, Vlad would hmmm his approval at one particularly sinister scene or another.

After the performance, they made their collective way out of the hall. Jack felt more nervously claustrophobic than ever. The four towering, black-suited behemoths seemed to surround him as they walked. His anxiety grew when they invited him into a black limousine, raising the partition between them and the driver.

"Where are we going?" he asked, trying to sound nonchalant.

"We have to fetch our little bird. Then we will have dinner . . . and many more drinks." Vlad laughed, and it was the first time Jack realized he had very white, almost luminous teeth.

The limousine pulled around to the dark alley that held the stage entrance and waited, seemingly forever.

Finally, thankfully, Sam emerged with several other dancers, some possessing that same fascinating allure that she held. Probably pixies, thought Jack, but Sam was special . . . to him, anyway.

She wore a filmy white silk skirt and a sky-blue silk blouse that matched her eyes. She smiled merrily at him, when he climbed out of the limousine to invite her in. He wanted to kiss her so badly! She gave each of the behemoths a hug and settled happily into the seat beside him, accepting their accolades and a glass of sparkling drink.

"And now, little bird, we take you to a dinner and a celebration," announced Vlad.

"Uh . . . well . . . I can't stay too late," said Jack.

"Why not?" challenged Sam. "You don't have to go to a job. And you deserve some fun after all that you've been through." She tossed her head and looked impishly at the four behemoths crowded in with them. "Besides, I can absolutely guarantee the party won't last past dawn."

"Why not?"

"Because they're vampires!"

.   .   .

"Stop the noise, fool!" scolded Senator Warren F. Lee, standing beside the truck and slapping its side window to stop the driver's honking.

The driver let down the window. "Open the garage door! My suit is dying. I've been stuck in it for five days!"

"Relax. Your suit will regenerate," said Lee, as he moved inside the warehouse, grabbed the controller and raised the overhead door. The driver gunned the truck in, and Lee closed the door, scanning out the window in the smaller door to make sure nobody had seen the truck approach.

The driver jumped down from the truck, the musky stench of five days' driving billowing out, and jabbed his chest to relax the flesh-suit. It sagged away from his muscular, furred frame, and he quickly but carefully stripped it off. He carried the limp, beige suit to a nutrient canister and plunged it in.

Now free of the suit, he yanked out his dentures to reveal a mouthful of needle-sharp fangs. He stretched luxuriantly, scratched his matted pelt to fluff it up, and yawned, peeling back his lips and growling contentedly. He turned to glare at Lee, who had also removed his suit, becoming the werewolf Flaktuckmetang.

"Why couldn't you have gotten an Ally to transport this thing?" demanded the driver. "We have them to do such common tasks."

"If any Ally saw the cargo and figured out what it was, we would face a full-scale revolt. *You* had to do it."

"Well, I've done it. I'm staying here for a few days to let the suit recuperate, then I'm gone back home."

He moved to leave, but Flaktuckmetang held up his claw to stop the departure. "Not just yet. Help me unload this and run diagnostics. We don't want the device to blow up when we first use it."

"We? What do you mean we?" I was told it will be only you. I'm out of here as soon as possible. I'm in too deep as it is. If my Warden finds out—"

"The Wardens have approved this test. And with a successful test, they will approve . . ." he didn't finish the sentence. It wasn't a good idea to bring up the planned fate of the planet's inhabitants, for somebody who didn't need to know—even if it was a fellow werewolf.

The driver sighed in resignation. "Okay, but if I'm helping, I'm getting time off my sentence."

"That's up to the Wardens. But you know we want to keep them happy. And this will make them happy. And that could mean time off your sentence. Help me unload."

Growling under his breath, the driver shoved the cargo door of the truck up, to reveal the shiny metal cylinder, strapped down with the parabolic reflector facing them. He lithely leaped into the back, unstrapped the cylinder, and pressed a button. With a faint hum, four legs unfolded from the cylinder, hefting it upward. Flaktuckmetang slid out the truck's ramp, and with the driver pressing a button on its control panel, the cylinder adroitly walked its way down to the concrete floor to the whine of its motors.

"There's meat in the refrigerator," said Flaktuckmetang. "Go feed. I'll run the diagnostics. Then we'll talk about a first target."

The driver checked his immersed flesh-suit to make sure it was getting nourishment and oxygen, then hurried off, driven by the prospect of gnawing on a hefty chunk of meat.

Flaktuckmetang moved to the control panel, touched a few glowing lights and stood back as a deep whine filled the warehouse. The weapon was coming to life.

• • •

The owner of the plush downtown steakhouse had greeted the vampires, the pixie, and the mixed-emotional Jack with delight and led them to a private room—with rich, ornately carved paneling, a crystal chandelier, upholstered chairs, and candles burning in silver candlesticks. If he didn't know better, Jack would swear he was in an ancient castle. It was probably the kind of environment that would make centuries-old vampires most comfortable.

"Very nice," pronounced Vlad, holding back Sam's chair for her to sit. The vampire sat between her and Jack, an arrangement that did not suit Jack. But he decided to say nothing to the blood-sucking creature.

Milorad, a hefty vampire with a pug nose and full lips, plunked himself down to Jack's right. Once more, Jack noted, he was hemmed in between vampires.

"Nice place," he said, trying to make conversation. "You know the owner?"

"He's an Ally. One of ours. A few years back, he happened upon Gennady enjoying a nighttime stroll . . . in the nude. And we vampires kind of glow in the dark, so he figured out what Gennady was. We asked him what he wanted out of life. He always wanted to own a restaurant, so we got him one. Besides, I supply him with meat. I own a meatpacking house." He started to continue, but a formally clad waiter appeared, and the table ordered drinks.

"And we'll have a cannibal mound," said Vlad. He noticed that Jack had stiffened, eyes widening a bit, and he explained: "Not to worry. That's another name for raw, minced meat."

"Oh," said Jack, not wanting to pursue the issue further. He subtly reached up and touched his neck, wondering if it would be punctured by bite marks at some point in the evening.

But the vampires seemed like cheerful company, and Sam's presence alleviated his unease. And, the waiter arrived quickly with the appetizers and six bottles of excellent drink, and they all ordered. Predictably, thought Jack, the vampires ordered their meat rare. He hoped he wasn't offending them by ordering his medium.

"So, you eat raw meat?" he asked.

"That's our diet," said Vlad, taking a bite of the minced meat with toast. "Raw meat. We need the hemoglobin."

Jack's relief grew, but still, there was the coming prospect of watching the vampires gnaw on bloody steak. "Well, it's kind of—"

"Disgusting? We find your diet *disgusting*. We don't eat baby animals. You do."

"No, we don't! That's *outrageous!*"

"And what of the young farm animals you consume as delicacies?"

"Oh, right."

"And you eat embryos."

"No we don't!"

"Eggs?"

"Oh." Jack took a drink of his cocktail and considered the relativism of cultural dietary preferences. Getting tipsier by the minute, he examined his black-garbed dinner partners.

"Do you have jobs?" he blurted out. "How can you hold down jobs? I mean, you can't come out in the daytime."

Vladimir smiled tolerantly. "Well, I tend to my business at the slaughterhouse largely at night. Doing the night shift."

"And I work the night shift at the hospital," said Radomir.

"Blood bank?" asked Jack.

"Emergency," said Radomir. "Blood doesn't bother me . . . obviously."

"Night watchman," volunteered Milorad, raising his glass.

"I'm a cop," said Gennady. "Love the graveyard shift!"

The vampires all chuckled at the old joke.

"Well, I guess you could pull off regular jobs," said Jack. "You look . . . normal."

"Hardly normal for our liking," said Milorad sourly. "You mean we look like your race. For us, this is disfigured."

"Well, yeah."

"It took some work, some pain," he said. "There's an Ally dentist who grinds down our fangs. And a plastic surgeon who rounds our lovely pointed ears to nubs. And the skin? Spray tans . . . every week, damned spray tans."

"You don't think our skin is handsome?"

Milorad made a disgusted face. "Pink, beige, brown . . . they look like skin that's not been cared for. And, oh how your species make such a big deal about skin color! This is what skin should look like!" The portly Milorad struggled to his feet, turned around, and dropped his pants to show a substantial, fish-belly-white butt.

The diners roared with laughter and derision, some flinging rolls at him.

"And now . . ." announced Gennady, standing up and unzipping his fly ". . . for the white whale!"

"No!" came back the shouted chorus, and Vladimir held up a butter knife to fend off the white whale, should it be unleashed.

"Your loss," shrugged Gennady, zipping back up.

Next, the increasingly tipsy vampires went around the table giving a succession of vampire toasts, each of which required a healthy drink.

"May you never reach body temperature!"

"Here's to our favorite relatives. *Blood* relatives!"

"Here's to never failing your blood test!"

"Here's to never suffering a tan!"

Finally, they had exhausted their toasts, their wine, and their laughter, which was replaced with occasional outbursts of satiated, happy chuckles.

"It's nearly dawn," said Vladimir tiredly to his fellow vampires. "We need to rest. We'll meet next Wednesday for the flight to the Convocation." An impish smile rose on his face, and he turned away, popping out contact lenses. He whipped back to reveal fiendish, glowing red eyes.

"*Shit!*" exclaimed Jack.

"We're taking the *redeye!*" exclaimed Vladimir, to a new wave of guffaws.

"What's the Convocation?" asked Jack.

The room abruptly grew silent.

"Oops," whispered Milorad. Jack sensed that a secret had nearly been revealed.

"You and Sam take our car," said Vladimir, ignoring the question. "We're going to sleep in the basement. And before you ask . . . no, we don't sleep in coffins. Very nice air beds."

Shortly, Jack and Sam were comfortably ensconced in the limousine, gliding through the capitol mall, past its many memorials.

"They were fun," said Jack. "Not what I expected. I'll admit, I was freaked at first."

"A'eiio wanted you to meet them."

"To intimidate me?"

"Not at all. To educate you. To show you that those whom you think are the worst are really good."

But Jack's attention had fully diverted from the vampires, riveted on the slim, beautiful, blue-eyed pixie seated so close beside him. "Sam. Is that short for Samantha?"

"No, it's Sam."

A cloud of worry descended on his face. "You're not really a male, are you?"

"No, it's a joke among pixies. Female pixies take male names and males take female names. We're poking fun at your tendency to be so absolutist about sex roles. Pixies don't make the distinctions you do, which has led your race to discrimination, even persecution."

She lowered the limousine's partition and told the driver to pull over. "This is near where I live." She opened the car door, preparing to leave.

"Can I come up?" Jack asked hopefully.

She smiled sweetly. "If we made love, you would become hopelessly lost in me." She stated it matter-of-factly, not as a boast. She kissed him. On the lips. And it supported her statement. His head began to swim, perhaps due to the alcohol, more likely her pheromones, and also because of his blossoming feelings toward her.

"Does that mean you like me?" he asked woozily.

But she was gone.

•   •   •

The badly hungover Jack understood what a vampire must feel like. He cringed at the sunlight streaming through the floor-to-ceiling windows of the offices of the Environmental Action Council. It seemed to penetrate like needles through to his brain, generating a throbbing ache. Fortunately, he had brought his sunglasses, which had been the only reason he had made it down the sunny streets to the transit station, and after an excruciating, noisy train ride, there to the offices.

However, the glasses didn't filter the sunny disposition of the pert receptionist, when he asked for Marc Bright. He smiled wryly when he said the name. Must everything be "bright" on the afternoon after an all-night partying binge!

Marc appeared, dressed in a dapper, dark suit and bright yellow tie. Would there be no comforting cloudiness in this day?

Marc took one look at him and asked the receptionist to fetch him a "vat" of coffee. "Deborah tells me you had quite a time with our mutual friends last night."

"How did she . . ." He didn't finish. The sound of his own voice rattled his skull.

"She and Sam have been conferring . . . about you."

Marc thankfully closed the curtains when they settled into his small office, and Jack thankfully sipped the hot, strong coffee. "Why did she want to meet me here?"

"Privacy," said Marc. "You cannot be seen together in public, and certainly not in her Senate office."

"I did a computer search on you," said Jack, struggling to make some minimal conversation, while the caffeine kicked in. "You're a big-time environmental lawyer."

"I try to make a difference. That's what our kind try to do while we're here."

"What are you in for?"

Marc shook his head in a warning. "A bit of advice," he counseled. "Never ask a Mythical what they did to be here. None of us wants to talk about what we did."

Deborah appeared, smiling, and kissed her husband. They closed the office door. Jack was recovering quickly, and fortifying himself for the bargaining that was to come.

"You look a bit the worse for wear," said Deborah. "Our friends do like to party."

"They are pretty stalwart."

"Well, you've seen an awful lot of us now. You have to make a decision. You have two good choices."

"Two choices that you've forced on me."

Deborah's eyes narrowed in accusation. "Remember, you brought on the situation."

"Well, I did what I learned to do. Investigate."

"Still . . ." She was impatient to get on with their discussion. "I talked to my Warden about your unorthodox proposal. He raised the issue with their Council. They decided to give you a trial run. We will give you full access to our exiles and our activities. And we will give you independence to report as you see fit, should the Council authorize it."

"That access includes the Convocation," he said. It was an old reporter's trick. Put a source off balance by hitting them with something unexpected.

"How did you hear about that?" asked Marc, anxiety tinging his voice.

"Does it include the Convocation?" Jack emphasized. "Can I attend it?"

Now Deborah paused, her expression grave, her lips pursed. "It is possible. But since it would be an unprecedented step, you would have to agree to an unprecedented step."

"What's that?"

"You must agree to implantation of a termination chip."

CHAPTER 7

J ack gingerly felt the base of his skull for the incision, which still hurt from the insertion of the termination chip. The incision for the adjacent coma chip had healed. He was now doubly controlled by the Mythicals.

He took little comfort that Wardens needed a unanimous vote to remotely trigger the termination chip to kill him. Nor was it comforting that he would be warned to stop whatever transgression he was committing by a shrill buzzing, like a bee embedded in his brain. If he did not comply with their wishes, a small explosive charge would sever his brain stem, causing instant death. He pondered whether the possibility of instant death was worth being at the Convocation of Mythicals. He wasn't even sure what this Convocation was, but it was clearly a major event for the Mythicals, and thus one he needed to attend.

He was distracted from his worrying by his company in the limousine and the passing sights outside its window. Beside him sat the alluring Sam, and across from him Marc and Deborah in their flesh-suits. They watched the crowds streaming along the sidewalks, and the resort city's blazing, swirling, vivid panoply of lights. This was only the beginning of a weeklong celebration that featured throngs of costumed revelers. The private jet had taken them over the vivid light show as it landed, and now he watched it from ground level.

The limousine left the main street and pulled up to the site of the Convocation, the Convention Center, where the driver quickly opened the doors for them. They negotiated the streaming crowd through the Grand Lobby to the North Hall, past a series of signs warning "Private Event, Invitation Only."

A burly, unsmiling guard passed them, clutching the arm of a skinny young man dressed like a large-headed alien, leading him away.

He protested, "But this is a costume ball, right? I heard that. And I'm wearing a costume."

But the guard forged ahead, escorting him to the Main Hall.

"We hold the Convocation a week before the city's main costume balls, to avoid dealing with the heaviest crowds," said Deborah. "The timing gives us cover. If somebody saw us out of our flesh-suits, they'd just think it was some early arrivals." She and Marc went ahead of them to confer with the phalanx of other black-garbed guards, who formed a solid wall of muscle to discourage outsiders.

"So, you've been given guard duty to watch over me?" he asked Sam.

"Yes," she said simply.

"Why? Did you volunteer?"

She tossed her head and smiled. "Because they know that I can handle you better than anybody else. Female pixies have that power over males of your species."

They reached a metal detector that didn't resemble any that Jack had seen before. It was a luminous blue archway that looked as if it had arrived from another planet . . . which it probably had. Deborah and Marc passed through ahead of them, and a guard on the other side, standing at a console, waved them through.

"It detects your chip," said Sam. "It knows who you are."

"Great," said Jack, wryly. "Under my alien masters' thumbs . . . or whatever passes for thumbs."

He entered a huge curtained room lined with hundreds of silver barrel-sized vats. There, Mythicals were shedding flesh-suits to reveal an alien menagerie—fairies, pixies, trolls, werewolves, elves, ogres, and a welter of creatures he did not recognize. They were carefully immersing the suits into the vats. They were exercising wings, stretching massive furred muscles, scratching gray-green skin, and generally chattering in a confusion of alien languages and enjoying the freedom from the disguises. The aroma was a sweetish, organic mélange of the nutrient liquid and of the bodies newly shed of their covering. A hint of spice from fairies, the animal musk of werewolves, a sour tang of ogres.

A'eiio and E'iouy approached Jack and Sam, their wings fluttering with pleasure and their lithesome alabaster bodies comfortably nude.

"I hope you've become used to our preference for lack of clothing," said A'eiio.

Jack started to speak, but was rendered temporarily mute by the mesmerizing sight of Sam, who had shed her dress, as well. "Uh, I'll try to adjust," he murmured.

"Well, that will be the least of your adjustments," said Sam, padding along, slim and barefoot, as they passed through the curtained area, into the main hall. "We'll be meeting with our own kind, and there will be an area for Allies. To your right."

"Just as well, I'm not sure I could take—" Jack stopped short, eyes widening.

Before him spread a vast hall crowded with a menagerie of Mythicals. In one area, fairies flitted about the girders of the two-story ceiling, their gossamer wings glimmering in the light. They sang to one another, their voices adding a melodic undertone to the crowd noise.

Another area was dark brown with a furry pack of werewolves, snarling at one another in some sort of angry debate.

Far across the vast hall, Jack could see the pure white of the feathery wings of angels, stretching magnificently, flapping, some soaring smoothly aloft, to circle and land.

Yet another area held a scritchy-screeching gaggle of elves, chattering to one another and bent over a collection of consoles.

Beyond them, a black-clad clot of vampires, toasting one another from a bar. Only a few days earlier, Jack would have been chilled at the sight. Now, he would have looked forward to their jolly company.

Other gangs of gnarled trolls and gnomes hunkered down among the taller creatures. Towering over all were the hideous ogres, looking like some living, gray-green outcropping, their booming growls reverberating through the hall. Marching past him into the hall came a cadre of small, orange-bearded creatures, like elves, but hairier and scruffier. Leprechauns, he guessed.

The far end of the huge hall held a stage, and standing on it was a representative of each species, distinguished as Wardens by the gold chains and control medallions around their necks. They sagely scanned the crowd as would creatures who had absolute control.

To the right, Jack spied a group of about fifty of his kind sitting around tables, and looking far more mundane than the crowd of exotic creatures surrounding them. They leaned together and talked quietly among themselves with some diffidence, no doubt intimidated by the stunning array of species.

He joined them, introducing himself as new to the business of being an Ally. He knew better than to whip out a tablet or laptop in front of this already skittish bunch. So, he did his best to remember names, and he passed out his cards with the name *Capital Herald* marked out. He received half a dozen in return—including a lawyer, a surgeon, a talent agent, and a hotel owner. If he could interview them, they would likely offer fascinating, even soul-shaking, stories of their first encounters with Mythicals.

The babble of alien voices quieted as the elderly, imposing vampire Warden called the Convocation to order. He obviously never had to go out in public: He still had his fangs, and his skin was dead-white. He didn't wear contacts, so his gleaming red eyes gave him a demonic glare.

He and the other Wardens began a litany of Mythicals' business—announcing new rules for the exiles, warning darkly of consequences for violating them, and discussing services for exiles to make their banishment tolerable.

Jack paid rapt attention, trying to store as much as he could in memory, anticipating typing the information furiously into his computer as soon as possible. The exiles used an array of ghostlike displays floating before them to take notes, perhaps to report to their fellows around the world who couldn't attend.

As the different Wardens raised their issues, the werewolves off to the left continued their loud, snarling discussion. Abruptly, one left the group and strode to the front of the hall, below the stage. The werewolf Warden bent down to him, and they had an intense, guttural discussion. The Warden mounted the stage, interrupting the elf Warden, who in strained, high-pitched English was discussing a new schedule for delivering supplies through wormholes around the world.

The Wardens retreated to the back of the stage to confer. The werewolf Warden returned to the front and announced in raspy tones, "The Allies are to leave immediately." The ogre Warden gestured at the mob of ogres, who moved ominously to herd the Allies from the hall.

"This has never happened before . . . ever!" whispered the lawyer.

"Something is going on!" exclaimed the surgeon, hurrying toward the exit before the looming ogres.

Waves of alien chatter swept through the hall, as each species reacted to the abrupt evacuation of the Allies.

Jack decided to take a very big chance. He took a deep breath and slipped off his jacket, reaching into the side pocket briefly, before bending down and slipping the coat beneath the hanging tablecloth. Fortunately, the closest Mythical was an approaching ogre, who was more interested in moving him from the hall than paying attention to his surreptitious action. He made for the exit with the rest, through the curtained area, out the door, beneath the luminescent archway and out into the Grand Lobby. There, the Allies discussed in dismayed tones what had happened, taking care not to be overheard by outsiders.

Were the Mythicals making some fateful decision about the Allies? Were they debating steps they didn't want the world to know about? Nobody had any firm idea, and Jack decided to return to the hotel, to pour his remembered experience into his computer.

He would return later for his coat and its contents. If his subterfuge wasn't discovered, maybe he would find out what was going on.

· · ·

From his vantage point high on a forested hill, Senator Warren F. Lee, dressed splendidly in his camouflage hunting gear, stood in the soft glow of a full moon, looking out over the small village.

"Perfect," he pronounced. "A clear shot, a good target."

"Yeah," said the driver, fidgeting at being once again shrouded in his own flesh-suit. "But once we do it, we've got to get out quick. They catch us, and the whole plan blows up. I don't get why we have to trigger this thing manually. Why not a remote?"

Lee gave the driver an annoyed look, as one might give an ignorant child. "That would leave the device vulnerable to jamming. The
orbiting generators will all be triggered manually when the time
comes. Foolproof." He turned his attention back to the village below.
"Peaceful, quiet . . . we'll fix that," he said.

"Yeah, the street lights will be an indicator," said the driver.
"They'll go out. And it's quiet, so we'll probably hear something,
like maybe car crashes."

"Not good enough. I'm going down there for some ground-truth
data."

"A stranger in town? When the place goes blooey? You are insane."

"I'll just say I'm passing through, doing some hunting. I'm a
senator, a celebrity. They won't connect the effects with me. Besides,
it's a full moon. I deserve some field time. I've got some nice chunks
of bloody meat in the truck. After the test, I'll come back up here,
take off this suit, and do some prowling, enjoy some meat."

"You're still crazy. But when we finish this, I can go home. That's
all I care about."

"Okay, give me an hour to get down there."

"Fine, but I'm taking some of that meat."

Lee had no problem finding a path down the mountain, given
his werewolf's keen night vision. He emerged on the two-lane road
leading into the village and passed a gas station, an auto repair shop,
and a general store. He reached the town square, seeing that the local
bar was open. A perfect vantage point for his observation. He checked
his watch. He had twenty minutes. Time enough to get in, order a
drink, and settle himself.

The comfortably battered barroom, smelling of alcohol and fried
foods, held a dozen customers, some sitting around tables drinking and
picking at baskets of snacks. Amid the cheerful, boozy camaraderie,

he took a seat at the bar, taking note of what the other denizens were ordering, before picking a drink.

"How's the huntin'?" he asked the bartender amiably.

"Pretty fair," the bartender replied. "Guy killed a big one last week. Up on the ridge."

Lee took note of that fact. He hadn't made a kill in a while. With all the commotion to distract the locals, he might be able to take a run in the forest and take down prey this night. He subtly checked his watch. Five minutes. He made sure to order another drink. Soon, there would be no drinks forthcoming.

"Well, I'm up here to do a little hunting, so I—"

Abruptly, the incandescent lights in the bar went out, wisps of smoke curled from the outlets, and the room was filled with the stench of ozone and smoldering plastic. Screams and shouts filled the bar, as the fluorescent lights and TV set over the bar took on a malevolent glow before plunging into darkness.

"Ow! SHIT!" bellowed a young man at the end of the bar, who had been making a cell phone call. He pitched the phone away, staring uncomprehending at his burned hand. A woman at one of the tables pitched her smoking purse away. The electronic cash register popped and sizzled.

"*What the hell is going on?*" exclaimed the bartender, amid the cacophony of frightened babble.

Smoke began to fill the bar, and the patrons rushed the door, shoving aside a small woman. Lee finished his drink, suppressing a satisfied smile, and followed them into a darkened street. A grizzled man in a floppy hat jumped into his truck, turning the key. Nothing. Others tried their cars, but all were dead.

The bartender rushed from the bar, a fire extinguisher in his hand. "*Get back!*" he yelled. "*Fire's all over in there! Too much to put out!*" Behind him, the orange flicker of flames lit the doorway.

Lee decided he'd seen enough. He edged away from the panicked creatures, starting his hike out of town and up the mountain. There, he'd strip off his flesh-suit and have a fine night running down some animal, any animal, to tear open its throat and gnaw at its warm flesh. He smirked in satisfaction at his new sense of freedom. He could go anywhere he wanted now. The test had gone well on two counts. It had proved the electromagnetic pulse generator as a weapon.

And as a bonus, it had almost certainly fried his coma chip, and even more fortunately, his termination chip.

• • •

In the darkness before sunrise, the main corridor of the convention center was deserted, dead-quiet. Jack managed to get in by discovering an unlocked service entrance at the back. He ducked into an alcove to avoid a janitor driving by in a sweeper, then sprinted to the North Hall. The blue archway was still there, evidence that the breakdown of the room hadn't yet begun. And he knew that the Mythicals' Convocation had run very late. He'd lurked outside the convention center until he saw what he thought were the last Mythicals leave.

The door to the hall was open, and he ducked through the empty, curtained antechamber that had held the nutrient vats and into the vast darkened hall.

He stood still, holding his breath, listening hard for any telltale noise that a Mythical had stayed behind, or that a cleanup crew had begun work. He heard only the gentle hiss of the ventilation system in the cavernous space. He peered upward. There might be some stray winged creature perched there. But the rafters appeared empty.

He pushed the button on his tiny key-chain flashlight and moved cautiously forward, feeling his way past tables, trying to remember exactly which one he'd been at. He guessed wrong twice, feeling under the table to find nothing. He stood up and reoriented himself. He had sat more to the right. Finally, he reached under a table to feel the fabric of his suit jacket.

He pulled out the coat, reached into the pocket and withdrew the digital recorder. He flicked it off and sat in a chair, deciding what to do next. He should really get out of there as soon as possible, but he had to know what had been so secret that the Allies had to be hustled out of the room.

He switched on the recorder, to hear the order to evacuate, the noise of the room being emptied of Allies. The sound was poor, muffled by the tablecloth and the coat. He recognized the deep, guttural voice of a werewolf. Must have been the werewolf Warden. He heard only snatches of what was said.

"We have . . . testing on a prototype . . . advocate . . . ." Now a cacophony of voices rose in the hall. Given that they were aliens speaking their own languages, he couldn't know who was talking, or certainly what they were saying. But he had a sense that the deep snarls were the cheers of werewolves, and the higher, lilting sounds were fairies and pixies objecting.

He heard more fragments of his own language from various Mythicals Wardens. They seemed to emphasize one particular word. Was it "palpitation?" That didn't make sense. No, it was *palliation.* He knew that "palliative care" was care that alleviated pain. But "palliation?" An abrupt buzzing in his head made it hard to hear the sound from the recorder.

Oh, no, no, no! He thought, realizing what it meant.

The hall was abruptly flooded with light, and he squinted and jerked his head around to see a line of Mythicals, all glaring at him. They all wore the large medallions that distinguished them as Wardens.

The werewolf's medallion glowed red!

The vampire's glowed red!

The ogre's glowed red!

The angel stood with a downcast expression, slowly bringing his hand to his medallion. He touched three of the glowing spots on it. It glowed red!

Of all the Wardens, only the medallions of the fairy and pixie Wardens remained dark!

He was only two votes away from death!

"Fool, don't you know that your chip enables us to track your movement!" growled the werewolf, stepping threateningly toward him. "You have violated our rules."

"My coat," said Jack weakly, holding up his jacket. "I just came back—"

The werewolf grabbed him by the neck with one claw, the talons digging into his flesh, and lifted him off the floor, snatching the recorder from his hand with the other. "This is what you came back for. Don't lie!" He crushed the recorder into pieces and flung them away.

Jack struggled for breath, flailing and clutching the werewolf's arm to try to support himself.

The buzzing stopped, replaced by the familiar hum of fairy wings. "Please, Wardens, he made a mistake!" It was A'eiio's voice.

"Yes, a mistake!" It was Sam's voice. "Please let him live! We will vouch for him!"

Still holding Jack aloft, the werewolf turned to the other Wardens, scowling. "He knows. We cannot allow him to live."

Jack gasped for breath, his conscious waning, his legs flailing for some support. He saw the lights on the Wardens' medallions begin to blink out.

The werewolf flung him across the table like a rag doll, and he tumbled off it, slamming to the floor, gagging.

"Very well," the werewolf snarled and stalked away.

"You are very fortunate," said the fairy Warden, as Jack managed to fill his lungs and drag himself onto a chair. "You have been the responsibility of this fairy and this pixie. Should you violate rules again, they will be punished, as well."

The Wardens moved away, leaving Sam and A'eiio to tend to him.

"I am sorry," Jack managed to gasp. "I just wanted to know . . ." but his voice failed him, and he couldn't finish the sentence.

• • •

Senator Warren F. Lee sat in his office, watching the news coverage of the mysterious calamity that had befallen the small town of Bellamini. He smiled at the video of the burning buildings, the smoking power transformers, the horrified residents holding up ruined cell phones, the immobile cars and trucks with their hoods open.

He continued smiling, as his thoughts turned to the pleasant memory of a night spent running free in the cold darkness of the thick woods. Of the headlong flight of his panicked quarry, crashing away through the brush. Of the feel of its muscled body collapsing under his attack. Of his jaws tearing away its throat. Of the delicious taste of its warm flesh torn from its body.

"Senator?" asked his aide, interrupting his reverie.

He almost growled. He had to catch himself; senators didn't growl. "Yes?" he answered. "I told you not to disturb me."

"You have a call. He didn't give a name, but he said you were expecting it. Will you take it?"

That would be his Warden. He *would* take that call.

"Lee," he answered curtly. He knew to speak this planet's language, even to a member of his own species. The telltale guttural language of werewolves would alert anybody who overheard.

105

"I am watching the news," said the Warden. "What is your assessment of the test?"

"I was in the target region. Optimal radiation intensity. Full coverage. Complete destruction of the electrical and electronic infrastructure."

"I don't have a location on you. I don't see any signal from your chip."

"So, it was, indeed, destroyed?" Lee's smile became a satisfied smirk.

"It appears so."

"Am I safe from the other Wardens?"

"Yes. Since I am your Warden, I am solely responsible for monitoring you. They are unaware of your chip's malfunction."

"I need you to explicitly state what you are giving me permission to do . . . for the record."

The Warden paused, likely working out the exact phrasing of the statement. "I formally give you permission as your Warden to take whatever steps you need to, in order to ensure the success of the Palliation."

CHAPTER 8

"It was no accident. It was an *attack!*" Senator Deborah Bright exclaimed to herself, vaulting from her desk chair, approaching the television screen showing the devastation in Bellamini. She paced back and forth, shaking her head, trying to figure out what to do next. *Lee must know about this, or be behind it!* She thought.

Within ten minutes, she had burst into Lee's Senate office, swept past his receptionist and into his inner chamber. Lee was just hanging up the phone.

"Your Warden told us at the Convocation that a test was being conducted. This was it?"

"Yes," said Lee, lounging back in his chair. "And a successful one."

"And the device I saw your partner loading onto a truck at the last rendezvous. That was the device you tested?"

"Yes."

"What are your plans?"

"Talk to your Warden. I'm not comfortable—"

"What are your plans?"

"I can only say that we are only preparing for the eventuality of the Palliation. Calibrating the equipment. We are at the service of the Wardens."

"Who's we?"

"Werewolves . . . and other species."

"And this test? This disaster you caused?"

"As you heard at the Convocation, the Wardens authorized it."

"This planet's inhabitants need to know about the Palliation."

"Why? There's nothing they can do about it. Even if there was, they wouldn't do what was necessary. You know that."

"I *don't* know that!" Deborah leaned forward over his desk, glaring at him. "It's *time*. You know it's *time*."

"To reveal ourselves? To tell these primitive creatures everything?"

"Yes. Everything."

Lee chuckled with the deep guttural resonance of a werewolf's voice. "*That* will cause quite a stir."

• • •

Senator Deborah Bright had just walked to the lectern, as Jack sat down in the Senate gallery, overlooking the semicircle of desks beneath the high, arched ceiling.

All was routine—or so the gathering of senators thought, as they chatted among themselves or gave instructions to their assistants. Today, the Senate business consisted only of routine speeches on behalf of the nominee for some minor government posts.

After four solid days and nights of writing, Jack slumped tiredly in his seat. The senator, or rather A'eiio, had instructed him to produce the most comprehensive article possible on the Mythicals. So, he'd pounded out a thirty-thousand-word opus, which he knew would never see the light of day. After all, who would believe the lunatic writings of an out-of-work, semi-alcoholic writer who had claimed to see a flying creature flit away from a dinner party?

In any case, as A'eiio had directed, he had brought his computer to the session and switched it on. With a tap of his finger, he could send the article to his former editor at the *Capital Herald*. But that tap would bring death.

But then, his reporter's instinct abruptly triggered him to alertness. Something indefinably odd was happening. Down on the floor, Senator Warren F. Lee appeared with two other senators, taking their seats. To his right up in the gallery, a distinctly motley mix of men and women entered and took seats.

They included a skinny guy in mechanics coveralls, a massive cop, a statuesque woman in clinical scrubs, a man in an expensive tailored suit, and an attractive young woman in a white silk dress.

Something about them, something in the way each of them moved, seemed familiar.

"Are you ready?" asked a feminine voice to his left, interrupting his puzzlement, and he turned to see Sam take the seat next to him.

She immediately riveted his attention. "Uh . . . for what?"

But Sam only smiled and laid her small hand on his.

Amid the murmur of routine business on the Senate floor, Bright went to the lectern and began to speak. "First of all, I assure you that you are all perfectly safe."

Here and there in the chamber, Senators turned from their chatting to look at her, puzzled expressions on their faces.

"At no time during my remarks, or the extraordinary events that will accompany them, will any of you be in any danger."

The presiding officer, William DeLucato, a slim, middle-aged senator with a head of wispy white hair, leaned forward and asked, "Senator, what are you saying?"

"If my esteemed colleagues will bear with me, I will today reveal a momentous truth about life on your planet."

Now murmurs arose across the Senate floor, as the senators whispered to one another about what their colleague might possibly be doing.

Bright took off her jacket, and began to unbutton her blouse, slipping it off. She unzipped her skirt and stepped out of it, quickly shedding her bra, slip, and underwear.

A shocked clamor arose from the floor, and DeLucato exclaimed a shocked *"Senator Bright! What are you doing?"*

Bright stood only a brief moment as a naked, pale, plump, middle-aged woman. She reached up, pressed a spot between her breasts, and her skin sagged loosely from her body. She reached beneath her chin and pulled off her mask, revealing a smooth, young face framed by silken silver hair.

Screams and shouts arose from the floor, as Senators bolted from their seats, unsure whether to run or stay and watch the unbelievable sight.

Shrugging her way out of the fleshy shroud, she stepped out of it and extended her transparent wings, fluttering them.

"What—!" began DeLucato, before his voice failed him.

"RUN! RUN!" bellowed the nearest senator, falling back over his chair and landing with a thud on the floor. Similar exclamations erupted throughout the chamber.

A'eiio lowered her head for a moment, popping out her contacts and carefully setting them on the lectern. She looked up to reveal glistening sapphire eyes. She smiled benignly, but that did not quiet the clamor.

Nor did a sudden, bone-chilling howl echoing from the other side of the chamber. All eyes had been riveted on the alien creature that Senator Bright had transformed into. Now, heads whipped around to see a naked Senator Warren F. Lee, standing on his desk howling. He punched his chest and shed his skin to reveal a fanged, hairy beast out of their nightmares.

Now the screams became terror-stricken. The former Senator Lee, now a werewolf, bared his fangs and howled again, gloriously enjoying the moment.

"You are not in any danger!" shouted A'eiio over the tumult.

In the gallery, the odd group of people sitting near Jack shed their clothes and flesh-suits to become a small, bald creature with pointed ears, a gnarled, white-haired creature, a short winged creature like the senator, a grotesque gray-green monster . . . and an angel!

He recognized them! They were Ryan the elf, Steve the troll, Robin the fairy, Mike the ogre, and Wendy the angel!

Wendy the angel—with long golden curls, mesmerizing cobalt-blue eyes, and milk-white skin—climbed onto the railing, spread her snowy white, feathered wings, and began to beat them with powerful strokes. She launched herself out over the floor, sailing upward and circling high in the ivory domed ceiling. A humming arose in the chamber, and she was followed by Robin the fairy, who flitted acrobatically through the air.

Three senators fainted. Several began to weep in fear. Others cowered beneath their desks. Yet others stood in paralyzed fascination, jaws agape.

A'eiio's wings became a blur, bearing her aloft. She hovered before the aghast DeLucato. "Please tell them they are in no danger."

"Who . . . what the hell are you?" he demanded, holding his gavel like a weapon.

The doors to the chamber burst open, and a dozen guards rushed down the aisles, guns drawn. They took aim at the circling angel, at A'eiio, at the werewolf, and up at the frightening creatures in the gallery.

"No!" shouted A'eiio. "DO NOT FIRE! ALBERT, DO NOT FIRE!" She commanded, calling the Sergeant at Arms by name. "IT'S ME! DEBORAH!"

The burly, balding man stared up at her, shocked at hearing a familiar voice emanating from this exotic, stunning creature.

"Senator Bright?" he managed to choke out. He lowered his pistol, and around the chamber, the other security men and women followed his lead.

A'eiio pivoted smoothly in midair and waved at Jack. "Send your article," she instructed. Jack grabbed his computer and began to type out a new lead to his story:

"Today, the Senate experienced the revelation that our world has been host to numerous species of alien creatures formerly thought to be only myths. These include . . ."

She lowered herself down behind the podium, taking DeLucato's hand. "Bill, it's okay," she said gently. "We're not going to harm you. I need to talk."

DeLucato stared down at the delicate hand holding his; at her slim, naked body; then up at her face, with its shimmering sapphire eyes. "Oh . . . uh . . . Senator Bright . . . or whatever—"

She smiled and turned to the stunned senators. "I am what you have called a fairy. In the chamber with me . . ."

She gestured at the werewolf who had once been Warren Lee, still standing imperiously on his desk, and up at the circling angel, the fairy, and the creatures in the gallery.

". . . are other representatives of what you might recognize as mythical beings. But we are real. We have shared your planet with you for a thousand years. We are now revealing ourselves to you.

"Why?" DeLucato managed to ask."

"We have determined that you are a terminal species."

• • •

A'eiio paced the floor of her small senate office, her wings fluttering in anxiety. *He* was coming. She had taken the incredibly dangerous step of revealing the existence of Mythicals, and now *he* was coming.

She was also agitated by the tension of having just met with her staff. Most of them stood in stunned, open-mouthed silence, as she explained who—or rather *what*—she really was.

Angie, her press secretary, normally a composed young woman, began to weep uncontrollably. Alejandro, her chief of staff, a dapper, no-nonsense man, periodically took a healthy swig out of a liquor bottle he had retrieved from his desk.

"Look, this is going to be a tornado," she had told them, gesturing at the television screen playing news footage showing her hovering before a horrified Senate. "You all decide what you want to do. Take your time. I'll understand perfectly if you want to resign."

They had filed silently out, but she heard an eruption of dismayed chatter in her outer office.

The talk faded, as the staff dispersed to their desks. After ten minutes, Jenny, her office manager, appeared in the doorway. Her wide-eyed staring at A'eiio portrayed her continuing consternation that what her boss of four years had transformed into.

"Uh . . . there's a man to see you. I know you didn't want to be disturbed, but—"

Jenny was interrupted by the appearance of a tall, grim-faced older man with a head of thick, curly gray hair. "I hate these suits," he said, walking past Jenny and into the room. "If you don't mind . . ." He disrobed, touched his chest, and the flesh-suit sagged from his body.

"Oh, dear!" Exclaimed Jenny. *"I just have to . . . I need to . . . . Oh, dear!"* She fled the room, and the Warden finished shedding

his flesh-suit, now standing before A'eiio as the tall, glowering fairy Warden who held her fate in his hands. He retrieved his control medallion from his jacket pocket and donned it. She stopped pacing and sat down, her knees weak, haunted by a vision of a bleak cell on a barren prison planet.

"What have you done?" he asked accusingly, towering over her. "This was not a decision for you to make."

"You know this was the best step to take," she said, placing her hands on her desk to steady herself. "I had to do it."

"Well, this borders on insurrection, and you know the consequences. And you persuaded the others. You put them in danger. Of course, it's up to their Wardens to decide what should be done with them."

"Please ask their Wardens not to punish them. I persuaded them. It's my fault."

"I will not advocate for them. That is not appropriate. But I don't think you realize what you have started."

"I know what I've started." Now her quavering voice took on a tone of defiance.

The Warden waved his hand, and a data screen materialized in midair. It showed an ornate paneled hall with rows of wizened men seated facing one another, some scrambling from their seats. An ogre stood stolidly in the middle, and a fairy circled overhead.

"You no doubt recognize this country's hall of government. A fairy and an ogre revealed themselves there today." He switched from scenes of one such imposing foreign government body after another, each showing various Mythicals panicking their occupants. "As you can see, the disobedience that you started has spread. Mythicals are revealing themselves all over the planet."

Recovering from the shock, A'eiio found she no longer worried over her own fate. "Well, doesn't it show that many of us question the wisdom of the Palliation? Let me at least tell the inhabitants what has been proposed. Let me try to help them avoid it."

The Warden's expression grew impassive, his face a mask, as he regarded her with cool detachment. Saying nothing, he waved his hand and the data screen disappeared.

"I will consult with the other Wardens. We will decide whether you may tell them. They will decide whether their exiles may participate. And I will decide whether you will be deported and imprisoned."

. . . .

Jack failed to suppress a cynical chuckle, as the standing ovation greeted his entrance into the sprawling, stark newsroom of the *Capital Herald*. He had departed just a week before to embarrassed silence, walking out the door carrying a pitiably small box of belongings.

As welcome as the applause was, it wasn't loud because there wasn't much of a crowd. Many of the desks in the regimented rows of low-walled cubicles were empty, and the reporters seemed to clap a little too heartily, almost desperately to make up for their reduced ranks.

Alan Roth, his editor, who had laid him off, approached smiling, and clapped him on the back. "Jack! What an amazing piece! It hit like lightning! Online page views skyrocketed!"

"Does this mean I've got my job back?"

Roth modulated his smile only slightly. "Of course. We were terribly sad to lose you. But, you know, it was just a part of this terrible economy for news media."

Lose me? Thought Jack. *It sounds like I left on my own. Or you misplaced me. Like a set of car keys.*

"Well, I'm glad to be back. We'll have to talk about salary. This is probably the biggest story ever, and I'm on the inside. There's much I haven't yet written about."

115

"Oh, certainly, of course, of course," said Roth, as they walked toward his office. "But first, tell me the back story here."

They sat in his office, while Jack described his ordeal from the first glimpse of A'eiio in the bedroom at the Congress of Nations headquarters; to his nightmarish encounter with the beasts in his own bedroom; to the drinking bout with the vampires; to the revelations in the Senate.

Roth sat back in his chair, nodding amiably, interjecting an occasional "Good." And "Good stuff."

But at the word "Ally," he leaned forward, his expression darkening, his hands clasped together on his desk.

"You mean you're actually in league with them, whatever their plans are?"

"I was forced to be. They implanted a termination chip in me. They know my location . . . they can track me, kill me at any time. Look, I'm telling you this in confidence. They have decided not to reveal the identity of Allies, for the Allies' own protection."

"Wow," said Roth, but it was an expression of shock rather than amazement. He shook his head. "Jack, that means you're not ours, you're *theirs*. In fact, you might well turn out to be an adversary in all this . . . even an enemy."

"Look, I stipulated in my agreement with them that I would be entirely independent. I would report what I saw as a journalist."

"With a chip in your head that means they could take you out at any time? I don't think so. At most, you're now just another source. And a compromised one."

"Alan, there is something going on . . . something they are up to . . . that I don't understand. I'm willing to risk my life to find out. And I need your resources to track it down. Your investigative reporters, your clout."

"Well, Jack, sorry, but we can't do it," said Roth.

Jack shook his head sadly. "Alan, this is a mistake. Something terrible is going to happen. I can feel it." He turned and left Roth's office, walking away yet again down the rows of cubicles to the puzzled stares of his former colleagues.

CHAPTER 9

As A'eiio and the seven other Mythicals walked, stalked, and flew onto the stage of the National Sciences Academy auditorium, even the jaded reporters and television crews gasped in awe.

Seated in the front row, Jack was the only reporter with any semblance of calm. He smiled in sympathy at the stunned consternation of the other reporters. He had, indeed, been where they were now.

Standing before them beneath the auditorium's dramatic geodesic dome of interlocking triangles was a menagerie of creatures that had, until today, been the stuff of dreams—or nightmares.

A'eiio knew how to quiet the crowd. With powerful beating of her diaphanous wings, she rose, hovering above the stage. Stunned silence fell; a barrage of camera flashes lit the hall; and television cameras zoomed in to broadcast the scene worldwide.

She settled back onto the stage. "I know this has been a shock," she said. "I know you have many, many questions. Some will not be answered here, but they all will be answered in time. My fellow Mythicals will introduce themselves."

One by one, the Mythicals gave their names and their species, to a continual buzz from the audience: Steve the troll, Robin the fairy, Mike the ogre, Wendy the angel, Ryan the elf, Vladimir the vampire. Finally came Warren Lee, free of his flesh-suit.

"I am Flaktuckmetang," he declared, grinning, showing glistening fangs, at the reporters' futile attempts to type the name into their laptops. "I am a werewolf. I am also Senator Warren F. Lee."

A'eiio began to speak, but the werewolf gave her a dismissive wave. He folded his thick furry arms, almost seeming to relish what he was about to say.

"We are all exiles, sent to your planet as punishment for transgressions on our home worlds. As you have learned, our species have been here for perhaps a thousand of your years. But what you haven't heard is what this experience has taught us about your species."

A'eiio's expression became grim, and the other Mythicals shook their heads in sad acceptance of what they knew would be said.

"You are a pathologically contradictory race. Your religions preach peace, but you fight horrific wars over those religions, killing millions. Many of your most prominent historical figures are warriors, tyrants, even mass murderers. Many of your signal technological achievements are those that enhance your ability to kill. You glorify murder in your entertainments. You obsess over it. Even my species, as warlike as our history, has not elevated slaughter to such a worshipful level."

The werewolf began to pace the stage like a prowling animal, continuing his diatribe.

"You are devastating your home planet. You disregard the effects of the torrent of pollutants that you unleash into your air and water . . . the carbon dioxide into the air . . . the acid it is creating in your oceans.

And you ignore the mass extinctions you are causing of species that have taken millions of years to evolve."

The werewolf strode to the front of the stage, pausing, scanning the reporters, his eyes gleaming. "You are committing suicide. Our computer models predict that you are a *terminal species.*"

Shouts rose from the reporters, as they reacted to the declaration and clamored to ask questions.

Giving the werewolf a somber look, A'eiio took over. "But we want to work with you to avoid this tragedy," she said. "We revealed ourselves so we could persuade you to prevent your own species' demise through your governments' action. We are all species that have succeeded. We have learned to live sustainably on our planets. We have avoided the very tragedies you are about to experience. Give us a chance to help you."

"Will you answer our questions?" exclaimed one reporter.

"Yes, as best we can," said A'eiio. "And I don't presume to speak for any other species. So, each of my fellow Mythicals will meet with you elsewhere, to answer your questions and give their own viewpoint."

With that, the creatures walked or flew from the stage, trailed by eager reporters, photographers, and video crews.

•   •   •

The elves spat out screechy-voiced epithets, as their spindly fingers skittered over the lighted controls to bring the wormhole sailing into a stationary position poised to orbit the planet. The wizened creatures hunched over the control panel outside the vacuum chamber that enclosed the wormhole and screwed up their small elf faces in displeasure and effort.

They hated releasing objects in orbit. It was no problem to accelerate the wormhole to match the incredible velocity required. The magnetic fields could propel the hole to just about any speed up to near the speed of light.

The really tricky, dangerous business was forcing a wormhole to maintain a curved orbital path. Holes had no mass, no inertia; and gravity did not affect them. So, the elves had to continually wrestle the controls to tweak the hole's course to hold an orbit around the planet—to hover over the target continent.

Even more risky was trying to shove an object through a wormhole in orbit from one universe to another. The object, in this case a massive cylinder, would grow progressively less affected by the gravity on their side and more by the weightlessness of orbit. The elf pilots were acutely aware of past disasters, in which a cargo had been sliced in two by the infinitely sharp, transdimensional edges of the hole.

They also hated working for the werewolves on this odious project. But they had been threatened with being gnawed into bloody elfin parts. The threat was personified by impatiently growling werewolves looming over them.

Finally, they rid themselves of the werewolves by skrittering angrily that the exit had been flattened, and the beasts could now depart to get on with the transfer.

One of the elf pilots gave the other an annoyed shake of the head, silently vowing to one another that once they finished the task and escaped the werewolves' hold, they would complain to their elfin governing council. This would be the last time they would agree to aid deployment of this horrific weapon.

The werewolves began donning their spacesuits over their muscular bodies, slipping the helmets over their pointed ears and down over their thickly furred faces. They made the seals tight and checked their integrity.

They wheeled the metal cylinder over to the large airlock, opened its door and hauled it in. Two elves closed the door and made it fast.

Elves didn't allow any species to operate the airlock in space except them. A careless ogre had once left a stray bolt lodged in the airlock door, compromising its seal. Six elf engineers had been sucked through the door into the vacuum chamber, squirting as a stream of reddish paste into the chamber and through the wormhole.

Once the suited werewolves had hauled the cylinder through the airlock and through the outer door into the vacuum chamber, they paused, panting heavily in their suits, waiting for the signal. Floating before them was the wormhole, the shimmering globe that was a transdimensional portal into the void above the planet.

The werewolves circled around the hole until the planet rotated into sight, its sprawling surface an abstract image of blue, brown, and white. That surface rotated slowly below them until their target continent slid into sight. Then it stopped, as the elf pilots managed to propel the hole into a curve that would become a stationary orbit.

A squawking screech erupted over their headsets—the voices of the elf pilots demanding that they begin the transfer as quickly as possible. They heaved the cylinder into place beneath the hole, hefting it upward through a metal framework and through the shimmering globe. Even with all their muscle, they had trouble holding it steady, as it shifted back and forth, coming into the gravity-free clutches of outer space.

Then the cylinder was through the wormhole, floating weightless. The werewolves followed, climbing the framework's ladder trailing their tethers, pushing off into space, grabbing handholds on the cylinder.

One of the werewolves hauled himself hand-over-hand to one end, opening a control panel. He pressed a button and a huge parabolic reflector unfurled itself like a shining, metal flower. The other werewolf floated around the reflector, inspecting it for any hitches. He poked one of the metal petals that had not snapped into place, popping it into position.

The werewolf at the control panel touched another button and the wings of solar panels slid smoothly from the cylinder's sides, deploying themselves as delicate obsidian extensions of the cylinder. The other werewolf floated along the extended panels, inspecting them. Again, he reached out and ever-so-gently tugged one of the joints that had not fully snapped into place.

Finally, he gave a thumbs up, and the werewolf at the control panel touched a large red button, triggering an array of indicator lights to glow on the control panel and faint vibrations signaling that the cylinder was coming to life. The werewolves pushed off to waft slowly away from the activated station. They watched the cylinder use its own jets to automatically skew it around to aim the huge reflector toward the planet surface and angle the solar panels to catch the energy from the planet's sun.

The werewolves floated back through the wormhole—their thirty-fourth deployment successful. Once back through the airlock, they used a secure communication line to report their success to their superiors—that the million-volt pulse generator they had deployed had begun charging its capacitor. They reported that all indications were that it would be operational shortly, capable of bombarding the continent with devastating blasts of electromagnetic waves.

They left the elves to the wormhole's controls, going to celebrate their progress toward deploying three hundred generators around the planet, capable of obliterating its technology.

•　•　•

Steve the troll grunted with the effort, as he hauled his squat body up onto the table of the hotel conference room so the reporters could see him. He plunked down, dangling his bow legs, and peered myopically through beady eyes out at the sparse crowd. With stubby fingers, he scratched his bulbous head, populated by its sparse crop of unkempt white hair. He started to pick his potato nose, but stopped, realizing he was being video recorded.

He grumbled, "You'd rather see the damn fairy, the angel . . . yeah, I know. You don't think trolls are as interesting."

"Well, you live under bridges, right?" asked a junior reporter from one magazine.

"Yeah, because we built the damn bridges long time ago. We build stuff, invent stuff, that's what we do. We invented the suits."

"What suits?" asked the restaurant critic, disappointed to have lost out in the choice of Mythicals to write about.

"Watch this." The troll pulled a metal canister onto the table and extracted out a flabby, wet mass of flesh-colored material. Shaking it dry, he poked his stubby legs into the mass, hauling what seemed to be some kind of skin up over his shoulders. He reached back and flipped up a mask that hung down the back. He tugged it down over his face, shifting it around until the mask was centered, its long, blond hair hanging down his back in damp strings. He pressed his chest, and the flesh tightened onto his body, the legs stretching out to make him taller. The face shaped itself, to transform the troll into an amply endowed, attractive, naked young woman.

"This suit is why we can live among you," said the troll, now in a breathy feminine voice.

"*Oh, dear God!*" exclaimed a male voice in the back of the room. "*Sandy!*" The young cameraman for a local television station dropped his camera in horror and bolted out the door, gagging.

•   •   •

Robin the fairy flitted gracefully around the ballroom, her wings a fluttering blur, her silver hair flowing behind her, making the crystal chandeliers tinkle with the breeze of her passing. She was perfectly amenable to giving flying demonstrations for the cameras.

She came to rest lightly on the stage, folding her wings back and spreading her delicate hands to invite questions from the throng of reporters.

"We thought you were all myths," said a reporter. "How did you ever keep your secret?"

Her sapphire eyes narrowed in amusement. "It wasn't as difficult as you might think. You see, centuries ago, there weren't any cameras, so we were the stuff of people's tales. Today, we wear the flesh-suits that make us blend. And even when there are sightings, media dismiss them. And everybody's too busy with crimes and celebrity scandals to pay attention to some crank who claims to have seen a weird creature.

"You are naked, and—" began a reporter.

"Yes I am," she interrupted. "We love our bodies. And we love sex."

"Fairies have sex?" he asked.

"Beautiful sex, lovely, aerial sex. We even have competitions on our home world. Like dance competitions. Frankly, to us, your sex looks like a couple of water balloons bumping together."

• • •

"Wanna see my balls?" asked Mike the ogre.

A shocked chorus of *"No!"* greeted the question—at first.

But then, the reporters realized that such a display would rocket their stories to the top of the news.

So, the consensus reversed to "Yes!" and the ogre happily obliged, grinning, showing stubby tusks.

He proudly thrust his crotch forward. His bulbous scrotum was dyed light blue and gaily decorated with jewels, and with hanging pendants on gold chains. He switched on two lights strapped to his legs, strategically aimed to illuminate the glittering testicles.

A multitude of still cameras strobed the scene, and video cameras zoomed in for close-ups.

"Why do you do that?" asked a reporter.

The ogre looked puzzled. "Because the balls are where life comes from. We don't understand why your species hides their balls. Or the other life-parts."

"It looks painful, all the jewelry and stuff."

"No more painful than what you pierce and decorate."

"Um . . . you seem to have . . . well . . . a somewhat . . . uh . . . small penis," diplomatically commented the reporter from *Medical Day*.

Mike looked down at the nub barely sticking out of his crotch. "Yes, isn't it excellent?" He grinned, once more showing his tusks.

"You don't want a large penis?"

"Oh, no! It overshadows the balls. I feel badly for your males with their great overhanging things. But it's sufficient when it expands for mating."

"How sufficient?" asked the reporter.

The ogre held up a massive foot. "Well, it gets as long as this."

A gasp rose from the male reporters and a chortle from the females. An abashed reporter from *Business Weekly* quickly changed the subject. "Do you have a name in your language?"

"Yes, it's . . ." With that, the ogre issued forth a deep-throated gargling sound. The reporters paused in their writing. Then many scribbled down a random succession of r's, g's, l's, and a few k's.

Asked another reporter, "Are ogres aggressive? I mean you're quite . . . um . . . imposing."

"Nobody argues with us. Not even the werewolves. That's why we're the managers."

"What do you manage?"

"Transport. The wormholes. Supplies. Whatever needs to be managed. Like I said, nobody messes with us. Wanna see the backside of my scrotum?"

• • •

Wendy the angel extended her wings, majestically stretching them out and fluffing their feathers before folding them against her body.

"Are you a messenger of God?" asked the writer for *Religion Reporter*.

"I am a messenger for my species," said Wendy sweetly. "We are just another intelligent species like you. We just have . . . well . . . a different form."

"But do you believe in God?"

"We believe in GOO."

"GOO?"

"Great Overarching Organism. There exists in the universe an intelligence so vast and unknowable that few species can hope to grasp it. There was one super-intelligent race that we encountered that does understand GOO. But they are so advanced, they couldn't really explain it in terms we could understand."

"Was our Messiah an alien?"

Wendy cocked her head and made a puzzled expression. "Well, he was on your planet before we arrived. He may have been. He does seem to have been someone other than your species. But then, as your religions believe, he may well have been the son of God."

"Or the son of GOO?"

"Or the son of GOO." Wendy nodded, agreeing.

• • •

Ryan the elf emitted an unpleasant creaking squawk like a rusty hinge, as he waved his spindly arms at the reporters assembled in the meeting hall. He donned his light-amplifying goggles so he could see in what to him was a dimly lit room.

Standing beside him, Sam translated, the cameras riveted on her: "He wishes you to understand that it is physically difficult for him to speak in the low register of your language. He understands you, though. Ask your questions, and I will translate his answers."

"Who are you?" asked the male reporter from National News Network, directing the cameraman to focus on Sam.

"I am a pixie. My name is Sam. But I don't wish to answer questions." Sam wore a modest pants suit, to avoid totally mesmerizing the males, and some of the females. Nevertheless, due to the pheromones emanating from her, the males—and some of the females—would not recall that there had been an elf in the room. They would sit staring longingly at Sam the entire time. Their editors would be furious at their lapse in reporting.

Almost all the questions directed at the elf came from women.

"What is the elf's name?" asked the female reporter from *The National Times*.

Ryan skreaked an answer.

"Well, his name here is Ryan," translated Sam. "But his real elvish name is Cvjmgrowfjhvvglehjhiiorddvmgtohq."

"Uh . . . how do you spell that?"

"Like it sounds," said Sam.

"You're kidding."

"Just call him Ryan," she said.

"How did you all get here?" asked the reporter from *Discovering Science*.

Ryan screeched at length, and Sam translated, "We have all formed a network of wormholes among our planets . . . transdimensional apertures that we elves pilot by guiding them using magnetic fields. The holes are not affected by gravity, so we can easily travel wherever we wish in your universe."

"The lights in the sky that people have seen. Are those wormholes?"

"Yes. But very, very rarely," translated Sam. "Sometimes we leave the lights on when we land at night. But very, very rarely. We are very careful. We are master pilots. And artists."

"Artists?" asked the reporter.

"We like to make art on your land."

"What does that mean?"

"Whenever we have time, and we're over farmland, we draw in the crops," translated Sam.

"You make the crop circles!" exclaimed a female reporter from the Alien Contact website.

"More than that. We can create a spinning plasma vortex with the magnetic field that guides the wormhole. We make very nice designs."

"Have you ever crashed?" asked the reporter. "We have this big meteor crater in the desert."

After a long bout of elfin screeching and skittering, Sam translated, "That was an elderly elf pilot. We once used landing craft and kept the wormholes outside the atmosphere. The old elf mistook the accelerator for the brakes. He crashed. He made that crater. Actually, we removed the ship debris and put some meteor pieces in it, to fool you."

"You look like the traditional aliens," commented the female reporter from the *National Investigator*. "Gray skin, big heads, little bodies, skinny arms and legs. Are you the aliens people have seen?"

More peevish screeching from the elf, then Sam's translation, "Yes, we are the beings so often reported by your race. But we have perfectly normal heads and limbs. You have tiny skulls, big monster limbs. *Ugly!*"

"Did your crashes ever result in bodies?" asked the reporter.

"Once. But it was the ogres' fault that the bodies were found. They didn't retrieve them. Your military did autopsies."

"There have been reports of abductions. Do you do anal probing?"

The elf drew himself up to his full diminutive height and indignantly shrieked and skrittered at considerable length.

Sam smiled and translated. "Yes, for very good reason. We needed intestinal samples. The exiles were having severe digestive problems, and we wanted to analyze your intestinal bacteria. But we only probed a little way."

"Sam, do you have a phone number?" asked the enamored male reporter from *Athletics* magazine. He would be among the reporters who didn't remember an elf in the room.

. . .

"You don't really look like a vampire," commented a reporter, straining to see Vladimir in the low light he had specified for the room. The television crews had even tried infrared cameras to capture his image. But those didn't work well, because the vampire's body emitted no heat.

"Ah, you mean this disgusting flesh color," Vlad gestured at his face. "Well, I will show you lovely skin. He stripped off his black suit to reveal a dead-white, faintly luminous body.

"Do you . . . uh . . . drink blood?" asked a timorous voice from the back of the hall.

"No, no, no! It's a myth that arose from one unfortunate soul, your planet's vampire of legend."

"How?"

"Ah, yes. Poor fellow. He wasn't evil. He just suffered bad luck about seven hundred years ago, and it ruined life for all of us. Back when he was serving his sentence as an exile, he took up with his rather delectable young girl of your species. They were . . . cuddling, you might say. Well, she sneezes and jerks her head back. His fangs just happen to nick her neck. He apologizes. They continue their cuddling. She goes home. Her father sees the marks and questions her. She doesn't want to admit she's been with a male. So she tells her father that the vampire was trying to drink her blood. *Bam!* We vampires become unfairly known as bloodsuckers!"

"And you don't turn into bats?"

The vampire laughed ruefully.

"Oh, that nonsense," he declared. "One of our kind was out one night enjoying the darkness, and he feels the urge—"

"To kill?" asked a reporter.

"—to defecate. We have to eliminate waste, same as you. Anyway, he finds a toilet. A boy sees him go in the door of the toilet. So, he is sitting there evacuating, and he looks up and sees a bat hanging from the rafters. He pushes open the door and shoos the bat out. Well, the boy, he runs to his house and tells everybody that a vampire turned into a bat! And there you are! The myth that we become bats!"

• • •

"Would you elaborate on your assertion that we are a 'terminal species'?" asked a reporter from the Federal Broadcasting Corporation.

"No," said the werewolf Flaktuckmetang, a.k.a. Senator Warren F. Lee. He stood glaring disdainfully at the crowd of reporters.

"You'll say nothing?" asked the reporter.

"No," said the werewolf, folding his thickly furred arms. "You are supposedly an intelligent species. You can figure it out for yourselves. Or, maybe not. I don't care."

"Shouldn't you resign from your Senate seat?" asked the reporter from the *Capital Post*. "You aren't one of us."

"Nowhere in the rules does it say a senator has to be any particular species . . . just intelligent. In fact, I suspect many of my colleagues would not meet an intelligence requirement."

"Well, then, you weren't born in this country."

"I have a birth certificate that says I was."

"It can't be real."

"Prove it."

"Do you transform into a werewolf when the moon is full?" interjected a reporter from *The Daily Star*.

"No, I wear a flesh-suit just like other Mythicals."

"But do you go out when the moon is full?"

"Yes, of course, because that's when I can see well enough not to run into trees."

The broadcast reporter returned relentlessly to his first question. "So do you really think we are a terminal species?"

"I'll put it this way. Among our race, your planet is known as *Krokatpof Topafog.*"

"What does that mean?"

"Roughly translated, Planet of the Morons."

CHAPTER 10

"This is great!" exclaimed Jack, as he sat in his apartment with Sam, going through the video feeds on the screen showing the massive coverage of the Mythicals' debut. The news channels had launched around-the-clock coverage documenting the historic events. Mythicals were interviewed, scientists were interviewed, religious scholars were interviewed—anyone who had even the slightest expertise was interviewed.

And the impact was global. Jack had visited channels he didn't even realize existed. All of the international channels showed interviews with their local Mythicals. Speaking the country's languages, fairies, ogres, and other Mythicals were interviewed about their species and their lives as exiles.

Sam's expression was stoic, as she watched the global coverage. She remained as Jack had found her in his apartment, folded into an armchair like a small, nesting bird. He didn't ask how she had managed to get into his apartment. He was too glad to see her.

"Wish I could tell what they're saying," said Jack as he proceeded through the channels.

Sam uncurled, sat up, and answered quietly. "Well, on this channel, the reporter asked the fairy about alien technology. The ogre was telling another station about their family structure. And the angel was explaining to a religious station how she is not a supernatural being."

"You speak those languages?"

"Mythicals know most languages. Some of our exile sentences are so long that we move from country to country, just to stay occupied."

"You don't look happy. Everybody loves the Mythicals. They're fascinated by you."

"It won't last."

"How do you know?

"We've seen it on other exile planets. When we're discovered, there's a period when they like us. Then something happens. Something always happens. That's why exiles remain hidden from the planet's inhabitants."

Jack wondered whether her pessimism had something to do with the "Palliation," whatever that was.

. . .

"Wow, the whole city is here!" exclaimed Jack, as they walked arm-in-arm into the sprawling Capital Convention Center ballroom. Every bit of its vastness was crammed with formally dressed luminaries. They were all eager to meet history's most famous celebrities: Mythicals.

The Wardens had requested—actually decreed—that the Mythicals worldwide would hold events to introduce themselves to the planet's inhabitants. As long as the Mythicals had revealed themselves, believed the Wardens, the best course was to try for acceptance. Otherwise, another exile planet would have to be located, and the exiles transferred—a massive logistical undertaking.

And so, Mythicals hosted hundreds of similar huge receptions in convention centers, city squares, and even stadiums.

As Jack and Sam negotiated the crowd, a circle of fascinated people would briefly part to reveal a glimpse of one or another Mythical. A fairy would be revealed fanning its wings; a hilariously drunk troll singing; an elf screeching a complaint at being jostled; an angel ascending above the crowd to admiring aahs.

Sam would not have been taken for an alien species at first glance, but just another stunningly beautiful young woman. She wore a ruby red gown that accentuated her delicate curves. Her eyes were green, indicating that she was exuding a pheromonal signal. So, as she glided through the throng with Jack, her exquisite emanations made the men forget whatever woman they happened to be with. They would turn toward Sam, beatific expressions on their faces, gazing longingly at her, until she was out of range, leaving them to a huffy scolding by their wives or girlfriends.

In his rented formal wear, Jack shook his head in sympathy. He had been under her spell long enough to at least try and appear poised.

"Can I leave you long enough to get you a drink?" he asked.

"I'll be fine," she said. "I'm fairly adept at dealing with the males of your species."

"I love you," said Jack, almost reflexively. It embarrassed him, but he couldn't seem to stop.

"I know."

He turned to find his way to the bar, but stopped, realizing he should ask a question he had never thought of before: "Are you of legal age?" He tried to make the ridiculous question sound offhanded, even joking. He'd never thought to ask. Sam looked young, but fully mature. But one never knew.

"It's been seventy-five years since I hatched," said Sam matter-of-factly.

Jack's expression morphed into a swirling maelstrom of bewilderment.

"*Oh God!*" he thought. "*I'm enchanted by a woman who's an alien . . . who looks too young for me . . . but is ancient . . . and was hatched!*"

He wandered off, befuddled, past Vlad the vampire, who was enjoying the flirtations of a flock of giggling young women.

At the bar, an ogre was downing two beers at a time, threatening the bartender if he didn't keep the drinks coming. It appeared to be Mike, but all ogres looked alike. It wasn't until the gray-green hulk clapped him on the shoulder that he was sure.

Mike returned to his prodigious imbibing, and Jack managed to secure drinks for Sam and himself, when an introduction came over the sound system from the distant stage of "two of the most prominent Mythicals, who would like to say a few words."

A'eiio and E'iouy stood resplendently naked on the stage, a sight that had become somewhat less disconcerting to Jack. But the shocked murmurs among the crowd conveyed their discomfort.

A'eiio began with a quietly recited list. "Fairies, pixies, trolls, werewolves, ogres, goblins, vampires, leprechauns, mermaids, angels, elves, gnomes, satyrs, bigfoot, sirens . . ."

The crowd grew dead silent.

". . . all of us were once a part of your lore. But now you know that we are real. We hope you understand that we have lived among you in peace. We hope you will understand that we mean to continue this peace, and to help your species prosper in any way we can. We hope you will consider the steps we have outlined to ensure your continued progress and prosperity."

Jack reached Sam to find her surrounded by swooning men who were ignoring the speech. He managed to extricate her and escort her to a place less crowded with susceptible males.

"Uh . . . we've got to talk. About the age difference . . . and . . . uh . . . about you being hatched."

Sam smiled, an amused twinkle in her green eyes. "Well, as for the age, that's pixie years. I'm still considered very young."

"Okay, but did you really hatch? Do you lay eggs?"

She laughed that alluring, melodious laugh. "It was a joke. Pixies can joke, you know. We give birth like your females. We are perfectly compatible with your species in *every* way. Our evolution was parallel enough for viable births. In fact, there are a fair number of offspring from such matings."

Jack had lost himself in considering the mating possibilities, and was startled by the eruption of applause when the fairies finished their speeches.

"See? People love you," he whispered in Sam's ear.

"I know. But not for long."

"Really. My people have accepted Mythicals, welcomed you. You're wrong."

"I wish I were." Now her expression grew somber, and she shook her head, looking around in sad resignation at those who, for now, regarded the Mythicals with wonder.

CHAPTER 11

Wendy the angel soared from the back of the Hall of Nations, high over the gathered delegates, coming to rest beside the lectern. She folded her snowy wings, smiling benevolently, as the awestruck delegates gasped at the sight.

Standing in the back, A'eiio watched her entrance with satisfaction. The fairy thought it best that the delegates' first formal sight of the Mythicals was a creature most revered as a comforting symbol of their religions. And, after all, it was the angels who had created the dire computer model predicting their species' terminal fate.

Fanning her wings to liftoff velocity, A'eiio rose and swept over the delegates and landed beside Wendy. She stepped to the lectern. The other Mythicals—Steve, Robin, Mike, Ryan, and Vlad—filed in, to another round of excited chatter.

Senator Warren Lee was notably absent. The werewolf had disappeared after the news conferences a week earlier. Nor were the delegates there that had formerly represented three of the countries.

They had been dismissed when they had revealed themselves to be Mythicals—a vampire, a male fairy, and a troll.

The General Secretary called the assembly to order, and invited A'eiio to speak.

"We have lived on your world in peace," she began. "Although we are not of your species, and are exiles from our home planets, we have come to you as fellow sentient beings that wish to help you survive on your own planet. The computer simulations done by the race you call angels have revealed that you will not survive to the next century. You are committing suicide. The angels are providing the data to your scientists, so you can verify them."

A'eiio paused, taking a deep breath. Now, she faced the critical moment when the frustrating creatures of this planet would either accept the measures necessary to save their species. Or, they would denounce the aliens who had presumed to prescribe to them. But the alternative advocated by the werewolves—the Palliation—was horrific.

"The damage you are doing to your ecosystems will soon be irreversible. So, our Wardens have given us permission to propose a Remediation. These steps, the models show, will preserve your planet and save your species. The Remediation comprises four laws that we urge your countries to enact:

"The Zero Carbon Law specifies that you will immediately begin to phase out all fossil fuel burning and launch a major initiative to replace it with solar, wind, and safe nuclear power. We will offer all the necessary technologies to enable this transition. Our own civilizations have made this change, and you are welcome to all our knowledge. We can dispose of any nuclear waste using our wormholes." A murmuring arose among the delegates, its tone dark.

"The Biodegradability and Health Law will specify that all artificial chemicals such as plastics will be formulated to biodegrade to harmless products and not be toxic for reproduction and health.

Again, our materials scientists will share with you any technologies necessary to render all your materials safe." Some of the delegates began to shake their heads, their expressions dour.

"The Ecosystem Preservation Law will require all nations to set aside sufficient areas to preserve your extraordinary diversity of species. Our ecosystem computer models can define those areas."

Now A'eiio hesitated. The next law would stun the delegates and their world, especially most of the leaders. But it was necessary.

"The Genetic Fitness for Leadership Law recognizes a sad reality about your species. Our analysis has shown that about half of you are genetically deficient. Unlike many of our species, you harbor a deviant population that possesses a truncated piece of genetic material . . . a sex chromosome . . . that causes them to be significantly more aggressive and less rational. As leaders, they have started all the wars among your species. They are the most murderous. They are responsible for almost all crime and violence. The Genetic Fitness Law would help protect your species from their aberrant behavior by training and equipping another clearly genetically superior group of your species to take most leadership posts in government and industry."

The General Secretary interrupted, his expression puzzled. "And who are these genetically superior ones?" he asked.

"Females."

"And who are these deviants?"

"Males."

●   ●   ●

Flaktuckmetang crouched in the thick brush of the woods, waiting on his prey. He felt only a slight twinge of conscience. After all, the denizens of this exile planet weren't as intelligent as his species. So, killing one, or perhaps several, would not be like killing one of his own, a practice which had been abolished centuries ago. Besides, as a soldier, he had killed many, many times on this planet's battlefields. This was like that killing—necessary for preservation. On the battlefield, he killed to give the advantage to whatever side he was fighting for. Now, he would kill to advance the Palliation, which was critical for the survival of the whole species.

So, killing today was permissible. And, in fact, since the prey wasn't his species, eating was permissible.

But he would give his prey a fighting chance. He would choose one that carried a weapon. So, it would be like killing in battle, but with a nourishing bonus.

And, in a sense, he had the permission of his Warden, who had told him he could do whatever was necessary to ensure the Palliation. And that meant sabotaging the Remediation that the faint-hearted fairies were proposing.

He yawned, peeling back coal-black lips to reveal his substantial fangs. He flexed his claws. He would need all his weapons.

The rattle of an engine rose in the distance. The sound grew, and an all-terrain vehicle came racing along the trail, carrying a large male. A rifle case was strapped behind him. Flaktuckmetang could have easily leaped out and torn him from the vehicle, but that would not satisfy his sense of fair play.

Instead, the werewolf launched himself on a parallel course, loping through the woods slightly behind the hunter's path. After a mile, the hunter stopped his machine, climbed off, and unpacked his rifle, loading it and slinging it on his back. Now he was armed. Now he was worthy prey.

But still the werewolf hesitated. He was glad he did. The hunter had mounted an automatic game camera on a tree so that it would capture any activity in the area.

Excellent! Even if the police were too stupid to conclude that the hunter had been killed by a werewolf, there would be incontrovertible images.

The hunter began to haul himself up the ladder to his tree stand. He settled his bulk into its seat, unslung his rifle and readied it for his hunt.

This would be an excellent kill. The werewolf circled around the area so that the camera would capture his attack. He tensed his muscles.

He leaped from the thicket and bounded across the clearing toward the tree, fangs bared, claws extended.

The hunter bellowed in alarm, bringing up his rifle and leveling it at the monster racing toward him.

The loud crack of a rifle shot echoed through the forest, but the werewolf had veered left, dodging the shot. Another explosion, but the werewolf evaded that bullet, as well.

He reached the bottom of the tree, and the hunter screamed in horror and sought to swing the rifle barrel downward. But the werewolf had already climbed near enough to reach up and tear the rifle from his hands.

The hunter barely managed to utter the beginning of another scream as, in one leap, the werewolf mounted the tree stand, tore open his throat with powerful jaws, and ripped his stomach open with razor-sharp claws.

The hunter hung from the tree stand, limp, bloody, and lifeless. Now he was dead prey. And Flaktuckmetang took his time feeding upon that prey, choosing the most delectable parts to tear off.

Once satiated, the werewolf climbed down, using leaves to wipe the blood from his muzzle and claws. He took one last look at the hunter's remains, now a well-gnawed corpse.

Plenty of evidence.

• • •

"Thank you for wearing clothes . . . *Senator*." President Amar Eller said the last word with a subtle sarcastic emphasis. He didn't smile, nor did A'eiio expect him to.

She stood at the door of the president's office, wearing a red silk dress that contrasted with her pale skin and silver hair, respectfully waiting to be asked to sit. Her wings opened and closed in gentle strokes.

Jack stood beside her, shifting uneasily from one foot to the other. He was trying to decide which was more nerve-wracking. Meeting the president or being seen in public with aliens.

"And this is . . . ?" asked the president.

"Jack March," said Jack. "I'm a reporter. I've asked to be the person to report on the Mythicals."

"You're one of us?"

"Yes."

"And you're in league with these . . ." The president didn't finish the sentence, leaving unsaid whatever epithet he'd considered using.

Eller was a tall, brawny figure with an erect bearing and a mane of white hair coiffed to a luxuriant pompadour. He waited some time before issuing the invitation for them to sit, standing beside his desk, regarding them coldly. He finally gestured for them to take the couch across from the presidential science adviser, Balin Litt, whose glasses, spare frame, and salt-and-pepper beard gave him a kind of sage authority.

The president moved to sit in one of the armchairs by the fireplace, where he had posed for photographs many times, across from some head of state in the other chair. He pointedly did not invite A'eiio to take the other chair, as portentous as was the first visit of a known alien to the White House. He left her sitting in the chair by his desk. And he pointedly had not asked the photographers in.

143

"I would have hoped you would have allowed other Mythicals to join us," said A'eiio.

The president shrugged. "My security agents were concerned enough having you here. But an ogre? A vampire? A troll? Even an angel? They decided the risk was too great."

"Mr. President, the Mythicals have lived among us for a thousand years," said Jack. "And there has never been an incident."

"They are criminals."

"We are exiles," said A'eiio, indignation thickening her voice. "Transgressions on our planets are quite different from the serial killers, rapists, and others you deem criminals."

"This Genetic Fitness Law you want us to enact . . ." The President leaned forward, his jaw tight in anger. "Basically you want us to pass a law that makes it harder for somebody like me to become president of the country!"

"Not at all," said A'eiio. "It merely remedies a deficiency in your race, by promoting the more peaceful ones to leadership positions."

He rose, looming over her, glaring. "I worked hard to get to this position, and you're telling me I'm genetically deficient?"

A'eiio regarded him coolly, deciding whether to provoke the president even more by pointing out that he was showing the very aggression that illustrated the species' males' lack of fitness for leadership. She decided to say nothing.

"I see that many delegates walked out on your speech when you suggested that males were unfit to lead," he said.

"Proving our—"

"And the other laws, the ecological laws," the president continued, pacing the room. "Politically unworkable."

"We have given your scientists all our data, all our models proving that all four laws are necessary for the survival of your species."

The science adviser Litt spoke up. "And as you know, there are doubts in our party that this climate change we are supposedly causing is real."

"*There are no doubts among your own scientists!*" declared A'eiio, her wings fanning in exasperation. "Your own computer models show the very same things . . . that unless you take the steps we have recommended, your species is on a suicidal course to extinction."

"Well, the response has not been positive," said the president. He picked up a tablet computer and swiped its screen. "The *National Business Journal* says, and I quote 'As stunning as was the revelation that we harbor a menagerie of alien species was their outrageous presumption in proposing a wholesale change in how we conduct our political affairs.'"

"Ah, but there is also support," said A'eiio. "The Environmental Action Council supports the environmental laws. And the National Women's Council says that, at first glance, the idea of discouraging males from positions of power seems silly. But when they looked at our data, they see it as a perfectly logical idea."

"They would."

"You should look at our data. The angels have created a comprehensive, detailed sociological analysis showing that the reduction in the wars alone would save millions of lives and prevent a vast amount of destruction. You know that wars do not create wealth; they destroy it. They do not enhance the lives of your species. They degrade it."

"Well, in any case, you'll have to deal with a lot of people who think your proposals will create havoc."

"Like the male legislators."

"Yes, and for the environmental laws, there's the oil industry, the coal industry, the plastics industry, and developers."

Jack leaned forward, his journalist's impulse to observe and report trumping his diffidence. "So, you're saying that you won't support any of these laws, even if all their data show their validity?"

"*Look, we've been invaded by aliens trying to tell us what to do with our own planet, our own society!*" exclaimed the president. "*Why should we listen to them?*"

"Because I've been to one of their planets. They are far more advanced than us. And, in fact, their societies have faced and overcome the same problems of sustainability we're facing."

"And you consider yourself loyal to us?"

Jack started to answer, but the door opened and an aide rushed in. "Mr. President, I believe there is news you should see," he said, moving to the video screen on the wall and switching it on.

The bright red breaking news banner at the bottom of the screen read "Werewolf commits murder."

The voice-over continued, ". . . you can clearly see in these images the perpetrator of the murder in this forest."

The series of grainy images showed a hulking creature leaping toward the camera, its fangs bared, its claws extended.

"I can't tell," said Jack "Is that . . . ?"

A'eiio looked stricken. "The werewolf Flaktuckmetang? Yes."

CHAPTER 12

The wormhole wafted down from the star-filled sky into the gloom of the clearing near the Pilgrim colony. The darkness was made even more absolute by the surrounding thick woods. Stealth was absolutely critical, so the men and women ringing the clearing did not switch on their flashlights. Nevertheless, some light emanated from the evanescent, shimmering aurora that played about the wormhole; and as always it emitted a steady, static-like crackling.

An eager murmuring rose among the gathered Pilgrims, conveying their eagerness at the arrival of the portal to their home planet.

"You sure the outsiders are asleep? They must not witness this," urgently whispered the thin, elderly man to his shorter, bearded companion, as they watched the wormhole coming to rest.

"Yeah, Robert," said the companion. "Anna is watching them. They've turned in for the night." He took a deep breath and smiled, no doubt relishing the fresh tang of ozone that the wormhole invariably brought with it.

"Do they suspect anything other than—"

"That we are just another colony of the Pilgrim cult," interrupted the companion. "Just like all the others around the world. They see us as harmless kooks. I gave them the usual spiel to get them to turn back, 'We have no motel here, no store, no gas station, no campground. We only wish to be left in peace.' I told them they should go right back where they came from."

"But they stayed," said Robert, shaking his head.

"Yes. They're just curious, like so many others. We couldn't very well threaten them. That would bring the police in. Tomorrow, I'll start giving them our indoctrination lecture. That usually prompts people to leave."

"If they don't leave, find out all you can about them," said Robert. "If nobody knows they're here, we can disappear them, if necessary."

The bearded man nodded in grim assent, as the wormhole halted its descent above the grassy clearing. Its lower side flattened, a ladder extended from its depths, and a figure climbed down, pausing in the still night, peering around.

Robert switched on his flashlight to guide the visitor, and he walked toward him.

"Welcome, Christopher, Brother Pilgrim," he said formally, embracing the man. "Welcome to our home." It was the appropriate ceremonial greeting for the executive director in charge of the Pilgrimage, whose job it was to oversee the colonization.

"*All* our homes . . . soon," replied Christopher, a portly man dressed in a black suit and tie. His silver pompadour seemed to float in the darkness as he moved about, smiling, warmly shaking the hands of the other Pilgrims. He carried his heft lightly, but with a reassuring authority. He showed no evidence that the weight of his species' survival was on his shoulders.

James, a slim, balding engineer followed Christopher down from the ladder, looking upward at the hole with the precise scrutiny of a pilot inspecting his airplane. He was a stark contrast to the jovial Christopher, his almost continually wrinkled brow portraying the worry over managing the only portal between his dying world and the promising new one.

"We had a problem with the steering field," James told Christopher. "But it's fixed. It's okay. And the containment field magnets will need replacing soon. We need to do that soon."

"Louisa can do that?"

"Of course," replied James, with a prideful emphasis, given that Louisa was his wife. "She's finishing a flight checklist."

Shortly, Louisa, a comfortably round woman with white hair held in a short, efficient bob, descended from the ladder. She wore the usual jumpsuit that wormhole engineers and pilots wore.

"We knew you were coming, but we didn't know why," said Robert. "We're happy to see you, but a transit is always risky."

"We've monitored the news here . . . about the Mythicals' revelations . . . their proposals to save the native species. We need to discuss steps to be taken."

"Certainly. Let's go to my house. There have been developments."

Christopher turned to James and Louisa. "I know you'd like to rest, but please join us. There's a matter I need to discuss with you. I wanted to wait until we were back in the colony."

As they walked, Christopher embraced some of the townsfolk, most of whom had no real business being present at the transit, but were drawn by homesickness. Even a possible glimpse of their home planet—as ruined as it was—through a wormhole was welcome. And, they wanted to see their leader Christopher. He was the symbol of their hope of colonizing this planet, and of the coming likely violent struggle to replace the native species.

They emerged from the woods to a small village of modest cottages with one main road, paved only through the town. The lights in the cottages began to blink out, as the people returned and retired for the night.

They entered one of the cottages and settled in the small living room, drinking the homemade liquor that was as close as they could come to their own whiskey.

Robert told Christopher, "Some very strange news. The intelligence we have is that the werewolves appear to be planning some drastic action. We have detected that they are orbiting what appear to be electromagnetic pulse devices . . . a great many of them. And they tested the effects of such a device on a small town."

"It sounds like a potentially devastating attack," said Christopher. "Could it accelerate the extinction?"

"Possibly," said Robert. "And a werewolf has committed at least one murder . . . I would guess in an attempt to thwart the Remediation that the Mythicals are proposing."

"So, if we were to contact them—the werewolves—could we trust them to be allies?" asked Christopher.

"We shouldn't. After all, they aren't human."

"Is there evidence that the Mythicals are aware of us?"

"Not so far. And I've been in contact with the other Pilgrim colonies. They see no evidence either that the Mythicals know we exist, although they may suspect. They could have detected our transits to the planet, and they would have known that our wormhole was not their own."

"Whether we trust them or not, we need to help the process along . . . whatever it is the werewolves are attempting," said Christopher. "Our models show that our ecosystem deterioration is accelerating. We have only a few years."

"How many of us are left at home?"

"Only a million worldwide."

"Maybe they would accept us here," interjected James. "Maybe we don't need to . . . well . . ." His voice trailed off. They almost never stated the drastic plan to save their dwindling population.

"Accept us? Would *we* accept *them?*" asked Christopher emphatically. "We've devastated our own planet, and now want to abandon it for theirs. They would see us as pariahs. No, the only way to survive is to take the planet. It's them or us. And we will be better stewards of the planet than them. We know what we did wrong. We know that they're on a suicidal course. We will fix that. And if the werewolves are planning a global attack, that could give us our chance at life."

"It's just that—" began Louisa, her expression downcast.

But Christopher interrupted. "I'm told that your son is deeply involved with the Mythicals . . . that he is one of their . . . what do they call them . . . Allies? What an excellent, fortuitous advantage for us! Does he know what he is?"

"No, Director, he does not," said James. "We are very careful not to reveal to him where he came from. As far as he knows, he grew up in a normal household. And that we moved into the Pilgrim cult after he left."

"Well, now it's time you told him. It's time you enlisted him in our cause . . . his cause. Remind me, what name did you give him?"

"Jack March."

CHAPTER 13

"We're eons older than these creatures," declared the werewolf Warden. "We know what's best for their pack. And that is for the weak to be culled."

The Warden stood at the window, enjoying the rise of his planet's ancient sun, as it cast a baleful orange glow across the stark, tortured, volcanic landscape. The sun was a looming ball of roiling red plasma, even in its death throes, which had lasted for a million years. A flare began to erupt from its surface, launching tendrils of luminescent, swirling gas.

"Some of us don't necessarily disagree with you," said the ogre Warden, sitting in the stone chair at the head of the conference table. "But you have gone too far. Testing your EMP weapon . . . dispatching your exile to murder and cannibalism! That is unconscionable!"

The werewolf turned from the window of the stone fortress. He showed his fangs. "I did not dispatch him. He is a rogue."

"Then trigger his coma chip," said the fairy Warden, shivering in the frigid temperature of the planet. He drew the coarse cloak he'd been given tightly around him.

The werewolf shrugged, tilting his thickly maned head in just a hint of disdain. "His chip was destroyed in the EMP test, as was his termination chip. It was unfortunate, but he decided to be at the target to gather ground-truth data."

"Nonsense," muttered the troll Warden. "You would have notified the Council the instant one of your exiles went off-line . . . unless, of course, you gave him permission."

"Prove it," the werewolf shot back.

The resounding crack of a lightning bolt signaled the beginning of a storm. It would yield magnificent violence, thought the werewolf. A fitting backdrop to support the defiant stance he would take.

The vampire Warden rose from his stone bench. "This is what you *will* do. You *will* find your exile, Flaktuckmetang. And you *will* banish him to the prison on your moon." A gale rose outside, its winds buffeting the thick window of the fortress.

The werewolf touched his wrist communicator with a clawed finger, and five guards entered the room—hulking creatures bred for battle. They carried the full complement of weapons—rifles, bomblets, missiles—that made them effective killing machines.

"My praetorians will escort you back to the transit station," he said coldly.

The elf Warden climbed upon the stone table—putting him at eye level with the werewolf, and stalked down its length to face him. He screeched an emphatic, furious answer.

The pixie Warden translated: "He said you risk a vote of the Warden Council to sanction you. Then you would face dire consequences."

"*I know what he said!*" snarled the werewolf. Another crack of lightning outside, and the winds rose to viciously batter the massive citadel walls. "*I will manage my own exiles. And we will take whatever steps necessary to prepare for the Palliation.*"

"Yes, but only *prepare,*" declared the ogre, drawing to his full height, looming over the werewolf. "You will take *no* further steps without the Council's permission, or you will face the likelihood of a conflict with all the other member worlds."

The ogre turned to face the phalanx of looming praetorians. He glared at them eye-to-eye. "And not even your engineered praetorians can overcome such foes."

"You have until our sun sets to depart," said the werewolf. He waved his claw at the guards, and they parted ranks, allowing the Wardens to leave. "The discussion is concluded."

●　●　●

Jack sat hunched over his computer, pecking away at his article on the latest events. Fortunately, he didn't have to rely on the *Capital Herald* to publish it. The online *Lightning News* had commissioned him to cover the most significant news story in centuries. Screw the *Herald!* But he couldn't concentrate. He kept switching to various other media sites, where a worrisome trending topic was "Dangerous Mythicals." The werewolf's cannibalistic murder had triggered a storm of rage. Jack scanned through the growing list of messages:

"Cannibal werewolves? What about the rest?"

"Should blood banks be checked for vampires?"

"Fairies could kidnap children! Lock doors!"

"A pixie made me crazy with her odor. True!"

"Heard of an ogre attacking cop!"

"They're evil creatures to be stopped!"

He willed himself away from the message feed, to write for half an hour, enough to upload his latest story on the worldwide receptions held for the Mythicals.

But he knew that positive story would change drastically, when he checked back. New topics were attracting massive followings: "Round up the Monsters," "Intern the Mythicals," and most frightening, "Death to Mythicals."

Then one message popped up that sent him leaping from his chair and rushing out the door:

"Heard Mythicals are being arrested all over. Major busts! Imprison the freaks!"

∙ ∙ ∙

A'eiio sat alone in the upstairs study, staring at the screen of her phone, but not seeing it. E'iouy, came in, fresh and naked from a shower, fluttering his wings to rid them of droplets of moisture. Seeing her distant stare, he bent down and kissed her on the cheek. She did not look up.

"What could we have possibly done?" she asked quietly.

"You have no control over the others," he said, sitting down in the armchair across from hers, leaning forward and placing his hand on her knee. "Especially the werewolves. They're so different from the other species. They barely survived their warlike period, as did this planet, with its nuclear arms race."

"Ah, well—" she began, but splintering crashes downstairs, from the front and back doors, interrupted her.

"POLICE!" bellowed a voice from downstairs, along with the thud of boots, and the faint metallic clink of weapons. The sounds of steps pounding up the stairs.

A'eiio stood, frozen in shock, but E'iouy sprang to the window.

155

"We can't let this happen!" he exclaimed. "If we're taken, we can't help the others!" He flung open the windows, his wings becoming a blur as he sliced through the air.

"No! Don't!" she exclaimed. "They have—"

But he had already lifted off, sailing out the window. She ran to look out at a phalanx of helmeted men arrayed on their front lawn. One raised the barrel of his weapon, which erupted a sharp crack.

E'iouy faltered in his flight, his wings flailing wildly, as he spiraled down to slam into the ground.

A'eiio screamed in agony, her hand over her mouth, tears welling in her eyes.

A sound behind her. She turned to face three hulking men in helmets, masks, and bulletproof vests. They leveled their weapons at her.

·   ·   ·

No answer! No answer! *No answer!* Again and again, Jack punched in the number for A'eiio, between bouts of urging the driver to speed up. The driver uttered a curse in some language Jack didn't understand, and hunched over the wheel. It was thirty minutes to the address A'eiio had given him.

The driver muttered another curse when Jack ordered him to stop before reaching the address, farther down the tree-shrouded avenue from the house. He shoved enough money at the driver to give him a good tip and leaped out, sprinting along the street.

His way was blocked by a large, black armored truck with "TAC-TICAL" painted on the side, parked on the street along with several vans. The truck's rear doors were open, and its rows of bench seats were empty. He was too late!

He turned to run up the broad lawn to the stone mansion, when a voice behind him shouted "STOP! POLICE!"

He ignored the warning and was slammed from behind and wrestled to the ground. A heavy body held him down, his face smashed against the thick grass. His hands were wrenched behind him, and his wrists bound with handcuffs that sliced into his wrists.

"Turn him over," said one of the body-armored policemen. "Poke him in the chest. If he's one of them, his skin will fall off."

"I'm a reporter! You want me reporting that you assaulted me?" Jack exclaimed, as he was flipped over and a finger began prodding his chest.

"Shut up," growled the cop, as he continued to jab at Jack's breast bone.

Abruptly bright lights lit the scene, and the cop straightened up, startled.

"Officer, what are you doing?" came a voice from behind the lights. It was a reporter with a camera. They were being videoed.

"He's assaulting a reporter!" Jack shouted.

But before he could say more, he was hauled to his feet, his cuffs snipped off, and he was shoved toward a growing crowd of video crews and reporters.

He turned to see in the glare of the lights two gurneys being wheeled down the driveway. Strapped on them were the pale forms of A'eiio and E'iouy. Both lay inert, their eyes closed.

"Did you kill them?" shouted Jack, running forward, but restrained by a burly officer. "DID YOU KILL THEM?"

A sergeant stepped forward, his hands raised. "No. They've been tranquilized. It was necessary. They tried to evade arrest."

"Arrest? Arrest? What the hell have they done?"

From the crowd came an angry babble, with phrases like *"dangerous aliens"* and *"protect us"* rising like glass shards from the chatter.

Jack pressed forward, leading the growing throng of reporters. "Do you even know what these drugs would do to them? Did you even know that you wouldn't kill them?"

A television reporter thrust her microphone at the sergeant. "Can you tell us why they were arrested?"

The sergeant shook his head. "Look, there'll be a news conference at headquarters tomorrow morning. They'll explain this stuff then."

He turned and left, as the two emergency vans bearing the unconscious fairies accelerated away, lights flashing, sirens blaring.

Jack decided he needed to call his editor, to add this stunning development to the story he had uploaded. But in his rush to get to the fairies' house, he had missed a message. It had been sent earlier from A'eiio. With trembling hands, he accessed it:

"They may come for us. You have to protect Sam! Her race cannot survive any captivity!"

·   ·   ·

The television truck careened around the corner and accelerated down the dark, narrow downtown street, lurching to a halt, nearly hitting a police car. The car was blocking the road, its emergency lights casting a whirling kaleidoscope of reflections off the houses on either side.

Jack leaped out, skirting the car and running toward the address A'eiio had given him, a modest structure nestled among the others. *"Poor, dear Sam!"* he thought. *"She's defenseless! She'll be traumatized!"*

The house's front window erupted in a cascade of glass as a blue-clad form erupted out of it. The flailing policeman landed in thick bushes at the curb and rolled over, groaning.

"What the hell did you do to her!" Jack shouted, trying to mount the steps.

"Awwww, shhhhitttt," moaned the cop, trying to haul himself to his feet.

Another cop burst from the doorway, eyes wide. *"Little monster is strong!"* he exclaimed. *"Call for backup!"*

Two more cops appeared, limping. Both of them showing bruised faces. One shoved Jack back down the steps.

"Don't go in there! Get back. This thing'll tear you apart!"

"What thing?" asked Jack. "An ogre?"

"Just get back. They sent us to pick up some girl. She's a whatcha-call-it. A pixie."

"She did this?" Jack stood transfixed at the sight of the injured policemen.

A static-filled radio message told the cops that Sam had been spotted. Bright lights switched on behind him, signaling that the TV crew had begun filming.

He followed the cops down the street, to find one pointing up at the roof. Jack looked up to see Sam, naked, running along the roof line, adeptly launching her small body in soaring leaps between buildings. Reaching a spot down the street from the officers, she vaulted herself off the roof into the thick branches of a large oak, leaped down, sprinted across the street, and began to scale the outside of a tall apartment house.

"I can't keep up!" exclaimed the television cameraman, trying to capture her acrobatic escape."

"SAM!" shouted Jack. "I'M COMING FOR YOU!" He heard a distant voice that he recognized as hers, but he couldn't tell what she had said.

Jack doubled back to the television van. The crew didn't see him, busy trying to video Sam. He climbed into the van, started the engine and slammed it into reverse, speeding backward down the street to the main intersection. He wrestled the van into a quick U-turn and found the emergency flashers and switched them on, hoping Sam would recognize that it was him.

Almost sideswiping a passing sports car, he accelerated to the next block in the direction he thought Sam might have headed. Slowing, he turned up the street. He reached the end of the block, turned left, and went up another block.

He was halfway down that block when a loud thump on the roof startled him. He stopped, and Sam swung down, opened the door and slid in.

"Thank God!" he exclaimed. "Are you okay?" He was startled by her eyes. He could swear that they had been a glowing red when she leaped into the van, but now they were the blue he had come to know so well.

"Yes. I hope the officers aren't too badly hurt."

"You did that? You beat them up?"

Sam smiled slightly and shrugged. "They wanted to capture me."

"We need to get you away from here. Are you strong or something?"

"When I need to be."

"Well, I sure won't challenge you to a wrestling match. Where can I take you that's safe?"

"There's a place, where we—"

She was interrupted by the warble of sirens, and three police cars zoomed in from side streets, lurching to a stop in front of the van. Jack checked the rear view mirror and saw two cars come up behind them, lights flashing.

Cops streamed out of the cars, leveling an arsenal of pistols, shotguns, and assault rifles at them.

"*Show your hands!*" shouted the cop who advanced, aiming a shotgun at the windshield. "*We will shoot you!*"

Jack raised his hands, glimpsing a movement out of the corner of his eye. Sam had opened the van door, and was sliding out.

"Don't!" he exclaimed.

"They might hurt you," said Sam calmly, padding toward the cops on bare feet.

CHAPTER 14

"You look like the creatures of this planet," declared the werewolf Flaktuckmetang suspiciously. He wore the battle armor he'd not been able to wear since he had been sentenced to exile. He had taken care to display the medals he had earned for performance of his duties before the exile.

"And dolphins look like fish," Christopher shot back, cocking his head and smiling. "But they are not. We are a far superior race."

They stood facing one another in the sunbaked desert, each standing at the front of a dozen of their species—Pilgrims and werewolves. Behind each group floated the huge, shimmering wormholes in which they had arrived.

The werewolves brandished weapons, because the surprise encounter with the Pilgrims' wormhole in orbit had nearly triggered a battle. After a tense standoff in the vacuum of space, they had warily landed their wormholes in the vast emptiness of the desert, and the blistering, dry winds gusting around them.

"Your ambush could have caused a disaster, intercepting us as we were deploying the . . . device. There could have been . . . consequences." The werewolf gestured to the pack of massive praetorians looming behind him, which aimed an array of their ornately decorated rifles, grenade launchers, and hand-cannons at the group.

"It was no ambush," said Christopher, raising his hands in an open gesture of conciliation. "It was a contact . . . to talk. We have been observing your deployment. We need to talk about what you are doing."

"What we are doing is no business of yours. And we don't know who . . . *what* . . . you are. You are not in the wormhole network . . . in the Alliance of species. Why have you kept yourself hidden?"

"We know your plans . . . of the Palliation," said Christopher. "We've observed your preparations. We want to help you."

"Help?" The werewolf gave a guttural, derisive laugh. "We don't need your help, whatever you are. Leave, or we will kill you."

"Our goals are the same. We both want to preserve this planet's environment; but to cull its population. The only difference between our goals is that you only want to preserve it for exiles. We seek to emigrate here from our home planet. Otherwise, our race will die. Here, we can better preserve the planet than these—"

"If you approach us again, we will see it as an act of war." The werewolf showed his fangs. "We haven't had a good war in a very long time."

"We can be of use to you. We can sabotage the Remediation. That will help ensure that the other species in the network will agree to your plan."

Flaktuckmetang gave another growling chuckle. "Haven't you been monitoring their news? About the one I killed? The arrests? The interning? There was even a death. They killed a fairy. No, the Remediation will not be implemented."

Christopher shrugged. "But you can't be certain. This planet's creatures may somehow decide to do the rational thing. We can ensure that there is absolutely *no* chance the Remediation will succeed."

"How? You are aliens on this planet. You have no role in their decisions."

"Actually, we do." Christopher smiled and shrugged. "We've been colonizing the planet covertly for decades. We have people high in government, in industry. They can advocate for special interests . . . oil, coal, plastics. They can deny that there is a disruption of their planet . . . a global heating. And they can very effectively campaign against the Remediation. We had planned to infiltrate and gradually take control before the planet was terminally ruined. But this is a better opportunity. For both our races." He gestured broadly at the expanse around them. "There is room on this planet for all of us. For all Mythicals and Pilgrims. Once . . ." he trailed off. There was no need to finish the sentence.

The werewolf gestured for the pack to lower their weapons. "I will take your proposal to my Warden. Until then, do not approach our operations or you will be attacked."

•   •   •

Smears of blood stained the glass, some being in the form of small hand prints. Jack felt a gut-wrenching knot of panic and fear, as he peered through the bloodstains and into the bio-containment cell holding Sam. She was curled up in a corner, handcuffed to a chain attached to the cinder block wall. She wore an orange prison jumpsuit and prison slippers.

"Sam!" he had to shout, because the cell was sealed. It was normally used to house prisoners with the most dangerous diseases. But

Sam's only "disease" was a pheromonal emanation that rendered the guards dopily smitten.

Sam raised her head and looked blearily up at him. Her normally glistening blue eyes were dull with depression, or maybe drugs, or both. She seemed not to recognize him at first; then her expression brightened and she gave him a wan smile.

"You came," she mouthed.

"I'm getting you out of here!" he exclaimed, as his fear transformed to utter rage.

He turned to the guard who had been hauling him, handcuffed, past the cell. *"Do you know what the hell you're doing to her? Do you even know how to take care of her? Do you even know what she needs to stay alive?"*

"She's dangerous," said the guard offhandedly. "She attacked our officers. And she's an alien, and we don't know what poisons she's spittin' out. So, it's up to the docs to figure out what to do."

He knew his options and credibility were limited, since he was in custody himself for trying to help Sam escape. But he hoped the phone call he'd made to the editor of *Lightning News* could bring a lawyer. After all, the online site was owned by the media conglomerate Bennett Communications. And, the site had a vested economic interest in getting him out. He was their reporter right in the middle of the hottest story on the planet.

Sure enough, only half an hour after he'd been deposited in the jail's interview room, a portly, balding, vest-suited lawyer, Donald Pearce, hustled into the room, declaring that he would be representing Jack.

But Jack already had his defense strategy mapped out. In his first reporting job on the court beat, he'd witnessed lots of defense lawyers spin webs of almost-truths to get their clients sprung. He'd already began spinning his own web.

"Okay, I was not helping her escape," he told Pearce, raising his eyebrows to signal the beginning of a concocted story.

"Right," said Pearce, smiling conspiratorially and scribbling notes.

"I was covering the story for *Lightning News,* and was looking for her, and she just jumped into the van."

"Yeah, sounds good," said Pearce, scribbling.

"And I didn't steal the van. The TV crew let me borrow it." Jack knew the television crew would readily agree to the small lie, in return for an exclusive interview.

"Okay," said Pearce. "I'll go see the TV crew and the prosecutor. We'll get you out of here." The lawyer stood to go, but Jack stopped him.

"I also want to give you a much bigger task. A tempting case for a lawyer. This is a civil rights case. These Mythicals are being held in custody for no good reason but their species. They haven't committed crimes. In fact, given that their jailers don't even know how to take care of them, they could die."

"So, what do you want me to do?"

"Get them out."

Pearce shrugged and shook his head. "Look, this is far beyond what my employers would go for. This is—"

"This is the biggest damned story *ever!* And getting these Mythicals out will get *Lightning News* the biggest exclusive *ever.*"

"Yeah, well, I'm telling you that as a news outlet, they wouldn't have a hell of a lot of influence with any judge. In fact, since this roundup was nationwide, it would be a matter for the Supreme Court."

"That's why I'm suggesting you go see a fairy by the name of E'iouy. He's in custody. He's a lawyer . . . a prominent lawyer. You work with him. He'll know how to proceed."

"Hell, you mean to tell me there could be a fairy . . . an alien . . . arguing before the Supreme Court?"

"That's exactly what I'm saying."

CHAPTER 15

Standing at the control panel, peering at the view screen, the Pilgrim wormhole pilot easily spotted the circle of lights beaming into the star-filled night sky from the expanse of the valley. Nearby, he could see the dimmer lights of the huge adjacent dwelling.

Christopher peered over the pilot's shoulder as he touched buttons to launch the wormhole sweeping down to waft gently into a hover just above the helicopter landing pad. Christopher passed through the airlock into the chamber that enclosed the hole and stood waiting while a technician extended a ladder down to the ground.

He laboriously lowered his portly bulk down to the ground, to see multibillionaire Nathan Clark standing on the broad porch of his massive log home. He wore his usual khaki pants, plaid shirt, and impassive expression. The tall, steel-gray-haired mogul had not come to dominate the country's energy markets by letting his emotions show.

Stepping up beside him, his slightly younger brother, David, shorter and seemingly less imposing in slacks and a polo shirt. But

Christopher had watched the younger Clark totally bulldoze a roomful of senators who foolishly tried to pass a bill that would affect profits of Clark Industries.

Particularly impressive about the brothers was that they had accrued their immense wealth in only two decades, since they had arrived through the wormhole as penniless Pilgrims.

Christopher approached them, and Nathan wasted no time getting to the point of their meeting. "Are the monsters planning what we thought?" he asked.

"Yes. They call it the Palliation." Christopher mounted the stairs, as the Clark brothers led him into the two-story great room of the log home.

"Palliation?" asked Nathan. "That means alleviate, right? What the hell do they want to alleviate?"

"The deterioration of the planet. The werewolves are now inserting an array of electromagnetic pulse weapons in orbit. At a given signal, they will trigger them to decimate the planet's electrical infrastructure . . . to destroy all power generation, communications, transportation. As a result, a huge percentage of the planet's population will die."

"Absolutely out of the question!" exclaimed Nathan. *"They would also destroy all that we have built!"*

"Yes, that would," said David in more measured tones. "We were quite prepared to evolve our business away from fossil fuels, toward ecologically sound sources. This catastrophic plan of these inhuman creatures would mean that we would inherit a ruined technological infrastructure. We have the means to stop this nonsense, do we not?"

"I'm not sure," said Christopher, as Nathan waved him to a seat on the leather couch before the massive stone fireplace, with its crackling fire. Nathan and David took seats in large armchairs.

"*Not sure?*" spat Nathan. "You mean to say after decades of monitoring this menagerie of freaks that you're not sure we can rid the planet of them?"

"It's not necessary to do that, for now. What I'm telling you is that I think our aims are currently consonant."

Nathan leaned forward, glaring at Christopher. "There are some twenty thousand of us in Pilgrim colonies around this planet. And we can arm them and use our own wormhole to attack these . . . *things.*"

Christopher's smile faded. He decided that—as powerful as these men were—it was time he asserted his authority. He pulled himself out of the chair and paced before them.

"You have been invaluable to our plans, no doubt," he said. "But I am responsible for this pilgrimage. Our own environment is now ruined. There are fewer than a million of us left. Our former plan to infiltrate and dominate is too slow. So your orders—"

"OUR ORDERS!" shouted Nathan, standing to tower over Christopher. "YOU DO NOT GIVE US ORDERS!"

Christopher remained imperturbable. "Actually we do. We made you . . . we can ruin you. So, your *orders* are to use your influence . . . bribery, blackmail, whatever is necessary . . . to ensure that this Remediation does not go forward. I have told the werewolves that we will do that. And I will ask them in return that we be given sufficient notice of the Palliation. We will temporarily evacuate or harden our colonies against the electromagnetic burst, and allow its consequences to unfold. We can then return to a more pristine, less populous planet that we will occupy."

"How can you do this?" asked Nathan. "How can you allow them to create such ruin on this planet? Why have you not allowed us to go public?"

"Never forget that we are alien to this planet just like these Mythicals. Just like them, we would be seen as enemies; identified,

hunted down, eliminated. This planet's inhabitants are full of preju-
dices and hatred . . . unfortunately more like us than I care to admit."

"Let's say we do accept what you say. What about the Mythicals?
They could become our enemies." David regarded him coldly,
strategically.

Christopher shrugged. "We will bargain with them. We will
agree that they can bring back their exiles. Until the time is right."

"What do you mean?" asked David.

"Once the beasts have destroyed the planet's infrastructure,
we will pledge to rebuild it. We will pledge to restore the planet's
ecology. We will restore our own population. Then, when we are of
sufficient numbers, we will 'palliate' the Mythicals . . . here, as well
as on their home planets. We have historically been quite effective
with our thermonuclear technology. We can confidently predict that
a missile directed through a wormhole will devastate the other side
and unleash an electromagnetic burst that will close the hole. And,
we would ask that you two lead the entire effort."

A red-faced Nathan, pacing back and forth across the large room,
started to speak. But David waved a hand at him to calm him.

David nodded his head resignedly, and said, "I think I speak
for my brother in saying that we will give this new direction serious
consideration."

•   •   •

A'eiio slumped on the cot in her cell, head bowed in despair, wings
folded tight against her naked body. Where was her husband? She
trembled at the memory of the horrifying sight of him plummeting to
the ground. And what had happened to Sam? The pixie would die in
captivity, she knew. But she could do nothing. The other Mythicals?
Her friends? She had only inklings of the fate, since she had been shot

with the tranquilizer gun. She had been barely conscious when she had been carried from the emergency van to the cell and left there.

No sound caused her to look up. Only a sense of presence. E'iouy! He stood at the solid steel door peering through the small window. She leaped to the door.

"How did you . . .? What has . . .?" she could not even form a coherent question. But he knew what that question was.

"Well, our friend Jack persuaded his employer that getting us a lawyer would be good business. And that lawyer persuaded a judge that, since I'm the lawyer for the Mythicals here, I should be free to advocate for them. There are some minor restrictions." He gestured at his neck, which had a large black rectangle strapped to it. Behind him stood a guard holding a remote.

"What is it?" she asked.

"A stun collar. If I try to fly away, I get zapped."

"That could kill you!"

"Don't worry about me. We need to get you out. We need to get you *all* out." He looked back at the guard expectantly. The guard nodded his assent and stepped back, waving to another guard in a control room overlooking the cell block. The cell door clicked to unlock, and A'eiio shoved it open and rushed to embrace him. They stood for a long time, not speaking, taking comfort in that embrace.

"The others?" she finally asked. "What's happened?"

He caressed her face sadly. "Robin," he whispered, shaking his head.

Her lip trembled; tears welled in her eyes. "What happened?"

"They went to take her. She was on a roof. She tried to fly. They shot her. Not with a tranquilizer. With a bullet."

He embraced his wife, as her body sagged in grief, and she began to sob.

"Is this happening all over?"

"Yes, globally. All the governments have conducted roundups. They're calling it 'precautionary detainment.' Some Mythicals are in prisons, others in camps. Thousands of us. But some aren't."

"They escaped?"

He smiled grimly. "Some hadn't revealed themselves in the first place. So, they got away. And, well, you know, nobody can keep a troll where he doesn't want to be. They managed to keep Steve in a cell for about an hour before he broke out. They can't find him. And Ryan and the other elves keep screwing up the alarm systems, the surveillance cameras. They couldn't find Vlad and the other vampires. Maybe they do turn into bats."

She smiled through the tears. "Not surprising. And Wendy?"

"They went to capture her, but there were some religious types among the agents. They just couldn't bring themselves to capture an angel. They hesitated long enough for her to take off."

"Good. Besides Sam, she's another who couldn't take confinement. And Flaktuckmetang?"

"Still missing. In fact, almost all the werewolves avoided capture. And some of the ogres. And others of various races."

"So, do you think they are working with the werewolves?"

"Likely. And they're certainly preparing the Palliation. We'll have to deal with that, but first, we have two tasks. We need to get you out. Especially because you're pregnant. And second, I'm filing a writ with the Supreme Court to demand all Mythicals' release."

●　　●　　●

"We absolutely have the best interests of the country in mind," declared Adrian Brenner, the "policy director" of the Clark brothers, picking up the bottle of very, very expensive sparkling wine. With his meticulously manicured hand, his wrist showing his very expensive watch, he poured the icy effervescent liquid into the senate leader's crystal goblet, smiling. The opalescent string of perfect, tiny bubbles spiraled to the surface of the liquid, as befitted a wine that cost more than the senator made in a month.

"I'm sure you do," said the senator, nodding amicably and taking a sip, raising his eyebrows in appreciation. Indeed, he had deeply appreciated the excellent meal at one of the capitol's most exclusive clubs.

Brenner was certain their conversation would not be overheard, ensconced as they were in the very private room of the very private club. However, Brenner also accepted reality that he did not have the full attention of the senate leader or the other guest, the vice president. He did not mind one bit. The two middle-aged politicians' attention was understandably distracted by their two lovely young companions for the evening.

The women had been chosen and procured per the details of the senator's and vice president's preferences in women, which had been extracted from Brenner's private data base. And that data base had been compiled by extensive investigations of the two men by the security firm owned by the Clark brothers. For the senator, there was a willowy, long-legged blond; for the vice president, a redhead with flawless ivory skin.

The vice president, a dumpy, balding man, briefly diverted his attention from the redhead to Brenner. "I take it you have discussed the matter with your counterparts elsewhere."

"Oh, yes," said Brenner, smiling the smile of one confident of the influence the massive wealth of the Clark brothers could buy. "My colleagues have been in discussion with leaders worldwide. They agree that these absurd proposals . . . the so-called Remediation . . . by these aliens do not merit serious consideration. And, of course, the arrests of the past week have proved that they are not to be trusted."

The slightest look of concern clouded the senate leader's deeply tanned face. "But still, the environmentalists, the scientists, they have confirmed the data these creatures provided."

Brenner made an offhanded wave. "Not to worry. My office has transmitted to you a set of talking points that speak to those issues."

He realized that he had only a brief window to discuss the subject before the two men departed with their companions. He ticked off the points on his fingers, keeping them simple:

"The Zero Carbon Law will profoundly disrupt our energy economy; the Biodegradability and Health Law will devastate our critical chemical industry; the Ecosystem Preservation Law will render vast tracts of land unavailable for development. And the Genetic Fitness for Leadership Law . . . well . . ." He paused, grinning. There was no need even to complete the sentence to persuade the two male leaders of the folly of that law.

Indeed, the senate leader and the vice president both chuckled and raised their glasses in tacit agreement.

"Gentlemen, I am delighted that you could join me this evening," said Brenner. He glanced at his assistant, who had entered the room, nodding. "I believe your limousines are waiting. And I trust you will let me know if there's anything I can do to assist you in ensuring that our country remains strong and its economy vibrant."

Again, he glanced at his assistant, who seemed to have a mild itch in his left eye, for he gently rubbed it. That telling signal reassured Brenner that the cameras had been installed in the bedrooms of the two palatial suites that the men would occupy that night with their willing and beguiling companions.

CHAPTER 16

Geniato Belligrado gave his round little mother a warm hug and took the lunch she had packed for him. He smiled because he knew it would include that very special sandwich she made for him; and she commented how nice it was to see him smile for the first time in a month.

And it had been a harrowing, exciting month. After his stunning encounter with the angel in his shabby room, and the life-changing offer the angel made, he had journeyed back to his little hometown of Vallipitano and shocked his mother with the news that he was taking her to his adopted country. At last he had the money, thanks to an angel. She had been puzzled at the last declaration. But he would not discuss the angel further.

He had presented her with all the necessary immigration papers, which had appeared mysteriously in his mailbox. He also proudly announced that he was now the owner of a small store at the other end of the country from where he had been working before. That information had also appeared in his mailbox, as part of the packet that included access to his new bank account and the information on his new life.

The angel had told him he could have his heart's desire, but he wasn't greedy. All he wanted was to run a family store. And, in return, he became what they called an Ally.

So, today, he walked out of the small house they had just moved into, and opened the door of the used car he'd gotten a good deal on.

"DOWN!" commanded a voice behind him, and he turned to see two suited men standing beside a black car, guns drawn and leveled at him. "DOWN ON YOUR KNEES, HANDS UP!"

"What—" he had begun to ask, when his mother scurried out of the house, a horrified look on her face.

The larger of the two men, swung his gun around and pointed it at his mother, causing her to scream. He moved forward, grabbing her and throwing her to the ground.

Geniato raised his hands, *"Don't hurt my mother!"*

Without explanation, the men handcuffed them both, shoved them into the back of the car, and sped away.

Geniato leaned toward his sobbing mother, trying to comfort her as best he could with his hands cuffed behind him. Where were they going? What had he done? He prayed that the angel would come to help them.

• • •

The shimmering wormhole sailed somewhat erratically over the craggy, black peaks of the polar mountains that thrust up from their snowy base. The hole reduced its altitude in awkward jerks, aiming toward the yawning entrance to the cavern blasted out of one of the sheer faces of the volcanic rock.

In the control room on the other side of the wormhole, the werewolf pilot poked tentatively at the controls, as the Warden glared at him. Werewolves were not nearly as adept at piloting the holes as elves. But after the EMP weapon deployment, the elf leaders had refused to cooperate further. Even the threat of a war with the fierce werewolves did not sway them. And the werewolves knew better than to further alienate a species with such technological capability.

"Are you finally stable?" asked the Warden. "Can you hold this course?"

"There are always magnetic anomalies," replied the pilot.

"The elves have no such difficulties. You can be replaced."

The pilot issued a throaty grunt. Replacement would not only mean disgrace, but likely imprisonment. Werewolves had no tolerance for even the slightest mistake. It showed weakness.

The wormhole slowly eased its way into the mountain's depths, still wobbling unsteadily, nearly touching one of the walls, which would have brought a shower of debris pouring into the chamber surrounding the wormhole, possibly damaging the guiding magnets, possibly destroying the hole.

"Incompetent mongrel!" exclaimed the Warden. "You are endangering the mission and the aperture!"

The pilot said nothing, bent over the controls. He finally managed to bring the wormhole to a stop hovering within the cavern and activated the autopilot to hold station.

"Stable, exit enabled," he mumbled, and the Warden growled and nodded to the Alpha praetorian.

"Deploy," commanded the Alpha praetorian, a massive, gray-furred werewolf, who wore the chainmail tunic that marked him as leader.

The Alpha wrenched open the airlock door into the chamber. Behind him stretched a line of one hundred praetorians, who began filing through the door into the large metal chamber enclosing the hole. They each hefted a full complement of weapons, and they took great care to lower themselves down the ladder onto the granite floor of the cavern base, on a planet that few of them had ever seen.

Over three hours, the regiment exited the wormhole. Only twice did a praetorian blunder, falling against the infinitely sharp edge of the hole—its transdimensional discontinuity. One soldier sliced his arm off, dark red blood spurting from the stump. His comrades leaped to his aid, managing to stanch the flow long enough to haul him back through the hole to the home planet, where the arm would be reattached.

The other praetorian was not so lucky. The wormhole sliced him in half—his upper torso falling back into their world; the lower torso into the cavern. The other soldiers impassively returned the two halves to their world for disposal. Praetorians showed no emotion, no remorse, no fear. They had been engineered that way. Their only reaction was a dark-humored debate over whether their body-severed comrade's family would receive full or half pay for deployment in a battle zone.

Finally all the soldiers had deployed, and they assumed formation in the cavern, their breath creating clouds of vapor in the bitterly cold weather. But they were perfectly comfortable, their thick pelts and armor offering sufficient protection, even against the frigid polar extreme.

They stood at attention, as the smaller, lower-class, indentured soldiers hauled the heavier weapons and components through the wormhole, lowering the cylindrical cases to the ground, where they were hauled away.

Because they were punier than the praetorians, and less able to handle loads, five indentures died in the process, sliced apart into bloody pieces when they stumbled into the transdimensional edges of the hole. Their bodies were hauled away to be burned. Indenture deaths didn't warrant military funerals.

Finally, the Alpha praetorian passed through, lowering his brawn down the ladder and onto the ground.

He stood scanning the formation critically, as his chief lieutenant went through the arrival check using a virtual display screen floating before him. One after another, a sequence of glowing green symbols, body silhouettes, verified the telemetry signals from the praetorians. Thus, the Alpha would know instantly how many of his warriors were functional, how many wounded, how many dead. A separate set of symbols, werewolf skulls, glowed to life on the screen, signaling that the praetorians' terminal chips were also activated. Prisoners, or even the extremely rare deserter, could be instantly dispatched.

The signal status verified, the Alpha gave a brief, brusque call to arms to the assembled phalanx and was answered by the expected thunderous roar of approval. They then watched the wormhole wobble slowly away to the cavern entrance and into the pitch-black sky, suddenly accelerating skyward with the velocity of an object with no mass.

The praetorians turned to their preparation of the area for its defense. The base had been empty for decades, so it had been stripped of its armaments. Not that defenses were needed in the vast empty reaches of the frigid continent.

As they installed the missile batteries and automated guns, they did so with the sense of satisfaction, even hope, that they would die on this strange planet, becoming martyrs to their species and heroes to their mates and pups.

Meanwhile, the Alpha summoned his lieutenants to a chamber off the main cavern. Bringing up a virtual display of the planet, he assigned each lieutenant to a region.

He formally gave the praetorians their mission: "Your assignment is to rid each region of any Mythicals who work for the Remediation and oppose the Palliation," he instructed. "You will prepare for the return of the wormhole from deploying the final EMP weapons. It will then transport your assault squads to their destinations. If you fail, shame will be upon you and your clan."

* * *

A'eiio sat beside Jack in her cell, her hands clasped tightly together, her wings folded. After Jack's release, he had immediately come to make sure she was all right.

"I have something terrible to tell you," she said. "I'm not sure what to do about it, but you deserve to know. You all deserve to know."

"Deserve to know what?" he asked.

"It's about the Palliation."

"I heard that term at the Convocation. It sounds bad."

"It's devastating. You know about the disaster in that village?"

"Where all the electrical systems failed?"

"Imagine that worldwide. Powerful electromagnetic pulses that could blanket the globe."

"That seems impossible."

"It's not only possible, but likely. Imagine huge electromagnetic pulse weapons directed at the planet, like the one that hit the village. That was only a small test."

"By who?"

"The werewolves." A'eiio took a deep, shaky breath. "They have orbited dozens, maybe hundreds of EMP weapons around the planet. They plan to use them. Soon."

Jack opened his mouth, but no words came out, only a shocked exhalation. He stared at the fairy in shock. She continued.

"The blasts would knock out the entire global infrastructure. Communications, computers, power generation, water treatment, vehicles, aircraft."

"It would mean mass deaths," Jack managed to choke out.

"Within two years ninety percent of the population would be dead."

"But why would they do this?"

"To preserve this planet as a prison for exiles. It's nothing more than a matter of convenience for them . . . to 'cull' a terminal species, as they put it."

"Cull," said Jack disgustedly. "Mass murder, and they call it culling." He stood, his fists clenched. "I have to tell everybody. But I need evidence. I have to—"

"They'll kill you!"

But Jack had already attracted the guard's attention, who opened the cell door for him to leave.

Her face grim, A'eiio wafted her wings slowly in anguish. Jack would not be deterred. She had to do something to protect him.

●   ●   ●

E'iouy wore the same suit he had worn many times before, so he could meet the standards of decorum for the Supreme Court. But now he wore no flesh-suit. And he'd had his tailor add slits at the shoulders to display his large, diaphanous wings.

The rather conservative chief justice scowled at the sight of the silver-haired, sapphire-eyed, winged alien standing before him. But his clerk had thoroughly researched the laws, and none said a lawyer arguing before the court had to be of the native species. Only that the lawyer had to be an accredited lawyer. And this bizarre *creature* was.

181

"I am petitioning the Court for a writ mandating the release of all the species known as Mythicals from their unlawful detention," declared E'iouy.

The chief justice, a spare, stooped man with a fringe of long white hair ringing a balding scalp, answered. "Please convince us . . . sir . . . that this petition has met the requirements for such an extraordinary writ."

"Indeed, it has." E'iouy consulted his notes. "As specified in the rules governing this court, the petition shows that it is in the Court's jurisdiction, that exceptional circumstances warrant the exercise of the Court's discretionary powers when no other court can provide adequate relief."

"If your honors please . . . ," interjected the government counsel, a stocky, ebullient man with a thick bush of curly hair. "We are faced with this . . . menagerie . . . of species of which we had no knowledge until very recently."

E'iouy stood, glaring at the opposing lawyer. *I object! Menagerie? This characterization is demeaning! We—*"

The government counsel interrupted, leaping to his feet. "Those species have proved murderous! For the protection of our population, we must quarantine them until such time as we determine they are no threat."

"And your species does not murder?" challenged E'iouy. "Yes, one species has committed murders . . . ghastly murders," said E'iouy. "But only one species. And only individual members of that species. Would the court intern all members of a given race if a few had committed crimes?" He answered his own question. "No, it would not. That would be illogical and cruel."

"It would be cruel to inflict these aliens on our citizens without understanding—"

Now E'iouy interrupted, his voice strained with barely concealed anger. "Mythicals have been on this planet for thousands of years. They have contributed to your societies . . . in some instances saved you from yourselves. And for that service, you would keep them in captivity in a state that will actually kill some?"

"We only ask that the court keep in mind the fact that this is our planet, and that these aliens are all criminals by definition. We hope—"

"The court has heard enough," interrupted the chief justice. "It will now begin deliberations."

"May I ask that these deliberations be done swiftly," declared E'iouy. "This is an urgent matter, since undoubtedly some of those imprisoned will die in captivity, given that their captors do not understand their physiology or their medical needs."

"We have your briefs. We have heard the arguments. You will have our ruling when we decide it," snapped the chief justice, rapping the gavel sharply to signal his displeasure with the presumptuousness of the alien standing before him.

Chapter 17

This was the most incredibly stupid thing he had ever done in his *entire life!* Jack shoved his way through the pitch-dark thicket, far from the nearest town, even far off the nearest paved road. He smiled ruefully. Interesting phrase, "entire life." His "entire life" could be over very, very soon. He suffered a severe bout of shivers, even though the night was warm.

But there was no other way to find out what he needed to know. If he was to credibly reveal the monstrous truth of the Palliation, he needed to have evidence from one of the monsters likely behind it— the murderous werewolf once known as Senator Warren Lee. To his utter surprise, a call to Lee's old office had brought a return message from the werewolf with instructions on meeting him.

The beam from his flashlight danced around the brush as he tripped and stumbled, stopping occasionally to check his location on his phone. It showed he was still a quarter mile from the destination.

He froze at a possible noise off to his left, maybe a very faint swish of shifting tree limbs, maybe the crackle of leaves being trod upon. He couldn't tell. He held his breath, listening. He reached around to his back, grasping the pistol stuffed into his belt. He thought about cocking it, flipping off the safety. But given his inexperience, he might just trip and literally blow his butt off.

No more sound. Must have been the wind. *But there was no wind, you idiot!* A foul, clinging odor assaulted his nostrils. Maybe a dead animal nearby. So, the sound might have been a small animal feeding at the carcass. Yeah, a *small* animal. He released his grasp on the pistol and scanned the flashlight in the direction of the sound. The light showed only impenetrable brush.

He continued on, until abruptly he emerged into a small clearing holding a shack. A faint light showed in the window. He called out, prepared to plunge back into the forest should anybody wielding weapons appear.

The door opened, and the doorway was filled with the massive silhouetted form of the werewolf that had become all-too-familiar to him. The werewolf's eyes gleamed in the darkness.

"You came," said Flaktuckmetang, chuckling darkly, folding his thick arms. "I thought you wouldn't have the guts."

"I know about the Palliation."

"Good for you." The werewolf closed the door behind him, walking out into the clearing. "Get that light out of my eyes."

Jack lowered the flashlight. "I'm going to expose its existence. But I wanted to hear from you first."

"And what do you expect me to say?"

Jack's voice shook as he uttered his standard reporter's line. "I want to confirm the story I'm going to write and get your side of it."

The werewolf chuckled again. "My side of it is that your terminal species has rendered or maybe willful ignorance has led your species to cause irreversible damage to all the planet's species. And now that you know of our existence, you will no doubt be intolerant of all our species that use this miserable rock as a planet of exile."

"And so the Palliation is your answer?"

The werewolf looked up at the pitch-black sky for a moment and sighed. "We have concluded that the only way to save your race is to sacrifice most of you . . . to reduce the population to a state of balance with your planet, so that you may begin anew, with greater respect for the fact that you live on a finite resource that must be preserved. It is drastic, but it is necessary. You would do the same if it were any other overpopulating species that was so profoundly and irreversibly damaging its habitat."

"Mass murder? You think we would launch mass murder?"

"You have done it before for less valid reasons. Actually, you're pretty good at genocide. But we're better."

"That's all I need," said Jack, beginning to turn to go.

"But that's not all *I* need," said the werewolf. He crouched and lunged at Jack, one leap covering the distance between them. Jack reached behind him and yanked the pistol from his belt, realizing with horror that he hadn't cocked it or flipped the safety off. With a powerful swipe, the werewolf tore the gun from his grasp, sending it flying into the darkness.

He slammed Jack onto the ground, and the light from the cabin showed an opening maw with slavering tongue beneath the glaring eyes. Now he would die. But the werewolf paused.

"I need a hunt," he said. "Haven't had a good hunt and a kill in a while. Get up. Run."

The werewolf stood up, towering over Jack. It was a futile act, Jack knew. But nevertheless, he hauled himself off the damp, cold ground and plunged wildly into the forest, tearing through the undergrowth. Branches slashed at his face, raising welts, as he scrambled wildly through the utter blackness. Rocks tripped him, and he slammed into a tree, but he kept running. He felt blood running down his face.

He had no idea which way to go, so he blundered blindly ahead, changing course in the hopes that he could evade the creature. He tripped on a root, crashing to the ground, knocking the breath out of him. But a chilling howl behind him and the sound of a huge animal ripping into the brush spurred him to his feet.

As he ran, he began to pant in both fear and exhaustion. Grunting sounds behind him, coming closer. Then silence. Eerie silence. He was being stalked. Now he would die. Now he would be torn apart, eaten.

He collided with a large tree. Feeling low branches in the darkness, he knew he could climb it. Maybe he could get above the animal, so he could slam its head with a kick, knock him out.

But as he grasped a branch, a huge claw clutched his shoulder, talons tearing into his flesh, blood soaking his shirt. Claws hauled him from the tree, spun him around, smashed him against its trunk. He smelled the musk of the werewolf's body.

"Not a very satisfying hunt," said the werewolf. "But it will do." He breathed in heavily. "Ah, the aroma of blood. So lovely."

Pinning Jack against the tree with one powerful arm, the werewolf reached down with the other claw to clutch at Jack's stomach. Jack braced himself for an agonizing death by disembowelment.

Then suddenly the werewolf was torn away, lifted up, bellowing, snarling, writhing helplessly. One flailing claw whipped out to deal Jack a vicious blow to the head.

Bleeding profusely, Jack slumped to the ground, consciousness fading, barely able to make out a massive, dark form twice as large as the werewolf, holding him aloft and shaking him like a rag doll.

Another monster come to kill me? He thought before unconsciousness enveloped him.

•   •   •

"Don't you touch her!" exclaimed A'eiio, beating her wings so furiously that they lifted her off the concrete floor of the cell block to hover above the guard. The stout guard lifted his hands, both for protection and in compliance, backing away.

E'iouy ducked into the cell, scooping up Sam's limp body and carrying her out of the cell. The guard's attention was suddenly, pheromonally riveted on the unconscious pixie.

"What can I do?" he asked solicitously.

"You've done enough," said A'eiio, as E'iouy carried Sam down the hall. "You never asked what would be the effect of imprisoning species you knew nothing about. For pixies, confinement induces profound, even life-threatening depression. They go into a coma. But you didn't care, did you?"

"It's not my fault," said the guard plaintively. "I was just doing—"

But the fairies were gone out the door.

E'iouy and A'eiio hurried to the waiting limousine with Sam; and with Ryan the elf driving, the car careened through downtown traffic to the fairies' home. Reaching their street, the limousine eased its way through the throng of reporters. E'iouy lifted Sam gently from the car and rushed for the front door.

He was immediately thronged by reporters, but abruptly the crowd parted, as the reporters gave forth yelps of pain. Steve the troll—who had emerged from his preferred riding place in the trunk—had begun viciously biting the legs of any reporters barring E'iouy's way.

They were even more disconcerted by the appearance of Mike the ogre at the front door. He stepped outside and ushered the fairies and their unconscious patient into the house, then planted himself alongside Steve outside the door, like two fantastic statues, one tall, one squat.

Inside the house, the two fairies took Sam to the bedroom and laid her on their bed.

"Open the windows," instructed A'eiio. "She needs light. She needs to feel free."

E'iouy did so, and the afternoon sun fell on Sam's inert body. A'eiio removed her prison garb, so she lay still and naked on the bed.

A'eiio bent over, whispering to her, "You are free, you are safe, you are with those who love you." She repeated the mantra over and over, as both fairies fanned their wings, creating a gentle breeze that wafted over Sam's body.

After half an hour, Sam stirred and groaned. She opened her eyes and weakly raised a hand. A'eiio took it in hers.

"Free?" she asked weakly.

"Yes," said A'eiio.

"All of us?"

"Yes. My husband argued for us in their Supreme Court. They ruled this morning that the internment was illegal and unwarranted."

"Jack?"

"He went to confront Flaktuckmetang. In the woods."

Sam struggled to rise. "He'll kill him! He'll—"

A'eiio placed a gentle hand on her shoulder. "Don't worry. I asked a friend to protect him. A very large friend."

* * *

Something was carrying Jack through the woods, crashing through thick brush as if it were straw. Something really big, thickly-furred. Something that smelled terrible. Jack's blood loss and the concussion made him weak, fuzzy. But he was vaguely aware that the odor was the same one he'd smelled before.

He managed to open his eyes to look up at a huge domed head with a hairy apelike face and deep-set eye sockets. He tried to move, but his weakness and the creature's powerful grip on his body prevented it.

"Who are you?" he managed to gasp.

The creature looked down at him with dark brown eyes. It answered with a guttural, rumbling sequence of syllables. From a large medallion on its chest came the words, "You were hurt. I am taking you to be treated."

"But who . . . *what* . . . are you?"

Another rumbling answer, followed by what was apparently a translation by the medallion. "The fairy sent me."

Fuzziness overcame him again, and he closed his eyes, his body sagging in the huge arms.

He became vaguely aware of the noise of passing vehicles. The creature had carried him from the thick woods into a small clearing near a highway. He felt his body being laid gently onto the ground.

Again, came the thick rumbling voice, followed by the translated words, "He is bad."

But now a mellifluous feminine voice answered, "I will take care of him. The car is coming." He opened his eyes to see hovering over him large, snow-white wings, a diaphanous tunic, a smiling, luminous face. Was he dying?

His eyes closed again. He felt bandages being applied. He felt himself being lifted into a car. He was enveloped again by the dark gray shroud of unconsciousness.

●   ●   ●

Geniato Belligrado slumped over, covering his face with his hands in utter despair, sitting on the concrete of the large prison yard, its high fence topped with razor wire, where he and the other Allies had been taken. The thought of his innocent, little mother in a similar pen haunted him. They had been brought in separate buses with barred windows, along with others who had been arrested, through a large gate and into what was probably a deserted military base.

Had she been questioned as brutally as he had been? He had been shackled in an interrogation room and harangued by a remorseless military officer who said his mother would die in prison if he didn't tell all he knew about the creatures called the Mythicals.

He had cried piteously, telling them she knew nothing about the creatures. He told the interrogator that he had only encountered a strange woman with some kind of torn disguise and an angel. And the angel had told him that there were many strange creatures on the planet; that they hid from people but were peaceful. And the angel had told him that he could decide to live on a planet with the angels. Or, they would grant him whatever he needed to have a happy life.

He chose the happy life with his mother. He trusted the angel. This was an angel with beautiful white wings and a golden smile who was offering him this good life. And the angel kept her word, and he promised to do things to help the Mythicals. The angel promised they would never ask him to violate any of his religious or moral beliefs.

So, he had agreed, and he had been happy with his mother, until the men in the suits had come and taken them to prison. He didn't dare say it to the military officer, but he wanted to ask him who were really the bad ones—the people who cruelly imprisoned him and his mother, or the angel.

Across the sunbaked, dusty courtyard, he heard a rising sound of excited babble from the other prisoners. They were staring upward and pointing. A faint hum rose from the sky, and Geniato stood and peered upward where the other men were looking.

The humming grew louder and above the roof of the prison building appeared dozens, perhaps hundreds of delicately built men and women, borne on fluttering wings that glimmered in the sunlight. Their fine silver hair blew in the breeze from their wings, and their perfect pale skin shone as if it had a light of its own.

They swooped down, circling smoothly over the compound, as the men whooped with joy.

He realized he had seen such a being before! It was the kind of being he had collided with at the embassy. He had not known what manner of creature she was, and now he knew that she was a beautiful, graceful creature of the air.

Geniato also saw appearing at the gate a gang of hulking gray-green creatures with massive heads and protruding jaws. He had never seen such monsters before, and he prepared to flee into the safety of the prison building. But many of the imprisoned Allies approached the creatures with welcoming shouts.

Geniato decided they must be friendly, despite their horrific appearance. In fact, it was apparently that appearance that made the guards—the ones who had been so cruel to him and the others—shrink away, leave their posts, and disappear.

The winged creatures landed outside the compound and, together with the gray-green creatures, swung open the gates.

The men began to stream out, and Geniato leaped up and followed them. He asked those around him what had happened. They said that the Mythicals had gotten them out, rescued them!

What were these creatures, he asked?

Fairies, he was told.

Amazing! He thought for a moment, before the worry over his mother reasserted itself.

He quickly followed the men out the gate between two lines of the male fairies, who thanked them and escorted them to waiting cars, to be returned to their homes.

But Geniato could not go home. He asked a fairy where the women were being held, and the fairy pointed at a distant building with a fenced yard. He ran toward it as fast as his legs would carry him, as did several other men. Ahead of him, he saw women streaming out through the gate, also walking between lines of welcoming fairies.

He reached the yard and scanned the crowd of women, seeing some old, some young, but not his mother.

The crowd thinned, but still he did not see his mother. He rushed into the prison yard frantically searching for her among the few women who were still preparing to leave. He asked several other women if they had seen her, describing her to them.

Finally, one of the women pointed into the prison building, and he rushed inside. He ran along the row of open cells, abruptly stopping at one in which a young woman was sitting with her back to him, bent over another woman lying on the bottom bunk. The woman moved, and he recognized his mother, rushing into the cell.

"Is she okay?" he asked. *"She is my mother!"*

The young woman turned toward him, smiling kindly. "She has not been well. Some kind of heart problem. But the doctor here has given her pills."

His mother stirred, looking up at him, smiling beatifically. "Geniato, my Geniato! You are all right!"

She struggled to sit up, and hugged him warmly.

"This wonderful girl has taken good care of me. We were in the same cell, and she took care of me when I had the pains in my chest. This is Meri."

And Geniato Belligrado found himself looking into the most beautiful brown eyes he had ever seen.

• • •

"You're okay, Jack. You lost a lot of blood, but you'll be fine." The smiling woman stood over Jack, as he opened his eyes, bringing the hospital room into focus. He tried lifting his arm to feel the wounds on his head, but failed—weakness permeating his body, like lead weights holding him down.

The woman wore the white coat of a doctor, and her golden curls were tied back. "You'll need to stay here a couple of days to regain your strength and check for infections."

"What happened?"

"We brought you into the hospital. I'm Dr. Wendy Burns."

Jack suddenly remembered that radiant face. "You're—"

Wendy brought her finger to her lips, still smiling warmly. "Shhh. I put on my flesh-suit before the emergency van came. These folks might be put off by seeing an angel, even though they know about us now."

Jack struggled to remember. "Somebody . . . some *thing* brought me out of the woods. Saved me from the werewolf."

"Yes, that was a friend whom A'eiio asked to watch over you. He went back into the forest. He's rather shy."

Jack was fully awake now. "He was rather *huge!*"

"They tend to be. But they're gentle."

"He wasn't very gentle with the werewolf."

"They are called bigfoot. They don't much like werewolves. They consider them too aggressive. It's ironic because bigfoot are quite peaceful unless they are angered. Then . . . look out!"

"So that's what he was? A bigfoot?"

194

"Yes. You may see him again. They're very faithful. Once they commit to a task, they stick with it. You have a friend for life."

"Useful friend to have." Now Jack was awake enough to begin peppering the angel with questions. "Where is the werewolf? Do you have to stay in hiding? Are the Mythicals still being interned?"

"The werewolf escaped. We've all been freed. E'iouy argued for us. The Supreme Court ruled that it was illegal and, in fact, dangerous to some species."

"Sam? Is Sam all right?"

"Not at first."

"What do you mean? I've got to see her!" Jack struggled to rise from the bed, snatching at the catheter in the back of his hand. But Wendy gently eased him back down.

"She's fine now. As a matter of fact . . ." Wendy backed away to reveal Sam standing in the doorway. "She's been waiting for you to wake up."

Wendy gave him a pat on the shoulder and departed. Sam approached the bed, a worried look on her face. She wore a brightly printed short dress and flowers in her ringleted hair, but the decoration didn't disguise her haggard appearance. She took Jack's hand.

"I was so worried about you," she said quietly. "I heard what happened."

"You were worried about me?" Jack chuckled. "Last time I saw you, you were near . . ." he stopped. He didn't want to use the word "death."

"We bounce back pretty quickly," she said.

"Hey, you did quite a bit of bouncing when the cops were after you."

"Pixies aren't weaklings."

"I love you," he said.

195

"I know," she answered matter-of-factly, tossing her head with the faintest of smiles. The declaration seemed to please her now, perhaps more than the several times he'd blurted it out before.

"What will you do now?" she asked.

"Tell everybody. Write the article. Can you get my computer? I need to start writing."

Sam bent down and kissed him gently on the forehead. He suddenly felt better. Much better. For some reason he could not fathom, she began to remove the bandage covering his lacerated shoulder. But before she could finish, a middle-aged couple appeared at the door—a spare, balding man and a short, matronly woman with white hair.

Now Jack forgot his weakness; even momentarily forgot Sam in his surprise. "Mom! Dad! What are you doing here?"

"We heard you'd been hurt," said his mother. "We were so worried! Are you all right?"

"I'm fine, Mom. This is Sam."

They made introductions, and Sam excused herself, telling him she'd be back with his computer and some better food than the hospital could offer. He watched her leave, distracted until she was out of sight. Then his attention returned to his parents. They hugged him and asked him if he was in pain, if he needed anything, that they were so worried about him. But a question puzzled him.

"How did you find out? It just happened."

"Well . . . uh—" his mother began to stammer, but his father interrupted.

"That doesn't matter. What does matter is that we know you're preparing to reveal something that needs to stay secret. For your sake, for our sake, for the sake of your people."

Jack felt the pang of uneasiness rise within him. "What does that mean *'my people'?*"

His mother took his hand, while his father closed the door to the room. He stood for a long while staring somberly at Jack, as if trying to find the words.

"You are not one of these people." He gestured at the door, indicating the outside world. "You are not even of this planet."

CHAPTER 18

Flaktuckmetang stood waiting for the praetorians, holding his broken arm close to his chest, refusing to wince in pain. It would be a sign of weakness, and werewolves killed weaklings. Having it set and cast was out of the question. These kinds of injuries were supposed to heal naturally—or not. They were badges of battle, and Flaktuckmetang would display a deformed arm as evidence of his fearlessness. He managed a pained grin in satisfaction. Perhaps it would even get his sentence reduced on this Planet of Morons.

On schedule, the wormhole descended from the cloud-filled night sky to hover over the lake. The hole was a pitch-black void in the heavens, an ominous portent for this planet's puny creatures, thought the werewolf.

Hovering above the water, the hole wafted to the shore where Flaktuckmetang had come after escaping the cursed monster that had robbed him of his kill.

The Alpha praetorian was the first to emerge from the hole. Climbing down its ladder to stand, sniffing the air for any whiff of an enemy. His olfactory reconnaissance completed, he turned to glare at this deplorable exile who stood tentatively before him, shaking his great head in disdain.

They proceeded to sniff one another, taking in each other's characteristic scents. Flaktuckmetang took care to keep his head lower than the Alpha, not a difficult task, given the Alpha's imposing height.

"You lost your prey," accused the Alpha, after they had finished. "You fled from your enemy, Warren Lee." The Alpha used the exile name as an epithet, not honoring him by saying his real name.

"I made a strategic retreat against an overwhelming foe," said Flaktuckmetang.

"You fled from one creature! *One!* And now we must track down your prey . . . what is its name?"

"Jack March."

"Yes, him, as well as the fairies, the vampires, the ogres . . . all those who work against the Palliation."

"But they cannot stop it, can they?" Lee realized he had made a linguistic error. Werewolves always made statements; never asked questions. Another sight of weakness.

The Alpha shook his head again in disdain. "Of course, they can. The other Wardens are not unanimous in supporting it. And even though they are of weaker species, they could cause serious problems in the Alliance. And we need the Alliance for the network it provides. We will find a way to neutralize the objectors without raising the Wardens' suspicions."

"Well, I shall—" began Flaktuckmetang, but the Alpha interrupted.

"Lead us to our target, Flaktuckmetang. And be prepared to report our victory."

The werewolf nodded enthusiastically. Now the Alpha had used his native name, indicating that his honor could potentially be restored.

The Alpha raised a claw to signal a lieutenant standing on the other side of the wormhole. The lieutenant began to send praetorians descending from the hole, hauling down their assault rifles, grenade packs, and missile launchers with them.

With Flaktuckmetang leading them, the commandos quickly moved from the narrow shore into the thicket.

From there, they would seek out and kill their prey.

• • •

"Jack, you must see your home planet," declared James March, as he drove with Jack sitting beside him through the winding country lanes.

Jack, still weak from the blood loss, shook his head in deep confusion. "I just don't understand. I can't even—"

Louisa leaned forward from the back seat, patting her son's shoulder. "You will, dearest. You'll see."

They reached the village where he had grown up while the sun was still rising, and the early morning light cast a golden glow on the farmhouse and the warehouse-sized barn.

They left the car and entered the barn to see, hovering high in the cavernous space, a shimmering wormhole, the aurora of colored lights playing around it.

Jack stood silently, trying to absorb the reality that his own family, the people in this village were aliens, and that they had arrived in a wormhole just like the ones the Mythicals used.

"You never told me about any of this. Why?"

"Yes, we never told any who were brought here as infants. We wanted you to feel that this planet was your home. Our strategy was to allow you to immerse yourself in its society, to become expert in its ways. And at the appropriate time we would reveal your heritage to you. To enlist you in our mutual cause. This is that time."

"Are you part of the Mythicals network . . . the Alliance?" asked Jack.

"No," said James. "They don't know about us. They can't know. Our aim is not to use this planet as a *prison*." He said the last word with derision. "Our aim is to make it our new *home*. Now, you will understand why."

With that, he signaled and a ladder descended from the hole. Louisa climbed upward, and James pulled himself onto its bottom step, turning to his son. "Come through with me. See your home."

He disappeared, and Jack followed, finding himself in a large, steel vacuum chamber much like the ones he had encountered when traversing to the fairy planet. The same magnetic probes extended from its interior, containing and guiding the wormhole.

His father unfastened the chamber's inner airlock hatch, and all three of them went through, and after sealing the hatch, exited through the outer door.

They stepped out into—not the pristine, soaring terminal of the Mythicals transfer station—but a scorched ruin of a building, its corrugated rusted metal sides full of holes, its dirty concrete floor scattered with metal parts and crates. Instead of the crisp coolness of his village, now he felt a dank, smothering heat.

A portly man dressed in a black suit introduced himself as Christopher, and the three began to speak in a language Jack did not understand.

Christopher turned to Jack and explained, "We call ourselves Pilgrims. We are seeking a new home for our race . . . your race, Jack. And we want to show you why."

They led Jack out of the building and into a sprawling fortress-like compound, with high steel walls topped by coils of razor wire. Guardposts were spaced along the wall, manned by ragged-looking soldiers with tripod-mounted machine guns. Armored personnel carriers were parked along one side of the compound, with grease-strained mechanics working on their engines.

"What is this place?" asked Jack.

"Our terminal," said Christopher. "It has to be well fortified against those who would thwart our mission."

They climbed a steel observation tower that reached above the wall, and Jack found himself looking out over a desolate, empty landscape of gnarled, dead trees. A lead-gray sky hung low overhead, with a faint brownish smog obscuring any long-range view. The air enveloped them like a smothering muggy shroud that reeked of smoke and organic decay. He felt a nausea rising when he realized that scattered on the cratered landscape beyond were what looked like corpses.

Jack stared in shock at the bleak landscape. "I am from here?"

"Yes, sweetheart," said Louisa. "This is your home."

"What is it called?"

"This is Earth."

CHAPTER 19

"They tried to kill us!" rasped Steve the troll in his guttural voice, punctuating the state-ment with an emphatic, furious grunt. He stalked back and forth in the warehouse that had been their clandestine meeting place for decades.

"They did kill Robin," said Vladimir, rising to address the gather-ing of exiled fairies, ogres, vampires, elves, angels, leprechauns, pixies, and trolls. "And they murdered her with no provocation. And they killed many others around the world."

"We can't really say there was no provocation," said A'eiio. "I am as sick as all of you over Robin's death . . . the other deaths . . . the imprisonments. But the creatures were frightened. The werewolves made sure of that."

"The werewolves merely triggered a blind, ignorant hatred that would have come out, anyway," said Vladimir. "Maybe the only solution is a final one. Maybe ironically, saving this species and their planet means instituting the Palliation."

"No, it does *not* mean that," declared Mike the ogre, in his resonant gurgle. "Some of my fellow exiles are also advocating that, but I do not."

"What about the Wardens?" squeaked Ryan the elf, managing a few words. "They are the final arbiters."

"The Council is divided," said E'iouy. "Some favor it, some oppose it. Those who oppose it hope to persuade the species to adopt the Remediation . . . to save themselves and their planet."

"So, the Council is deadlocked," said Vladimir. "Meanwhile, we are stuck on this planet between those who would destroy it and those who would save it. We are the ones in the middle of this problem."

"Vote," said Sam. "Let us all vote."

"The pixie is right," said Wendy the angel. "Let us call for a global vote. All the exiles. It will influence the Council."

"You can vote all you want, but in the end, it will be the werewolves who decide," said Vladimir. "Them and the others who side with them. Maybe us."

"And maybe even some of us," said Mike.

Several of the Mythicals voiced the sounds of their species signaling their agreement.

"Then, at least we can agree—" began E'iouy, but he was interrupted by a burst of weapon fire from outside and a scream from one of the Allies who had been guarding the warehouse. The scream abruptly stopped. More gunfire, and the howling of werewolves.

A young woman burst into the warehouse, blood streaming from a wound on her shoulder.

"They're Outside! They want to kill all of us!" she shouted.

.   .   .

Standing on the tower, gripping its rusty railing so hard that its sharp grit bit into his hands, Jack stared in unbelieving shock out at the desolation that stretched away beyond the walls of the Pilgrim compound. He lowered his stunned gaze to the battered hulk of a building harboring the wormhole that had transported them here. On the other side of that wormhole was the planet he had thought was his home—Thera.

"So, I am not of that planet? I was not born on Thera?"

"No," said his father. "You are not a Theran. You were born here and we brought you to Thera as a baby. Earth is your home. We are your species . . . humans."

"Humans? That's what our species is called?"

"Yes," said Christopher. "And we call our group Pilgrims. Our mission is to emigrate to Thera. To make it what we call New Earth."

"But Thera . . . it's a planet like ours?"

"Yes," said Christopher. "Many decades ago, before the environmental catastrophe you see here . . . ," he gestured out over the ruined landscape ". . . some scientists discovered and captured wormholes that appeared on Earth. The holes opened when the solar system moved through a region of space that we think contained concentrations of dark matter. It's invisible, except for its gravitational effects. It basically created localized holes in space-time . . . wormholes."

"The same wormholes as the Mythicals use?"

"Exactly. The scientists explored the other side of these wormholes. They discovered that they were transdimensional apertures to parallel universes . . . some much like ours . . . some very different."

"But the Mythicals don't know that," said Jack.

"They're not sure. But we know that all these universes connected by wormholes are parallel. And each universe in these multiverses evolves slightly differently. Now, we have had legends of mythical creatures here on Earth, like the ones on Thera. But apparently, they just visited. They didn't use Earth as a penal colony the way they used Thera."

"So, the Mythicals are—"

"—what might have evolved on Earth-like planets, given different environments, different courses of evolution. They are alternate versions of us," said Christopher.

"But they're fairies, werewolves, and so forth. The people of Thera are exactly like us."

"Some universes evolved in closer parallel than others. Through the most incredible luck, our scientists found that one of our captured holes opened into the universe that contained a close parallel to Earth . . . Thera. It was a godsend for us. A way to save our race."

"But Thera isn't ruined. Why is Earth?"

"Apparently, the different universes can be on different timelines. There can be different conditions. Here on Earth it's the year 2080. On Thera, it seems to be earlier in their civilization. They have not yet ruined their planet."

"What happened on Earth?"

"Basically, we were stupid. Stunningly foolish. We kept burning, polluting. We allowed carbon dioxide levels to rise . . . the planet warmed . . . and it triggered a catastrophic, positive feedback effect."

"Positive feedback?" Asked Jack, his voice thickening with emotion.

"Runaway climate change. As Earth warmed, the polar ice melted reducing heat reflection back into space, making it even hotter. The Arctic permafrost melted; and lightning triggered vast fires in the tundra, producing what's called the Carbon Bomb . . . a massive release of carbon dioxide. The warming caused Earth's huge peat bogs to dry out, and lightning sparked fires in those bogs that have burned for decades. They released billions of tons more of carbon dioxide . . . and created the smog that you see. All this produced the death blow. The clathrate gun."

Jack felt a rising nausea, as he tried to process the stunning revelations. Shaking his head, he had just enough voice to ask, "Clathrate?"

"Huge deposits of methane frozen in the depths of the seabeds. Billions upon billions of tons thawed, and the methane eruptions essentially killed the oceans, turned the Earth into hell. Billions of people died of starvation, heat, cancer, wars."

"Didn't the governments do anything?"

Christopher shrugged and shook his head in resignation. "Our scientists warned them of the dire future. But the politicians . . . the corporations . . . none of them had the will or the courage to take the necessary measures. Too little, far too late. Then the governments collapsed. Now we are trying to save the remnants of our civilization."

"How many?" Jack asked, his voice now only a whisper.

"Maybe a million, scattered in fortifications around the world. We've been sending as many people through the wormhole to Thera as we can. They're in isolated villages scattered over the planet. But some of us are in positions of power."

"And you planned to just take over?"

Christopher turned to James and Louisa and began to speak in a language Jack did not understand.

"What are you saying?" demanded Jack. "What language is that?"

"English," said Christopher. "Your native language. We will teach it to you when we are all on Thera."

"Why don't you just ask the Therans for refuge?"

"We knew we would be treated like an invading force. We—"

"You *are* an invading force!"

Christopher ignored the outburst. "We believe this discovery of a refuge planet was a sign from God. That we have been chosen to save it from the creatures that would destroy it. We decided that we would disguise our identity as a Theran cult . . . Pilgrims. It was a useful subterfuge. We would work to save Therans from themselves. And if that didn't work . . . well . . ."

"The Palliation? You are working for the deaths of billions of these . . . people?"

"The Palliation wasn't our idea," said James. "But since the Mythicals are launching it, we must save ourselves. We will repopulate Thera with humans who have learned the consequences of what happened on our planet. The Therans are not human, after all. They just look human."

"So what are you asking me?"

James took his son by the shoulders. "We're asking you to save us. We're asking you *not* to reveal the Palliation . . . the plan that will save your own people."

. . .

A fusillade of bullets raked the warehouse from the attacking werewolves penetrating the walls and shattering windows, erupting razor-sharp shards of glass onto the cowering Mythicals.

Steve shrieked in pain as a bullet struck him in the gut, sending the troll staggering back, yellowish blood streaming from the wound. Wendy, who had been tending to the wounded young woman Ally, emerged from the apartment to rush to his side. Her feathered wings beating furiously, she lofted him back to the safety of the interior apartment, and began to treat him.

A bullet shattered the skull of a leprechaun, sending him to the floor, his eyes staring sightlessly.

Another bullet slammed into Mike's chest. The ogre looked down at the wound, uttered a dismissive hmph, and burst out the door, thundering toward the werewolf positions.

A razor-sharp piece of glass slashed Sam's shoulder, sending blood streaming down her arm. As she grabbed a cloth and knotted it tightly around the wound, her eyes transformed from blue to a gleaming fiery red. She bolted to the shattered window, and stared outside for a long moment. Then, seeming to spot her target, she leaped out and disappeared.

A'eiio and E'iouy bent to the wounded, helping them to the safety of the inner apartment. There, they found Wendy tending the wounded Ally. Satisfied that the young woman was stable, Wendy turned the Ally over to them and spreading her wings vaulted upward to the ceiling, drawing from her white tunic a gleaming sword.

None of them noticed that Vladimir had vanished, slipping out a back door.

Outside, Mike took two more bullets before reaching the nearest praetorian and wrapping a massive gray-green hand around his throat, snapping his neck. A nearby werewolf raised an assault rifle to fire a fatal volley at the ogre. But an instant before he could pull the trigger, a white blur swooped down from the black sky, snatching away the rifle and sending it flying into Mike's hands. He swung the weapon around and began emptying its explosive rounds into a knot of attacking werewolves, who collapsed, dead before the withering salvo.

Wendy banked into a tight turn and attacked again, sailing along a line of praetorians, slashing with her sword, sending one after another of them slumping to the ground like furry rag dolls, their black blood soaking the ground.

The doors to the building flung open, and a roiling gang of Mythicals erupted out of it, rushing the werewolves, who fired wildly.

Some Mythicals collapsed, dead or wounded. But others managed to reach the werewolves, swarming over them.

The remaining werewolves fought off their attackers and retreated to gather into a tight defensive formation, their backs against the thick woods. Together they raised rocket and grenade launchers, preparing to obliterate the enemy.

But even as they raised their launch tubes, the praetorian nearest the forest uttered a surprised yelp and disappeared into the darkness, to the sound of the dull thud of flesh slamming against wood. Another praetorian was flung high into the air slamming into the building, his shattered corpse collapsing onto the ground.

Giant, furred bodies emerged from the depths of the forest, grasping werewolves and flinging them like dolls. One werewolf managed to launch a rocket into the attackers, a flash of light from the fiery blast revealed a dozen bigfoot wading into the cadre of praetorians, smashing them against the tree trunks, shattering their bodies.

The air outside the building was filled with the rattle of gunfire, the howls of werewolves attacking, the shrieks of their dying.

The Alpha and his lieutenant, however, stole away from the battle, circling around to find an open window. They knew their real targets were not among the combatants. They sought the leaders, the fairies. They slipped into the bullet-riddled building, listening for the sounds of their quarry. Amid the shouts, screams, and gunfire of the battle outside, they heard faint, urgent voices from deep within the structure.

They made their way toward the voices, finding the door to the apartment. The lieutenant slammed his huge body against the door, sending it crashing into the room. The Alpha plunged in ahead of him. Both brought their weapons to the ready.

They found A'eiio, E'iouy, and four other fairies tending to wounded. Elves and leprechauns huddled against one another in fright.

"Please don't," said E'iouy. "Please don't shoot her." He gestured at his wife. "She's pregnant." He moved his body between the werewolves and A'eiio, his jaw set, ready for the bullets that would come.

"Good," said the Alpha. "It will make more of an impact on the others when they find your bodies."

He signaled to the lieutenant flanking him, who clicked his rifle on automatic, and raised it to fire.

But he didn't. His arm ripped away from his body and slammed against the wall, still gripping the weapon. The eight-foot praetorian unleashed an agonized shriek, as his massive body lifted into the air and sailed against the far wall, smashing against it and falling to the floor, now only a quivering carcass.

The Alpha whirled around to face the doorway behind him and raised his weapon to fire at whatever had torn apart his lieutenant. But his body jerked and shuddered, and his head flung back, lolling on his neck. He managed only an agonized grunt. Those in the room heard the crunch of bone and the wet sound of ripping flesh, but could not see what was happening, until the Alpha's body fell backward into the room, his chest torn open, his fangs bared in the rictus of death.

Sam stood there, her eyes gleaming red, her wounded left arm wrapped in a bloody cloth, her right hand grasping the Alpha's still-beating heart. Her small, naked body was covered in black, glistening werewolf blood.

CHAPTER 20

J ack stood leaning on the door of his apartment after he'd closed it behind him, his head bowed for a long time. He needed the support. The shock of what he'd just seen and learned drained him of even the will to go to his couch and collapse.

After his time on Earth, he'd told his parents and the man Christopher that he needed time to think. His quiet apartment was the best place. Even though at one time his rooms had been the site of a horrifying attack by monsters. But these Mythicals were monsters no more. They were friends on what he now knew was an alien planet.

Thera, his so-called home, was an alien planet! He shook his head, still trying to wrap his mind around the idea that the forests and cities of Thera, where he had grown up and gone to school, were not his real home.

Earth was his "home"—that ruined, polluted, dying planet. And he was human, not Theran.

He needed a drink. He went to the kitchen, pulled out a glass and opened the cabinet to get the bottle of liquor. The room suddenly darkened. He closed the cabinet to see, hanging outside the window, a fat, grinning vampire.

"What are you doing?" he exclaimed backing through the kitchen toward the living room. He realized the large, grinning, pug-nosed face was that of Milorad. And somehow, the large vampire had managed to climb a sheer building wall all the way to the fourth floor.

Milorad tapped on the window, still grinning pointing to the latch, asking to be let in.

"You should let him in," said a deep voice behind him. He whirled to see the vampire Gennady looming at his bedroom door. "He doesn't climb very well," said Gennady, nodding at Milorad. "Your bedroom window was unlatched, however. I didn't think you'd mind if I let myself in."

"What do you want? Why are you here?" was all Jack could think to ask.

A knock on the door, prompted Gennady to action. "You get that," said the vampire matter-of-factly. "I'll get the window." He glided into the kitchen, as Jack realized his only escape was through the door that likely had another vampire on the other side. His only option was to open that door, whatever his next move would be.

Standing in the doorway were Vladimir and Radomir, who continually swiveled his neck back and forth to peer up and down the hall.

"What do you mean breaking in? What's this about?"

"We are sorry," said Vladimir. "The werewolves have brought in soldiers. They attacked us at our building. I knew we would beat them, but I figured they would come after you, so I contacted the others, and we came here. I couldn't get you on the phone. Where were you?"

"Attack?" Jack backed away into the apartment, the vampire intrusion forgotten for the moment. "Was anybody hurt?"

"Yes, and some were killed."

"Sam! Is Sam okay?"

"Last time I saw her, she was wounded, but she had gone red. So, she will be fine."

"Gone red? What's that?"

"It's a hyper-aggressive state that pixies transform into when they're enraged or threatened. Their eyes turn red. They attain incredible strength and agility. I suspect she is stalking the leader of the attackers."

"But she's not badly hurt."

"I'm sure not. Can't say the same for whoever she goes after."

"And you think the werewolves will come here?"

"I'm certain of it. That's why we had to scout all the possible entrances, coming through your windows. We're here to guard you."

"But there's no fire escape. Did you—"

"Turn into bats?" interrupted Vladimir, smiling. "No, we don't fly. But we are pretty adept at climbing sheer surfaces. We evolved in the mountains of our planet."

Milorad came into the room, still panting from climbing the building and hanging outside the window. "We were worried that we couldn't reach you," he puffed.

"I wasn't here," said Jack. "I was out of phone range."

Vladimir frowned in puzzlement. "In this area? Was the signal blocked?"

"I was on another planet."

Vladimir's frown deepened. "You went through a wormhole? The Wardens allowed it?"

"It was not one that the Wardens . . . in fact none of the Mythicals . . . know about. It was to my home planet."

"Home planet?" Vladimir paused for a moment, his pale brow wrinkling. Then he nodded in realization, smiling. "Ah . . . there *are* others! For decades, our Wardens have sighted wormholes that were not ours. The Wardens suspected that other races were coming to Thera, but the others evaded any contact."

"They're doing more than just coming to Thera," said Jack. "They're invading it." He proceeded to tell the vampires all that he had learned from his parents, Christopher, and from his visit to the dying planet Earth.

There was a long, uncharacteristic silence among the vampires, as they sat in the living room and tried to absorb the enormity of what Jack had told them.

Vladimir broke the silence, declaring, "I need a drink."

Milorad quickly fetched glasses and every bottle of liquor in Jack's cabinet. They proceeded to pour themselves generous helpings, providing a particularly large one for Jack. He thankfully began to drink it.

"Your home planet's name. How do you spell it?" asked Vladimir.

Jack spelled "Earth," and Vladimir rolled his eyes and chuckled. "What a terrible name for a planet. *Earth.*" He pronounced the name with a guttural grunt. "It's like the sound somebody makes when they're sick to their stomach."

Milorad took up the theme. "A sound like when somebody gets struck in the testicles."

Radomir chimed in. "Like the name for a really ugly person. 'Boy, that person Earth really is homely.'"

Gennady grinned, adding, "Like the surprised sound somebody makes when they've eaten something foul. Ewww, Earth!"

Vladimir became serious. "We've been frankly undecided about saving the Therans. But we're pretty unanimous about saving you. Sam seems to have taken a liking to you."

"I love her," said Jack, unable to contain the sentence even when out of range of Sam's pheromonal charms.

"She knows."

"We need to stop drinking," said Radomir, decisively clunking his glass on the coffee table. "We know the werewolves will come here, and there's nothing more useless than a drunk vampire."

"Drunken elves are worse," said Milorad defensively. But then he, too, put down his glass.

"Well, in any case, we're almost out of liquor," said Gennady.

"And we need food," said Vladimir. "Go get some, Milorad. You look the least like a guard."

"I beg to differ. I am a most *imposing* guard."

"You are fat," said Gennady.

"I am substantial, robust."

"Please take your substantial, robust self and get food."

"I'll go," said Jack. "I know the neighborhood." He began to rise, but Vladimir placed a restraining hand on his shoulder. "But you do not know the enemy like we do."

"What's to know?" asked Jack. "They're werewolves."

"Just let us do our jobs," said Vladimir.

Milorad laboriously hauled himself out of the chair and proceeded to carefully unlock the front door and peer cautiously out. He left, and Vladimir locked the door behind him.

"You need rest," said Vladimir to Jack. "Go, sleep. We'll be here."

At the vampire's words, Jack seemed to deflate, burdened by the combined effect of the last few days' traumas and the alcohol. He wobbled into the bedroom and collapsed onto the bed, falling immediately into a deep, grateful sleep, lulled by the comforting voices of the vampires arguing over the implications of the Pilgrims' plans for Thera.

He was in profound, dreamless slumber when the sound of a scream pierced his conscious, bringing him to bolt upright in the bed. Another scream, this one higher than the first, followed by wretched sobs.

He leaped off the bed and ran into the living room, to find Milorad holding a young boy and girl by the necks, as Radomir slammed his fist into the boy's face.

"WHERE ARE THEY?" he bellowed.

"What are you doing!" exclaimed Jack. "Let them go!"

"I found them in your hall when I returned with the food," said Milorad.

"*Please!*" begged the girl, who was in her early twenties, with long blond hair. Tears welled in her wide brown eyes. "Please don't hit him again!"

"*We weren't doing anything!*" declared the boy, who was the same age, with curly brown hair and an acne-scarred face showing frightened eyes.

Radomir slammed his fist into that face, snapping the boy's head back. "Where are they?" he asked again.

"Stop!" commanded Jack. "Do you hear me?"

Vladimir stepped forward and punched the boy's chest.

Jack's jaw dropped in shock, as the flesh-suits sagged off the boy's body. Vladimir ripped away the suit to reveal a small werewolf, black blood streaming from his swollen mouth.

"But he isn't big?" was all Jack managed to say.

"No," said Vladimir coldly regarding the werewolf, who sagged in Milorad's grip. "He's an indenture. Normal-sized creatures, not the genetically enhanced soldiers. He, and probably others, were sent here because he is small enough to blend in with Therans when they wear flesh-suits."

"What about her?"

"Please don't hurt me!" exclaimed the girl. *"I'm an Ally. They made me! They're going to—"*

She was interrupted by simultaneous crashes of shattering glass from the bedroom and kitchen.

Still standing in the doorway to his bedroom, Jack spun around to see a gang of furred, muscular bodies erupting through the window, showing gleaming eyes and bared fangs.

• • •

Sam sat quietly, breathing hard, trying to "go blue," her body still covered in dried werewolf blood. Around her, the fairies and other Mythicals continued to tend the wounded, as the blood-red eye color marking her rage gradually gave way to her more tranquil sky-blue. To help her recover, the other Mythicals had quickly removed the werewolf bodies and remnant organs. A'eiio had gingerly pried the Alpha werewolf heart from her small hand, handing it to an elf, who with a disgusted squeal, carried it away.

Mike the ogre staggered into the apartment, green blood oozing from his wounds, helped by Wendy.

"I'm going to operate," she said, fetching her medical kit, enlisting the others to lift Mike onto the apartment's dining table, which creaked under Mike's weight.

He looked up at her, screwing his massive bulldog face into an expression of impatience. "I've got things to do," he rumbled. "Hurry it up."

She scrutinized the ogre's wounds, and without looking up, said, "I'll need different instruments."

"I think we may have something," said E'iouy, hurrying away into the main room of the building. He returned with a toolbox, and Wendy opened it, selecting a large hammer, a chisel, pliers, and a crowbar.

Placing the chisel on one of the wounds, she lofted the hammer and slammed it down, making a small slice in Mike's skin. He stared down at the wound with annoyance.

"Can't you do better than that?" he asked.

Wendy scowled at him, and uttered a mellifluous angelic curse, smashing the hammer down seven more times, managing to slice open the wound enough to insinuate the needle-nose pliers. She dug around in the wound for some minutes, finally extracting the bullet and dropping it into a bowl E'iouy had brought.

"I need to disinfect and seal the wound," she said. "Thermal-seal."

"I've seen it done with ogres," said A'eiio. "I know something that can do it." She left and returned with a propane torch and lighter.

Wendy turned on the torch and lit its flame, which hissed to life, glowing a deep blue. She held the torch to the wound, and it began to scorch and smoke, emitting the stench of burning ogre flesh.

"*Ow!*" complained Mike. "That stings!"

"I should think so," said Wendy, examining the sealed wound as she shut off the torch. "If my experience treating ogres is correct, this should scab over soon. But I'll make sure it stays closed."

Wendy rummaged in the toolbox and came up with a battery-powered nail gun and a roll of steel wire. Grasping the edges of the wound with the pliers, she fired nails through Mike's flesh to create holes for sutures. Then, using a screwdriver, she pushed the wire through the holes, lacing up the wound, and twisting the wires together with the pliers.

She repeated the procedure for Mike's other wounds. The elephantine ogre inspected the results, rolled off the creaking table and lumbered away, muttering about how slow Wendy had been.

"Wait until you get the bill!" she called after him.

Wendy, A'eiio, and E'iouy finished treating the other wounded and checked on Sam, who was already showering off the blood, her eyes a delicate azure.

"Can Sam help?" Wendy asked A'eiio. "You know, by doing what pixies do?"

"No, not after she's been red. It takes a while for her therapeutic ability to return."

"Too bad," said Wendy, as they finished bandaging the last wounded elf.

They left the building, emerging into the scene of the battle, the broad field surrounding the building.

Where the field met the surrounding woods, four bigfoot were huddled over the fallen body of one of their own. Their rumbling voices resonated with the sound of sobbing. They lifted the body and disappeared into the woods.

Near the front of the building, four small, red-bearded leprechauns sat in a circle around their fallen comrade. They rifled his pockets, as the dead leprechaun was already decomposing into dust, a characteristic reaction to the atmosphere of the alien planet. Taking mementos of a dead friend was a custom among their species.

Mike had already joined the trolls and other ogres in pitching the werewolf corpses onto a pile for cremation. An elf drove up on a large front-end loader, which would crush the skulls into dust. There would be no return of their heads to their planet for ritual funerals to honor their sacrifice.

Other groups were collecting the weapons and piling them beside the building.

The two fairies and the angel surveyed the scene.

"We need to report this to the Wardens," said E'iouy. "This may convince them to renounce the Palliation."

"More importantly, we need to ask them to allow us to arm ourselves," said E'iouy. "This is only the first battle."

* * *

The young, blond Theran Ally, who gave her name as Meri, was curled up trembling with fright in the corner of Jack's living room when the police pounded on the door.

"*Hurry! Hurry!*" urged Jack, holding his bleeding arm, wounded in the fight, as Radomir quickly finished dressing it.

"You really need to stay away from werewolves," said the vampire doctor. "They are definitely not good for your health."

Milorad pulled the girl up and took her into the bedroom, warning her to be silent. Jack scanned the apartment, realizing that its shambles would reveal the battle that had taken place. Lamps were knocked over, furniture was smashed, black blood stained the walls, and tufts of werewolf fur littered the floor.

"*Open up!*" demanded the voice on the other side of the door. "*Police!*"

Vladimir hauled the last of the werewolf bodies into the bedroom, and he and Milorad slammed the bedroom door, leaving Jack with Radomir and Gennady. Jack opened the door, careful to keep his bandaged shoulder concealed behind it, to see two large uniformed patrolmen staring coldly at him.

"We got reports from the neighbors of a disturbance here," said one of the cops. "What's going on?"

"Nothing officer," said Jack. "Just a party. Were we too loud?"

"We need to come in."

"It was just a party," said Jack lamely.

"The report didn't sound like it. We're coming in." The officers both drew their weapons and began to shove their way through the door.

Gennady stepped forward, holding up his police badge. "Sorry guys. It was a party that got too loud. And we were playing a video game with explosions. We had it turned up, and we were hollering."

At the sight of the badge, the two officers holstered their pistols, and one said, "Okay . . . well . . . keep it down."

Jack gingerly closed the door, leaning against it for support for the second time. His left arm throbbed from the latest werewolf attack, his right shoulder hurt from the attack in the woods. And, his whole body ached to the bone from the trauma of the last days. But as he stared at the bedroom door, he knew the trauma wasn't over.

As Radomir and Gennady went to fetch Meri the Ally to question her about the werewolves' plans, Jack followed them into the bedroom to see a pile of seven bloody werewolf corpses piled on his bed and lying inert on the floor.

Vladimir and Milorad were too busy rifling through their uniforms to notice him.

"What am I supposed to do now?" he demanded. "What am I supposed to do with a room full of corpses?"

"Nothing," said Vladimir, straightening up and patting Jack's good shoulder. "We know how to handle these things."

"What? You mean you routinely take care of piles of corpses?" Jack felt a serious case of the shakes overcoming him.

"Well, not the transport," said Vladimir, shrugging his shoulders nonchalantly. "Some of our troll friends have a moving company. I've already called them. They'll be here soon with crates and a truck. It'll just look like you're moving some things."

"And then?"

"Remember, I have a meatpacking plant."

Jack lurched into the bathroom and threw up.

CHAPTER 21

t first Meri refused to open the door when Geniato arrived at her apartment.

"I can't trust you," she said, her voice breaking. "You're an Ally for angels."

"But I love you. I want to protect you," said Geniato. "Please let me in!"

After more entreaties, he heard the sound of locks unbolting, and she opened the door. Her brown eyes were wide with panic, her face puffy from crying, her hands trembling. He took her in his arms.

"What happened?" he asked gently. "You wouldn't tell me on the phone."

Meri wouldn't answer at first, instead asking, "Your mother . . . is she all right?"

"I took her back home and made sure she had help. Then you called, and I came. Tell me what happened. Please!"

"You know I am an Ally for the werewolves. They call me an indenture. They make me do things."

"What things?"

"They wanted me to help them kill a man who was going to reveal the bad thing they were planning."

"The Palliation. You mean the reporter, Jack March? He could reveal it to the world. And they wanted you to help kill him?"

"Yes, and his friends stopped them. Vampires. It was horrible. They killed the werewolves who were attacking. They realized I was there against my will, so they let me go."

"So you're safe." He hugged her closer, kissed her forehead, and helped her to the couch.

"No, I'm not." She bowed her head and shook it dismally. "The werewolves have more plans for me. Horrible plans."

"Well, I have plans, too. I'm contacting my angel."

· · ·

"He was a fool," declared the new Alpha, who had just emerged from the wormhole into the icy depths of the werewolves' cavern base. He strode briskly away from the hole, as a new cadre of praetorians began to emerge, moving quickly into formation.

Flaktuckmetang shivered in the unaccustomed cold, but as they ritually smelled one another, tried his best not to show discomfort. "But there were successes," he declared, trying to sound dominant.

"Did you secure the Alpha's body, at least his head?" The Alpha crossed his arms and glared at the werewolf who was not a praetorian, but only a puny exile.

"No, I was instructed only to observe and report back. I was in the woods when the Alpha was killed."

"As I would have expected," snarled the Alpha. "One would not expect someone like you to engage an enemy."

"It was too late to retrieve the head. Of course, the Mythicals know that we venerate the heads of fallen warriors as monuments to their valor. So, they destroyed them immediately."

"*Barbarians!*" exclaimed the new Alpha with disgust, turning his wrath to the Mythicals. "They have no honor!"

"Indeed, the desecration was carried out around the globe when praetorians were killed, and their comrades could not retrieve their heads."

"How many successes did we have?"

Flaktuckmetang hesitated, knowing that sometimes bearers of bad news were killed, in the superstitious belief that they also carried a remnant of the curse of that news. He took a deep, tremulous breath. "I've been in contact with other exiles who accompanied the raids. There were successes. Many of those who opposed the Palliation were killed."

"But the one Ally who could reveal it? Jack March?"

"We've heard nothing from that mission."

"Again he was a fool, my predecessor, for dispatching indentures, not to mention a Theran Ally."

"It has always been done that way. Indentures attract little attention. And Allies know the Therans and their customs."

The new Alpha growled a curse and turned to his lieutenants to plan the next mission.

The transfer was almost complete, with three hundred praetorians standing at attention in the vast cavern, as their equipment was brought through the hole by indentures.

"Well, now that I am in command, we will attract much attention."

"You're . . . *our* . . . orders?" asked Flaktuckmetang.

"Stop the news of the Palliation from spreading. If not, prepare for its launch."

• • •

"Have you decided to reveal the Palliation?" asked Sam, sitting down beside Jack.

"Yes," he said. He lay on his bed, still wearing the same goofy smile produced by Sam's arrival. He had changed the sheets, given that they had been spattered with black werewolf blood. The vampires slept in the living room, having fallen into their daytime stupor.

He began to answer, but she interrupted. "You are hurt . . . again." She touched his bandaged arm, then his shoulder. "I should have helped you in the hospital."

"What do you mean?"

"I'll show you." She gently lifted away the bandage on his arm to reveal the nasty slash that had been meted out by an attacking werewolf, before Vladimir had throttled it. Then, she slipped off his shirt and did the same with the bandage on his shoulder, revealing the older wound from the attack in the forest.

She bent down and began to kiss his shoulder.

"That's nice," he said, feeling an odd tingling in the wound. "I haven't seen you this affectionate."

She paused. "I'm not being affectionate. It's therapy."

"Well, it feels good. But I'm still glad of the antibiotics."

She finished kissing his shoulder and moved to his arm. His shoulder continued to tingle strangely, the ache now disappearing.

"You haven't heard the phrase 'healing as a pixie's kiss'?" she asked between kisses.

"If that's a Mythicals saying, I guess I haven't been around them long enough to hear it."

She kissed his arm several times, then straightened up. "Purely medicinal. Pixie saliva is healing. Especially to Therans. We're not sure why, but we've actually saved many Therans from pain, even death."

"Oh . . . well . . . I need to tell you something. I'm not Theran."

Sam sat up, her expression puzzled. "What else would you be?"

"I just found out. There are those here who look like Therans . . . exactly like Therans. But they're . . . *we're* . . . from a planet called Earth. We came through a wormhole from there, me as a baby. It's a dying planet. They ruined it. Now, they want to colonize Thera. Sam, they want the Palliation to go forward. They've tried to persuade me not to reveal the Palliation. They said their lives . . . the lives of my people . . . depend on it."

"And what would happen to us . . . the Mythicals."

Jack merely shook his head.

Sam stood up, her body stiffening in shock, staring at him with deep anguish. "And what did you say?" Her eyes began to take on a greenish tint.

Jack recognized the meaning of the change. "You would use your . . . influence . . . on me?"

"To save billions of Therans? To save Mythicals? Yes, I would."

"You asked me if I made a decision." Jack reached over to his bedside table and picked up his computer. He swung it around so Sam could see the screen. It displayed an article with the headline. "Werewolves Plan Devastating EMP Attack." A subhead read, "Other Mythicals Battling to Save Thera."

Laying his finger on the touchpad, he moved the cursor to a button on the screen marked "Send." He tapped his finger.

CHAPTER 22

H is body tensed, the vampire Warden stood gazing out the window across the vast plain below his government's mountaintop citadel. The planet's dim sun was setting, and he was thankful for the coming darkness. He felt more comfortable in the gloom.

The other Wardens would arrive soon, and he had just dispatched a hunter to harvest one of the stubby-legged grazers for their dinner. It was a welcome distraction, watching a harvest. The Council meeting could be disastrous, marking the end of the Alliance, perhaps even war. And vampires had held themselves to be neutral thus far about the Palliation. But that couldn't last.

A rotary-wing flier thundered out of the launch bay of the black marble castle, swooping down to skim above the herd of grazers, which began to stampede at the onslaught from above.

"I will designate," instructed the Warden.

"Order received," came the answer from the hunter, and the flier paused, hovering.

The Warden made a gesture with his fingers, and the window transformed into a magnified display of the landscape. A wave of his hand triggered the display to scan across the herd. He spied a particularly large cow and gestured with his finger to designate it. Very nice. The werewolf Warden would enjoy the fresh, raw meat, as would the vampire, perhaps making the discussion that would accompany the meal go more smoothly. But some meat would have to be cooked for the ogre and troll Wardens—a distasteful task for the chef.

But the fairies and several others would need imported fruits, and the pixie Warden would need that peculiar gelatinous concoction that his species preferred when not on their planet. As for the elf, the angel, and the leprechaun Wardens, they seldom ate at a Council meeting. The elf always complained that the food was not adequate; the angel never ate in public, as was the custom. And the leprechaun was usually too skittish to do anything but fidget.

The Warden watched as the flier began to swerve back and forth, tracking the fleeing target animal, and the hunter efficiently stunned it with an anesthetic arrow. The animal collapsed onto the ground and was quickly hoisted aboard.

"Good capture," thought the Warden. The animal would be alive until it was butchered, fresh enough for any werewolf or vampire.

The distraction was short-lived. A wormhole silently materialized from the depths of the slate-gray clouds, its interior lights agleam. A shimmering aurora of evanescent reds, yellows, and blues played about its surface. Its hissing and crackling rising from the background noise, it sailed into the citadel's hangar bay below, and the vampire Warden quickly made his way down to greet the delegation.

After the usual ceremonial Warden greeting, they seated themselves at the long onyx table covered by red cloth, the food placed before them. The hunter barely had time to recite the prayer honoring the fallen animal before the werewolf had begun to feed. He ignored the others, who waited for a tank to be wheeled in, and the mermaid Warden transferred into it, floating gracefully inside, ogling them with his large, limpid eyes.

This was a rare full Council meeting, including not just the usual Wardens—vampire, werewolf, fairy, pixie, troll, ogre, elf. Even the Wardens who hated to travel via wormhole had attended—angel, leprechaun, mermaid, demon, gnome, bigfoot. Most brought their own native foods, not trusting the likes of a vampire to meet their needs.

The leprechaun wasted no time in challenging the werewolf. "You murdered one of our exiles!" he exclaimed in the high, keening voice.

The werewolf waved a bloody rib in the air gruffly declaring, "An exile. What do you care about exiles?"

The leprechaun leaped onto the table, preparing to scramble its length to confront the werewolf. But the angel Warden gently restrained him, settling him back in the chair.

"Besides, these beasts . . ." said the werewolf, waving his claw at the bigfoot. ". . . these beasts killed many of our praetorians."

The bigfoot Warden leaned forward, eyes glaring, and began a rumbling speech. He touched his translation medallion, replying "I would be most happy to add one more to the count. Your unprovoked attack was reprehensible." His pungent aroma wafted across the room.

The answer made the werewolf pause in his feed and bare his fangs.

"As host, I am interlocutor of the meeting," warned the vampire. "And I would ask that we focus on the broader issue of the Palliation. As I've indicated before, the vampires have been neutral in this matter—"

"As have the leprechauns," interrupted the leprechaun.

"*However* . . ." continued the vampire emphatically, ". . . while we had previously believed it was a rogue operation, a matter for your species to handle, it is now clear that this Palliation is sanctioned by your species. The equipment and the warriors you have committed show that. You have lied to the Council."

The elf skrittered an angry declaration, translated by the pixie as, "We have proof that you brought your soldiers through a wormhole."

"We were forced to take unilateral action," said the werewolf. "The Council is allowing Thera to be devastated by the Therans themselves. So, the Palliation offers a way to preserve the planet."

"By devastating the population?" asked the fairy Warden. "The Therans now know of the Palliation. They are outraged, fearful. They wanted to launch an attack on you. But we told their leaders that any assault will risk the enmity of all Mythicals, who have already suffered from internment and will not tolerate another persecution. We pointed out that Mythical technology is powerful, and Therans would risk a devastating war."

"We have a new ally," said the werewolf, finishing the rib, and as was the custom, rubbing the remaining blood on his pelt. He took up another clawful of meat and began to gnaw on it.

"You can't mean Therans," said the fairy.

"I mean a previously unknown species called humans," said the werewolf. "We've long suspected an unidentified interdimensional-traveling species existed but did not know for sure. The group calls themselves Pilgrims."

"And why would they become allies in the Palliation?"

"Their planet is beyond saving. They have been covertly colonizing Thera. They propose to become caretakers of the planet. To preserve it for the remaining Therans, for themselves, and for the Mythicals."

"And they would countenance the death of billions of Therans?" asked the fairy.

"They are like us. They see no other way," said the werewolf.

"You shall not proceed!" declared the fairy Warden, his wings beating furiously, lifting him above the group.

"I have a solution," said the vampire. "Give the Therans some time . . . say ten of their days . . . to decide on the Remediation. If they are still determined to ruin their planet, then the case for the Palliation is stronger."

The werewolf pitched down the chunk of raw carcass and stood. "They will not agree to the Remediation. They are fools. But we will give them those days. Then, we will bring our engineers through our wormhole to trigger the EMP generators."

The fairy Warden immediately launched himself out the door and toward the wormhole, to transit back to his planet. He had a dire message to deliver.

• • •

"You killed our indentures!" snarled Flaktuckmetang. He glared out from the view screen at Vladimir, his werewolf's black lips curling back to show ivory fangs. Behind him in the cavern of the werewolves' polar base, the massive praetorians moved about the business of helping their wounded comrades into their wormhole.

"We were protecting a friend," said Vladimir, standing easily before the screen in his house, the other vampires lounging behind him in his large, windowless living room.

"Jack March is no friend. He revealed the Palliation. He has made our plan more difficult."

"Well, first of all, as you said yourself, we *only* killed indentures. What do you care about them? They were not the praetorians that the other Mythicals killed in battle. The ones whose heads they destroyed. You know we were not involved in that battle. We have remained neutral. And we ask your help."

"You do not need our transport," said the werewolf. "You are taking care of your own."

"Yes, many of our kind are evacuating worldwide. They're ones the Wardens decreed were far enough along in their sentences. But you know there are simply not enough wormholes for us all to transit in time. And we know you are using your own to move your exiles to safety. Look at it this way. By launching the Palliation, you are risking the collapse of the Mythicals Alliance. But if you show good faith by helping to save other exiled Mythicals than your own . . . specifically us . . . it may yet still hold. We vampires . . . ," Vladimir gestured around the room at the others ". . . have at least some sympathy for the Palliation."

The werewolf shifted slightly, betraying some discomfort with the situation. He was not used to handling political issues. He preferred killing. Then, he seemed to recover his authority, declaring, "I will consult with our Warden and the Alpha praetorian. We will determine whether we have the capacity, and the inclination."

"Fine," said Vlad. "We will await your decision. But I ask your Alpha to consider the consequences of refusing."

The screen went blank, and Jack appeared from the other room, followed by Sam and Ryan. Ryan was busy chattering in the squeaky tones of elvish into his phone.

"Did the werewolves believe your ruse?" asked Jack.

"Vampires are pretty good liars," said Vladimir. "I think they'll ultimately agree to bring their wormhole within range."

"From what I'm told, Therans have the missile technology to destroy it. But the reverse is also true."

"And that is?" asked Vlad.

"Since we plan to destroy *their* wormhole with missiles, *they* could just as easily do the same to the Mythicals' apertures. You need some way to protect your wormholes. I think I've figured how to engineer such a defensive system."

Finishing his phone call, Ryan skrittered an elvish answer, which Sam translated as, "He has proposed your defensive technology to the Wardens and the trolls. They can engineer it."

"Do they know whether the werewolves are preparing to launch the Palliation?" asked Jack.

The elf squeaked out an extended answer, which Sam translated: "The elves and trolls can't tell from the orbital scans whether the werewolves have transited their engineers through to Thera. That is necessary to trigger the EMP generators. But he says they have not moved their wormhole to orbit, which would also be an indication they plan to launch the Palliation. Now, they appear to be only evacuating their exiles. But we need to know for sure. If their engineers are on this side, they can still devastate the planet."

"But in the end, we have to close that hole," said Jack. "We have to shut them off from Thera."

"It's up to you to persuade the Therans to help us do that," said A'eiio. She placed her hands on Jack's shoulders, her sapphire eyes staring into his. "You are the only one to do it. They still believe you are one of them."

"True, the Therans don't know of the Pilgrims . . . of humans," said Jack. "And I won't tell them. If they knew I was human, they would think I was betraying them somehow. And in any case, there are appeasers among them . . . those who do not want any aggression against the werewolves; those who will see our plan as provoking the werewolves . . . as triggering the Palliation."

"Well, then, make them see they have no choice."

CHAPTER 23

Vladimir smiled an ivory-fanged vampire smile. He had allowed his teeth to grow to their natural length since the revelation of the Mythicals' existence on Thera. The towering vampire spoke into the radio to Jack, as he stood in the welcome gloom with his fellow vampires in the broad parking lot outside his meatpacking plant.

"The beasts will be quite attracted to this landing site," he said. "We have activated fans from the building. Now the place smells of raw flesh. And it will mask the other scents."

Normally, the building bustled with the carnivorous daytime traffic of carcasses being hauled in, and butchered meat shipped out. But tonight it was quiet, except for the hum of the compressors from the lines of refrigerator trucks parked at the loading docks. The sound added an ominous undertone to the scene.

The vampires counted on this noise and the darkness of the moonless night to mask the stealthy maneuvers now taking place around the plant.

The vampires intently scanned the sky. After a long wait, the werewolves' wormhole appeared as a faint blotch in the distance, growing rapidly. Its faint-colored aurora defined it against the ink-black sky, as it dropped toward them. Abruptly, its lights switched on, and the vampires winced at the light. Milorad donned sunglasses against the glare.

The hole slowed its descent coming to a stop above them, and a ladder extended down. The furred form of Flaktuckmetang descended from it, and he was followed immediately by the Alpha, leading a squad of praetorians, who fanned out around the hole, their bulky, ornate rifles at the ready, aimed outward.

"You are ready to depart?" asked the Alpha, peering around suspiciously raising his snout to sniff the air.

Vladimir shrugged. "We have to settle an issue first."

"There are no issues to settle. We have agreed to evacuate you . . . to give you the privilege of using our aperture. Board now." The werewolf stepped back and gestured impatiently with a taloned claw for the vampires to climb the ladder to enter their world.

"Oh, but there *is* an issue as far as the Therans are concerned," said Jack, appearing from behind one of the trucks. "They want to stop this horrible thing you plan."

The Alpha crouched into an attack posture, and the praetorians swung their rifles around to aim at Jack.

"*What are you doing here? I can have you killed!*" snarled Flaktuckmetang.

"I know . . . Flak," said Jack, using the truncated version of the werewolf's name, knowing it was a profound insult. He spread his hands to show that he held no weapon. The werewolves likely didn't shoot unarmed people. But they could take him prisoner, and the Alpha signaled two of his guards to do just that.

But as they moved forward, Jack backed away, and a squad of Theran soldiers materialized in the broad circle of light cast by the glowing wormhole. Their own weapons at the ready, they encircled the werewolves. The vampires backed away, as well.

The Alpha's ears pricked up, and he bellowed a command in the guttural language of his race. The praetorians began a retreat to the ladder, weapons still aimed outward at the much larger encircling force.

"I should have known you would betray us!" exclaimed Flaktuckmetang. "We will never—"

A brilliant flare erupted from the gloom beyond the lighted circle, followed instantly by the loud whoosh of a rocket launch. Trailing its blazing exhaust, the rocket streaked like a fiery lance toward the wormhole.

The missile penetrated the wormhole, detonating with an ear-shattering blast that flung the werewolves back.

The wormhole was enveloped by a blinding fireball, but only for an instant.

The wormhole vanished, its magnetic containment destroyed, leaving only utter darkness, the pungent aroma of smoke, a disconcerting stillness.

Blasts of wild gunfire shattered that stillness, erupting both from the blinded werewolves and their equally blind Theran enemy. Screams of wounded soldiers and the explosions of grenades punctuated the gunfire.

A sudden glare of light overhead flooded the area, revealing a bloody scene of dead and dying Therans and werewolves.

It also revealed Jack and the vampires hunkered down, frozen by the sudden assault.

"It's another wormhole!" exclaimed Jack, peering upward, squinting at the light. He held the radio to his mouth. "Can you target it? Can you hit it?" he asked the Theran missile team.

237

From the hovering wormhole erupted a fusillade of gunfire that raked the Theran soldiers, wounding and killing many, and scattering them, opening a way for the werewolves to escape.

Before Jack could receive an answer from the missile team, the werewolf Flaktuckmetang loomed before him, raising a rifle, leveling it at him and Vladimir.

"We thought you might try something like this!" he exclaimed. "Now you'll pay!"

Jack and Vladimir both steeled themselves for death, as the werewolf pulled the trigger.

But with a bellowed "No!" a large form leaped in front of them, shuddering as the bullets impacted his body. The werewolf ceased firing, as gunfire from the Therans drove him back. He and the praetorians shot their way out of the ring of Theran soldiers and toward the glowing wormhole, as it lowered to the ground, enabling them to climb its ladder.

Unbound by gravity or inertia, the wormhole streaked into the black sky, shrinking to a star before blinking out.

Lights from the Theran soldiers flicked on, playing over the bodies of their fallen comrades, tending to the wounded and beginning to evacuate the dead.

The Theran colonel approached, shining a light on Jack and Vladimir. The light also revealed the bloody corpse of Milorad, his eyes fixed, his mouth gaping open, now silent. Radomir bent over him, searching in vain for any signs of life. He looked up at them with a grim expression, and shook his head.

"He saved us," breathed Jack.

"I would have expected nothing less," said Vladimir, tears welling in his eyes as he knelt over his fallen friend. Gennady knelt beside Vladimir, putting his arm around him.

Jack stood and surveyed the scene, his brow knitted in puzzlement. Then he realized.

"The Pilgrims! It was their wormhole! The werewolves have enlisted them!"

"It appears so," said Vladimir, reaching to gently close Milorad's unseeing eyes.

"My own people," said Jack, his head lowered.

"Your own people," echoed the vampire.

"And the Palliation . . . the werewolves will launch it."

"Yes, and that werewolf exile will certainly try his best to make sure you are killed."

"I'm already under a death sentence," said Jack, tentatively touching the back of his neck, feeling the bump of the scar where his termination chip had been implanted.

· · ·

Having just emerged from the Pilgrim wormhole, Flaktuckmetang stood beside the towering Alpha praetorian and stared with disgust beyond the rusting steel walls of the Pilgrim compound. They looked out over a desolate landscape, the pall of pollution obscuring the sun. The dull, yellowish light revealed the dead trees and the craters that littered the bare ground outside the compound. The Alpha snorted, trying to expel the foul stench of the planet from his nostrils.

"They did this to their planet." Flaktuckmetang shook his head. "And they expect to become the dominant species on Thera. We should destroy their aperture after this is over."

"Perhaps," said the Alpha distractedly. He had turned his gaze downward, staring with grave reflection at his praetorians arrayed below the tower.

They stood in a Circle of Honor around one of their dead comrades, chanting the ceremonial Ode to a Fallen Warrior. The chant complete, the praetorian priest moved to the werewolf's corpse, and pulled out a gleaming combat ax. Holding it high, he uttered the benediction, and with a powerful stroke, severed the head.

From a crowd of Pilgrims watching the werewolf ceremony came a shocked, collective gasp, punctuated with sounds of retching.

The head rolled away from the body, where the chaplain retrieved it and placed it in a preservation sack. It would normally have been sent home, to be displayed with honor in the Hall of Heroes. But now the werewolves were marooned from their world, the hated Therans having destroyed their only way home.

As the circle re-formed around another body for the next ceremony, the Alpha turned to Flaktuckmetang, his expression furious.

"These soldiers will not have died in vain," he declared. "We will go forward with this cleansing of that enemy planet, so that at least our exiles and the remaining praetorians will have a livable place."

"And the humans?" asked Flaktuckmetang.

Before the Alpha could answer, a voice behind them replied, "We are prepared."

They turned to see the short, squat Pilgrim leader, Christopher. He continued. "Our colonies on Thera report that they have completed hardening their systems against electromagnetic pulses. And those not in colonies have either retreated to safe shelter or returned here." He gestured across the compound at a line of refugees streaming from the building housing the Pilgrim wormhole. They exited the compound gates, to a village of tents erected outside the walls.

Christopher gestured at two middle-aged humans, who stood behind him staring with unabashed anxiety at the werewolves.

"This is Nathan and David Clark. They are our liaisons with the Pilgrims on Thera. And they will work with you to help as you wish with the Palliation."

"We need no help," said the Alpha curtly. "Our engineers are with us and have the trigger codes and the necessary expertise to use them."

Nathan stepped forward, offering a hand, which the Alpha did not take in his claw, staring distastefully at the pale, fleshy human appendage.

"We are so sorry that the Therans destroyed the portal to your planet," he said. "Is there anything that we can do for your . . . men?"

"No. Our mission was to enable the Palliation. We will carry it out. We only need access to orbit."

"Good. Very good," said Nathan. "I'm sure the other Mythicals opposed to the Palliation may present problems. So—"

"Nothing we cannot overcome," said the Alpha. "The outcome of the Palliation . . . a healing planet . . . will eventually persuade them." His attention shifted to a load of long, slim cylinders the Pilgrims were now hauling into the building housing the wormhole.

"Are those weapons?" he asked the Alpha, gesturing to the containers. "Why do you need weapons?"

"No, they're not," said Nathan, shaking his head, a gesture mimicked by his brother. "Those are final shipments of hardened electronic equipment . . . radios and so forth . . . that we are sending through to our colonies for communication."

The Alpha gave Flaktuckmetang a suspicious sidelong glance, and he nodded at the unspoken signal that the cylinders were to be investigated further.

Flaktuckmetang, as a seasoned politician on Thera, also knew to deflect the issue, to allay any suspicion by the humans.

"This human, Jack March," he said quickly. "He has done considerable damage to your cause."

David Clark moved up beside them, gesturing in agreement. "We will take care of him."

"No, *we* will," said Flaktuckmetang emphatically. "We just want to inform you that he will be killed. He is one of you, but he has become an enemy."

"Killing him will be difficult," said David. "The Mythicals protect him."

"Not really," said the Alpha. "He has a termination chip. We were the ones who developed that technology for the Mythicals. We know how to circumvent the safeguard system that required a unanimous vote of the Wardens. Once we've launched the Palliation, he will be terminated."

CHAPTER 24

Jack struggled to contain his nausea at the scene in the huge hall, his stomach roiling. Whether he was reacting to the sight of the grisly funeral ceremony taking place there, or the profoundly disturbing smell of cooked vampire flesh, he could not say.

Sam took his arm, and A'eiio placed her calming hand on his shoulder.

They looked out over the expanse of round tables, all occupied by black-suited vampires, poised with their forks aloft holding small bits of flesh.

At the center of the hall, on a raised platform, lay Milorad's body covered with a red silk sheet, only his face showing. But the sheet was not draped over the familiar bulk of his round body. Rather it sagged over a sunken form, as if covering a skeleton.

Which it was.

Jack stifled a gag reflex and managed to gasp out, *"They're really eating him!"*

"Their custom," said Sam quietly, as the vampires took the morsels of Milorad the vampire into their mouths. They chewed solemnly, as a vampire choir began to sing a melodious hymn, their rich voices filling the hall.

"Why?" asked Jack.

E'iouy moved up beside them to answer. "Well, as you may have gathered, they revere flesh. They believe it to be sacred. And, they believe the flesh of their loved ones to be especially sacred. It's their way of honoring him by incorporating bits of him into their body."

Jack took a deep breath to recover. "Well, if they don't mind, I'll honor him in my own way, with a good bottle of his favorite liquor."

"Well, they don't drink liquor in the ceremony," said E'iouy. "On the table there, you do see the glasses of—"

"*Dear!*" interrupted A'eiio, rather emphatically. "I do think Jack has had quite enough of vampire customs. We need to tend to much more urgent matters. The Palliation. The werewolves have only been set back temporarily. They will no doubt go ahead with the effort."

Having mourned Milorad as much as Jack could stomach, they left the hall and drove quickly to the presidential mansion, a marble edifice fronted with massive pillars sitting on a broad, manicured lawn. Entering the main hall, occupied by heavily armed soldiers, they joined Steve the troll, Mike the ogre, Ryan the elf, and Wendy the angel.

A uniformed aide led them to a conference room, where they met President Eller. Standing beside him was science adviser Balin Litt; and behind them a cadre of dark-suited security men, holsters visible under their jackets. They eyed the Mythicals suspiciously, especially the hulking ogre. They glared pointedly at Mike, who had decorated his testicles with glimmering lights for the occasion.

E'iouy, his wings wafting slowly behind him, chuckled at the armed security. "So do you feel safe with all that firepower against a few Mythicals?"

Eller did not smile. "The urgency of the situation has dictated that I accede to your requirements that all these . . ." He seemed not able to find the word ". . . well . . . that they all attend. Shall we discuss what is to be done?"

Eller sat down at the head of the conference table, and the others took their places. The fairies and the angel tucked in their wings as best they could against the backs of the tall armchairs.

Litt tapped briefly on a tablet computer, then handed it to the president, whose impassive expression evolved into a deep glower.

"I have the after-action report from our military," he said darkly. "It reports that our missile destroyed the werewolves' portal to their planet. It also reports that the werewolves were rescued by yet another wormhole. Am I to assume that means that other creatures are supporting them in this attack?"

Jack stood, his hands gripping the table, steeling himself for what he was about to reveal. "Not Mythicals. There is another group of aliens that you have not been made aware of. They are called Pilgrims. They—"

"The Pilgrim cult?" asked Litt. "They are aliens?"

"Yes. They are from a parallel planet, called Earth. Its species are called humans. They have been infiltrating Thera for decades, with a view toward colonizing it. And, Mr. President, I have been informed since we last met that I am one of them. I am human, not Theran."

Eller leaped to his feet and launched an enraged tirade, with Jack and the Mythicals trying to convince the president and the science adviser that Jack's actions had proved his loyalty to Therans and his sincerity in preventing the Palliation.

Finally, Eller sat down, his expression one of smoldering anger. "Perhaps you are not a traitor to us; but you are certainly a traitor to your own species," he said.

"I didn't even know my species until recently," said Jack, holding his hands wide in a placating gesture. "Mr. President, let me continue to help Thera, to help the Mythicals. Let me continue to prove myself."

Litt, who had been staring coldly, analytically at Jack through Eller's tirade, said quietly, "Prove yourself by giving us actionable intelligence. For example, did closing the werewolves' interdimensional aperture prevent them from launching their attack?"

Jack shook his head emphatically. "Not at all. We have to assume that they made sure they had the technicians on this side to launch the Palliation."

"Can we jam any triggering signal?"

"Probably not. We have to assume they engineered the orbiting devices to be triggered manually, to avoid such jamming."

"Then we must immediately launch our missiles to destroy the generators," declared the science adviser.

"It's worth a try," said Jack. "But again, the werewolves are excellent military strategists. We have to believe they will have defensive mechanisms in place."

"Our missiles are fast enough to penetrate any defenses," declared Eller, beckoning to an assistant. He instructed her to pass on his order to the military to organize a global missile attack on the orbiting generators.

"My generals have told me it will take about a day to target the missiles, and coordinate a simultaneous worldwide attack," he said.

Ryan uttered a series of raspy screeches, which Sam translated as, "He says that the missile attack shouldn't happen just yet. We still have six more days left on the ultimatum the werewolves gave. We should use that time for another approach to stopping the Palliation."

"Surely, the werewolves will not honor their deadline," said Eller.

"You can be certain that they will," said A'eiio. "Whatever you think of their barbarity, they live by a code of honor. And their leaders have pledged to give Thera time to decide to implement the Remediation. You must reconsider your decision against it."

"We will *not*," said Eller coldly. "We will not suffer the huge political and economic damage of such a drastic change in our energy sources. And as you well know, the Remediation includes oppressive social strictures that we can simply not abide by. We will manage our future as we see fit."

The president stood, preparing to leave, signaling that the discussion was closed. "I know that my colleagues around the globe feel the same."

"It's your planet," said A'eiio. "We can only help you escape its destruction by other Mythicals. Your own fate is in your hands."

"As it should be," said Eller. "Now, let's say our missiles are not completely successful. They will—"

He was interrupted by a loud complaining grunt from Steve. The troll hauled his squat body onto the conference table, and faced the president.

"The human Jack March has told you it will not be successful," he rumbled. "And the elf would tell you the same, if you could understand him." Ryan the elf made a high-pitched creaking sound in assent. Steve continued. "We have gleaned what knowledge we can about the structure of these generators. They are hardened. They are protected. Your race will die, unless you do something besides send your primitive rockets at them."

"Primitive? I hardly think so," said Eller. "They will be successful. Besides, there is no other way."

During the arguments, Jack had sat with his head bowed in thought.

"Maybe there is," he said. He stood and turned his back to the group, reaching up to lift the hair on his neck to reveal a small pink scar. "The Mythicals Wardens inserted this chip into me. A termination chip, so they could kill me anywhere, anytime. Do the werewolves have such chips?"

"They do," said the troll. "In fact, we adapted their technology for the chip that you and other unmanageable Mythicals . . . like me for instance . . . have." The troll turned his head and lifted his mop of stringy white hair to reveal a similar scar in his leathery brown skin.

"Could we somehow activate *their* chips?" asked Jack.

"No chance," said the troll. "The codes are in the high-security control center . . . impossible to access by anybody but a werewolf . . . and a werewolf controller at that."

The elf skrittered in agreement.

"But there is a chance," said Jack, tapping his fingers emphatically on the table. "I know how we might get those codes!" He turned to Wendy, smiling.

CHAPTER 25

"I can't," sobbed Meri, shaking her head in despair. "I just can't! They will kill me. They will kill my family! They will kill *him*." Nestling against Geniato, the fragile-looking young girl wiped her eyes, and Geniato put his arm around her.

"You could cause Meri's death," Geniato declared. "And you are asking her to risk the lives of her loved ones. She is not equipped to do this. She only became an Ally of the werewolves because she stumbled on one in the forest taking off his disguise. She did not put herself in this terrible position. They call her an indenture, lowest form of life, and they would kill her with no thought."

He looked up with a pleading expression at Wendy the angel, who had only months earlier invaded his cramped apartment, upending his life and recruiting him as an Ally.

Wendy protectively folded her white wings around the two of them as they sat on the couch, and regarded them sadly.

Across from them in the hotel suite sat Jack, Sam, A'eiio, and E'iouy. Not present were the more frightening Mythicals—the troll, the elf, and the ogre. And certainly not the vampires, whom Meri had witnessed cold-bloodedly killing a cadre of indenture werewolves in Jack's apartment. Those Mythicals' presence would have thwarted the plan to enlist the timorous Meri.

"We know we are asking you to risk everything," said Wendy gently. "But this would save Thera and all the people in it."

Jack leaned forward and took her hand. "The termination codes that you could take from the werewolves could stop the Palliation. You understand what a catastrophe the Palliation would be. You and all your loved ones . . ." Jack raised his hand in an expansive gesture, ". . . *all* our loved ones, would perish."

Sam sat beside the diminutive girl and embraced her. "You are strong, Meri," she said gently. "You have endured working for those beasts. You *can* do this."

All of them tacitly decided that silence was the best persuader—that simply letting the enormity of the Palliation sink in would bring the girl around.

Meri leaned forward, placing her hands over her face, shaking her head. Then, after a long moment, the shaking stopped. She looked up, tears welling in her brown eyes, her hands trembling.

"I will try," she declared, her voice quavering. "I will try."

.   .   .

The werewolf praetorians towered over the humans, as they stood at the controls of the Pilgrim wormhole in the battered, cavernous hangar on the Earth side. As they piloted the wormhole, the view screen showed the thickly wooded landscape of Thera passing beneath. They brought the aperture to hover just above the forest floor, in a clearing outside a Pilgrim colony. They held position, as the humans transported through the airlock and to the colony the last cylinders containing what the Pilgrims described as hardened electronic equipment.

Flaktuckmetang could not resist a veiled insult aimed at the Pilgrims.

"It is such a beautiful planet," he said. "Fortunately, *that* one will remain so." He curled his black lips and pointedly glanced around at the ruined building surrounding them. Out a large window in the building rose the scarred steel wall of the Pilgrim compound, a reminder that this was a last bastion, under constant siege, of a species that had ruined its own world.

Christopher ignored the taunt. "You are prepared, I take it," he said tersely.

The Alpha praetorian answered just as coldly. "Of course. Complete your tasks quickly. We must trigger the generators before they figure a way to stop us."

"I thought you were confident in your engineering," said Christopher. Now it was his turn to taunt.

"Just finish," grumped the Alpha. To emphasize his impatience, he flicked a claw at Flaktuckmetang.

"I am ready to monitor the activation," answered Flaktuckmetang, a touch too much eagerness in his voice.

"No," said the Alpha. "You are to go through to Thera. You are to report to the commander of our camp. You are to coordinate any necessary surgical strikes on any Theran missiles."

"Sir, I could offer—" began Flaktuckmetang, but the Alpha cut him off by turning away and signaling that the werewolf engineers should be fetched.

They appeared immediately, and the lead engineer began donning the pressure suit, while the others checked its fittings and attached the tools he would need.

Careful to keep his scowl to himself, Flaktuckmetang obediently entered the chamber and made his way through the hole to the Theran side.

"All right, all right," said Christopher. "We are ready. Give us the coordinates of the first generator."

The lieutenant stepped forward, handing a tablet computer to the wormhole's pilot. The Pilgrim typed in the coordinates, and on the view screen, the Theran landscape instantly fell away, as the wormhole leaped into the sky, speeding into space.

An involuntary grunt arose from some of the observers, both Pilgrim and werewolf. They could not avoid feeling the sense of vertigo from the stunning acceleration of the hole in the other universe, while their side remained still.

After mere minutes, one shining, star-like object appeared in the obsidian, star-filled sky on the view screen. It quickly grew and resolved itself into the large cylinder of an EMP generator, its solar wings spread, its parabolic dish pointed at Thera.

The Alpha allowed himself a smile. "Now, we can begin to cleanse this planet," he said.

·   ·   ·

"I am going in," whispered Meri, pushing through the thick brush toward the distant sounds of snarling werewolf speech.

"Okay, you're fine," said Jack gently in her earpiece. He had been enlisted as communicator, since Meri had been so anxious about working with any Mythicals. So, she heard only in the background the gruff voice of Steve the troll.

"Tell her the camera is working fine and to hurry it up," said Steve. "She'll get caught."

Meri touched her ear to make sure the earpiece was snugly inserted and not visible. Then, she touched the tiny camera attached to her dress. "Tell me where to go," she said, almost pleadingly. "I don't know where to go."

"Don't worry," said Jack. "These Mythicals know enough about werewolf camps to direct you."

She had taken a dozen steps forward, when a massive figure loomed before her, a praetorian sentinel. She gasped and shrank back against a tree, as the armored soldier raised his rifle, aiming it at her chest.

"Tell me why I shouldn't shoot you and drag your body into the woods," he said in accented, guttural Theran. "Even make a meal of you."

"I'm an Ally!" she exclaimed.

"You mean an indenture. Who is your master?"

"Your Alpha. He'll want to see me." She took a deep breath to steady herself; to make her commands sound authoritative. "Let me through."

"He is not at the camp. So, we will put you in with the other indentures until he returns."

"Call him. Tell him I have returned with intelligence he needs."

"He is on the other side of a wormhole . . . out of range." With that the praetorian grabbed Meri by the arm and lifted her off the ground, turning toward camp.

In her ear, she heard Jack say, "You can't be imprisoned! You need to be free! Tell him something!"

As she was being dragged through the brush, the pain from the praetorian's vice-like grip lancing through her arm, Meri thought furiously, then declared, "He has an assignment for me that requires me to get information from others in the camp."

The guard stopped, held her up to his fanged face, and demanded "What assignment? What is it?"

"I am not to divulge that."

The guard shook her violently, snapping her head back and forth. *"What assignment!"* He smiled, perhaps at the enjoyment of threatening the Alpha's indenture.

Breathless with fear, Meri managed to stammer out a retort that she hoped would stop him. "I am instructed to tell no one . . . especially an ordinary praetorian. Shall I tell the Alpha that his commands were not honored?"

The praetorian's eyes widened slightly, his fanged grin disappearing. He knew that countermanding an Alpha would bring summary disembowelment and discarding of his corpse, including his head—the ultimate shame to his clan. He lowered Meri to the ground, giving her an annoyed shove toward the camp.

She stumbled to the ground, hauled herself up, and turned back to the guard, saying submissively, "Thank you, sir. I shall tell the Alpha that you aided my assignment."

"Clever girl," she heard Jack say. "You may need him later. Now just walk through the camp. We're with you all the way. We need to find the communications center. That would have the controls for their termination chips."

Meri entered the camp, a collection of several dozen huge, gray inflatable airdomes, some glowing from the lights inside. The paths between them were crowded with praetorians hauling equipment, cleaning their weapons, or lounging in front of their airdome barracks watching a blood-feud battle between champions of two rival packs.

She passed several other airdomes, peering into each one. Jack and Steve examined them through the camera and urged her on, the impatient troll muttering, "Go! Go! Keep looking."

She passed the armory dome with its racks of assault rifles, and finally the feeding dome. There hundreds of werewolves gathered according to their pack, around large carcasses, tearing at the raw meat, squabbling, and growling. The combined odor of flesh and the musk of male werewolves exuded from its doorway.

"Good," she heard Jack say. "It's feeding time. That may give you access. Just stay calm."

She came to two interconnected domes that had three guards posted at the entrance, and they glared suspiciously at her. A praetorian emerged with a tablet in his hand, scrutinizing its screen.

"That could be it," said Steve. "It's a big one, and they'd want that for the control center."

Jack added encouragingly. "You did it! Can you get closer?"

Trying to show an air of confidence, as if she were really on assignment from the Alpha, she walked toward the dome entrance.

The guard praetorians, moved to block her way, glaring down at her from their imposing height.

"Keep moving, indenture. You have no business here."

Meri stopped, not sure what to do next. Luckily, Jack's voice in her ear gave her a way in.

"Tell them you have information about the Palliation for the controllers."

Meri drew herself to her full modest height, declaring, "The Alpha dispatched me among my people to gather information on their response to the ultimatum. The controllers will want to know what I found. The Alpha will need the information when he returns."

"You are not to enter," declared the guard.

Now, Meri decided, was the time to use their low opinion of her. "Do I look like a risk to you . . . to the controllers?" she asked, in a soft, vulnerable tone. "Me? An indenture? I only want to please. To fulfill the terms of my agreement."

One of the guards shifted slightly, which Meri took as a sign of their uncertainty. She stepped tentatively forward, and the two behemoths finally gave a dismissive wave and let her through.

"Great!" said Jack. "Now, you'll want to make yourself as inconspicuous as possible . . . and try to find the control console for the termination system."

"What does it look like?" she asked.

Now, she heard Steve's voice, but her adventure had made her confident enough that she was no longer frightened of the troll. "It'll have a view screen showing maps and icons where all their soldiers are," said the troll.

Meri entered the dome, scanning the inside surface. It was covered with a profusion of projected maps, video images of praetorians, and other data.

The dome was also crowded with uniformed werewolves, who sat in an outward-facing ring of throne-like, control-studded chairs. Through the camera and microphone on Meri, Jack and the others could tell they were intently monitoring werewolf patrols around the planet and dispatching commands. The dome was also redolent with the cloying musky odor of werewolf bodies.

Despite the disquieting aroma, Meri breathed a sigh of relief. Nobody was looking at her, a mere indenture. Their attention was on the displays, as they went about their duties.

"Scan the dome with the camera," instructed Steve. "Let me see the projections."

Moving slowly, trying to look as casual and inconspicuous as possible, Meri slipped past werewolves standing in the dome and to the dome's center. Now with the full dome and its projections visible, she slowly turned a full circle, hoping that none of the soldiers noticed the strange behavior.

"There!" exclaimed Steve. "There's the projection from the termination system."

"What do I do now?" she asked.

"Try to figure out which of those beasts is paying attention to that specific display," said Steve.

Meri scrutinized the werewolves occupying the chairs. She finally saw that one of the controllers, an obese, gray-furred werewolf, had his eyes riveted on that display. Periodically, he would touch a button, or wave his claw in the air, to zoom in on one map or bring up another, apparently tracking the movements of the praetorians.

"I see him," whispered Meri, turning so that the camera was aimed at the controller.

"Yes, that's him," said Steve. "Get yourself into position. You have the comm-chip ready?"

"Yes." Meri fished the fingernail-sized chip from the pocket in her dress and clutched it tightly.

"I'll tell you where it needs to go. Just stay low. Get as close to the control console as you can."

Meri scanned nervously about, looking for a way to get near the monitoring chair. A way presented itself when one of the controllers heaved himself out of his chair, and trundled away, scratching between his legs and growling. That left two chairs empty.

"I can get between those chairs into the center consoles," said Meri.

"Do it!" exclaimed Steve.

Waiting until as many gleaming yellow werewolf eyes as possible were aimed in the other direction, Meri ducked down and crawled between the empty chairs. She managed to nestle herself next to the huge collection of cylinders that were the werewolves' master control computers. An electronic warmth emanated from the computers, heightening the musky werewolf-smell in the dome.

"I'm there," she whispered.

"I can see that," said Steve. "Now try to make it around to the computer just behind the controller who's monitoring the termination chips."

257

Meri crawled slowly past the empty chair, then taking a tremulous breath, crawled behind those occupied by controller-werewolves. Fortunately, they were intent on their work, emitting only an occasional guttural growl.

She reached her target, holding up the comm-chip that would enable Steve to remotely tap into the computer and download the termination codes.

"What do I do?" she asked, pleadingly. "I don't have much time."

"Aim the camera toward the computer. I need to see the access panels."

Meri did as she was told.

"Now, you see the small panel on the left side? Pull it open."

Meri did so, revealing a confusion of wires and electronic circuit boards.

"That's it!" exclaimed Steve. "See the circuit in the middle? See the chip slots? Put the chip into the lower slot next to the red light! Hurry!"

Meri found the slot, and shoved the chip into it. She quickly snapped the cover back into place.

"Wait!" commanded Steve. "You didn't let me test the link!"

"Well, I had to—" began Meri. But then she began to scream, the sound quickly stifled by a claw clutching her neck. Strangling, she was dragged from behind the chair out into the dome.

She was surrounded by snarling, slavering werewolves, but only one face mattered.

Flaktuckmetang held her up struggling before him, his fangs bared, his face so close she could smell his fetid breath. "What are you doing here!" he growled. "What treachery are you committing?"

CHAPTER 26

"*The picture is dark!*" exclaimed Geniato. "The picture is all dark! What happened?"

He stood with Jack and the Mythicals in the control room of the Theran military command, staring desperately at the large screen. It showed *nothing*. As the werewolves had dragged Meri from their control dome, the view screen had shown the camera attached to her dress gyrating wildly. The speakers in the control room had reverberated with her cries for help. But now the screen was dark, the speaker silent.

"They could be smashed! She could be dead!" exclaimed Geniato.

"Or, she could just be in a dark place . . . a cell," said Jack. "She could be all right."

"We can't worry about her now," said Steve. The troll feverishly waved his gnarly fingers in the air to manipulate the virtual symbols—attempting to decipher the termination codes he had managed to steal from the werewolves' computer. As he worked, he muttered to himself in the gravelly language of trolls.

Ryan looked over the troll's shoulder, his elfin, goggle-covered eyes fixed on the screen. He squeaked some suggestions, which were translated by Sam into troll language. The troll answered with an occasional grunt, and continued.

"Do you have the codes?" asked Jack.

"He's not sure," said Sam. "The werewolves could have detected the spy chip and fed him false codes. Or, the codes could be outdated by the time we try to use them."

The Theran defense minister—a spindly man with an angular face and a bush of gray hair—interrupted, pointing at another wall-sized screen. It showed the blue and white ball of Thera hanging in space. The orbital space surrounding the planet was festooned with blinking red dots marking the EMP generators.

"We've now pinpointed all the generators," said the minister. "We can see their image in both visible light and microwaves, to detect any pulse they produce. Couldn't we scan them to find the Pilgrim wormhole and destroy it the way we did the werewolves'?"

"Not likely," said E'iouy. "Nobody . . . at least no Theran . . . has tracked a wormhole in flight. They're stealthy; very little electromagnetic signature. That's why wormholes could remain undetected for so long."

"But you closed the werewolf aperture," said Jack.

"They were stationary. Easy, visual target. They had no idea what we were planning."

On the screen, a shimmering cone of light erupted from one of the blinking dots, coursing downward to splash a blood-red circle on the planet's surface. The circle turned black.

"No!" shouted the defense minister. "THEY'VE TRIGGERED ONE!"

A frightened clamor echoed through the center, as the Theran engineers urgently scrutinized their console screens for clues to the target.

"Aslandia is struck!" exclaimed one of the engineers. "It is devastated. All signals lost."

"Well, if we can't destroy the wormhole, we must target the generators," said the defense minister. "Can we launch?"

One of the engineers tapped a key on his console to bring up on the wall screen the image of the activated generator. The gleaming cylinder was suspended against the blackness of space, its solar panels extended. Next to it lurked the glowing wormhole. "It's stationary! We can target it!" exclaimed the engineer. "Aslandia's neighboring country has a missile targeted."

On another screen, a white missile streaked aloft on a pillar of smoke and flame from a desert base into an azure sky.

Within minutes, the screen depicted the missile homing on the generator and wormhole.

"On target!" exclaimed the engineer.

The missile exploded—a silent, blast that spewed an expanding cloud of debris.

"Got it!" exclaimed Jack.

But A'eiio's expression remained grave. "No, we didn't."

Sure enough, the generator remained as before, intact.

As if in answer, the screen displaying the globe of Thera showed yet another red dot abruptly expanding, transmitting another cone of death onto the planet below.

"Bajanta is hit," declared one of the engineers grimly.

"Population ten million," said the defense minister, slumping into a chair.

"As I thought," said A'eiio, her wings sadly wafting back and forth. "The generators have protective mechanisms . . . some kind of high-energy beam that can detonate incoming missiles before impact. And we can't possibly target the wormhole. We can't detect it when

261

stationary. And since it has no mass, it can instantly accelerate far away, after a generator is triggered."

Another dot blossomed on the screen, to cries of despair. The burst targeted Tralia and surrounding countries, announced the engineer, putting his hands to his face in despair.

A screen showed another missile arcing upward from a launch pad near the country, only to detonate ineffectually far from the generator.

"We're helpless," said A'eiio. "Unless we can get the termination codes, we can only watch the planet die, country by country."

"Maybe there is something we can do," said Jack, turning to the defense minister. "I remember when I did a piece on missile technology, that your defense directorate was developing new, multiple-warhead targeting capability."

"Well, yes," said the defense minister, his brow furrowing. "The missiles were originally meant to aim at separate ground targets. But it was decided to upgrade their capability to hit multiple targets in space, in case we had to take out, for example, a collection of satellites. But these EMP generators are too far apart to use that technology."

"No, you don't target the separate generators with a missile. You target *one* generator with *multiple* warheads, including the dummies that I believe are on each booster!"

A'eiio interjected, "That might overwhelm the generators' defenses!"

Nodding his head in realization, the defense minister issued an order to the engineers, who turned to their controls, taking on the urgent task of programming a multiple-warhead missile to home its payloads on a single target.

Another dot blossomed on the screen, marking another country attacked.

"Do other countries have the multiple-warhead capability?" asked Jack.

"Not sure," said the defense minister tersely. "Nations keep their technology secret."

"But you can tell them what we're trying, right?"

"And give them classified information?" The defense minister shook his head decisively.

E'iouy laughed derisively. "You're worried about secrets when your planet is under attack? Minister, you have a responsibility beyond your own country."

Scowling at E'iouy for a long moment, the minister finally turned to his communication officer and instructed him to transmit globally the data on the multiple-warhead plan.

"The programming is done," announced the chief engineer. "But for now, we can only target one of several generators over our country."

"Launch what you can then!" exclaimed the minister.

Within moments, a view screen showed the fiery blast of a large intercontinental missile bursting from its silo in a roiling cloud of vapor and accelerating skyward.

Another screen showed its target, an orbiting EMP generator, ominously with a wormhole hovering alongside it.

"They're targeting us!" exclaimed an engineer, closely scrutinizing the image. "I see a figure at the wormhole, preparing to come through!"

Silence shrouded the control room, as the screen showed the missile vaulting upward, an onboard camera showing ejection of the broad nose cone that was its payload. That payload separated into a dozen warheads. First, one of the warheads disintegrated, then another, as the phalanx sped toward the generator. But then two warheads penetrated the generator's defense, exploding it into a myriad shimmering pieces that spun away into space.

The room erupted in cheers, stopping only when Steve, who had been crouched over a console, typing furiously, waved his gnarled hand and grunted loudly for attention.

"I think I have the codes!" he exclaimed. Ryan the elf emitted an emphatic screech, signaling his agreement.

"Only one way to find out," said Jack. "Try them!"

Steve activated a wall screen showing a map of Thera festooned with black, werewolf-skull icons.

"Those mark the positions of the werewolf soldiers," said the troll. "The warriors with active termination chips."

"But they are all on the planet," said the defense minister. "None in orbit. We must target those . . . the engineers . . . not the soldiers on the planet."

"The engineers are out of range, on the other side of the Pilgrim aperture," said Jack. "Their positions wouldn't show. They have to come through. Just wait. They'll come."

"Then take out whoever you can," said the minister coldly.

•   •   •

The Pilgrim wormhole sped through space toward the orbiting EMP generator, periodically adjusting its course to rendezvous. The generator's large parabolic dish was aimed at the daytime face of Thera below, with its blue oceans, wispy clouds, and continents tinged with green and brown.

The hole halted instantly, as would an aperture in space-time that possessed no mass, no inertia. A space-suited werewolf praetorian emerged from the hole's shimmering surface, floating, trailing a safety line, propelling himself with a precise shove from the exit ladder toward the generator's control panel.

"Skip the system check," commanded the Alpha over his suit communicator. "They might launch more missiles. Just trigger the generator so we can escape."

"Yes, Alpha," said the praetorian, his gaze warily sweeping the planet's surface for approaching missiles. Using the wrench strung on his wrist, he deftly opened the control panel, revealing the keypad and red button that would trigger the generator.

"This will be perhaps the most satisfying of all," said the Alpha. "The Confederated States have been our most annoying adversaries."

Hanging onto the cylinder with one hand, the suited werewolf laboriously punched in the activation code, a task made difficult by his bulky suit glove. But even as he completed keying in the code, his movement suddenly ceased, his hand hovering motionless over the red button. The other hand released its grasp on the cylinder, and the werewolf floated inertly in space.

"Push the button," commanded the Alpha from the Pilgrim control room on the other side of the hole.

The suited werewolf did not move.

"Push the button!" he commanded even more forcefully.

Still no movement.

Then, to his lieutenant, the Alpha growled, "He must be hesitating because there are Mythicals down there he may know."

"But he's dead!" exclaimed the Pilgrim pointing to a display of the praetorian's vital signs. The line registering the heartbeat was flat.

"Dead?" asked the Alpha in surprise. But after only a brief pause, he waved his claw in casual dismissal. "Perhaps a suit malfunction. Send another. He was a praetorian. He will be honored in death. His clan will be proud."

The dead engineer was hauled in by a space-suited Pilgrim from within the wormhole. The engineer's face was a mask of death, droplets of blood floating inside the helmet.

Outside the outer airlock of the Pilgrim chamber, another praetorian climbed into a suit. Given the fate of his comrade, he meticulously fastened its seals and rechecked them. He stepped through the door into the airlock chamber, and after it depressurized, moved through the inner door into the airless vacuum surrounding the wormhole. He pulled himself up the ladder and pushed off through the hole toward the generator.

"Alpha, I am now—" but then the second engineer went limp, floating inertly past the generator, tugging his safety line taught.

"What is happening?" exclaimed the Alpha. "Check the suits for sabotage! Send another!"

One after another praetorian engineer was dispatched through the hole, each immediately dying, until the vacuum chamber became piled with the dead bodies of five suited praetorians.

"You shouldn't send any more, until we figure out what is going on," suggested the Pilgrim operating the wormhole.

"Contact our surface force," instructed the Alpha. "They may know what is causing this problem." The Alpha paced the control room, muttering darkly.

An antenna was extended through the wormhole. After a long moment, the lieutenant looked up from the comm station, saying, "I have received only one reply,"

"Who?"

"Flaktuckmetang. He says all the others are dead. He says their termination chips were somehow activated. He says he was spared because his had been destroyed in the first EMP experiment."

. . .

The werewolf once known as Senator Warren Lee—what seemed like a lifetime ago—stood stunned amid hundreds of corpses of his species. The foul stink of death rose from the jumble of furred bodies. Some still clutched weapons, ready to enter the Pilgrim wormhole once it returned from its mission. Now, they were a battalion of the dead. Others had been hauling crates of explosives and had collapsed silently beside them.

How dishonorable a death! thought Flaktuckmetang. *How cowardly were these Therans, this human Jack March, to mass-murder his fellow warriors in such a despicable manner! They had not died in battle. Their clans would not honor them. Their heads would not be displayed in the Hall of the Fallen Warriors.*

True, he was no warrior, but he would avenge this perfidy. Someday, when he had died a natural death after a long and richly rewarded life, his valor would be remembered. Somehow, he would navigate the network of Mythicals wormholes back to his home planet, and would die there, his head to be severed and displayed.

He made one more reconnoiter of the camp to make sure that all the praetorians were, indeed, dead. Then, he returned to the control dome, where the image of the furious Alpha was projected on the wall.

He made his report, and the Alpha replied, "The Therans are targeting the generators with multiple warheads. You must stop the missiles. We cannot return through the aperture, so it is also up to you to avenge the cowardly act of killing our comrades."

Flaktuckmetang shifted uneasily before the large image. He didn't want to appear anything less that stalwart. But he had to ask an obvious question. "How shall I proceed, given that I am only one?"

The Alpha glared at him for a long moment, then said, "You are bordering on insubordination to even ask that question of your superior. But I have an agreement from the Pilgrims. There are two brothers on the planet, the Clarks. They are sending Theran mercenaries to your site. They will aid you in your mission."

"Excellent! Excellent!" declared Flaktuckmetang with renewed eagerness. "I apologize for the presumption, Alpha. I should have known you were making strategic plans that would lead to glorious success. I can—"

"I have also begun communication with the Mythical Wardens," interrupted the Alpha. "I am seeking to persuade them that the human Jack March has committed a capital offense against the Alliance by participating with the Therans in the mass-murder of our praetorians. I am asking that they supply the termination code for him, so that you may end his life as ignominiously as he did our brave comrades."

Flaktuckmetang grinned, showing his fangs. This would be a marvelous revenge! He saluted the Alpha and moved quickly out of the control dome, past the dozens of bodies to the prison dome. There, he walked down the rows of isolation cells, where prisoners were kept in pitch dark and sensory-deprived silence. All the werewolf prisoners were dead. But the Theran was not. She would be his way to glory.

He opened the door to see, laying inert on the plastic floor, the indenture Meri. She remained unconscious from the beating he and the other werewolves had administered. He hauled her up and clasped her bruised, puffy face in his claw, shaking and slapping it, until her less swollen eye opened, staring at him dully.

"Where is Jack March?" he demanded. "Where can I find him?"

Her head lolled forward, and she mumbled something he did not understand. He leaned closer.

She took a deep breath and spit in his face.

With a roar of rage, he slammed his claw into her head, lifted her up, and flung her over his shoulder. He did not notice her small ear piece dislodge itself and fall to the floor. Nor did he notice the camera that had ripped away from her dress and was also on the floor.

"I will bring you around," he declared. "I will make you tell me what I need to know." He stalked out, with her body hanging limp, swaying with each step, like a rag doll.

CHAPTER 27

"The werewolves were not . . . shall we say . . . as cooperative as we would have liked," said the rotund Christopher, settling his bulk into a chair in Nathan and David Clark's log-home mansion. He took a sip from the glass of very expensive, well-aged Theran liquor, as Nathan Clark sitting on the couch across from him did the same.

"You mean they were too untrusting to give you the trigger codes for the EMP generators," said David, sitting beside his brother, swirling his drink around in the glass, contemplating its rich amber hue.

"I tried to convince them. I pointed out that if their troops on Thera were compromised . . . or their engineers . . . they could not trigger the Palliation," said Christopher. "And that is exactly what happened. The Mythicals obtained the codes for their termination chips. We watched the werewolf ground troops die. We watched the engineers die in orbit. Now they cannot transit from Earth to Thera without being killed."

"Hmph. *Mythicals*," muttered David, taking a sip, as if to rid his mouth of the taste of the word.

"We need the generator trigger codes," said Christopher. "How will you accomplish that?"

"We can persuade the creatures," answered another voice. It was from a bald, muscular man in green fatigues and wearing a black machine pistol as a sidearm. "Even these animals' pride won't last long with our methods of persuasion," said Allan Roberson. The mercenary leaned forward in the leather chair beside Christopher.

Christopher grunted sarcastically. "You Therans believe that torture is the only way. That really is your style, isn't it?"

"You pay, we give results," said Roberson matter-of-factly.

"And, indeed, we are happy to procure your services and those of your fellow Theran soldiers," said Nathan. He turned to Christopher. "Captain Roberson and his security group have served us well in past missions, and I am sure they will serve us well this time."

"And I need to get my men into the field, to begin the mission, to meet the animals," said Roberson. "So, I need to know the parameters of that mission."

"Certainly," said Nathan, rising to stoke the fire in the massive stone fireplace. "First of all, you are to give the creature who is your contact . . . the werewolf with the absurd name . . . Flak-something . . . the impression that you have been dispatched to aid him in his quest. You are to help him obtain the codes from his leader so he can trigger the Palliation. And failing that, you are to obtain the codes by whatever means, so we can do it ourselves."

"I require a sufficient force," said Roberson. "I have recruited a thousand men . . . all professional, all battle-hardened. You will pay?"

"Whatever you require; whatever equipment you need," said Nathan.

Roberson turned to Christopher. "And I expect my men to be in command of sufficient forces from your own human colonies."

"Agreed," said Christopher.

"So, then, I need you to explicitly state our mission," said Roberson.

"As you know, the beasts have orbited several hundred electromagnetic pulse generators," said Christopher. "They are capable of obliterating the infrastructure of the nations they target. They have already struck several regions. Your mission is to take whatever steps necessary to make sure that their so-called Palliation is successful, and that Thera is cleansed."

"*Cleansed?*" spat Roberson. "So, you are asking us to ensure the destruction of our own people?" The mercenary now rose to tower over the group, his hand on his pistol, his eyes moving from man to man, as if deciding whom to target first.

"Yes," said David coolly. "And you and your men . . . and whatever companions and family they wish to include . . . will be fully protected from any danger. Either evacuated through our wormhole to Earth or safely housed in our colonies here. And once the Palliation has run its course, you will be offered wealth beyond any you have ever conceived of. And you will be among those leading the rebuilding of your civilization . . . the power elite . . . oligarchs."

After a long moment staring impassively at them, Roberson took his hand off his pistol and folded his arms. "Hmm," he said, a faint smile now rising on his face. He cocked his head in satisfied assent. "Well, then, I will speak to my men, and I'm sure that they will agree to those terms."

"And those who don't?" asked Christopher.

"I guarantee security. Accidents happen," said Roberson.

Nathan leaned against the fireplace, ruefully shaking his head. "I see that Therans are more like we humans than I had appreciated."

"I understand there is more to the mission," said Roberson.

"We have secretly transported about a hundred thermonuclear surface-to-air missiles to our colonies," said Christopher. "We will use them to close the Mythicals' wormholes. When targeted to those apertures, they will also devastate the terminals and the cities on the other side."

"And you want us to launch those missiles?"

"Yes, just after the Palliation and when the Mythicals' wormholes have arrived at the planet surface, to return their creatures," said Christopher.

"Leaving this planet to humans."

"And to select Therans such as you and your men."

Roberson laughed sarcastically. "And, of course, if anything goes wrong, we are giving you humans deniability. It will have been those 'monsters' the Theran mercenaries . . . *us* . . . who attempted this heinous act."

Nathan waved his hands dismissively. "But nothing will go wrong, we trust, given your expertise, and given that you have the incentive of immense wealth and power."

"Incentive doesn't aim missiles," said Roberson. "I know enough about these wormholes to know that they have never been tracked."

"Until now," said Christopher. "An engineer in one of our colonies has identified a characteristic electromagnetic signature of the wormholes. He has developed a targeting technique. Even now, our missiles are being programmed with the necessary targeting data."

"And you're sure it will work?"

"The missiles will target the wormholes, they will penetrate them, and the blast will close them and devastate the other side." Christopher poured himself another drink and took a healthy sip.

. . .

Flaktuckmetang braced himself against the vicious gale buffeting his body and let it blow away all the frustration and disappointment that had seemed to engulf him like a shroud. Standing on a ledge, he peered out over the wind-blasted landscape of the ogre planet, with its thick mat of low vegetation that had evolved to resist the constant winds.

He grinned, showing fangs. This was exactly the punishing climate he needed for the Warden Council meeting; and since he had requested the meeting, he was allowed to specify the location. The crushing gravity, the winds, the deluges of pelting rain, and the smothering heat would all be highly uncomfortable for those puny Mythical species that had been the werewolves' most implacable opponents—notably, the fairies, pixies, elves, angels, and leprechauns.

He had arrived earlier to prepare, and now the wormhole approached that brought those species to the planet. It paused before the yawning entrance to the vast subterranean city excavated into the mountain range that was the ogre's regional capitol. The ogres were diggers by nature, and over the eons they had tunneled far, creating a planet of subterranean metropolises.

The near-lethal weather—for his enemies—meant there would be no ceremonial exit onto the surface and procession into the meeting hall. The wormhole would not disgorge the Council members until it had sailed deep into the caverns, coming to rest in a protected hangar.

The wormhole hovered before the steel hangar door as it slid ponderously upward. The wormhole drifted slowly inside, the swirling colored auroras playing about its shimmering surface.

A fleet of hawk-like ogre aircraft sailed after the wormhole into the mountain, whose surface had been polished by eons of winds into a smooth, undulating sculpture.

Flaktuckmetang took a last triumphant breath and allowed himself a full-throated howl, to energize himself for the meeting.

He turned and shoved open the metal door back into the meeting hall, which had a floor-to-ceiling window looking out over the wind-whipped planet surface. He had chosen this hall, too. He could have requested a room nestled deep within the mountain city, where the Mythicals would feel more secure.

But he wanted the hated enemies to be constantly reminded that they were on a planet that would kill them if they took one step outside. Their constant feeling of disquiet would work to his advantage. They would want to make a quick decision.

The semicircular table in the hall was heaped with piles of ogre fare. As was the custom, guests were expected to grab chunks of meat, whole squirming creatures, vegetables, and other edibles from the common pile. Ogres paid little attention to their guests' sensibilities or customs.

The interior door opened, and the ogre Warden thumped into the room, his decorated testicles jangling, followed by his fellow Council members—vampire, fairy, troll, pixie, elf, angel, leprechaun, demon, gnome, bigfoot.

Each took a place around the table, some choosing to dig into a food pile, others visibly unsettled by the undifferentiated mounds.

As host, it fell to the ogre Warden to conduct the meeting. With a gargling rumble, he cleared his throat, and began.

"You are an exile," he said to the werewolf, his thick brow knitted in consternation. "Why are you here instead of a Warden?"

"Two reasons," answered Flaktuckmetang, pacing before the Council. "The Therans destroyed our aperture to their planet, leaving us stranded with no Warden. Many of us took refuge on the Pilgrim planet. And most damning, all of my fellow werewolves are dead at the hands of the Therans. I am the only one of my species that survived. And the only one that can safely remain there. They murdered all of my comrades by stealing the codes to our termination chips and activating them. My chip was accidentally neutralized some time ago."

"So, we will assume for the moment that you have some standing before us," said the ogre. "What do you request of the Council?"

"Justice," declared the werewolf. "The murder of hundreds of our kind demands the application of our laws. So, I request you to give me the Wardens' code for the termination chip for the one creature chiefly responsible for these evil acts. Its name is Jack March."

"How do we know that he was responsible for these crimes?" asked the ogre.

"I have proof," said Flaktuckmetang. "I captured a traitor." He stepped over to the side of the hall, grabbing a large carrying case and hauling it to the center of the room. He unlatched it and hauled out a battered Meri, standing her up before the Council.

"This creature entered our control center and planted a spying device in our system. It transmitted the termination codes that resulted in the mass murder of our praetorians."

"What have you done to this woman!" exclaimed the fairy Warden. "You have clearly tortured her. This is barbaric!"

Flaktuckmetang snorted derisively. "It is an indenture, of little significance in our culture." He flung Meri back into the case, slamming the cover and latching it.

"This is not—" began the ogre, but Flaktuckmetang cut him off.

"So, I demand the termination code for Jack March. And I further request that the vampires, the fairies, the pixies—all those Mythicals engaged in this crime—be punished to the maximum extent of your laws. We are magnanimously requesting only that justice for them be done according to their own species' laws."

"Magnanimous?" exclaimed the fairy Warden. "So, basically, you are allowing us to apply our *own* laws to our *own* citizens. Instead of attacking them yourself, as you have been known to do. How civilized." The fairy vibrated his wings in a sign of disgust.

The vampire Warden stood, glaring at the werewolf. "Our information is that your soldiers were the attackers. The responses by the Therans and the human Jack March were defensive, to stop you from devastating their planet. This Palliation of yours, I might add, was not authorized by this Council. If so, you are requesting revenge, not justice."

"*Devastating* their planet? No . . . ridding the planet of the burden of the population that was devastating it," declared Flaktuckmetang. "And I should point out that, as the Council requested, we gave the Therans time to save themselves . . . to mount a Remediation. But there was no other way but to save their planet with this extreme action. So, we ask for this limited justice for mass murder of our—"

"ENOUGH!" bellowed the troll. "This Council will countenance no further killing, even if it is according to your code. I call for a vote."

As Flaktuckmetang stood transferring his glare from one Warden to another, each voted to refuse to give him the code he requested. And each Warden declared that their species' exiles would not be punished.

The Wardens then stood and exited the hall, leaving the werewolf with a strange smile. He had lost the vote. But he had another plan.

Finally, only the ogre Warden was left, staring at Flaktuckmetang impatiently.

"You may depart with the others now," rumbled the ogre. "The decision has been made. I do not want you on this planet."

The werewolf folded his thick, furred arms, cocked his head, and grinned. "There is one small matter that should be settled . . . just between us."

"There are no matters between us . . . only Council matters."

"You have a son who is an exile. His Theran name, I believe is Mike. I believe he was wounded in a battle."

"He was sentenced for a youthful mistake. And the fact that he is my son has never compromised my duties as a Warden," declared the ogre.

"Do you love your son?"

"Of course I do."

"And you would not want to see any harm come to him . . . even perhaps being killed."

The ogre vaulted the table between them and thundered forward, clutching the werewolf by the neck and slamming him against the wall. Flaktuckmetang merely raised his claws, offering no resistance.

"You are threatening my son?" The ogre thrust his fanged, gray-green face into the werewolf's, his black eyes narrowing with hatred.

"Give me the code," whispered the werewolf conspiratorially. "It is a simple thing to give me the code to kill Jack March. And no one will know how the human died. The Pilgrims are supplying an army of mercenaries, which I will command. They will protect your son from whatever danger, from whatever . . . source . . . he might encounter." The werewolf hissed the word "source," rendering it a dire threat.

●   ●   ●

"The other countries have multiple-warhead targeting," said the Theran defense minister, a relieved expression on his face. "Six countries either have multiple-warhead targeting, or they can engineer their missile defenses to launch multiple missiles simultaneously. Aslandia had already taken out the generator that targeted its population. They had EMP-hardened missile facilities."

"It's a good start," said Jack. "But there are hundreds of generators. We have to target them, as well as make sure any werewolf engineers who try to trigger them are killed."

As he spoke, wall screens around the vast control room were showing missiles launched, and generator after generator exploding into whirling chunks of metal that careened away into the blackness of space.

"Well, they have ceased attempting to trigger the generators," said Steve, peering myopically at the wall screen map of Thera. It showed a mass of black icons overlain with X's, marking where werewolf praetorians had been killed via their termination chips.

"Now can we look for Meri?" asked Geniato pleadingly.

Sam comforted him, placing her hand on his shoulder. "We know that the werewolf has her. Wherever they are, we'll find them."

"But you don't have a clue," said Geniato.

Jack shook his head sadly. "I'm sorry. We don't know. Her camera and microphone are still in the cell."

An eerie, faint whine interrupted them, emanating from the ceiling of the control center.

They looked up in horror to see a hole abruptly begin growing in the ceiling, expanding rapidly, the roof seeming to disappear into an utter blackness.

Before any could react, a shower of grenades erupted from the hole, scattering across the expanse of the control center.

"RUN!" shouted Jack, grabbing Sam by the hand and sprinting for the door. He slammed it open, and they dove through, followed by the two fairies—A'eiio yanking Ryan after her, and E'iouy clutching Steve.

A few engineers followed, as they barely made it through the doors, when a rapid-fire succession of blasts gutted the building. An acrid smoke burst from the door, and the roof began to smolder.

"WE HAVE TO LEAVE!" Jack exclaimed as bursts of automatic rifle fire sounded from within the building.

Sam wrenched herself away from him and ran back toward the building, following Theran soldiers, their rifles at the ready.

"They're killing the survivors!" she exclaimed over her shoulder. "Geniato is still there!" She glanced back at him, and he could see that her eyes now shone with a demonic red glow.

Trucks began to rumble up to the building, carrying Theran soldiers, who began surrounding the center, preparing to breach.

"What the hell happened?" asked Jack, as they watched the battle unfold.

"The Pilgrim wormhole," said A'eiio. "It's the perfect assault weapon. It doesn't reflect radio waves, it's nearly silent compared to aircraft, and in its spherical form, it can slice through even the thickest armor."

"But who—" began Jack, who stopped, his eyes widening in fright.

"What is it?" asked A'eiio.

"A buzz!" he exclaimed. *"There's a buzzing in my head!"*

CHAPTER 28

Jack stood paralyzed with fear, as the buzzing intensified, becoming a searing pain piercing to the depths of his skull. He realized he had only moments before the termination chip would trigger the explosion that would sever his brain stem, plunging him into the ultimate blackness of death.

Immersed in the terror and the searing agony in his head, he was only vaguely aware of Sam emerging from the building, carrying Geniato. They were followed what appeared to be a mercenary, who leveled an assault rifle at the two, preparing to fire. But a gust of wind from gossamer wings swept past Jack, and the soldier's head separated from his body, his corpse collapsing to the ground. More mercenaries poured from the control center, as the wormhole that had transported them lifted skyward from the building, hovering overhead, gunfire spewing from within it, raking the area.

Jack collapsed to the ground in agony, as he saw Flaktuckmetang follow a troop of mercenaries out of the building, his eyes gleaming, holding a small control box, as he ducked behind a truck.

As his mind clouded, Jack felt powerful arms lift him up, hauling him backward. Gunfire and explosions erupted, and as he was being carried away, his pain-dulled gaze shifted upward, to see a constellation of wormholes sailing into view above the base, billowing, multihued auroras playing about their edges. They sank rapidly to the ground, and legions of Mythicals poured from their depths—vampires, trolls, angels, ogres, fairies—to attack the growing horde of invaders. They joined the Theran soldiers in a tumultuous, bloody battle against the mercenaries.

Fairies and angels swooped overhead in deft aerobatic maneuvers, evading the barrage of gunfire. They wielded gleaming swords that they slashed with brutal efficiency at the soldiers, cutting them down.

Vampires sprinted across the battlefield, lightning-fast reflexes enabling them to evade a mercenary's hail of bullets until they reached their target, their jaws gaping wide to clamp onto throats, tearing them out, leaving the mercenaries slumping to the ground, dead.

Naked pixies, their eyes glowing crimson, darted through the turmoil of combatants, their petite bodies only flesh-colored blurs. A pixie picked a target mercenary, reached him before he could bring his rifle to bear, hoisted his body into the air, and slammed him to the ground with such force to shatter his body into a lifeless, broken hulk.

Bellowing ogres were not so agile, allowing bullets to slam into their bodies as only annoyances, as they seized mercenaries, tearing their bodies in half.

Then suddenly, he was no longer amid the battle on the sprawling military base; no longer engulfed in the melee. He had been pulled back through a wormhole, now resting against a large, gray-green body in its surrounding chamber, the noise of conflict now distant, peering back through the wormhole to a battlefield that rapidly shrank away as the wormhole vaulted upward.

The pain, the buzzing, began to thankfully subside. He panted in relief, turning to see who had saved him.

Coal-black eyes stared down at him, and Mike the ogre grinned showing his stubby fangs.

"You are getting better?" he asked.

"What happened?"

"The werewolf got your termination code," he explained in his guttural voice. As the atmosphere thinned with the increasing altitude, the ogre helped him through the inner airlock door, through the outer door, and into the control room of the wormhole. They appeared to be on the ogre planet, although an elf was hunched over at the controls, his small hands busily operating the controls, his goggled-eyes staring intently at the view screen.

The hulking ogre carried Jack gently over to a chair, hefting him as easily as a child would a doll.

"Why am I still alive?" Jack asked woozily.

"It was the fairy. A'eiio. She called us when the attack began. We got here quick. Wormholes can move pretty fast. You rest. We go back when things have settled down." Mike then turned to complain to the elf about the too-fast ascent, to which the elf replied with an annoyed screech that was obviously an insult.

"Are they all right . . . Sam, A'eiio, the others?" Jack called after the retreating ogre. "

The ogre turned back briefly, shrugging his massive shoulders and chuckling. "They might be a little tired. And the other ogres will have to have some bullets removed."

∙   ∙   ∙

"You failed!" snarled the Alpha, as Flaktuckmetang slumped on the floor of the Pilgrim warehouse, leaning against the steel wall of the vacuum chamber containing the Pilgrim wormhole.

Flaktuckmetang looked dully up at the huge werewolf, raising the control box in weak triumph. "But I'm sure I killed the human, Jack March. I saw him in agony. I'm sure his brain is destroyed."

Roberson the mercenary emerged from the outer chamber door, hauling a fellow mercenary whose chest oozed with blood from a bullet wound. Roberson himself limped from a deep, bleeding gash in his thigh. He pulled the other soldier across the floor of the warehouse, to join a bedraggled, wounded group of other mercenaries being tended by their medic. Binding a clotting pad against his wound, he returned to the two werewolves, thrusting his battle-grimed face into the Alpha's.

"Your intelligence was shit!" he spat. "You sent us into a killing field!"

He clutched the Alpha's battle harness as if to attack him, but the much larger werewolf easily ripped his hands away.

Christopher hurried up to them, waving his pudgy hands in an attempt to calm the two.

"They did the best they could," he said. "They could not have known the Mythicals would be so quick to respond."

Not taking his furious gaze from the Alpha, Roberson commanded, "Pilot your wormhole to your main colony. We have operatives there. We will launch the missiles . . . *now.*"

"*Missiles?*" asked the Alpha. "Those *electronic components* were missiles? Is that what you were transporting to your colonies? What do you plan to do with them?"

"We will destroy the Mythicals' wormholes, eliminate this threat," said Roberson.

The Alpha unleashed a furious bellow and reached for his pistol. Christopher backed away, panic rising on his face. But before the Alpha could draw his weapon, Roberson leveled his sidearm at the werewolf, snapping off the safety. His comrades, seeing his action, snatched up their weapons. Flaktuckmetang struggled to his feet, his eyes widening at both the news of the missiles and the threat to his Alpha.

The Alpha's sergeant leaped forward to intervene, and Roberson's gaze briefly diverted from the Alpha. Taking advantage of the distraction, the Alpha slipped a small object into Flaktuckmetang's claw.

The diversion was short-lived, as a mercenary slammed his rifle butt against the sergeant's head shattering his skull, and he collapsed, dead. Flaktuckmetang took the opportunity to slink away, ducking behind a pillar and out the door.

"Find him!" commanded Roberson, his gaze still riveted on the Alpha. "Secure the other beasts!"

A platoon of mercenaries rushed from the building to the praetorian encampment in the Pilgrim compound. The Alpha stood in furious impotence as shouts, snarls, and bursts of gunfire arose outside.

"This is unconscionable!" exclaimed the Alpha. "You know those missiles will not only close the wormholes. You will destroy the vacuum chambers . . . the entire terminal complexes . . . entire cities of the Alliance."

"What do you care about the Alliance? You and your fellow . . . *creatures* . . . have worked against that very Alliance . . . against the other species."

The Alpha opened his claws, signaling an eagerness to embed them in the mercenary's neck, to tear out his throat. "We have been faithful to the Alliance. We have done what we believed necessary to preserve the planet Thera for the Alliance."

"You have no power to stop us from closing those wormholes," said Roberson. "But you do have the power to enable us to trigger the generators. Give us the codes. We will cleanse the planet. You will have revenge. We're not endangered by termination chips." Leveling his rifle at the Alpha, he signaled two of the mercenaries to seize the hulking werewolf, dragging him to a chair and binding him.

Now Christopher felt brave enough to approach the restrained Alpha. "Your race engineered the Palliation," he said. "We can make it succeed. After all, the Therans murdered your comrades."

"That was a military action against praetorians who had pledged their lives to service. Your missiles will kill innocents, trap Mythicals species on Thera to die, destroy their cities. I will not give you the codes to aid your depraved plan."

Christopher nodded to Roberson, then turned to leave. "This is your operation. You do what must be done."

Roberson pulled out a knife, leaned close to the Alpha's face, smiling. He slowly, excruciatingly pushed the knife into the flesh of the Alpha's shoulder.

The Alpha roared in both agony and defiance, as black blood flowed from the wound down his furred chest. He peeled back his lips to defiantly bare his fangs, straining against his bonds and snapping viciously at the mercenary.

. . .

The Alpha's roar reverberating from the building spurred Flaktuckmetang to even greater speed in escaping. Hearing the rattle of gunfire, he stopped at the building's corner and peered around to the praetorian encampment to see the violent turmoil of a massacre. Mercenaries fired their assault rifles at captive praetorians, hauling their bodies into a bleeding pile. Two mercenaries strode among fallen werewolves, firing rounds into the writhing bodies of the wounded. Enraged howls arose from the wounded survivors when the mercenaries slammed their boots down on the heads of the fallen, crushing them, preventing forever their display in the Hall of Heroes.

Flaktuckmetang took a deep breath to calm himself, deciding his next move. Two alternatives. He could attack. Or, he could wait until nightfall. Then he could kill as many mercenary guards as possible, avenging the praetorians, earning the Alpha's acceptance, perhaps even honor.

He chose a third; to run.

He pulled out the small, silver memory chip that the Alpha had given him and contemplated it. It held the EMP generator activation codes, which would make him a prime quarry in an intensive search, and also the subject of torture by the mercenaries. And even if he gave the codes up, he would receive a quick, casual bullet to the brain.

He backed away from the corner, figuring a plan. He had to think ahead. He was probably safe from the other Mythicals. But they were smart. So, there was a slight chance they might somehow transit through the Pilgrim wormhole to this hell of a planet. If they did, he could use his hostage to bargain for his life, maybe even for safe passage. So, he needed to keep the Theran indenture alive, to bring her with him.

The mercenaries were still occupied with murdering wounded praetorians, so he could easily sneak around to the back of the airdome barracks where he had chained Meri.

He sprinted swiftly to the structure, and taking out his knife, slit the fabric, taking care not to puncture any of the air cells that maintained the dome's shape. Meri was huddled on the floor beside his bunk, her food and water bowl beside her, the chain around her ankle.

"Make a sound and you die," he hissed, unlocking the chain and transferring it to her wrist. He attached the other end to the belt of his harness.

"Where are we going?" she asked in a voice weakened by the trauma inflicted upon her. "I am no use to you. I have no information. Let me go."

"You *are* of use to me," he said. "We're leaving." He drew his knife from its scabbard. "If you slow me down, I can quickly detach that small wrist."

He wrenched the chain, dragging her out through the slit in the tent. She whimpered in pain, and he turned and clutched her throat, punching her hard in the face.

"Another sound, you die."

Then, taking care not to alert the mercenaries, he loped across the compound to the line of armored personnel carriers the Pilgrims used to venture outside the compound. Meri managed to keep up, limping along on bare, bloodied feet.

Flaktuckmetang ducked from one vehicle to another along the line, stopping to allow a sentry to pass by.

Then, a minor problem dawned on him. Actually, a couple of problems. For one thing, the Theran mercenaries were after him. And for another, the compound gates were built to withstand any vehicle impact. So, even if he managed to steal a vehicle, he would be trapped!

Hauling Meri to his side by her chain, he crouched on the ground, pondering what to do next.

The rumble of vehicle engines starting up caused him to stand up to see exhaust billowing from the front three armored carriers in the line. They were leaving! *Luck!*

He ducked along a row of parked carriers until he reached the last one in the line.

More luck! No guards patrolled near the idling vehicles, all of them occupied with killing the werewolves or searching for him. He yanked open the back cargo door of the last carrier and dragged Meri in. He drew his knife and leaped forward, holding it at the throat of the driver, who gasped in terror.

"I just want to get out," he whispered, his muzzle close to the driver's ear. "Get me out, I free you with no harm."

The driver nodded gingerly, given that the knife was hard against his throat.

Flaktuckmetang grinned. He would relish—once the convoy was well away from the compound—burying his fangs in the driver's throat and tearing it out. And making a meal of the driver. He was hungry. And he hadn't tasted human flesh, only Theran.

No doubt he would survive just fine, perhaps even prosper, on this planet of weak, degenerate creatures.

CHAPTER 29

"You *can* go back to Thera," Sam said gently, her small arm encircling Jack's waist. "The werewolf is gone. The trigger is gone. We're sure."

"Yeah, well, they say the body forgets pain," said Jack, standing with her before the airlock door of the ogre wormhole. "It's not true. I'll never forget that feeling, like a hot poker stabbing into my brain."

"I understand if you don't go through."

"I didn't say I wouldn't. I'll try to forget the pain. But I will remember the hell that monster put me through . . . what he put *everybody* through. And I'll remember that he still has Meri. I'll go."

With that, he pulled open the airlock door, and they stepped into it and through the inner door to stand before the wormhole. The interdimensional bubble hovered in the center of the chamber, drifting slowly back and forth, held by the magnetic fields produced by the metal probes encircling it. The faint swirling aurora of colored lights played about its edges.

"We've flattened the exit zone," said the voice over the speaker. They could see that the magnetic field had been adjusted to warp one side of the hole into a flat surface that wormhole-travelers could safely traverse without being sliced by the infinitely sharp interdimensional edge.

Jack and Sam stepped through to find themselves outside the main defense control center of the Theran nation, Califana. Walking through its doors, they found that the huge hall resembled the now-destroyed center of the Confederated States. It held rows upon rows of glowing monitoring consoles crowded with images, arrays of constantly changing numbers, and the hieroglyphics of equations. Each station was manned by an engineer who alternately scrutinized his individual screens and glanced nervously up at the array of wall-sized displays depicting the Califanan defense installations. One screen in particular attracted the most attention. It showed the map of the Theran globe encircled with blinking red dots marking the remaining EMP generators. Another screen that warranted frequent scrutiny showed a fleet of missiles poised on their launch pads. The row of white obelisks resembled some arcane historical monuments, but the missiles' tips held the latest nuclear warheads capable of obliterating cities—or hopefully orbiting EMP generators.

Wendy approached them wearing a physician's white jacket, her snowy wings extending through slits in the back.

"No buzzing," Jack breathed thankfully to her, taking a deep, relieved breath and letting it out.

"Excellent," said Wendy. "We have procured the device to extract the chip. We found it in the werewolf camp when we searched for Meri. We hope this torture will be over for you."

"Great!" With that, Jack began to follow the angel from the control center to the military base's clinic. But Sam took his hand, squeezing it, in an unspoken message that she would come with him.

He smiled in gratitude, and together they made the walk across the military base to the clinic building.

Entering a surgical suite there, Wendy directed him to lay face-down on the operating table, while she positioned a small wand over the base of his skull. He felt the sting of a needle, as she administrated a local anesthetic.

"What's the wand do?" he asked.

"Without the wand, the chip activates," she said softly, as she leaned down to scrutinize the incision made to install the chip. "It's why I can't just go in and remove the chip surgically."

"Could it activate anyway?"

She said nothing for a long, tense moment. "I have to be honest. We're not sure the werewolves didn't program a security code into the extractor. If such a code were not entered, there's a possibility the device could trigger the chip. And it looks like the chip itself has a trigger that prevents tampering. Do you want me to continue?"

Jack clenched his jaw. He felt Sam's small hand on his back. "I have to get this thing out," he said quietly. "Otherwise, I won't be of use to anybody."

"All right, then," said Wendy. "Here's what I'll do. I've studied the extractor, and I'm fairly sure I know how it works. It will pinpoint the chip and insert an extraction probe, attach it, inactivate the chip's tampering trigger, and pull it out. Ready?"

"Ready," said Jack.

He heard the whine of the extractor powering up, felt pressure on his anesthetized skin, felt his flesh being pierced.

A faint buzz arose in his skull.

Chapter 30

Roberson limped down the row of monitors in the Pilgrim control room, peering over the shoulders of the mercenary technicians. The monitors showed the Pilgrim surface-to-air missiles, mounted on their wheeled carriers, arrayed around the globe. Some showed the missiles enveloped in the gloom of a local night, as faintly visible white cylinders rising vertically. Others showed the missiles gleaming brightly in the Theran daytime. At those sites, mercenaries were busily stringing cables leading to the control huts and plugging them in.

"Tell them to hurry up!" Roberson commanded the technicians. "The Therans could have tapped our communications."

"No worries, sir," said one of the technicians. "These guys want their revenge."

"When those missiles hit those wormholes . . . sweet, sweet revenge!" exclaimed another.

The others nodded in grim agreement, still vivid in their memories were the devastating firefights in which Mythicals and Theran soldiers had wounded or killed many of their comrades.

Roberson stepped outside to check on the missiles at his own site. They would not be needed. No Mythicals wormholes would show up here. If all went as planned, they would be lured to the military sites around the globe, to be destroyed by the missiles.

Beyond the missile array, the Pilgrim wormhole now floated in a clearing in the thick woods of the Pilgrim colony in the Confederated States. It shimmered faintly in the moonless night.

Satisfied that the missiles were ready, Roberson returned to the control hut, a barn on the colony's outskirts. Now, the Clark brothers and Christopher had appeared, peering over the shoulders of the technicians.

"Are they ready?" asked Christopher.

"Nearly," said Roberson curtly. "You can see as well as I can," he said, gesturing at the technicians.

Nathan Clark leaned against the barn wall, crossing his arms, staring coolly at Roberson. "You have failed so far. Let's see if you can get this attack right."

"Failure? We successfully engaged the enemy," Roberson shot back. "And we lost men. That's the business we're in. We account for losses in our plans."

David Clark chuckled wryly. "Yes, but not those kinds of losses. We're here to review your plan, which we hope is adequate to accomplish the mission. We frankly don't see how this plan will lure the Mythicals' wormholes into missile range."

"I don't expect you to understand military tactics," said Roberson, intently scanning the monitors. "We will launch multiple simultaneous attacks on the Theran bases, precisely coordinated. I've dispatched a squad to each base. We know the last attack drew the creatures in. They will believe the new attacks are merely repeats. And, they will believe that since they repelled the first one by bringing in their wormholes, the same tactic will work again. And since all the launches are triggered from here, we can make them as close to simultaneous as possible, to avoid the creatures warning one another."

"Are the missiles sufficient?" asked David Clark.

"Three missiles are deployed near each base . . . thermonuclear. We have the targeting algorithm your technician developed programmed in to detect the wormholes and launch the instant any are in range."

"And if those missiles are inadequate? Or, if they're destroyed?"

"My men have shoulder-mounted missiles. If the wormholes approach the base, they can launch them to close the apertures. Not as much damage on the other side, but sufficient."

Nathan Clark added, "Well, you also failed to obtain the codes from the werewolf's leader. That needs to be done while there are still enough generators to significantly damage the planet's infrastructure. They are being rapidly destroyed."

Roberson resisted the urge to pull out his pistol and simply dispatch these annoying humans. A simple bullet to the forehead for each of these aliens.

After all, he was a Theran, albeit a traitor to his species. He had done everything possible to extract the EMP generator activating codes. Every violent thing.

He flashed back to the bloody, gutted corpse of the werewolf Alpha, sagging in the chair to which he was bound. He remembered the grisly business of crushing the creature's skull in front of his captive soldiers, to persuade them to cooperate. He knew that was the ultimate, horrifying act to the creatures. They didn't fear death, but they did fear not having their heads returned to their Hall of Heroes, to be displayed.

But none of his tactics worked. Not even executing those soldiers, one by one, and crushing their skulls with an assault vehicle, while the others looked on.

He answered Clark. "The missile attacks will serve two purposes. They'll cut off the Mythicals. And, they'll stop the destruction of the generators long enough for us to get the codes. After all, there is one werewolf left. He escaped your compound. He is somewhere on Earth and likely has the codes. Once the Mythicals' wormholes are closed, and we risk no interference from them, we will pursue him."

With that, Roberson instructed the technicians to confirm once again that the mercenary-led human commando teams were in place at the other Theran defense sites. One after another, the technicians signaled readiness.

"Launch," commanded Roberson.

. . .

The specter of sudden death that had haunted Jack was gone! With Sam beside him, he strode back into the Califanan base control room with a renewed energy, a grim determination.

"The chip is out!" he exclaimed, and A'eiio hugged him with relief.

"More good news," said the fairy. "We took out two more EMP generators. We're down to a hundred or so. They're still an active threat to many nations, but we're getting there. And, there's no evidence that werewolves are attempting to passage through the Pilgrim wormhole to trigger them."

Now crouching over the control consoles were Steve the troll, Ryan the elf, and many of their fellow Mythicals. They had joined the Califanan technicians at the monitors.

The wall screens periodically showed a salvo of missile launches from a Theran base. They streaked toward another generator, leaving contrails in the azure sky. Moments later, another screen showed a generator's destruction, as one of the missiles managed to penetrate the machine's defenses. The cylinder silently exploded into a rapidly expanding cloud of metal pieces, its solar wings and parabolic reflector tumbling, glimmering away into space.

E'iouy returned from checking the status of the monitoring stations. He shook his head in worry.

"There are still many generators in stationary orbits over regions not reachable by the missiles," he said. "And there are still the ones over nations that have already been attacked. If the Pilgrims get the operational codes, they could re-deploy the generators."

"So, there's still the possibility of a global Palliation?" asked Jack.

"Unfortunately, yes."

"How about using the Mythicals' wormholes to take them out? Like the Pilgrim wormhole that attacked the control center?" he asked.

"We can't risk it. There's the very real possibility that the generators have defenses against the wormholes. While we're fairly sure wormholes can't be detected at a distance, a generator could identify one up close. One EMP burst would close a wormhole, which would be catastrophic."

"Then use the wormholes to transport the missiles into range."

E'iouy shook his head. "They're intercontinental missiles. Far too large to pass through a wormhole."

The Califanan general, a squat, barrel-chested man with a mop of white hair, entered the center, approaching the group.

"We've started transporting missiles to put them in range of the generators," he said. "But it'll be many days before they're positioned and launched."

"Well, we can only hope that—" began E'iouy, when the general held up a hand, his brow furrowing. He touched a communicator earpiece.

"I'm getting a call from base security," he said, frowning. "There's a breach from the south."

A loud thud shook the building, as the elves scrutinizing their consoles skrittered a warning. The trolls and Theran technicians sounded alarms, as well.

The general scanned their consoles. "We're getting multiple attacks around the globe," he announced. "They're coordinated."

Another thud of a distant explosion shook the building; and Jack, Sam, E'iouy, and A'eiio rushed outside to see truckloads of soldiers speeding toward the south fence of the sprawling base.

An explosion reverberated to the north, one to the west, then one to the east.

"They're attacking from all sides," declared E'iouy. "We need to contact our Wardens, to have the wormholes deployed to bring in our reinforcements."

He turned to re-enter the building, but Jack remained, a puzzled look on his face. He shook his head as sporadic bursts of gunfire sounded from the four directions. Mike loomed behind him, preparing to join soldiers headed for the battle. Jack grasped his massive arm to stop him.

"You were a soldier?" he asked.

"Yes, before my exile."

"What would you think of multiple attacks on widely separated targets by relatively small forces? These sound like only small numbers of attackers, right?"

Mike thought for a long moment, his great ogre head swiveling about, scanning the base.

"Trap," he growled and turned to lumber back into the building. Jack followed, to find E'iouy leaning over a communication console manned by Ryan.

"They've given permission," he said. "The wormholes have been dispatched with reinforcements. They will be on station very quickly."

"*Trap!*" repeated Mike emphatically. "They want the wormholes in range."

E'iouy shook his head in puzzlement. "But there's no way they can track them if they are moving. Only if they're stationary and nearby. Like the werewolf wormhole was when it was targeted. And we've developed maneuvers to prevent that."

"*Still* feels like a trap," repeated Mike insistently.

"Then we'll spring it," said Jack, turning to Ryan. "Message the Wardens to expect a missile attack . . . to activate the defenses."

The elf launched into a frenzy of screechy phone calls.

E'iouy joined him, asking, "How can you possibly guard against missiles? Aren't you endangering the wormholes?"

"We prepared," said Jack. "When we were planning to close the werewolf wormhole with missiles, I realized that all the wormholes were vulnerable, including the Mythicals'. So, I asked the trolls to work with the elves to devise a defense system. You'll see. It'll be pretty spectacular."

The explosions and the rattle of automatic gunfire drew closer, and Jack and the others sprinted outside, taking cover behind a troop carrier. They hunkered down as bullets ricocheted off the carrier with loud clangs.

"Look up!" directed Jack, and they saw above them, a wormhole gliding down through the clouds, growing into the shimmering transparent orb they had seen so often. But inside the hole, they could see—instead of the usual vacuum chamber interior—a large black sphere, studded with cylinders.

"What—" began E'iouy, but Mike interrupted him, bellowing,

"MISSILES INCOMING!" He threw his massive body over the others to shield them. Three missiles materialized from three directions, speeding toward the wormhole, leaving white contrails.

"They'll destroy the hole!" exclaimed E'iouy.

"They won't," declared Jack. "Shield your eyes!"

Just as the missiles reached the wormhole, it erupted in a seething fireball of blinding, white-hot light, spewing cascades of sparks.

E'iouy and the others gasped as the fireball hissed and sputtered, radiating waves of blistering heat.

As the missiles penetrated the roiling fireball, their casings melted, exploding into harmless fragments that showered down, rattling against the metal of the troop carrier and littering the ground. A large fragment slammed into Mike, bouncing harmlessly off his armored skin.

A pall of gray smoke obscured the sky where the wormhole had been, and they peered upward, trying to see through it. Finally, it began to clear.

"It's gone!" cried Sam. *"It's destroyed!"*

"That's what the attackers will believe," said Jack. "But the instant the grenades were launched from inside the wormhole, it accelerated away. It's fine."

"Grenades?" asked E'iouy.

"Thermite grenades," said Jack. "The big sphere you saw inside the wormhole was a grenade launcher. It was triggered by radar to shoot out a hundred thermite grenades the instant the missiles grew close enough. They burn at several thousand degrees. They created a fireball hot enough to detonate and destroy the missiles, shielding the wormhole. We should get back inside. The missiles were probably thermonuclear, and there is likely radiation that needs to be cleaned up."

They rushed back into the control room, to find the general conferring with Ryan, Steve, and others at the monitoring consoles.

"Did all the defenses work?" asked Jack. "Were all the missiles destroyed?"

"Yes," rumbled Steve. "All the wormholes survived . . . globally. We could tell that all the missiles were launched at precisely the same time. *Precisely!* That means they were triggered from the same place."

"That means there's a central Pilgrim control center," said Jack. "And that means the Pilgrim wormhole is probably there. And *that* means we can find it, capture it, and transit to Earth to go after the werewolf Flak and save Meri." He turned to Steve, who was overseeing the consoles. "Can you pinpoint the headquarters?"

The troll began ranging up and down the rows of consoles, issuing instructions, querying the operators. He returned, nodding his gnarled head and grinning with brown teeth.

"We're gathering signal data from the other sites. We should be able to triangulate a position," he said.

"But how could we possibly capture a wormhole?" asked Sam.

"I may have an idea," said Jack, taking up his laptop and retreating to make a phone call.

CHAPTER 31

"*Nothing!*" triumphantly declared the Theran mercenary Roberson, striding from monitor to monitor in the Pilgrim control room. "Nothing left of the wormholes. They're *gone*. Now the only Mythicals we have to deal with are those left behind."

"You're sure?" asked Christopher regarding Roberson dubiously.

The soldier shot him an annoyed look and tapped one of the screens decisively. "Just look at the feed from our drones."

With that, the technician called up video showing a wormhole hovering above a missile base. A trio of speeding missiles etched contrails across the landscape toward their target; then a blinding flash of light, and an empty sky.

"You can review all the other sites. All the same. All show the wormholes closing in a flash. The Mythicals threat is gone. Now, we can concentrate on capturing that werewolf, Flak-whatever, and getting those trigger codes."

"But they're going to continue to destroy the generators," said David Clark.

"They won't be nearly as successful as they have been," said Roberson. "Our forces around the globe have withdrawn with acceptable casualties. Shortly, I'll order them repositioned to attack the Theran missiles. Our reconnaissance indicated many are vulnerable, because they're being transported over land. Many won't reach their destinations."

"So, the next step?" asked Nathan Clark.

"I've got a platoon of a dozen men armed and ready to go through your aperture and pursue the werewolf. And if you have no more questions, I've got to launch that mission."

Before any of the others could react, Roberson donned his armored vest heavy with grenades and ammunition pouches, took up his assault rifle and left. On a control room video screen, a dozen heavily armed mercenaries sprinted to the Pilgrim wormhole and began hauling themselves up its ladder.

.   .   .

James and Louisa March stood frozen at the controls on the Earth side of the Pilgrim wormhole, as the mercenaries filed from the vacuum chamber into the warehouse. The brawny soldiers quickly assembled at the building entrance, checking their imposing arsenal of rifles, grenade launchers, and shoulder-mounted missiles. Echoing through the warehouse came the decisive metallic click of rifle bolts being drawn and the terse commands of orders being given.

"Can we do this?" Louisa whispered timorously, grasping James's arm. "Can we pilot this wormhole to Jack? *Should* we do this?"

"You know how we feel about what's been happening. And Jack needs us to do this . . . to find the werewolf . . . to stop the Palliation. We promised him."

"We're betraying our own kind."

"We're trying to stop a massacre of global proportions."

"And, we'll have to go . . . out *there*," she said, shivering at the prospect of venturing into the ecological wasteland outside the compound.

"We have to. Jack will go, and so must we. He's never been out there. He would die. So would the others."

The middle-aged couple briefly held hands to bolster their resolve, and James turned back to the control panel. He mentally rehearsed the rapid sequence of control commands needed to hijack the wormhole, instantly vaulting it away from the Pilgrim colony on Thera. What if somebody was in the chamber with the wormhole, exposed to the vacuum of space? He steeled himself against the possibility. That person would explode into unrecognizable fleshy pulp.

He scrutinized the video screen showing the inside of the chamber. The wormhole floated in the middle, imprisoned by the magnetic fields emanating from the hundreds of cylindrical electromagnets dotting the sides of the chamber. Through the wormhole he could see the clearing in the woods where the wormhole now floated on Thera.

He checked the status of the magnets. All were stable. He nodded to Louisa, who bent to the task of checking the propulsion electromagnets at the ends of long, robotic arms that rapidly adjusted themselves in the chamber to drive the wormhole in the other universe.

"Let's turn off the shaping field," whispered Louisa. "Nobody will notice. It will keep anybody from entering the wormhole from the other side."

James shook his head decisively. "We'd have to withdraw the ladder first. They would notice that in the control room."

He glanced at the mercenaries in the warehouse to see if he and Louisa had attracted any attention with their nervous fidgeting and whispering. But the soldiers were busily shouldering their weapons, preparing to deploy. James shrugged nervously, changing his mind.

"All right. The instant they're gone, I'll retract the ladder. Then, you turn off the shaping field. That'll stop anybody from coming up. I'll make an excuse."

"What?" she asked.

James shook his head, beads of sweat rising on his forehead.

"Make sure you're ready for our return," said a voice behind them, making them both flinch. It was Roberson, staring at them suspiciously, holding his rifle. "We'll need to get back through quickly."

"Uh . . . sure . . . of course," said James.

"You look nervous," said Roberson. "Something wrong?"

Louisa answered. "A bit of a fluctuation in one of the containment magnets. We just need to make sure it's replaced before any transit."

"Do whatever you need to quickly. Once we get those generator codes from the werewolf, we'll want to come back through . . . to apply them."

He turned and left, barking orders to his men and exiting the warehouse. The roar of engines starting up told James and Louisa the mercenaries were preparing to exit the compound on their mission. Sure enough, the next sounds were the deep whine of the front gate's electric motor; the rattle of the gates opening; and the sound of the troop carrier engines fading.

"Ready?" asked James.

Louisa peered at the dials, ensuring that the fields were all stable. "Now!" she exclaimed.

James flipped switches, twirled dials, and shoved the two joysticks forward. The video screen showed the Theran forest plummet away, the colony shrinking to a mere opening in the woods, then the curvature of Thera as the wormhole vaulted into space. Without the friction of the atmosphere, James could now accelerate to enormous velocity, streaking toward the destination.

"*What is this?*" he heard a voice exclaim. He turned to see the captain of the compound, glaring at him, pulling out his pistol.

• • •

"JESUS CHRIST!" exclaimed Christopher, waddling out of the control building as fast as his short legs would carry him. He reached the darkened, empty field where their wormhole had once hovered, jerking his head comically around in all directions, his chin wattle quivering, peering into the surrounding gloom.

Nathan and David Clark rushed up behind him, followed by security men wielding rifles, as if the weapons would prove useful. All stood puzzled at the wormhole's sudden departure.

"What the hell happened?" asked Nathan.

"The mercenaries?" asked David. "Did they double-cross us?"

"Don't know why they would," said Christopher, pacing back and forth, his head down. "They stood to gain a lot by staying loyal. And, they know that any disloyalty would bring disaster for their families. We have a list."

"Okay, then, one of our own? The Marches? After all, they are Jack's parents."

Christopher stopped pacing, his expression grim. "Maybe. But we won't know until the aperture returns. There's no communication through a wormhole."

"So, what do we do now?" asked David.

"Preserve the generators. Stop those missiles. So, the instant the mercenaries return with those codes, we resume the Palliation."

"And the wormhole. Is it lost?"

Christopher smiled conspiratorially. "Not at all. We know how to track them now. We'll track ours. And when we locate it, we'll attack."

• • •

James March froze, panicked, opening and closing his mouth soundlessly, trying to find the right words, as he looked down the barrel of the pistol the captain was pointing at him.

"What the hell are you doing moving the wormhole?" the captain demanded. He glanced at the view screen, which showed the oceans and continents of Thera sliding past, as the wormhole transited the planet's face.

Fortunately, Louisa had the presence of mind to answer. "Put down the gun," she commanded. "The answer is we don't know what's going on. We were instructed to relocate the wormhole, and nobody bothered to tell us why. Maybe there's a threat; maybe it's some tactical move. *So, put the gun down!*"

Perhaps the captain accepted the explanation. Or, perhaps the matronly, middle-aged Louisa reminded him of his mother, whom he always obeyed. But for whatever reason, he lowered the pistol, although he kept it out of its holster.

James took the distraction to surreptitiously press a button that would automatically pilot the wormhole to the rendezvous point. So, if anything happened to them, it would still reach its destination.

The captain's voice was distinctly less angry now. Again, he scrutinized the view screen. "So, where are you headed? You do know that, right?"

"All they said was to land at these coordinates . . ." James gestured at a set of numbers on one of the screens. ". . . and we're to pick up some . . ." James paused for just an instant. He hadn't figured out his lie thoroughly. He hoped the captain didn't notice. ". . . creatures who have agreed to help."

"Why would they do that?"

"Same reason as the mercenaries. Protection. Wealth."

Two other guards arrived, and the captain turned and murmured something to them. James only hoped it wasn't a shoot-to-kill order.

The image of Thera on the screen loomed ever larger, as the wormhole swooped into the atmosphere, slowing to prevent damage, but still traveling at an enormous speed. The landscape rushed up to reveal a Theran military base, and the captain backed up and raised the pistol once more. The other two guards did the same.

The view screen revealed seven figures—a human, two Therans, an ogre, a pixie, a fairy, and an elf—waiting below the wormhole. The fish-eye distortion of the scene resolved into clarity, as the magnetic field flattened one side of the wormhole to allow access.

The ladder descended, and the figures began climbing upward, the view screen showing them crowding into the vacuum chamber.

"These are enemy!" declared the captain to the guards, now joined by two more to level their weapons at the metal airlock door. "We're not taking any chances. On my command, open fire!"

The large hatch swung open with a groaning creak, and the hatchway filled with the gray-green bulk of an ogre. He regarded the guards with his onyx eyes, his massive brow furrowing at the sight of the guns. He grinned, his tusks becoming more prominent.

"Fire!" commanded the captain. James and Louisa slammed to the ground, as the guards launched a volley of bullets at the monster. The rounds slammed into his body and his arms raised in defense, driving him back into the chamber.

The firing paused, as the guards assessed the damage they had wrought.

The ogre reemerged from the chamber, his thick hide pocked with the marks of bullets that had not penetrated.

"Ouch," he growled, his tone scolding. "That hurt."

CHAPTER 32

S am crouched in the troop compartment of the speed- ing armored personnel carrier, sponging blood from her arms and legs. Her eyes were beginning to transform from their angry scarlet back into sky blue. She had fol- lowed Mike the ogre through the wormhole, with devastating results for the human guards, despite their weapons.

Across from her, occupying two seats, Mike calmly scratched at the dents in his hide from the hail of bullets that the Pilgrim guard had blasted at him. He dislodged three bullets, and they clinked to the floor of the carrier.

From the driver's seat emanated the screechy voice of Ryan, as the elf drove the carrier speeding away from the Pilgrim compound as fast as the fifteen-ton carrier could go. Beside him, James March issued directions, and behind him Louisa March consulted a digital map. She also relayed radio messages from E'iouy, who flew far overhead, surveying the landscape ahead.

Above them, Geniato Belligrado perched in the open hatch, scanning the terrain on either side of the road. He couldn't stand to be in the troop compartment, when he might be able to catch a first glimpse of the werewolf and his captive, the cherished Meri. He also filmed the passing scene, the bleak wasteland that was Earth, to document the ruined planet for Thera's leaders.

Vlad had assumed the best vantage point, manning the fifty-caliber machine gun. The vampire's acute vision meant he could distinguish the most distant objects in the dimmest of light.

In the troop compartment, Jack leaned toward Sam, his brow knitted in worry.

"Are you bleeding?" he asked.

She smiled faintly, finishing her cleansing. "Don't worry. This blood is red . . . human. Mine is bright blue, luminous, in fact."

Leaving Jack shaking his head at yet another revelation about the exotic, fascinating pixie, she moved forward to sit between Ryan and James, to translate the elf's skritterings.

Handing the radio up to Geniato, Louisa moved beside her son. She hugged Jack warmly. "My dear, I was so worried about you! And that chip . . . that termination chip. Why didn't you tell your father and me?"

"I didn't want you to worry."

"True, we would have been beside ourselves."

Jack looked out the carrier's port at the dismal landscape sliding by. He shook his head. "I can't imagine being trapped on this planet."

Louisa patted his hand. "Not to worry. We won't be. The Pilgrims in the compound won't interfere with the wormhole controls. We forced them to lay down their weapons by threatening to close it. And your father and I told them we installed a destruct code."

"But you didn't, right?"

"No, but we couldn't take the chance that one of the fools would attempt an escape to Thera and collapse it. That's our only way back home . . . well, your home."

"What do you and Dad know about this area . . . where we're going?"

"We've been on scouting parties . . . well, more like raids . . . to confiscate fuel, weapons, and food. So, we know the terrain. The problem is, we're passing through territory ruled by warlords. That's good news and bad news."

"What do you mean?"

"Well, it's good that these warlords know everything that goes on in their area. They're constantly battling over boundaries, so they have scouts everywhere. They could tell us whether the mercenaries or the werewolf passed through."

"And the bad news?"

"They're more likely to murder us for the vehicle and our equipment than to offer any help."

From the hatchway came Geniato's voice. "E'iouy says there's a village ahead. And people."

"That's likely a landfill village," said Louisa.

"Landfill village?"

"Many settlements have grown up around old landfills. They tap the methane for fuel. And they mine them for metal, plastic . . . anything they can sell or barter. Even food."

"Food in the garbage?"

"Sometimes a package of dried soup or noodles. Sometimes even a can of food. Quite a prize for somebody who starves most of the time," she said, as they moved forward to crowd behind the others peering out the carrier's windshield.

After ten minutes, they saw a cluster of ramshackle huts made from discarded junk come into sight. The ragged, hunched figure of a young woman holding a baby stood beside the road, waving piteously.

"We'll go out to talk. You should stay inside," Jack told the Mythicals. "They might be frightened by your presence."

Jack and his father took up assault rifles and made their way to the rear hatch. They stepped out onto the rubble-strewn road and into the hellscape that was Earth.

As always, the suffocating heat engulfed them, raising a sweat that soaked their clothes into sticky, clinging shrouds. The heat was so incongruous, given that the weak sun shone only as a smothered disk of wan light through the oppressive clouds. A choking smog clawed at their lungs and obscured any long-distance view of the gray-brown wasteland. Nearby, the only landmarks were the gnarled shapes of dead trees. A stream of scummy, fetid water trickled along a ditch which ran beneath what had once been a superhighway.

From the shacks emerged still more gaunt, ragged people, shuffling determinedly toward the carrier.

"My child needs food," pleaded the woman, holding the little girl close to her tattered dress. "Can you spare any?" She glanced fearfully behind her as she spoke. James began translating from English to Theran for Jack.

Jack steeled himself against the heartrending sight of the mother and starving child. "We have some food that we can give you. But we need information," he said.

"Yes, yes," whimpered the woman. "Food for my baby. I'll tell you what—"

She was cut short by the arrival of a mob of tattered, gaunt villagers, who also began begging for food.

Jack was about to make them the same offer when a shout came from the top of the carrier.

"GUNS!" bellowed Vlad.

Bursts of automatic weapon fire erupted from the crowd ricocheting off the carrier with metallic clangs. Jack and his father ducked behind the carrier, aiming their rifles, but holding fire.

"The people . . . we can't just shoot into the crowd!" Jack exclaimed.

From behind them erupted another round of bullets slamming into the carrier. They were surrounded. They scrambled beneath the carrier.

Jack pulled a grenade from his belt, but James stopped him.

"They're using the people as shields," he said. "You'd kill innocents."

"So, basically, we're trapped out here," said Jack, stowing the grenade. "We'll just have to take our chances and try to make it back inside."

Above them, the machine gun roared to life, Vlad launching a fusillade of rounds that ripped into the shacks, exploding holes in their sides and shredding their roofs. He aimed above the crowd, making them drop as one, scrambling away in the dirt, screaming and crying.

But still the gunfire continued from the cover of the human shields.

"We've got to make the carrier!" exclaimed Jack. "Take the chance of being shot."

They leaped up, to see Vlad determinedly holding down the machine gun's trigger, raking the area with machine gun fire. Beside him, Geniato fed the ammunition belt into the smoking machine gun.

But the attackers continued their barrage, now targeting Vlad. Round after round careened off the metal of the carrier near him, but he kept shooting. Periodically, he ducked an incoming round, marshaling his lightning reflexes.

Abruptly, Geniato disappeared into the carrier; and rising up through the hatch came the massive bulk of Mike, shielding Vlad from bullets that slammed into his body.

James plunged into the back of the carrier, and Jack was about to follow. But he paused when he glimpsed a shimmering reflection of light streaking downward from the sky toward a spot distant from the road.

The enemy gunfire abruptly stopped.

Realizing the silence, Vlad stopped firing. The only sound was the sobbing of the villagers.

Jack stood warily up, and James emerged from the carrier. They looked at each other with puzzled expressions, but both held their rifles at the ready.

They quickly brought them up again when, throughout the crowd, gunmen began to stand up, holding their weapons above them, as in surrender. One by one, they began to back away from the carrier, as the people took the chance to scramble for the safety of the huts, leaving the carrier sitting isolated amid an empty expanse.

A figure stepped from behind one of the shacks, a hulking, bearded man with a scar slashing through one blinded eye and down across his face. He held his hands at his side.

Behind him appeared the alabaster body and gossamer wings of E'iouy. The fairy held a dagger hard at the throat of the man, shoving him toward the carrier.

"They didn't expect an air assault," said E'iouy, smiling. "I'd like you to meet . . . what is your name?" James translated the question.

"Bardolph," muttered the man.

"Ah, yes, Bardolph," said E'iouy. "He is the leader of these thugs. They apparently obey him."

E'iouy shoved Bardolph up to the carrier, as James and Jack leveled their weapons at him. From the village, they heard alarmed shouts, and the warlord's men appeared from behind the shack walls, leveling their rifles at the group.

"You could have been killed," Jack scolded E'iouy.

"I'm pretty fast."

"Well, you're going to be a father. You really shouldn't have come, you know."

E'iouy grinned and nodded. "True. But you needed me, obviously. A'eiio is safe on Thera. That's what matters."

Jack confronted the warlord, and with James translating, saying, "Here's our offer, Bardolph. You give us the information we need, and we take you with us down the road far enough until we're sure none of your men are around. Then we let you go. It's that simple."

"You will kill me."

"No," said Jack. "We give our word."

Bardolph glared up at him, uttering a guttural grunt of disbelief. "The others killed. They killed five of my men."

"Others?"

"Soldiers. They also came in two of these." He gestured at the carrier. "They came at night. They took men from their families. They killed the families. Then they killed the men."

"We're different," said Jack. "They are our enemies."

Ryan and Sam appeared from within the carrier, and the warlord regarded the elf and the pixie with a widened eye, snorting in disbelief. "Yes, you are," he said. "What are these creatures?"

"Tell us what your men told the soldiers."

The warlord paused, regarding the invaders with a calculated stare, finally nodding in agreement. "They told them about the cannibal beast that came and killed."

Geniato leaped forward, grabbing the warlord before being pulled away. *"What about the beast?"* he demanded. *"Was there a girl with the beast? Where did they go?"*

Bardolph glared at him, then shrugged. "The creature came at night. One of the girls saw it, as it dragged away her mother from their hut. It had fur . . . and fangs . . . an animal, but like a human.

We found the mother's body. It had been eaten. And we found others dead and eaten at its feeding ground. One was my kin."

Geniato slumped in dejection against the side of the carrier.

"Where did the beast go?" asked Jack, repeating Geniato's question.

"South."

"That's not helpful."

"That's all I know. And that will let you find them. They can only go so far south before they reach the ocean. The beast may be trying to get there and take a boat."

"There are boats there," confirmed James. "If he manages to steal a boat, he can escape to open water. This is the only road there. The others were destroyed in the civil wars, when the government collapsed."

"Then we go south," declared Jack.

CHAPTER 33

"He's gone. She's dead." Geniato slumped between Jack and James on the muddy shore of the flat, gray sea. They had reached the end of the highway, only to find a total emptiness both to the east and west as far as the eye could see.

Jack put his arm around Geniato, declaring. "Don't give up hope. E'iouy is up there. He can see for miles."

"Well, I need to do something," said Geniato. "I'm going to scout."

Jack considered stopping Geniato from going off on his own, but thought better of it. The sorrowful young man needed to be doing something. "Okay, but take a weapon." Jack waved to the ogre, who was tromping up and down in the scummy water. "Take Mike with you."

Geniato nodded and returned to the carrier to fetch an assault rifle, and followed by the hulking ogre, hiked off down the mud flat.

Sam and Vlad emerged from the carrier to join them, Sam shaking her head to indicate there had been no word from E'iouy of any sighting.

"Could the werewolf have taken a boat from here?" Jack asked his father.

"Not likely. There are no villages here. No reason to be. The ocean is dead. Few fish, except for sharks. Little life."

"What happened?" asked Jack.

"It started back in the two thousand and twenties, when global temperatures were rising, including the ocean water temperature," said James. "Carbon dioxide levels were going up, and the ocean was absorbing it and becoming acidified. It began killing fish, coral reefs. The warmer waters reached down into the deep ocean, where frozen methane ice had been collecting for millions of years. The deposits thawed and over maybe decades there were these huge eruptions of methane. That was the death blow."

"So, there aren't many boats?"

"Not the last time we were here, years ago on an expedition. But there were boats in some villages up and down the coast . . . trading boats that go south to flooded cities, where there are still buildings sticking out of the water. They trade . . ." James's voice trailed off, as if he didn't want to explain further.

"So, this wasn't always ocean?"

"No. It was all land from here for several hundred miles south. It was a giant peninsula. It was called Florida."

.   .   .

E'iouy skimmed above the decaying landscape, along the shoreline where the gray mud flats met the ocean's brown waters. He struggled to breathe in the muggy, dank air, but was determined to fly on, especially because he had glimpsed what appeared to be a village in the distance.

He willed his wings to beat harder to carry him higher in the murk, to make it less likely that a bullet would find him. It was a laborious task, given that he had decided to carry a belt full of grenades. Even the relatively small load made flying harder, but he had decided for this flight, he might need aerial munitions.

Armored carriers! He spotted a pair of armored personnel carriers parked among a collection of ramshackle buildings below. At first he could make out no people around them, but as he began to circle, he saw that camouflaged mercenaries were ducking their way down the streets. They were converging on another carrier parked near the water.

Then, he saw why they were advancing. It was the werewolf! The creature was scrambling for a boat dock, dragging Meri behind him. E'iouy could see villagers fleeing, probably terrified of the monster that had appeared among them. E'iouy pulled out the radio and told the others of his discovery. Louisa replied that they would head for the scene immediately.

The mercenaries were nearly on the werewolf, making it likely he would not reach the boat in time.

E'iouy banked into a sharp turn, to stay above the scene. He realized that, as absurd as it might seem, he had to help this beast who was a cannibal, and who had abducted an innocent girl. If the mercenaries reached them, they would kill the werewolf, which was not a bad thing. But they would no doubt kill Meri. And, if the monster had the codes for the Palliation, it would be the death of an entire planet's population.

So, he pulled two grenades from the belt, yanked out their pins, and held the triggers tightly. He calculated where the nearest mercenaries were approaching the boat dock. He banked into a steep dive, counting on the whisper-quiet of his wings to enable surprise. He whipped across the roofs of the village, releasing a grenade in front of one contingent of advancing mercenaries. And on the next parallel street, he dropped the other.

He willed his diaphanous wings into a furious whir to bear him upward, hoping that the mercenaries had not detected him.

From below rose the sharp report of exploding grenades and the crackle of automatic gunfire. He scanned the area, trying to discern whether any of the shots were directed upward. But they seemed to be aimed at the dock. The mercenaries must have believed the werewolf had launched the grenades.

The werewolf had reached a boat and clambered in with his captive. Still the mercenaries advanced. They would be on him before he could launch.

Now E'iouy had a choke point; the dock entrance. He pulled out two more grenades and pulled their pins, banking around and sailing low along the shoreline, calculating precisely when he would reach the dock.

Now!

He released the grenades, watching them plummet downward, bouncing on the dock, coming to rest.

But now, more gunfire, and aimed at him. Bullets whizzed past him with a piercing whine. He quickly banked left, then right, then left, to evade the bullets. A round pierced his wing, bringing a stinging pain, the tattered hole rendering it less aerodynamic. He adjusted his flight to compensate.

As he swooped down to take himself out of the line of fire, the grenades exploded with a louder bang, given his lower altitude. Now that he was beyond the village, he gained altitude to see the result.

Success! The werewolf had boarded the boat and flung the girl onto its deck. But the beast didn't leave immediately. He turned and flung a small bag onto the dock. Then he returned to the boat's small open cabin, started the engine and sped away in a spray of brown water.

The mercenaries reached the dock and began firing at the fleeing craft, but E'iouy could tell that the boat was far enough out that the bullets had little chance of reaching their target.

Two mercenaries aimed their weapons upward, spraying the air with gunfire. As bullets whizzed past him, E'iouy struggled upward, hindered by the injured wing.

Finally, he was at a safe altitude, which the soldiers likely realized, because they ceased firing.

But even at this height, E'iouy could see that the mercenaries were taking no steps to follow the werewolf. Even though numerous boats were docked nearby, the soldiers showed no interest. Instead, they gathered around the bag.

The leader stood, shouldered the bag and signaled the men to move off. They sprinted through the deserted streets back to the carriers, boarded them and roared away over the mud flats, heading north.

E'iouy felt a deep fatigue overtake him. The injured wing, the evasive maneuvers, the choking atmosphere had drained his energy. He fluttered down to land on the dock, its approach now shattered by the grenade. He scanned the ocean for any sign of the boat.

The werewolf was gone.

• • •

Hunched over in the passenger compartment of the wildly lurching armored carrier, Roberson punched the laptop computer's power button to bring it to life. The next minute would tell him whether he had accomplished the mission and obtained the generator codes. Either he and his remaining men would be rich and powerful beyond their wildest dreams. Or they would be fugitives branded as traitors to their race when the Palliation failed.

The carrier lurched again, as it sped along the trackless mud flats, and Roberson clutched the computer to keep it steady. He had ordered that the two vehicles avoid the highway. That's where their pursuers would look for them. And that's where the warlords would expect them.

Four of his hardened veterans sat impassively in the passenger compartment, checking their weapons, reloading, and napping, even amid the roar and jerking of the carrier. They had been in these situations before. They knew how to survive, to fight their way out, to kill the enemy.

The computer screen showed icons indicating it was operational, and Roberson inserted the memory chip into its slot. He typed commands to access its contents. There was a pause, during which he contemplated the possibility that the werewolf had given them a bogus chip when he had flung the satchel at them on the dock. The treachery would mean turning back, finding the animal, obtaining the real chip, and killing him in the most painful way possible. Inconvenient.

He smiled, though, when an array of werewolf symbols scrolled down the screen. He'd been briefed on what the codes might look like, and these appeared to be valid.

He gave a triumphant nod and thumbs up to the other mercenaries, and one of them radioed the other vehicle that the codes were good. Next would come a takeover of the Pilgrim wormhole and piloting it to the Pilgrim colony.

There, he and his men would re-confirm the deal with the humans. Their families and those of their fallen comrades would be shepherded into safe havens. And, of course, they would divide up the Theran territories. They would become kings, emperors in their world.

He settled back for a nap himself. He would relieve the driver afterward. The jouncing continued for some half an hour.

He had settled into sleep when a massive thud shook the carrier, jolting him awake to grab his rifle in an automatic reflex.

Another thud, and the carrier careened to the left, slamming the soldiers against the bulkhead. As Roberson was stowing the bag containing the chip, one of the mercenaries kicked open the rear door. The three flipped their weapons off safety, aiming out. Above them, the soldier manning the machine gun triggered a series of rapid-fire bursts that reverberated through the carrier.

Then he screamed in agony, as a torrent of flaming oil cascaded down through the hatch into the interior to engulf it in searing flames.

CHAPTER 34

Ryan wrestled with the wheel of the commandeered boat with his skinny elf arms, piloting it at the highest speed possible, skimming across the flat sea. Droplets of greenish elf sweat dotted his forehead, as he crouched behind the windshield. The others stood thankfully in the fetid breeze that flowed over their bodies, a welcome relief from the oppressive heat.

Vlad scanned the horizon ahead, with Sam beside him. Jack joined them and together they scoured the featureless expanse.

But they saw nothing ahead, not even the line of a horizon, which was obscured by the blanketing smog.

"We don't know where we're going, do we?" shouted Mike, from the deck.

"Neither does the werewolf," Jack shouted back. "So, we're betting he just heads south."

"Yah . . . *betting*," grumped the ogre, settling his bulk for the ride.

"Buildings ahead!" exclaimed Louisa, listening to the radio message from E'iouy, flying high above. "He says there are buildings ahead and to the left!"

"I see them!" exclaimed Vlad, and Jack pointed at the undifferentiated bumps materializing from smog. The vague forms resolved into an archipelago of ruined skyscrapers jutting out of the waters.

"Pretty sure it's what was called Jacksonville," said James, consulting the map on the boat's navigational computer screen.

"Anything?" Jack asked Louisa, who relayed the question to E'iouy.

The flooded buildings grew closer, now towering above the boat. Their ground floors awash, they were stained green with algae and black with mold. Many of the huge windows had been knocked out, the gaps looking like missing teeth.

"I would guess hurricanes did this," said Jack, peering up at the broken windows.

"More likely gun battles," said his father. "There were bad ones all over the country after the martial law, when the government was trying to keep order. Before the warlords took over. Now, there are only Pilgrims in authority."

Occasionally, they would glimpse a lurking figure in a window far above them, but there was no sound except the faint slap of low waves against the scummy walls.

Ryan slowed the boat to lower the engine sound, and the group listened intently, all scrutinizing the waters around the buildings for any sign of the boat that had brought Flaktuckmetang and his captive Meri.

They passed a tattered band of people huddled on the window sill of what had once been a second floor. They stood beside a makeshift crane whose steel cable extended into the water. The people did not wave, but glared fearfully at the boat.

"Have you seen a boat carrying a monster?" shouted Jack. "And a girl?"

At the sight of the ogre, the people scrambled back into the darkened interior. But one remained, a tall, gaunt man, standing tentatively.

"Do you have a corpse?" he shouted. "We have shark to trade. If no corpse, go away!"

Jack turned to his father. "Corpses?" he asked.

James shook his head in disgust. "I didn't want to tell about the fishing here. The only remaining food source are great white sharks. The people have nothing to attract them but . . ." his father paused and took a deep breath, ". . . corpses. They have shark traps that they bait with the dead. The sharks come, and if one takes the bait and enters the trap, they haul it up."

Jack blew out a breath to rid himself of the grisly information. "Have you seen—" he began, but Louisa interrupted him, relaying a message from the fairy.

"He's spotted the boat!" she exclaimed. "At the building with the pointed top. There!" She pointed at a glass-walled skyscraper two buildings beyond, and Ryan gunned the engine, throwing up a rooster tail of spray, heading for it.

Mike stirred his massive body to make room, as E'iouy fluttered down to land on the deck, slumping onto a bench, breathing heavily.

They drew closer, and Ryan began to circle around the building.

"There!" exclaimed Sam, as the boat came into sight, moored to the building.

The elf eased the boat up to a broken window, and Jack hitched a line to a metal rod jutting from the building. James, Louisa, and Geniato took up assault rifles. Figuring that close combat was possible, Jack chose an automatic pistol and extra ammunition clips.

They hauled themselves up through the shattered window and into the interior. E'iouy and Ryan remained aboard, the fairy to recover, and the elf to guard the boat.

The dank, dark interior of the ruined building smelled of rotten, organic decay and was strewn with the garbage of human occupation. A moldy, ripped couch sat beside the window, and blankets and stained mattresses occupied places around the walls, where people had been sleeping.

"We'll never find him in this—" began Louisa walking into the room, but Vlad interrupted her.

"Over there," he said, peering into a pitch black corner of the room. "Bodies."

Jack switched on a light, to see two bodies, a young man and a young woman, lying on a blood-soaked blanket. Both had their throats torn out, and the man had large chunks of flesh missing from his arms and legs.

Retching, Louisa staggered across to the window, bent over trying to recover.

Jack struggled to maintain his composure, backing away from the horrific sight.

"We need to split up," he declared coldly, taking a deep breath. He asked his father to fetch radios and flashlights from the boat, and directed three teams to begin searching the building: he went with Geniato; Mike, Sam, and James struck off together; and Vlad and Louisa joined to search.

Mike, Sam, and James struck out for the lower floor; Vlad and Louisa began to explore the middle; and Jack and Geniato began the long hike to the top floors.

Jack and Geniato climbed the darkened stairs as quietly as they could, despite the grit crunching under their feet. They stopped periodically to contact the other groups and listen for any telltale animal sounds that might betray the werewolf's position.

They reached the top floor, pushing through the metal fire door to find themselves looking out over the ruined city, with its flooded buildings and the distant pylons of a submerged bridge. Broken glass littered the floor, and almost all the windows were shattered.

"If he's here, we'll hear him," whispered Jack, as they made their way from room to room.

But they heard nothing. No sound, no sign of the werewolf or Meri.

Jack saw that Geniato was trembling, and he clasped him gently on the shoulder in reassurance. "He would have kept her alive," he said. "He knows he might need her."

They moved quietly down to the next floor and searched along the hallway, ducking into rooms, finding nothing but more gutted interiors, more shattered glass.

But on the next floor down, a faint sound echoed down the hall. Indefinable, but not a natural sound. Something moving about far down the hallway.

A growl!

Jack and Geniato stepped quietly down a darkened hallway, illuminated only by pale light filtering through the open doorways of offices that had windows.

Now, they could hear more sounds, a growling, a shuffling.

A sob! It was Meri!

Geniato leaped ahead, grasping his assault rifle, with Jack unable to grab his arm to stop him. He ran down the hall, just reaching an open doorway, when a massive furry arm reached out, clutching him, and snatching him in.

He yelled, as Jack drew his pistol and sprinted to the doorway, rounding its corner. He saw Geniato lying in a crumpled, barely conscious heap, on the floor by the far wall.

As Jack entered the room, the werewolf, who had flattened himself against the wall by the doorway, tore the pistol from his hand and flung it out the open window.

Jack backed away, desperately seeking a weapon among the debris.

"You!" exclaimed the werewolf in shock. "I killed you!"

"Obviously not," said Jack. "And now I am here to kill *you*."

With an enraged roar, the werewolf slammed Jack against the wall, clamping his claw over Jack's face and yanking his head back to reveal Jack's throat. The claw was a suffocating shroud that reeked of animal musk.

"Now you will *really* die! Now, there is no beast to save you."

Jack fought back, bringing up his fist to pound the werewolf's face, slamming it to the side, briefly loosening the grip.

But that grip tightened again, wrenching Jack's head back even more.

"You will taste so good," said Flaktuckmetang.

Jack steeled himself for death, but abruptly the werewolf howled in pain, his body lurching away, careening around the room.

Jack realized that it was Meri clinging with one hand to the thick fur on the werewolf's shoulder, stabbing him again and again with a shard of glass she had snatched from the littered floor. She hacked at his back again and again, oblivious to the blood streaming from her own hand from the shard's razor-sharp edges. She barely held on, as the snarling werewolf twisted around, grasping at her, trying to dislodge her.

With a vicious bellow, the werewolf finally managed to tear the young girl's grip loose, hauled her around and slammed her to the floor, standing over her, grinning.

"So, then, you shall go first." He bent down and raised his claw to tear Meri's throat open. She held up the glass shard, a feeble weapon against those claws.

But the werewolf abruptly stopped his attack and stood up, a puzzled, pained look on his face. He pawed at a long dagger of glass jutting out of the side of his neck, his eyes growing glassy. Black blood flowed down his shoulder onto his chest.

Jack had also found a shard of glass.

"What—" began the werewolf, but Jack didn't allow him to finish. Grabbing another shard, he leaped at the werewolf, slashing at his body.

The glass found its target, and blood began to spurt from the werewolf's arm. Weakening from pain and blood loss, the werewolf swung clumsily at Jack. But Jack ducked beneath that blow, quickly circling behind the creature, reaching up, and hacking as hard as he could at the beast.

Meri pulled herself up, her expression one of maddened rage. She circled the werewolf, taking advantage of her small stature and quickness to inflict her own wounds on the lumbering creature.

Time after time, the werewolf swiped his huge claws at his attackers. Time after time, they evaded the lethal blows, inflicting more slashing wounds.

The werewolf staggered back near the open window, and Jack took advantage of the positioning. Leaping forward, he slammed into the werewolf's chest, sending the beast vaulting out the window, plummeting down into the ocean far below.

Jack and Meri held onto one another, peering out the window to see the werewolf struggling to swim to the building, his blood flowing from his wounds into the waters around him. He had just reached the base of the building, stretching up with one claw to grasp its side, when the water around him erupted in a volcano of spray.

The werewolf's massive body vaulted upward, clamped in the jaws of an even more massive great white shark. The werewolf's arms and legs flailed lifelessly, his head lolling, his fanged mouth gaping open, as the shark bit down again and again on his body. The shark finally dragged the body down into the flat gray ocean. The waters continued to roil as the shark fed amid the black stain of blood and scattered floating body parts rendered buoyant by air trapped in their fur.

Jack pitched down the glass shard and quickly moved to check on Geniato, who was pulling himself up. Meri embraced him, and they both sobbed with relief. Jack managed to radio the others, telling them what had happened.

And as Geniato bound Jack's and Meri's wounds, all three sat recovering, gazing out at the dead ocean and down at the now-calm area of its surface where the hated werewolf had been torn to shreds.

CHAPTER 35

Vlad manned the machine gun, with Sam beside him scanning the landscape, as the carrier sped along the desolate highway, back toward the Pilgrim colony.

Inside, Geniato embraced Meri, who rested her head on his chest, sleeping. She had been given water and food, and her wounds bandaged.

E'iouy rested, too, his injured wing temporarily mended; and Mike occupied the entire back of the passenger compartment, snoring loudly.

Jack and his parents huddled together at the front, making plans, as Ryan zig-zagged the carrier, avoiding the many abandoned wrecks and other obstacles on the highway.

"Can we get back through to the wormhole?" asked Jack.

"It won't be easy," said his father. "We'll have to keep them believing that we installed a self-destruct sequence. In any case, they can't use the aperture, because I implemented an access code. So, we're all right. They know that losing their wormhole would mean losing humanity's last chance at survival. You've seen the conditions here. In a matter of years, Earth will be unsurvivable for humans."

They had just begun to plot tactics, when Sam shouted from above, "Smoke! There's smoke!"

Jack pulled himself up through the hatch beside her to see a tendril of smoke rising in the gray sky off the highway to the right.

"Two carriers burning, "said Vlad, peering intently at the scene.

"It's the mercenaries," Jack called down. "We need to find out what's happened to them."

"Is that wise?" James called up. "Remember the warlords."

"We need to find out what happened," Jack repeated emphatically. "Roberson has the generator codes."

He instructed the elf to home in on the smoke plume, and shortly, Ryan brought the carrier slowly up to the two gutted vehicles.

The group exited the passenger compartment, to inspect them, finding a grisly sight. The interiors were burned-out ruins, holding the charred corpses of a dozen men. The acrid stench of burned flesh rolling out of the carrier caused them to gag.

But Jack climbed into the first carrier, making his way into the interior, searching for any sign of the satchel containing the code chip. He had just begun poking through the ash around the charred bodies when shouting and gunfire drew him back out.

He emerged to find the carriers surrounded by a ragtag mob of armed men and vehicles—battered cars, trucks, and motorcycles.

Vlad shot the bolt of the machine gun, swiveling it around to aim at the thugs. They did not retreat.

Mike stalked back and forth before them, growling, baring his massive fangs. An impulsive young thug leaped toward him, thrusting a spear into his belly. The tip broke off.

Mike grinned and chuckled. "Maybe you should poke harder," as the man shrank away in shock.

The others, however, maintained their distance, until the gang parted, and Bardolph emerged, wielding his rifle. He shouted a command, which James translated into English as, *"You will all die as these did! You come to our land, you kill our people!"*

Bardolph raised his rifle, and his men followed, leveling their weapons at the group.

"Tell him we killed no one," said Jack, and James translated. "Tell him we brought him a gift."

A dozen rifles trained on them, Jack gestured to Mike, who fetched a blanket-wrapped object from the carrier and pitched it to the ground before the warlord. The ogre ripped away the blanket to reveal the shark-gnawed head of Flaktuckmetang, his staring eyes milky, his jaws gaping in death rictus.

Jack kicked at the head. "This is the creature that killed your people. This was all that was left after a shark got him. We offer you revenge. We offer you justice."

The warlord stared at the water-soaked head for a long moment, then transferred his impassive gaze to Jack. Jack held his ground, not sure whether the next moment would bring permission to pass or a hail of bullets.

Finally, the scarred, hulking man lowered his rifle, and saying nothing, waved his hand at his gang.

The crowd in front of the carrier parted, and Jack and the others boarded the vehicle. The elf eased the carrier slowly forward past them, then once clear, gunned it back toward the highway.

"I figured the werewolf's head would come in handy," said Jack, as they slumped, relieved in the carrier's passenger compartment.

After a day speeding across the barren, gray landscape, constantly vigilant for other gangs, they reached the rusted steel gates of the walled Pilgrim compound.

From the guardhouses atop the concrete walls, machine guns swiveled around to bear on them, and the sound of their bolts being snapped echoed down.

James and Louisa climbed out of the carrier and stood before the gate.

James issued a challenge. "You know we hold the key to your future," he declared. "Only we can disarm the destruct mechanism and allow you to escape to Thera. Open up, or you will die with Earth."

After a long moment came the clank of the gates being unlocked, and the whine of their electric motors as they swung ponderously open. James and Louisa walked through, followed by the carrier.

Inside, they found themselves proceeding between two ranks of heavily armed Pilgrims. The colonel commanding the compound stepped forward, his expression one of barely contained fury.

"You will release the controls!" he commanded. *"You will return the wormhole to functionality."*

"Of course," said James matter-of-factly. "We are Pilgrims, too. We just could not agree with what the leadership planned . . . joining with those monsters to kill billions of innocent Therans. We will ensure that all Pilgrims . . . here and at the other compounds around the globe . . . can transit safely to our new home."

After a long moment, the captain curtly issued a command dispatching the four men to accompany the group to the wormhole, where James and Louisa began operating the controls to prepare it for transit.

As they typed commands into the console, the main view screen came to life, showing the gently curved surface of Thera far below. James and Louisa plotted a course that would bring the wormhole down from orbital height to the planet surface—specifically, to the Califanan defense center.

The wormhole began to descend, and the Theran landscape loomed closer, the defense center appearing on the view screen. It was a sprawling array of windowless, one-story buildings, surrounded by tanks and troop transports.

Geniato and Meri embraced, relieved to be home. Jack put his arm around Sam—a bit diffidently, given that he had witnessed this petite, beautiful pixie decimate a cadre of burly, well-armed soldiers. But she nestled against him, warmly affectionate. She brought up his bandaged hand that had been wounded by his grip on the glass shard that had wounded the werewolf. She unwrapped the bandage and began to kiss it lightly, and Jack felt a strange tingling, as his torn flesh began to heal itself.

Finally, the wormhole had settled near the ground, and James operated controls to magnetically warp one section into a flat surface that would allow safe passage.

The wormhole's ladder extended, and they all made their way down, with E'iouy going first, given that he needed medical attention. Indeed, A'eiio was waiting anxiously, her slim figure now rounder with her pregnancy. They embraced, their wings wafting back and forth in the pleasure of their touch.

Jack, Sam, Geniato, Meri, and Mike all took their turns climbing down onto the Theran surface. The defense minister met them, making arrangements for a debriefing and a meeting with his country's president.

But Jack left them to greet A'eiio, and make sure she was well, and her unborn babies healthy. After a warm embrace, he saw them over to another waiting wormhole—the fairies'—and up its ladder. On the other side was the fairy terminal, where E'iouy could be transported to a medical facility to receive treatment for his injured wing.

But when Jack turned back to the Pilgrim wormhole floating nearby, his brow knitted in unease. Something wasn't right.

"My mother and father . . ." he began worriedly, shaking his head. "They should have followed us through."

He started back toward the wormhole, when the ladder abruptly retracted, and with the stunning acceleration, the wormhole vaulted into the sky, speeding away so quickly that in only seconds, it shrank to a small orb, then to a dot, then to nothing.

"MY GOD!" exclaimed Jack, as the others also shouted in alarm. "WHAT HAPPENED?"

• • •

"You thought I was dead," said Roberson, standing beside the wormhole control console on the Earth side. He aimed his pistol at James and Louisa. "You thought the codes were gone. You thought you had won. All wrong."

He leaned heavily against the console, favoring the wounded leg he had bandaged with rags. He panted in bone-deep pain; the narcotics he had demanded from the Pilgrims hadn't yet kicked in. His right arm and the right side of his face were both blistered from the fire that had engulfed the carrier, as he leaped out of it and into the clutches of the warlord's men.

Even as his uniform had smoldered, he had shot three, slashed the throats of two more, and taken a bullet to the leg before he had reached the motorcycle of one of the warlord's men. He had leaped on, and hunkering down to avoid the hail of bullets, sped away across the mud flats.

Compared to that escape, he'd had little problem scaling the wall of the Pilgrim compound, killing four guards, and making it into the wormhole control room.

Now, he loomed over James and Louisa, having demanded that they pilot the wormhole away from its landing spot on Thera.

He had ordered the colonel and the other Pilgrims out of the building. They readily complied, given that he had slapped an explosive charge onto the control panel and held the trigger in his hand. And it was a dead-man's switch. If he released it, or lost consciousness, the building would be obliterated and the wormhole closed.

In fact, the colonel was just as happy to comply, because the mercenary wanted the wormhole directed to a destination that was perfectly fine with the colonel—the Pilgrim colony in the Confederated States.

"What do you think you will do?" asked James, his gaze intent on the controls, as the wormhole plummeted toward Thera.

"What I was contracted to do. I'll have the techs at the colony check the trigger codes . . . make sure they'll actually activate the generators. Then, we will all take a trip into orbit. And Thera will suffer the consequences."

CHAPTER 36

"*Where is it? Where is it? Where is it?*" The defense minister repeated the question over and over, as much to himself as to the others crowded into the Califanan defense center. A crowd of Theran scientists, Mythicals, and one lone human—Jack—stared desperately at the large view screens, as elf, troll, and Theran technicians worked feverishly at the monitoring consoles to find the Pilgrim wormhole.

"Can't we find it?" asked Jack grimly. "We know how to detect a wormhole. We have the electromagnetic signature."

Scrutinizing his console, Ryan skrittered an answer, which Sam translated as, "He says the problem is that the sensors can't differentiate among wormholes. There's no fingerprint that identifies the Pilgrim wormhole. To the sensors, the fairy wormhole outside this building looks just like the Pilgrim wormhole."

From another console, Steve said, "We're trying a process of elimination. We are notifying the Wardens to take the Mythicals apertures to orbital height. The Pilgrim one will be the only one left on the planet."

"Assuming the Pilgrim wormhole is on the planet," said Jack.

A'eiio and E'iouy entered the hall, E'iouy's injured wing wrapped in a clear bandage. A'eiio gently clasped Jack's shoulder.

"Your parents. Would they have done this?"

"No, I think something happened on the Earth side," he replied. "I don't know what."

"There!" exclaimed the troll, and he punched a button to bring up, on one of the wall view screens, a satellite image of a Theran forest showing the familiar layout of the Pilgrim compound in the Confederated States. The shimmering image of a wormhole was visible in a clearing near a large barn.

"Zoom in," commanded the defense minister. "We need to know what's going on."

The image magnified, to reveal several figures surrounding the wormhole, setting what looked like spacesuits beside the ladder, in preparation for loading.

"Why would they need those?" asked the minister.

"Obvious," said E'iouy. "They are planning spacewalks. The only reason they would do that is if they were going to trigger the remaining EMP generators."

"But that's not possible," said Jack. "They don't—" he stopped, staring intently at the screen.

On the satellite view, several figures emerged from the large barn, one limping.

"Roberson! The mercenary!" exclaimed Jack. "He survived the warlord attack!"

"And he must have saved the trigger codes. They're going to activate the generators!"

The defense minister sat heavily into a chair. "It would mean disaster," he said. "We were not able to destroy enough of them. The Theran mercenaries and their allies prevented it. They could trigger a generator and redeploy over another region . . . over and over. They could destroy our civilization."

"We have missiles," declared one of the generals. "We have the wormhole outside. We could have the missiles on station instantly. We could launch within an hour . . . close the Pilgrim wormhole!"

"No!" declared Jack. "My parents are on the other side. And as much as the Pilgrims have done against us, we cannot simply kill them."

"Well, then, do you have an alternative?" shot back the defense minister. Without waiting for a reply, he turned to the general and ordered him to ask the fairy Warden to use their wormhole to transport missiles to orbit.

Jack shook his head in impotent frustration. "Even if you did attempt to come within range of the wormhole, remember they know how to detect them, as well. They'll immediately pilot the wormhole out of range, and Thera will be lost."

"Then what?" asked the minister.

Jack sat at a console, rubbing his face, thinking. He needed a way to get near enough to the wormhole without triggering an attempt to escape. It had to be an approach that seemed benign to the Pilgrims.

And he needed a way to disrupt the precisely controlled magnetic fields that maintained the wormhole stability. The disruption need not be violent. Even a minor magnetic instability could destabilize and close the wormhole. Even though it would mean the loss of his own parents.

As an engineer, he tried to focus on closing the wormhole as an engineering problem. Since magnetic fields maintained the wormholes, his analysis drew on his understanding of electromagnetic equations . . . electromagnetic induction. That seemed promising—creating an electrical field using electromagnetic induction.

The room had grown heavy with tension, quiet except for low, urgent chatter among the elves, trolls, and Therans at the consoles.

Abruptly, Jack sat up straight, then leaped from the chair. "I think I know how to close the wormhole!" he exclaimed, turning to A'eiio and E'iouy, and leading them over to confer with Wendy.

"I need all the fairies, and all the angels you can possibly muster," he said. "I need you to gather them on the other side of the fairy wormhole . . . to prepare for transport to the Pilgrim colony."

At first the fairies and the angel shook their head in puzzlement. But as Jack outlined his plan of attack, and as its logic dawned on them, they began to smile and nod. They left immediately to contact their Wardens.

Jack next approached the general. He sketched a set of engineering specifications on a tablet computer, showing it to the general before transmitting it to him.

"Produce as many of these devices as you can make," he declared.

"But this is ridiculous!" exclaimed the general, staring with consternation at his own tablet. "How can these possibly be used as weapons?"

"Payloads," said Jack. "Payloads carried by fairies and angels."

"What can they possibly do? They can't possibly close a wormhole!"

"That's exactly what the Pilgrims will think."

• • •

His face and arm bandaged, Roberson leaned over the console, scrutinizing the display showing the Theran globe. An array of red dots arrayed around the planet marked the positions of the remaining EMP generators.

"You're sure you can program a fire-and-reposition sequence?" he asked the technician.

"Absolutely," replied the young mercenary. "We experimented on a spare generator we found in the werewolf base . . . and used the information from the captive soldiers on their system. That gave us enough knowledge to automate the whole process."

"By automate you mean . . . ?" asked Christopher, who had joined them with the Clark brothers.

"We've enhanced the activation codes Captain Roberson brought us," said the technician. "Once a generator is triggered to unleash its pulse, it will automatically shift orbit to target another region . . . pulse again . . . then shift again."

"And all the regions of the planet are covered," said Roberson.

"Each generator has its own assigned targets. The impact on the planet will be as if none of the generators was destroyed."

"So, now we launch the wormhole to rendezvous with the generators to reprogram them," said Roberson.

"We have an intrusion!" exclaimed another technician, pointing to one of the security camera screens. It showed an array of glimmers in the sky of sunlight reflected off shimmering wings.

Roberson and the others rushed outside to see a fairy fluttering smoothly into a landing near the barn, his silver hair wafted by the breeze from his wings. He stood quietly, as he was surrounded by rifle-wielding soldiers. Given that he was naked, he clearly carried no weapons, so Christopher waved off the soldiers and approached him.

E'iouy opened his arms in a gesture of surrender.

"I see your wing is damaged," said Roberson. "You are the one who attacked me and my men."

"I am," said E'iouy. "But we were only trying to save the beast's captive. And our purpose was only to stop you from injuring the young girl we were protecting. We injured none of your men. And you got your trigger codes."

"What do you want?"

"As you know, all Mythicals are trapped here . . . when you closed our apertures."

"And why should we care?" asked Nathan Clark. "Why should we not let you perish along with the Therans?"

"We have technology you do not," said E'iouy. "In return for keeping us safe, we will offer our expertise."

"You will offer only revenge . . . ," spat Roberson, ". . . revenge for marooning you here. We should just kill you. Another enemy neutralized."

Christopher waved his hand in dismissal. "Captain Roberson, I understand that as a soldier you see that as a valid tactic. But it is not a valid strategy. What harm can these creatures possibly do?"

"Yes, what harm?" asked A'eiio. "And, we also can give you a human you have sought . . . Jack March. You have his parents."

"We do," said Christopher. "They are traitors. They will die."

"He is willing to trade his life for theirs."

Christopher and the Clark brothers moved away to confer, quietly arguing among themselves, glancing periodically back at the fairy.

When they returned, Christopher nodded his assent.

"And where are his parents?" asked E'iouy.

"Nearby," answered Christopher. "Over in the colony. In a room . . . guarded."

"They are not on the Earth side?"

"No."

"Good," said E'iouy. He touched his finger to an earpiece, announcing into it, "They are here."

"INTRUSION!" shouted the tech monitoring the security cameras. "MASSIVE!"

Roberson and the others leaped to the screens, to see a sky alive with flying creatures.

"Mobilize everyone!" exclaimed Christopher, and they rushed outside, as if not believing what appeared on the screens.

They were immersed in the whir of fairy wings and the whoosh of angel wings. Above them, swooping, wheeling, and banking overhead, filling the sky, flew hundreds of fairies, hundreds of angels.

. . .

"What is happening?" demanded Christopher. "What are these creatures doing?"

E'iouy did not answer, instead launching himself to soar upward, joining the throng.

"Is this an attack?" he demanded of Roberson.

"If it were an attack, there would be other species," replied the mercenary. "True, these creatures can do battle, but not effectively."

Then the flock of flying Mythicals released clouds of gray powder that began to waft downward in a thick metallic fog.

The first curling tendrils of powder settled toward the wormhole, triggering a crackling of electrical discharge around the orb.

A technician burst from the barn, shouting, *"Metal powder! They're dropping metal powder! It's destabilizing! The wormhole is destabilizing!"*

"Launch!" exclaimed Christopher, and a wormhole pilot leaped for the ladder, beginning to climb through the surface of the wormhole, now alive with swaths of fiery electrical sparks. But Christopher grabbed the pilot's arm and shouted something into his ear, before dispatching him through the hole.

Within seconds the wormhole began to lift skyward, but its movement grew sluggish, erratic.

"The metal is affecting the guidance magnets!" exclaimed Christopher. "Shoot down the creatures!"

Roberson signaled to the mercenaries, and Pilgrim soldiers began peppering the sky with a hail of automatic weapon fire. The bullets brought scores of fairies and angels fluttering to the ground, wounded or dead. Several of the mercenaries took up grenade launchers, firing grenades that burst among the flight, ripping into fairies and angels, bringing them also plummeting to earth.

The wormhole slowly became airborne. But instead of streaking skyward away from the assault, it abruptly veered sideways, aiming straight for a formation of Mythicals. Plowing through their bodies, it was the ultimate sword, its infinitely sharp edges slicing them apart, creating a bloody rain of wings, legs, torsos, heads, which littered the ground below.

"What did you tell the pilot?" demanded Nathan Clark.

"I reminded him that a wormhole is not only an aperture but a weapon," said Christopher coldly. "We need to stop this attack so we can finish loading the equipment and carry out the Palliation."

The wormhole sailed away from the flight of Mythicals, with sparks shooting from its surface. But its shape began to undulate with instability caused by the faltering magnetic field. Then it instantly reversed course, paused and swooped back toward the fairies and angels.

But as it bore down upon the creatures, its pilot failed to notice another squadron of the creatures plummeting from above. They pulled up above the wormhole, unleashing another thick cloud of the gray dust, and the wormhole sailed at high speed into the cloud. It abruptly lurched to a stop, beginning to wobble back and forth, its surface warping and contorting, no longer a perfect sphere.

The electrical sparks swirling around the sphere grew into lightning bolts that engulfed it. It began to deform into a series of malformed shapes, and to shrink down—smaller and smaller and smaller.

Then it was gone, leaving only the faintest swirling, colored aurora.

"KILL THEM!" bellowed Christopher, his face purple with rage, glaring at the point in the sky where his only passage to home had evaporated. "KILL THEM ALL!"

But even as the mercenaries reloaded their weapons and aimed them skyward, they heard a shout from within the barn.

"WORMHOLES! WORMHOLES! ALL AROUND US!"

Christopher, the Clarks, and Roberson sprinted back into the barn to find the computer tech, having leaped out of his chair, staring unbelieving at the security monitors.

"What do you mean *wormholes?*" demanded Christopher.

But the tech was speechless, able only to gesture mutely at the screens. They showed giant, glowing orbs surrounding the entire colony, floating toward the ground.

"You said you destroyed them!" bellowed Christopher, clutching Roberson's jacket, shaking him. *"Those are Mythicals wormholes!"* he shouted, his face contorted in fury.

The mercenary tore the pudgy hands from his jacket and took up his rifle. "A setback," he said coldly. "But one that can be remedied." He touched his communication earpiece, speaking into it. "Form a defensive perimeter around the colony. Position the heavy ordnance. Any wormhole that comes within range, take it out."

CHAPTER 37

"*F*ind him!" pleaded A'eiio. "*Please find my husband!*"

Jack hugged her reassuringly, as they stood among the assault team in the wormhole control room. He enfolded her trembling body, and steeled himself against the agonizing possibility that E'iouy lay dead somewhere in the forest, either shot down or killed by the marauding Pilgrim wormhole.

"I will. I promise," Jack managed to choke out.

"He hasn't answered radio calls since the raid!" she said. "And Wendy couldn't find him afterward. And there was such—" She began to cry, unable to finish the sentence. Another female fairy embraced her, leading her away into the main fairy terminal, where crowds of fairies and their Allies waited for the outcome of the looming battles to come.

Jack's heart pounded with his own soul-deep anguish. Not only would his dear friends face what would be a final battleground—the Pilgrim colony deep in the thick forest. But his parents were being held prisoner somewhere in the compound, as traitors who would no doubt be executed if they weren't rescued.

Around him stood Sam, Mike, Steve, Wendy, and Vlad, readying for battle along with a troop of other Mythicals. Sam's eyes were assuming a reddish glow. While some Mythicals wielded weapons, most, like Sam, would employ only their strength and agility. The teams also included Theran soldiers. Lacking the natural physical power of the Mythicals, like Jack they carried rifles, grenades, and shoulder-mounted missiles.

Together, they would face the Theran mercenaries and the Pilgrim soldiers, all heavily armed.

Other such Mythicals battalions had been formed from the varied species, under the strategy that each race had its own skills, its own powers, to bolster the attack. And so poised to deploy from other wormholes would be squads comprising fairies, pixies, trolls, ogres, goblins, vampires, leprechauns, demons, angels, elves, and gnomes.

Even a clan of reclusive bigfoot had volunteered—invaluable not only for their strength, but also for their ability to stealthily maneuver in thick woods. In fact, looming behind Jack was the massive creature who had rescued him from the werewolf—its pungent aroma now actually quite comforting. The bigfoot had first silently appeared at the Theran base to shadow him, seeming to materialize out of nowhere. What Wendy had said was true. He apparently had a friend for life.

Ryan, piloting the fairy wormhole, issued a warbling screech telling them that the aperture had reached the deployment point. It wafted down into a clearing far enough from the colony to be a safe launching point for their offensive.

The team exited, and the wormhole vaulted away into the sky to land near other Pilgrim bases throughout Thera. All the other Mythicals wormholes had done the same, deploying assault teams planet-wide. This would be a global battle to subdue the human invaders and Theran mercenaries who would decimate the planet.

Jack and the others crouched silently amid the thick forest, listening for any sign that their arrival had been detected. But he heard only the forest sounds he had become so accustomed to growing up in that same colony.

The faint whisper of wings, and the glimpse of white off to his left told him that Wendy had launched to circle high above them, to act as an aerial scout. He fervently hoped Wendy could also find E'iouy alive.

He touched the button on his earpiece, to contact the others.

"I want to find my parents. They're likely being held in their house. It's on this end of town. Can we do that?"

He received instant, wholehearted agreement over the radio and described the house. Sam sprinted away to scout ahead, deftly scurrying through the underbrush, keeping low. The rest of the group spread out, and made their way as stealthily as they could through the forest. Glimpses of the colony buildings appeared through the trees.

A rifle shot echoed from a thicket to the right, and a human scream, cut short.

"What happened?" asked Jack.

Mike answered over the radio. "Tried to shoot me. He's a good shot. Or *was* a good shot."

The shot was followed instantly by more gunfire erupting from the town, and a fusillade of bullets began to rake the forest, tearing through the underbrush, ricocheting off trees. An explosion tore into a nearby tree trunk, and the tree cracked and splintered, plummeting toward Jack. He looked up to see falling death, but a massive arm reached out to stop the tree.

The bigfoot looked down at him, smiling slightly, as he held the tree just above Jack's body.

Jack scrambled out of the way, and raced forward, hearing behind him the ground-shaking thud of the tree striking the ground, as the bigfoot released it. Behind him also came the crunch of footsteps through the forest, as the creature followed after him.

"I see the house," whispered Sam through his earpiece. "There are guards posted outside."

Another voice in his ear, this time Wendy's. *"I see E'iouy! He's on the ground in a clearing to your left. He's not moving."*

In the distance, the hollow thunk of a grenade launcher sounded, and Jack glimpsed a projectile arcing toward them. This time, it was Steve who intervened to save them.

The powerful, squat troll scrambled forward, scooped up the grenade, and with all the power of his thick arms, hurled it back to its launch point. A scream and an explosion revealed that his throw had been accurate.

Now, Jack had a decision to make. Intense gunfire and explosions from the colony told him his friends were in the thick of battle in the direction of his parents' house, and he had to save his parents. But he also had to save E'iouy. If E'iouy was not already dead, he was gravely injured.

"Guide me to him," he instructed Wendy, and the angel began to give guidance on precisely where to find the fallen fairy.

Then Jack issued more instructions to the rest of the team. "Surround the house. Try to take out the guards. I'll come back."

A sudden searing pain in his arm told him a bullet had found him. He slumped to the ground, his head swimming from the shock. He managed to recover enough to roll onto his back, catching sight of an approaching mercenary, taking aim for a kill shot. But Jack was quicker, firing a burst that caught the mercenary in the chest, and he collapsed dead.

The familiar grunt of the bigfoot resounded to his left, and a body flew past his field of vision, slamming into a tree, the mercenary's back breaking with the impact. He, too, fell to the ground, dead.

351

The shock of the wound was beginning to cloud Jack's conscious, and he felt the bigfoot's huge arms lift him up. He was being hauled back away from the battle, but he struggled to his feet, waving off the creature.

A fluttering of white wings told him Wendy had alighted next to him.

"Just bind it up," he said to the angel. "Just stop the bleeding."

"But you—" began Wendy.

"Please," he said. "We need to find him."

The angel nodded reluctantly, and bound a bandage tightly around the arm. Blood immediately began to soak through it.

Managing to recover himself, Jack signaled for the angel to resume her aerial guidance, and she vaulted upward, bullets tearing into the trees around her.

The rattle of gunfire from the direction of his house told him the assault team was attacking.

He and the bigfoot continued their headlong plunge through the forest, arriving at the clearing just as the angel was landing, bending over E'iouy.

Jack joined her, as she examined the frighteningly inert form. One of the fairy's wings was sheared away, and incandescent red blood was oozing from his chest and mouth.

Wendy shook her head. "He's barely alive. He must reach his people soon. I can't carry him."

"But he can," said Jack, gesturing at the bigfoot. Then, to Wendy, "You try to contact the fairy Warden at their wormhole." He instructed the bigfoot, "Take him. Follow Wendy."

The powerful creature hesitated, and touched his translation medallion. The answer came. "You need me."

"He needs you more."

The bigfoot leaned down and gently lifted E'iouy's limp body, cradling the fairy in his arms. Wendy flapped her snowy wings, sailing away to guide him. Peering upward at the flash of white through the trees, the bigfoot followed, pounding away through the woods.

Now to save his parents! His bleeding arm on fire, he stumbled through the familiar woods and toward the house that was now their prison.

As he ran, he was startled to see Vlad appear running beside him, as if materializing out of thin air.

"We have them cornered," he said. "Your parents are in the house. Mercenaries are guarding them."

Jack felt a shiver of fear. The mercenaries would do anything to save themselves; even use his parents as shields.

Jack touched his earpiece and contacted the heads of the other assault teams. They reported making major incursions into the colony, and were on the verge of overrunning it. But the house was still a stronghold.

He and Vlad clambered up a brush-choked hill to the back of the house, its stone walls rendering it a virtual fortress.

Vlad paused, laying a hand on Jack's arm, cocking an ear toward the house, listening.

"I hear eight people," he said. "Two in a small room in the back—"

"Probably my parents."

"Two more at the front door, two at the back door, two in the main room."

Mike appeared beside him, plumping his gray-green bulk down, picking a bullet out of his hide. "You're hurt," said the ogre, touching Jack's wound. "You need Sam."

"Where is she?" asked Jack.

"She went to help with a battle by the big control building."

Despite his knowledge of Sam's prowess, Jack had to force himself to quiet his worry over her fate.

"We need to go in," he said. "We need to figure out a plan."

"Well, there's one way in," said the ogre. He pointed at the roof of the house, where Steve the troll crouched, scratching himself, waiting. "He'll take care of the guards at the front door."

Jack smiled, despite the gravity of the situation, at the idea of the squat, ungainly troll doing battle. But he knew that trolls were adept engineers, so this one would know how to un-engineer a roof.

"Good," he said. "Vlad and I can take the back door. But my parents will still be in danger."

"I'll take care of them," said the ogre.

"How will you get into the house?"

With that the ogre shrugged, hauled his bulk to his feet, took a deep breath, grunted loudly, and launched himself at full tilt toward the back wall. He struck with a resounding crash, penetrating the solid stone wall and disappearing inside.

"Well, I guess the assault has begun!" declared Jack, leaping to his feet, and with Vlad beside him, sprinting toward the back door of the house.

He glanced up in time to see the troll tear a gaping hole in the roof and leap through it. The explosion of gunfire sounded from inside.

Jack and Vlad reached the back door, and Jack kicked it in. The guards' attention had been diverted into the back room by Mike's bursting through its wall. The guards stood down a hallway, glaring into the doorway to the room that held his parents.

They unleashed a spray of gunfire into the room, just as Jack brought up his rifle and fired, killing them.

Behind him, he heard a sharp snap, whirling around in time to see a mercenary collapse to the floor, his neck broken by a powerful twist from the vampire.

He rushed down the hall to the room holding his parents, over-come by a gut-wrenching panic that they might have been hit, even killed.

But he had neglected to take into account Mike's presence. When he reached the doorway, the ogre's broad back was to him, his hide pocked with the marks of bullets that had ricocheted off. The ogre stepped aside to reveal James and Louisa, crouching in the corner.

When they saw their son, their fearful expressions were replaced with relieved smiles. They embraced each other, and relished the moment of relief from the trauma that had enveloped them.

Vlad appeared at the door, a grim expression on his face.

"What is it?" asked Jack.

"There was a battle at the control building." Vlad stopped, his voice faltering.

"What happened? *Vlad, what happened?*"

"The leaders are captured. The mercenary Roberson was killed."

"Good. Great."

"But . . . he killed a pixie."

CHAPTER 38

J ack lay in the bed, his body totally spent, his soul seeming to waft from his body—as if it needed time to recuperate from the wrenching emotional ups and downs of the last two days. He had suffered utter, gut-wrenching panic, followed by profound relief, then utter bliss.

The panic had overwhelmed him during the battle, when he had faced the prospect of Sam's death. At first, he had staggered against the wall of the house, overcome with fear. He had managed to will himself to action, dashing headlong across the village, even as the tumult of last-ditch battles raged around him.

He had reached the control building to see a blood-soaked scene—scattered, broken bodies of mercenaries, of Theran soldiers, and of some Mythicals. And to his horror, he had come upon pixies sobbing over the body of one of their own, lying frail and small and still on the ground.

With a soul-searing anguish, he had rushed over to the group, crouching down, dreading that the body would be Sam's.

But it was not Sam! The body was of another pixie.

Then came relief and utter joy when he heard the familiar voice behind him. "You are injured," Sam said simply, her eyes still showing a tinge of red. "You need help."

He had leaped up and embraced her, and she returned that embrace, her warm body against his.

They had been inseparable during the whirlwind of events that followed.

They learned the blessed news that E'iouy had made it to his planet, with A'eiio beside him, where his life had been saved. He was now healing. They would see him soon.

They learned that the Pilgrim colonies all over Thera had been captured, and any threats to the planet neutralized. And that casualties among both Mythicals and Theran soldiers had been minimal, thanks to the ability of the Mythicals to instantly deploy their wormholes to the battle.

They learned, thankfully, that the Theran governments had ruled that the Pilgrims already on Thera, including his parents, could stay as refugees, as long as they remained peaceful.

Then came the bliss, when Jack and Sam returned to his apartment. They had made love for the first time—transcendent, intoxicating love. More sublime than any Jack had ever experienced.

They had joined their bodies in unions that were by turns urgent and gentle, softly tender, and wildly abandoned.

Her body was unimaginably delicious, a softness beyond softness. Her pixie fragrance, an intoxicating mélange of the most delicate flowers, the sweetest spices. And he found himself moved to emotional depths he didn't know existed.

When they had paused to rest, they nestled sensuously against one another, sharing their dreams, sharing their love.

And they had made love again.

357

And then talked.

And made love again.

And repeated, until they were both exquisitely, profoundly fulfilled.

And now, after a shower that had included yet another voluptuous fusion of their bodies lubricated by the warm, streaming cascade of water, they lay nestled in bed. He put his arm around her, feeling little of the pain of the bullet wound, given that she had applied her pixie's healing kiss.

He managed to find his voice, but he could only manage single words. "Wonderful. Happy. Amazing."

"Yes," she said simply.

"Pheromones," he whispered. "Amazing."

She propped herself up onto one elbow and looked into his eyes, smiling impishly. "What do you see?"

"You. Lovely."

"I mean my eyes. What color are my eyes?"

"Blue."

"Yes, blue. They never turned green, did they?"

"Uh . . . I don't think so. I don't remember."

"They only turn green when I'm producing pheromones. I never did that. What we had . . . what we did . . . was just *us*. Together."

He grinned stupidly at the ceiling. "Wow, you mean it was just us making love with no chemical . . . uh . . . influence?"

"That's what I said."

"I love you."

"I know," she replied casually, as she had said so many times.

"I mean I really love *you!* For *you!* It's not me being an enchanted human. It's me in love!"

"I know."

They laid together for a long time, enjoying the present, imagining the future.

His cell phone intruded with its ring. He let it ring for a long time before answering.

His expression began with a smile, but faded to sobriety, then became grim. He ended the call, downcast.

"What is it?" she asked.

"That was A'eiio. The Wardens Council has met. They have ruled that Therans remain a terminal species, and they will inevitably devastate the planet's environment, rendering it unlivable. They showed the Theran leaders the video we took of dying Earth. But the Theran leaders were dismissive. They still reject the Remediation."

"What does that mean?"

"The Wardens have decreed that all Mythicals are to evacuate the planet."

●　　●　　●

The bleak, smog-enshrouded landscape of Earth slid by on the giant screen, as the members of the Theran Congress of Nations watched the video in silence. There would be no narration. None was needed.

The scene cut wordlessly to the squalid village along the potholed highway; then to the starving, ragged people; then to the lifeless ocean, then to the flooded, mold-encrusted buildings.

Months earlier, in the same hall, the same delegates had been stunned to see the alien Mythicals who had lived anonymously among them for all of their history.

Today, standing before them was another alien, Jack, but one who looked just like them. And, one who had defied his race to help save their planet from devastation. Behind him stood the Mythicals who had become such a cherished part of his life—Sam, Mike, Steve, Vlad, Wendy, Ryan, and A'eiio. Even E'iouy had come, his slim, pale body still encased in the transparent healing film that was used by fairy doctors.

As the video finished, Jack stood at the lectern, allowing the images of his dying home planet to sink in. This was a last chance to persuade the Therans to save themselves.

"Your planet is a sister planet to my home, Earth," he began. "It has evolved in a parallel universe, and you see the fate Earth has suffered at the hands of its people . . . the result of their ignorant foolhardiness, allowing their technology to bring it to ruin.

"Thera has not evolved as quickly as Earth, but the same forces are at work here that threaten your planet. Rising levels of planet-warming gases, melting of polar ice, acidification of the oceans."

Jack paused, smiling sadly. "Soon you will catch up to Earth. Soon you will see the devastating consequences of your folly."

He went on to show the charts and graphs that Theran scientists had developed from their masses of unequivocal data that pointed to Thera's looming fate.

"I beg you, as do all the Mythicals, to implement the Remediation, to save your planet from environmental ruin."

He and the others then moved to the gallery, to hear the speeches in response. The reaction from some of the delegates was supportive. But from most, the statements were disheartening:

". . . an interference in our affairs by these monsters from other worlds . . ."

". . . an economic burden that would cost jobs and disrupt the carbon-based energy industry that has served us so well."

". . . merely theories that need to be studied more before we take any drastic steps."

". . . an attempt by scientists to justify their existence and enjoy their generous research funding."

". . . a massive hoax perpetrated by those who would profit from these so-called clean energy sources."

". . . a warped and incomplete picture of that planet that probably leaves out all the successful adaptation that has taken place."

In the end Jack and the others left the hall in defeat, walking slowly out into the cool night air of the capitol. They stood silently together, their resolve drained.

A'eiio helped her husband walk to their waiting car, then returned to Jack, who stood with Sam.

"You tried your best," she said softly, shaking her head. "The Wardens were watching the convocation. We will all try to dissuade them of their decision. But remember, we are all exiles. We have no say in our fate."

Jack said nothing, but hand-in-hand with Sam, walked away into the night.

CHAPTER 39

The wormhole, a lighted, shimmering globe against the night sky, settled slowly down to hover above the lawn of the vast green-space that extended from the capitol building to the Hall of the President of the Confederated States.

The ogre who waited to manage its landing did not complain tonight about the elves leaving the lights on. Tonight, the Mythicals wanted the world to see them depart.

Similar landings were occurring throughout the planet, in all the major capitols. Each interdimensional aperture would take on board the Mythicals species that lived there. They would then all rendezvous in a vast, empty plain in the southern hemisphere. At that transfer point, each species would reboard the wormhole that would take them back to their home planets.

And so, around the landing site on the capitol lawn had gathered a vast multifarious crowd of fairies, pixies, trolls, ogres, goblins, vampires, leprechauns, demons, angels, elves, and gnomes. Even the reclusive bigfoot had emerged from the deep forests to go home.

Beyond them stood an even larger crowd of hundreds of thousands of Therans, some cheering the departure, others seeing the event as tragic evidence of their planet's dire fate.

As a human, and therefore an alien, Jack had been allowed access to the Mythicals departure area. And he had managed to find his friends among the departing exiles—all but the one he wanted to see most. Each said their farewells as they boarded the wormhole.

He hugged A'eiio, and she placed his hand on her swelling belly. He felt fluttering.

"The little ones are trying to fly," she said. "You would be amazed to see a fairy birth. It has to take place in a netted enclosure, because they can fly immediately."

He embraced E'iouy gingerly, given his healing injuries. His wing was showing regrowth. Soon, he would take to the skies of the fairy planet again. The fairy hugged him back harder.

"We're not as fragile as we look," he chuckled. "I can take a good hug. You know you are welcome to live on our planet."

"But my parents are here . . . what remains of my race. And maybe we can convince the Therans to save themselves."

Then Mike lumbered up and lifted him off the ground, so the ogre could look him in the eye.

"You are rather puny," he growled. "But you have been a worthy Ally. And I am sorry I frightened you so at the beginning."

The three vampires, Vladimir, Radomir, and Gennady crowded around, bidding hearty goodbyes, not very successfully hiding their sadness, recalling their dinner together. It made him long even more for the absent Sam.

Even Ryan approached and emitted a scritchy screech that Jack took to be a fond farewell.

The whisper of breeze from above signaled the arrival of Wendy, who sailed gracefully down, smiling angelically, and enfolded him in her wings.

"We all wish you well," she said. "We will all be so happy to be back in our home worlds. But we will all be sad that you are no longer with us."

"Sam?" he asked hopefully. "Did you see her?"

Wendy shook her head sadly. "No. Maybe she could not bear to say goodbye."

Jack felt the soul-wrenching pang of utter sorrow, barely able to hold back tears. Tears at their leaving, but more so because he had lost the magical creature who had brought such light to his life.

Finally, all had boarded, including the ogre who had guided the wormhole to ground.

Jack stood back to watch the wormhole glide up into the pitch-black sky, a glowing sphere that shrank and shrank, until it was but a star. Then, having ascended beyond the atmosphere, it accelerated to stunning speed and was instantly gone.

The crowd of Therans began to disperse, but Jack could not bring himself to leave. He sat down on a bench in the growing quiet, to be alone with his heartbreak. Finally, the only sound was the whoosh of trees in the night breeze and the thrum of traffic.

"We should go home," he heard a whispered voice say.

He gasped. Sam sat down beside him.

"You're here!" He stammered. *"Oh . . . you're here!"*

He embraced her, not letting go, as if to do so would lose her.

"Obviously," she said.

"Why? How? What . . ." his words failed him.

"I'm sorry I wasn't here earlier. I was meeting with my Warden. I had asked to stay. I told him that the Mythicals still needed an ambassador on Thera. To report back any progress. I asked to be that ambassador."

Jack's heart pounded with joy. He would have leaped up to dance, but he absolutely refused to let this pixie out of his embrace.

"But really, you gave up your chance to go back to your own planet . . . your home . . . your people . . . to be with *me?*"

"I love you," she said.

He grinned ecstatically. Now it was his turn to say the words: "I know."

www.ingramcontent.com/pod-product-compliance
Lightning Source LLC
Chambersburg PA
CBHW051526250626
47156CB00001B/243